Spinster of Th

CW01064677

W. B. Maxwell

Alpha Editions

This edition published in 2024

ISBN : 9789361479120

Design and Setting By
Alpha Editions
www.alphaedis.com
Email - info@alphaedis.com

Contents

AUTHOR'S NOTE

NEITHER the characters nor the incidents of this story are in any way drawn from persons or events of real life; and in passages where the names of the living or the dead have been mentioned, they thus appear merely because the omission of them seemed impossible (in such a context) by reason of the world-wide fame of their holders.

CHAPTER I

IT had been an odd impulse that made little Mildred Parker seek counsel and advice, or at least sympathy, from Miss Verinder in the first great crisis of her young life. The imperious necessity of opening her heart to somebody had of course lain behind the impulse, and Miss Verinder, although really only an acquaintance of Mildred's parents, had been unusually kind and friendly to Mildred herself; but now, sitting in the drawing-room of Miss Verinder's flat, listening to Miss Verinder's pleasant emotionless voice, watching Miss Verinder with methodic care put away small odds and ends in an antique bureau, she felt the huge incongruity that there would be in speaking of love to an old maid of fifty.

"I won't be a minute," said Miss Verinder.

"I am not in the least hurry," said Mildred quite untruthfully.

Waiting and watching, she thought that fifty years of age is nothing nowadays—if you are not an old maid, and if you decorate yourself properly. Some women of fifty are still dangerously attractive—they act leading parts on the stage, they appear in divorce cases, they marry their third husbands. But when once you have allowed old maidishness to take possession of you!

"A place for everything and everything in its place," said Miss Verinder, closing a drawer and speaking as if to herself rather than to a visitor. "That is a good motto, isn't it?" And she began to flick a silk handkerchief. "These are souvenirs—with only a sentimental value."

Mildred glanced round the room. At the far end there were windows, through which one saw the shredded stem and drooping branches of a large plane tree, all transparent green and fiery orange now in the sunlight of a September afternoon; near the window at the other end there was a cage with a somnolent grey parrot; a singularly clean white cat lay stretching itself lazily on the seat of a chintz-covered chair; and everywhere there showed the neatness and order as well as the prettiness and taste that are only possible in rooms altogether free from the disturbing presence of clumsy man. Mildred, feeling more and more enervated, spoke admiringly but abruptly.

"I do like your flat, Miss Verinder."

"It is convenient, isn't it?" said Miss Verinder. "So close to the Brompton Road, so near everything. Strictly speaking," she added with gentle precision, "it is not a flat at all, but what they call a maisonette. That straight staircase—almost like a ladder, isn't it?—has been as it were stolen from the auctioneer's offices on the ground floor; and it forms quite a private entrance. I prefer that. It gives a feeling,"—and she made a graceful vague gesture. "I think Oratory Gardens is the only place where you find flats constructed on this principle. I considered myself lucky in securing the lease—many years ago, you know. I wanted to be just here, because I have so many associations with this neighbourhood—the whole neighbourhood—as far as Kensington Gore and Knightsbridge, but not south or west, you know. I like the sight of the tree too."

For a few moments she ceased dusting the small objects on the flap of the bureau and stood at the window, looking out; a tall thin dark figure with the sunlight behind her.

"It sometimes makes me feel as if I were miles away from Kensington"; and she gently nodded her head and half closed her eyes. "Far in the country. On the other side of the world, even."

She was really a very charming, well-bred, elegant woman; and once upon a time, a long while ago, when those eyes of hers were full of brightness and lustre, when her sensitive lips were redder, when her pale unwrinkled cheeks had permanent colour instead of the fitful pinkness that now came and went so delicately, she must have been quite good-looking. Possibly she might then have been fascinating also. Her hair was really good, dark and strong, rolled in bulky waves about her forehead and in a lump at the back of her neck.

It was the demureness, the air of patience, endurance, and submissiveness proper to her age and condition, that spoilt her general effect and made her just a little dowdy, although always beautifully dressed. Even in the moment of recognising a certain natural feminine charm one sought for and found the stigmata of spinsterhood. She had no mannerisms, affectations, or silly tricks; and nevertheless.—But there is the bother of it. How and why do we judge people or form any opinion concerning them? As soon as you think you know what a woman is you begin to think she looks like what you have decided her to be. Perhaps one merely imagined and did not really see that outward suggestion of untilled fields, autumn leaves, and faded flowers, which has come to symbolise a particular combination of loneliness and neglect.

Essentially, she appeared to be spinsterhood personified. She stood so very much alone. Although, as was known, she had relatives, she did not appear to preserve any close intercourse with them. One never met robust full-blooded nieces putting up at the flat with "darling Aunt Emmeline" for a night or two; she showed you no portraits of middle-aged brothers and sisters, or snap-shots of children in embroidered aprons and sailor hats, the representatives of a budding generation; there was not even a ne'er-do-well nephew in the background, emerging into the foreground from time to time and extracting financial assistance as he passed through London on the way from Harrow to Sandhurst and from Sandhurst to his regiment.

Thus it seemed that the attitude of uninvolved spectator or disinterested critic of all that matters in life had been irrevocably forced upon her, and that, as in all such typical cases, she had taken up feeble little secondary interests to fill the vast blank spaces that should have been occupied by prime ones. She attended concerts, lectures, classes; played bridge for mild points; drank weak tea and nibbled dry biscuits at afternoon parties. Sometimes, abruptly going away by herself, she was absent for long periods; and one imagined her, charmingly and suitably dressed as usual, say in the solitude of Dartmoor, translating its purple heather and golden skies into the wishy-washy tints of her sketch-book; or gathering a sprig of fern near the Castle of Chillon in order to place it later between the pages of Byron's poem—in a word, one imagined her travelling as old maids with ample means have always done, changing the outward scene but never the mental atmosphere. Occasionally, too, she shut herself in the flat, for weeks at a time, refusing to see anybody; and then one surmised that she was passing through those phases of nervous distress or semi-hysteria from the experience of which old maids can scarcely hope to escape altogether.

Naturally she offered a strong contrast to the very modern young lady of twenty sitting on one of the sofas, playing with her gauntlet gloves, and brimming over with youthfulness and ardent irrepressible life.

Mildred looked very pretty in her scant frock, low bodice, and short sleeves; after the manner of modern girls seeming, perhaps, a little commonplace or ordinary because so like so many others of her class and years, at once doll-like and self-possessed, shrewd and yet innocent. She was, or at least believed herself to be, entirely modern; although at the moment occupied with elemental things.

"Now," said Miss Verinder, "I am all attention," and she came from the bureau and drew a chair to the sofa.

"I'm so glad I've caught you alone," said Mildred feebly.

"Well, my dear Mildred," said Miss Verinder, "I am purposely alone, because, when I received your little note saying you wished to see me—I don't know why—but somehow I had the suspicion that there was something you wanted to tell me, or to talk about."

"Oh, Miss Verinder! How kind—how very kind!" said Mildred in a gush of gratitude.

Indeed this divination seemed to her a most striking proof of Miss Verinder's power of sympathy; her own instinct had been correct; she was glad she had come here. She went on impulsively and confidently; telling Miss Verinder how she had half mooted the subject of her troubles to two comfortable matrons, but in each case she had felt rebuffed and had immediately "curled up," feeling certain that neither would give her any help, but rather take the side of her family against her. Then she had made up her mind to tell Miss Verinder all about it.

"I knew you'd help me if you could, dear Miss Verinder. You *have* been so nice to me ever since we first met—and, I know it sounds conceited, but I felt you did really like me."

"I do like you very much," said Miss Verinder simply and affectionately; and she stretched out her hand and gave a little squeeze to one of Mildred's soft warm paws. Then she folded her hands on her lap again.

"Thank you so much. I think you're just an angel, Miss Verinder."

"Why always Miss Verinder? Why don't you call me Emmeline?"

"Oh, I *couldn't*," said Mildred, flattered but overwhelmed by this surprising invitation. "It would seem such awful cheek."

"Am I so venerable and forbidding?" asked Miss Verinder, with mild reproach.

"Of *course* not," said Mildred eagerly. "No, I shall be delighted, if you'll really let me. I think it's absolutely sweet of you—Emmeline. Well now, Emmeline,"—and Mildred repeated the name firmly, as if feeling great satisfaction in using this unceremonious form of address;—"The fact is, Emmeline—"

And with a voluble flood she narrated how she had fallen deeply and perhaps even foolishly in love with a young man; how Mr. and Mrs. Parker had made a monstrous absurd fuss about it; and how, because of it, the once comfortable home in Ennismore Gardens was swept with tempest, wrath, and pain.

"You understand, Emmeline? I mean to say, they really are behaving like people who have been bitten by a mad dog. In one way, I mean to say— you know—it's all too ridiculous for words. The things they say! The things, don't you know, they threaten to do. Well, I mean to say—"

Mildred's eyes were flashing, she pulled her gloves from hand to hand, and, prattling on, became so involved with mean-to-says and don't-you-knows that she floundered suddenly to silence.

"Emmeline," and she changed her position on the sofa, "I think I'd better start at the very beginning."

"That is always a good place to start at," said Miss Verinder, smiling sympathetically.

"Then what I want you to understand is that I'm very much in earnest. It's no silliness—or infatuation, as mother says—or any rot of that sort. It's the real thing." As she said this Mildred's pretty commonplace little face became all soft and tender, her lips quivered, and in spite of her modernity she had the aspect of a quite small child who will burst into tears if you speak harshly to it. "You must understand," and she suddenly turned her head away, "I wasn't even thinking of love—much less hunting for it. It came upon me like a thunderclap."

"Like a thunderclap!" Miss Verinder echoed the words, and drew in her breath, making the sound of a faint sigh. "Go on, Mildred dear."

"Well then," and Mildred looked round again, with a child-like air of triumph. "I would have you to know also that the man I've fallen in love with is very famous."

Miss Verinder started and looked at her intently.

"But it's nothing to do with his fame that has made me love him."

Again Miss Verinder started, slightly.

"Of course I don't mean to say that I wasn't influenced by all that. You know what I mean? Seeing his photographs in the papers! Hearing what other girls said about him. And I own that I admired him before I knew him, but it was for himself and nothing else that I fell in love with him directly I did get to know him. The fact that he was celebrated and a favourite of the public was nothing then."

And, now fairly started, Mildred opened her heart as she had never done before. She told Miss Verinder all she felt of the torturing bliss and exquisite pain that honest straightforward young girls suffer when this most potent of fevers catches them without warning, like a thunderclap. The tale of Mildred's frenzied longings and cravings and hopes and fears brought faint old-maidish blushes to the smooth ivory of Miss Verinder's cheeks. It was as though Mildred, like a small house on fire, had lit up a faint reflection in the far distance of a tranquil evening sky.

"There," said Mildred, ceasing to flash and becoming quite calm. "Oh, Emmeline, that *has* done me good—even if you can't help me. You know what I mean? Just to get it off one's chest for once." And then she laughed in a deprecating manner. "But I'm afraid I'm shocking you most frightfully."

"No, my dear," said Miss Verinder, "you are not shocking me in the least."

"You *are* so kind. Well then, now you *do* see I'm in earnest, and how ridiculous it is for one's people—"

"Yes. But who is he, Mildred? You haven't told me yet."

"Alwyn Beckett," said Mildred looking confident and triumphant.

But great as was Miss Verinder's sympathy, she could not make her face show any signs of intelligent recognition. She reminded Mildred that she lived very much out of the world. It would naturally appear ignorant and stupid, but she felt forced again to ask the question: Who is he?

"The actor," said Mildred.

"Oh, yes," said Miss Verinder. "You must not be surprised if I don't know him by reputation, because I never go to the play, and am quite out of touch with theatrical people"; and she paused, smiling as if involuntarily amused by some secret thought. "The utmost I do in that direction is occasionally to go to one of these cinema theatres."

"Oh, but he is on the films too," said Mildred proudly.

"In what piece is he acting at the present time?"

"He is understudying the two big parts in *Five Old Men and a Dog*."

"Ah, yes?"

Then Mildred burst forth about her family. "Of course I know they can't keep us apart. Of course they've no right to interfere with me. But it isn't exactly that. Good gracious, no, this is 1920, not 1820. Of course they can do what they're doing now—I mean to say, just making hell for me at home. It's irritating, but I must put up with it. Only I simply can't stand their attitude to Alwyn"; and Mildred grew warm. "What are they, I'd like to know—to look down upon the stage!"

Miss Verinder said that the notion of treating the stage with contempt did certainly sound rather old-fashioned nowadays.

"Old-fashioned! I should think so. Even if they were anybody—which they aren't. Do you know what my grandfather was? No. Well, I don't myself. Father's been jolly careful to prevent us knowing; but I know this—he wasn't a gentleman. I mean, he hadn't the smallest pretensions to being one. It was up in the north, and I believe he was just a person in a shop; you know, not owning the shop, but serving behind the counter—and he married grannie for her money. She wasn't anything either. The elderly ugly daughter of some manufacturing people. But by a fluke of luck her share in the business somehow turned up trumps, so that while father was still a boy they were rich, and able to send him to Rugby and Cambridge. Then, when grandfather died, he and mother came to London, and bought the house in Ennismore Gardens." Saying this, Mildred laughed scornfully. "Yes, and amused themselves by pretending that they've lived in it for ten generations."

"They could hardly have done that," said Miss Verinder, smiling; "because Ennismore Gardens have not been built long enough."

"No, exactly. But you know what I mean"; and Mildred spoke with almost tragic force. "Father's just a snob, and mother's every bit as bad."

Miss Verinder reproved her for speaking disrespectfully of her parents.

"I know, I know, Emmeline;" and Mildred hastened to assure her that till now she had always been fond of her parents—"poor dears." She had been loyal too, entering into their little foolishnesses, never giving the show away; and she could feel fond of them again, if only they would behave decently.

Miss Verinder asked, "Do they really base their objections to—Forgive me, dear. What is his name again? Mr. Beckett. Yes, of course. Well, do they only base their objection on the fact that he is an actor?"

A crimson wave of indignation flowed upward from Mildred's neck to her forehead, while she explained how they had the effrontery to say their real objection was—not so much that he was an actor, as that he was a bad actor.

"Who are they to judge?" said Mildred hotly; and for a space she held forth concerning the young man's brilliant talent.

Miss Verinder asking how matters stood at the moment, Mildred told her that the outrageous Mr. Parker had simply forbidden them to meet. "But we *do* meet of course." And with a few words she conjured up a picture of their clandestine meetings late at night in Ennismore Gardens itself—he driving as fast as taxi-cab would bring him from the theatre, she slipping out of the house to wait for him, and the two of them pacing slowly through that columned entrance by the mews and along the passage by the churchyard, in the warm darkness beneath the trees; peered at curiously by soft-footed policemen; encountering, as it seemed, all the servant-maids of the neighbourhood similarly engaged with *their* sweethearts. "Isn't it degrading, Emmeline, to be forced to do such a thing?"

And again she spoke of love and its invincible claims. She knew, she said, that her destiny was all in her own hands. If she lost Alwyn, she would have herself to thank, and it would be no use to put the blame on anybody else. It was this thought that sometimes made her feel desperate—and Alwyn too. Her parents could not of course really come between them. But then there is the money question. What they *can* do is just to cut her off without a penny; and really, seeing them behave like such pigs, one could believe them capable of doing it. Well, that is not fair. That is tommy rot. Suppose, after all, darling Alwyn should prove, not a bad actor, but hardly quite the tremendous one that she hopes he is; then, in that case, if they had a proper settlement—"the usual thing," with parents as well-off as hers—she could take him off the stage. There were heaps of things she could do with him. Or if—as is far more probable—he makes a colossal success, money will be useful to set him up in management. You must look ahead; although, when you are madly in love, it is difficult to do so.

Miss Verinder, watching her thoughtfully, inquired if all these ideas had been prompted by Alwyn himself; and Mildred said no, he was a thousand miles above such considerations. He cared for nothing but her.

"Emmeline—as I say, you're so awfully kind, and I do feel that I need a word of advice from someone older than myself." At this point of the interview, it was curious to observe in Mildred that mixture of shrewdness and innocence which makes the typical modern girl seem at once so shallow and so baffling. She still playfully tormented the yellow gauntlet gloves; her eyes shone with childish candour; but there was something a little hard and business-like about the red lips that only a moment ago had been pouting petulantly. "My own inclination is to chuck over everything and do something desperate—you know, just to run off with him."

"And marry him without your parents' consent?"

"Or *not* marry him," said Mildred, pulling at her gloves.

"Mildred!" said Miss Verinder, with a little cry. "What *do* you mean?"

"Well, what I mean," said Mildred, "is that if they're so damned old-fashioned, I don't see why they shouldn't stew in their own gravy—at least for a bit. Don't you see? When they find I'm gone, in *that* way, if they're really genuine in their feelings, it will be the regular Mid-Victorian business. The lost child—our daughter gone to perdition. Get her married now to the scoundrel that has lured her away. Make her an honest woman at any price—and, by Jove," said Mildred, with a little ripple of innocent laughter, "I'll jolly well make them pay the price. You know, no more than is right—the usual. I don't mean blackmailing them or anything like that."

"Mildred," said Miss Verinder, with an unexpectedly firm tone of voice, "you and I must talk very seriously. And you must listen to me, dear, and not be impatient if what I urge—Ah, yes."

Interrupted by the opening of the door, she checked herself.

It was the faithful maid Louisa—a grey-haired woman older than Miss Verinder, neat yet stately in her black dress and black silk apron; just such an efficient long-tried maid-housekeeper as one would expect such a mistress to have. Louisa was bringing them tea. At sight of her the white cat dropped heavily from its easy chair, stalked forward, and rubbed itself against Miss Verinder's ankles; while the grey parrot as promptly awoke, flapped its wings, and screamed. Tea meant something to these two dependents.

"Look sharp, Louisa," said the parrot, expressing the wish of both in a gruff monotone. "Look sharp, Louisa. Louisa. Louisa."

Louisa, bringing a collapsible table from the wall, smiled sedately.

"He always says that," Miss Verinder explained. "It was taught to him a long time ago—and with great difficulty. Only as a joke," she added. "For Louisa is always up to time—very much on the spot, as you young people say."

Louisa opened the table in front of her mistress, brought the tea tray with kettle and tea-pot; went out again and returned with trays carrying cakes, bread and butter, and so forth, which she placed on smaller tables; finally brought a silver tea-caddy, and lit the lamp under the kettle.

"It is just on the boil, miss."

"Thank you, Louisa."

Then Miss Verinder made the tea. Mildred watched her, fascinated although preoccupied; it was all so neat and careful and methodic. "One spoonful for you and one for me." After warming the tea-pot with a very little hot water, Miss Verinder was using not a spoon but a queer little silver shovel to put in the tea. "One for the pot—and one for luck! Now, dear, you see that bolt beneath the kettle? Pull it out for me, will you? That's it." And for a moment she was almost invisible as the steam rose. "Louisa never fails me. She knows the proverb that 'If the water not boiling be, filling the tea-pot spoils the tea.' One lump or two?"

In spite of emotion, or because of it, Mildred was hungry; and she ate freely of the thin bread and butter and the sugar-covered cake, till gradually these dainties seemed to turn to dust and ashes in her mouth while she listened to Miss Verinder's advice.

Miss Verinder indeed displayed an astoundingly accurate comprehension of her young friend's state of mind; but truly every word she said might have been heard with cordial approval by Mr. and Mrs. Parker themselves had they been present.

Mildred must not be silly; Mildred must be a sensible girl; Mildred must summon patience to her aid, consider other people's feelings as well as her own, allow time to work on her behalf.

Mildred put down her tea-cup with a nervous jerk; she was bitterly disappointed; and yet what different sort of advice could she have expected from the owner of this room, with its caged bird, its cat of dubious gender, its chintzes, water colour drawings, and embroidered footstool—this room used only by elderly women, in which the sound of a real man's voice had never once been heard? Clergymen came here no doubt for subscriptions; and faded old bachelors, like old maids themselves, to gossip amiably—of books, china, pictures, or anything else without any real life in it. Completely enervated, Mildred felt again that sense of fantastic incongruity between the subject of her late discourse and its auditor. As well might she have gone to the nuns at Roehampton and told her tale there.

Moreover, while talking, Miss Verinder performed certain little actions which, as Mildred guessed, had become purely automatic from long habit— such as pouring out milk and tea in a saucer and placing it on the floor for the cat, going across the room and inserting morsels of the sugary cake between the cage bars for the parrot. Nevertheless, although thus to be interpreted, they added to the girl's distress.

Miss Verinder went on talking with earnestness and affection. She would help, to the best of her ability, she would take the first chance of a chat with Mrs. Parker. But really and truly it is all nonsense to speak of kicking over the traces, outraging propriety or convention, and that sort of thing. Mildred must wait. At any rate, one must not give way to one's passions.

Then Mildred blurted it out; clothed her thought in very plain words. "But, dear Miss Verinder, perhaps you don't know what the passions are."

"Why should you assume that?" said Miss Verinder gently.

Mildred apologised for a stupid phrase or explained it away. Unconsciously she had ceased to address Miss Verinder by her Christian name, and she pleaded with great strength for her own point of view. It was the fiery cry of youth. Whatever else you can do when you are young—so she said in effect—there is one thing you cannot do, and that is, *wait*.

"Miss Verinder, I feel that I want us to be bound together—now—and forever. Suppose we put it off, who can say what would happen? Accidents—anything—He might grow tired of waiting—or—or change his mind."

"Oh, no, dear. If there is any chance of that, it is all the more reason for not being in a hurry."

"Miss Verinder, I believe you think I'm horrid about it; but on my honour I'm not. My love for Alwyn and his for me is a *nice* love. Really and truly it is."

"I'm quite sure yours is."

"His too." Suddenly and unexpectedly Mildred began to cry. She did not gasp or sob; her lips trembled, her eyes filled with tears, overflowed, and in a moment her whole face was wet, looking like the face of a child of six who has been caught in an April shower. She dabbed it with a totally inadequate handkerchief to prevent the drops from falling on her pretty frock, and continued talking. She herself looked prettier now than at any time during the visit; that touch of calculating sagacity, with all other attributes of modernness, had gone; only the natural innocence and simplicity remained. "When we have been together for hours and hours— alone together—up the river—anywhere—sometimes he hasn't even once kissed me. And at the time I haven't even noticed it. I've only thought of it afterwards, you know. We have been just perfectly happy being together— not wanting anything else on earth. Miss Verinder, you see what I mean? I only tell you to *make* you see what our love is. It's because of it that I'm sure of myself—yes, Miss Verinder, I am really."

And dabbing her eyes with vigour, she emphasised the argument that in linking yourself to anyone of the other sex you are quite safe when you find the desired companion as well as the lover. Companionship with Alwyn was the essential thing for which she longed. It would be too dreadful to lose it—to risk losing it. Suppose she let the chance slip, suppose she allowed Fate acting under the more usual title of Accident to rob her of this felicity, it was probable that she would never meet anybody else for whom she could care in the same way, or even so much as "the snuff of a candle." She would be spiritually alone forever. Under such conditions she felt that she simply could not face her life; and, carried away with emotion and momentarily forgetful of the personage she addressed, she sketched vividly the situation of a middle-aged, soon-to-be old spinster—alone, with nothing to hope for.

"But one always goes on hoping," said Miss Verinder firmly.

She said the words indeed with such quiet strength that Mildred, startled and surprised, asked her what she meant.

Miss Verinder did not answer explicitly. She came and sat beside Mildred on the sofa, put her arm round the girl's slim waist, and began to repeat or sum up the counsel that she had already given.

Mildred for a minute was quite unable to listen; she sat looking at her wondering. One always goes on hoping! What an extraordinary queer thing to say. Could it be possible that Miss Verinder still tried to brighten the cold monotony of life with sentimental or romantic dreams—did she at her age still cherish the idea that a knight would one day come to smash the prison bars of solitude, break the chains of habit, and lead her out into freedom and light—did she, poor dear kind soul, still really hope there was somewhere on this broad strange earth a man stout enough and bold enough to save her from dying as an old maid? These questioning thoughts touched little Mildred's heart with something far removed from mirth, rather a pitying pain. They drove away her self-absorbed emotion; they steadied her.

"Yes, Miss Verinder, I am really giving weight to everything you say."

Miss Verinder was gently yet firmly summing up. Mildred must promise not to act rashly. In time—the young man proving patient and worthy—her parents may agree to an engagement. In time—they shewing themselves obdurate and unreasonable—one can begin to think of marriage without their consent. But this suggestion of an unsanctified bolt, an irregular union, entered into for whatever aim or purpose—oh, no, never.

"Believe me, Mildred dear, it is only the very strongest characters that can brave public opinion—and you must remember, public opinion is represented by your father and mother. Yes, I am sure—to go right through with anything of that kind, immense self-control, really almost an iron nerve is required. That is, if it is to be done successfully.

"And, Mildred," said Miss Verinder, with an affectionate pressure of the surrounding arm, "You mustn't think I don't know what I am talking about. I don't want you to dismiss me as antiquated and squeamish."

"Oh, no, Miss Verinder."

"As you said, this is 1920; and people are always saying how tremendously the world has changed; but I often think the changes are not as big as people pretend—I think they are most of them on the surface, as it were, and not going deep. Of course, when I was young, girls had much less freedom. Oh, yes, much less—and people will tell you that girls now can do what they like, and do do it." Saying this, Miss Verinder had a demure little smile. "So to speak, girls are allowed to govern almost everything—but then they must never omit to govern themselves. Oh, no, Mildred," and she shook her head. "In *that*, public opinion is quite unchanged. I mean for people of *our* class, Mildred. For those above us and below us it may be quite different. I can't say. But you're not a barmaid or a duchess either—are you?"

"No, Miss Verinder," said Mildred meekly.

"And you have to think of your Alwyn and the effect it might produce on him. There is the danger that he might fail you in a way you haven't considered. No, no—I don't for a moment mean play you false. Oh, no. But, perhaps, it is only the very finest natures that can—accept—ah—this particular kind of surrender or self-sacrifice from a woman and still hold her quite as high in their minds as they did before—ah—the surrender occurred.

"There, Mildred dear. I am going to help you for all I am worth, and you are going to be wise. And don't—I beg you—forget this. I have my reasons for all I have said."

Mildred, nipping through the traffic of the Brompton Road with the composure and agility of up-to-date girls, and then making her way thoughtfully past the Oratory and into Ennismore Gardens, was wondering what were Miss Verinder's reasons.

CHAPTER II

MISS VERINDER'S reasons were as follows: In the year 1895, when Queen Victoria still reigned upon the throne, when people still talked of the London season and described it as being good or bad, a brilliant season or a dull season, Emmeline Verinder was living very comfortably with her parents in one of the largest houses of Prince's Gate. Then, unexpectedly and for the first time, she and love bowed, touched hands, and made acquaintance. The thing came upon her like a thunder-clap.

It began on a June evening just before midnight; and Mr. Verinder, her father, thinking afterwards of that summer night, used to feel a kind of warm prickly irritation, as though one of Destiny's invisible imps was teasing the back of his stout neck with stinging nettles. It might have happened anyhow, but he could not banish the annoying recollection that he himself had assisted in getting it started. When his wife placidly asked whether the effort was worth while, it was he who had decided that, having accepted the invitation, they must certainly go to Mrs. Clutton's musical party.

And he had said so not truly because he desired to go, but because of vague, almost organic sensations which told him that if you are a well-preserved man of sixty who is also a personage of a certain importance, who lives in Prince's Gate, with plenty of money, horses, carriages, an ample ornate wife, one charming beautifully dressed single daughter, and another daughter, married, but now staying on a visit under your roof—when you find yourself so situated and so surrounded, there is something inadequate and unimpressive if you go to bed at eleven o'clock in the height of the London season.

They went, then, the four of them; he, Mrs. Verinder, Emmeline, and Margaret Pratt, her married sister—down the newly-named Exhibition Road, round the corner to one of the largest houses in the Cromwell Road. There would have been space in the closed landau for Eustace, the son and brother; he could have sat between Emmeline and Margaret; but he was attending a banquet as the guest of a city company.

There had been a dinner-party at Mrs. Clutton's and the Verinders with many others were asked for the music. The concluding strains of Tosti's *Good-Bye* floated down the staircase to meet them as they entered the inner hall, through which Mr. Verinder's ladies swept onward to some library or boudoir at the back of the building, now organised as a place for depositing velvet coats and feathered wraps. Mr. Verinder, having been relieved of his coat and opera hat, stood waiting for them—large, grey-headed, dignified, and yet urbane, exchanging suave civilities with other prosperous ladies and gentlemen, who had arrived just before him. It was a typical evening party of the period—awning, drugget, and linkmen outside; inside, a full pressure on the electric light; large palms, together with masses of flowers brought in for the occasion; extraneous help also in the dining-room, now set as a brilliant supper scene; the servants of the house obliterated, or, at least, standing back behind the numerous grave hirelings in white waistcoats, who, but for their solemnity, might so easily have been mistaken for some of Mrs. Clutton's visitors.

It should be noted that at this period the neighbourhood still had a distinct society of its own; not, of course, because the antiquated country custom of calling on one another merely as neighbours was practised by its residents, but because this modern spacious end of the town, with no traditions earlier than the Prince Consort, seemed to have been planned and constructed for a particular class of which the members were likely to foregather—fairly rich prosperous people, eminently respectable if somewhat colourless people; merchants, bankers, judges of the High Court, Queen's counsel of the Parliamentary bar, heads of departments in the civil service; here and there a doctor who had been made a baronet, a successful recently knighted architect, a chartered accountant doing government work, and so on. These and their families meddled not at all, in the year 1895, with fashion and aristocracy; punctual in the regulation attendance at drawing-rooms and levées, but bringing no influence to bear in order to secure command for state concerts and balls; prompt with bouquet or curtsey when a princess opened one of their bazaars, but never fawning on the lady-in-waiting with hints that it would be a pleasure as well as an honour if her Royal Highness would come to luncheon one day, at number so-and-so Prince's Gardens; they felt and were sufficient for themselves. Untempted by the lure of a vanishing Bohemia, they did not traffic either with artistic circles; they bought pictures and read books without desiring to know the creators of such amenities; they enjoyed the play, but thought a row of footlights a very sensible, useful barrier between comedians of both sexes and the rest of the world.

Thus Mr. Verinder found himself immediately among his friends, and soon learned of something a little unusual about to-night's assembly. Anthony Dyke, the famous explorer, was here. He had dined here, and was now upstairs listening to the music.

"Oh, *that* fellow," said Mr. Verinder. "What a fuss they're making about him. You see his name everywhere. By the way, I rather thought he was booked to dine with the Salmon-Curers' Company this evening. My son went there, quite expecting to have a peep at him."

But old Sir Timothy Smith, given a knighthood last Christmas for designing the market-hall of a northern city, assured Mr. Verinder that the great man had dined with Mrs. Clutton and no one else.

"Refresh my memory about him," said Mr. Verinder. "I remember the Antarctic voyages. But what's his latest?"

"Well, nothing since that astounding performance in the Andes."

"Some of that has been questioned, hasn't it? Travellers' tales, what!" said Mr. Verinder, with a large tolerant smile. "Ah, there you are, my dear."

Mrs. Verinder, sailing forth splendidly from the cloak-room, was at his elbow.

"Dyke, the explorer, is here," she said.

"Yes, so Sir Timothy was telling me. Lead on, my dear."

And Mrs. Verinder led on, broad but splendid still in the back-view, carrying her train with a stout round forearm, followed by the grand young married lady and the slim demurely graceful girl, and lastly by Mr. Verinder. As they went upstairs, the music took a classical turn—a turn for the worse, Mr. Verinder considered.

After an ill-timed stentorian announcement, they were received in the midst of a few hushes, with silent cordiality by Mrs. Clutton. She was amiable and friendly as ever, leading Mrs. Verinder to a seat when the music stopped, but a little nervous or self-conscious by reason of the presence of the lion of the season.

"Yes, the big man leaning against the wall."

It would have been impossible to make any mistake. You could not see him without recognising him—since his portrait had become so familiar in the illustrated newspapers, as well as on the cover of that remarkable book of his. And seeing him you could scarcely help struggling hard to form a clear conception of what the man really might be.

In size he was very big, but looking still bigger than the true iron frame of him because of his loose garments—and one thought at once that of course he hated all confinements and restrictions, even those entailed by well-cut neatly-fitting clothes; with dark hair, blue eyes, a reddish beard, and shoulders that seemed too heavy; of enormous energy, the fire or lust for effort that seems incomprehensibly to renew itself in the grossest excesses of gratification; explosive and uncontrollable, as men like him must always be, but with that curious streak of softness, even of sentimentality, which goes sometimes with such characters. Just as he looked bigger than his size, he looked older than his years; but this impression may have been derived less from the marks and tints left upon him by tempest and strife than from the known record of his achievements. It was difficult to believe that he had done so much and yet was only thirty-seven. Above all else, unavoidably confusing judgment and driving one back to intuitions, there was a glamour cast about him by the deeply proved quality of courage—a glamour, it should be remembered, very much more rare and therefore very much more potent and alluring then than now.

"Did you hear him laugh?"

Everybody was whispering about him, thinking of him, ostentatiously taking no notice of him—except the privileged few who from time to time were being presented to him.

After twenty minutes or so Mrs. Clutton introduced Mr. Verinder to him, and they seemed to get on well together. Mr. Verinder, pleased to show that he knew a good deal of geography, asked intelligent questions, and felt flattered by the adventurer's eager expansive manner of giving full details in reply. Though he made you feel small physically, he did not make you feel small mentally. He said it was pleasant to be back in the old country, and agreed with Mr. Verinder that—all said and done—there was no place like London. Asked how long he intended to honour the metropolis with his presence, he laughed, and said it depended on circumstances, but he certainly should not stay more than a month or two. He was "taking the hat round," as he explained with a laugh, trying to raise funds towards another Antarctic expedition. "The fact is, Mr. Verinder"—and Mr. Verinder was not ill-pleased to observe that his name had been picked up so quickly and correctly—"in my trade, capital is very necessary. The most successful ventures are those that are best fitted out. The more money you have behind you, the further you go."

"I'm afraid," said Mr. Verinder, laughing in his turn, "that that may be said of all other trades, Mr. Dyke, as well as yours; but I quite understand what you mean. Equipment. Equipment. And no doubt many risks could be minimized by foresight and wise outlay."

Dyke became quite exuberant at finding Mr. Verinder so intelligent and sympathetic; his loud open-air voice could be heard throughout the length of Mrs. Clutton's double drawing-room. He was giving Mr. Verinder more and more details, with a child-like enthusiasm, and he would not stop when the music began again. No one dared say hush to him, but the decorum of Mr. Verinder's manner gradually restrained him. In regard to such interruptions, he pleased Mr. Verinder most of all by declaring that this music was incomprehensible to him—over his head; and at once concurring in Mr. Verinder's opinion that a ballad concert at the Albert Hall was the real stuff, and laughing most heartily when Mr. Verinder said that a just finished arrangement of Bach for the violin and piano might, in the popular phrase, have been the tune the old cow died of. Then, their relations having reached this very cordial stage, Anthony Dyke said abruptly—"I'm a fish out of water here. I wonder if by chance you could tell me the name of that girl over there."

"Which one?" asked Mr. Verinder.

"That one," said Dyke, not of course pointing with his hand in an uncouth manner, but only making slight yet significant signs with his dark eyebrows and blue eyes. "Now—the one using her fan. I'd like to get somebody to introduce me to her."

"I can supply the information, and gratify your wish," said Mr. Verinder, in a tone so urbane that it was robbed of any pompousness. "She is my daughter."

"Oh, really!" said Dyke, suddenly staring at him as if he didn't believe it. Then he laughed once more, but not loudly, shyly. "I hope it didn't sound odd my saying that. From living alone so much, I bang out whatever comes into my mind. You must look on me as the untutored savage and make excuses for me."

"None are necessary," said Mr. Verinder.

Emmeline, on the other side of the room, was engaged in conversation with their friend Mrs. Bell, whose house was one of the biggest in Queen's Gate. Her father beckoned her; and as she did not observe the signal, went across to fetch her, bringing her back with him and feeling proud of her as something that belonged to him and did him credit. Indeed, the circumstance that in a room full of other well-dressed women she had drawn the attention of this simple middle-aged wanderer, seemed a compliment to the whole family.

He thought that she looked very nice as she stood there smiling, after Mr. Dyke shook hands; so modest and quiet, so essentially *ladylike*, so completely everything he would have wished; her eyes shining, and a little colour in her usually rather pale cheeks, brought there from the excitement caused by meeting a really celebrated person; but with no shyness or awkwardness perceptible in voice or manner—just a raising of the arched eyebrows above the straight well-cut nose and that frank smile about the sweetly gentle mouth in order to show courteous interest in everything that was being said. The cream satin dress, too, with the silver and pearl ornamentation straight across the bodice, the shoulder puffs, the long white gloves, and the enormous fan, were all exactly the right thing, all very becoming. Mr. Verinder liked also, now that he considered the matter, this method of arranging the dark hair—quite low on the forehead and ascending beneath bands of gold ribbon to a high crest, brushed up from the back of her neck, as you saw when she turned round, and secured by a broad jewelled comb. This, the very latest mode, suited Emmeline. She had plenty of hair. Her father felt well satisfied with Emmeline's appearance.

They all three remained talking together, and Dyke would not relinquish the father and daughter when his hostess came and made further introductions. He drew the new people into the talk or let them slide altogether, but he hung on to the other two, moving with them if they moved. Mr. Verinder had a good-humoured gratified feeling that the lion had taken to him, and natural fierceness had disappeared in impulsive affection; it was, so to speak, a tame lion following him about, ready to eat out of his hand. But lionising, like everything else in a well-regulated world, must have its limits; you cannot neglect your duties at an evening party to gratify a stranger's hunger for your society, however famous that stranger may be. Mr. Verinder wished to rejoin his wife, and, using tact, he extricated himself. Yet his tact was not sufficient to extricate Emmeline as well.

One saw them standing together on the staircase, and later they were sitting together in a remote corner of the supper-room; he still telling her wonderful things, so that one heard the boom of his eager tones and the sound of her pretty girlish voice chiming in—a flute helping, not interrupting the 'cello or the bigger reeds. "Oh, but how exciting that must have been! Did you really, Mr. Dyke? What presence of mind."

When Mrs. Verinder with Margaret broke up the chat and said it was time to go, Emmeline gave a little start and looked at her as if for the moment she did not recognize her; then, as if remembering, she made the traveller known to her.

In the carriage, going up Exhibition Road, Mr. Verinder praised him. He said that he was a breezy, open hearted, engaging creature, and he would like to ask him to dinner. Get a few friends to meet him, what?

Mrs. Verinder said, "He has asked Margaret and Emmeline to tea to-morrow at Hurlingham. They could give him a message."

"Oh," said Mr. Verinder, "has he asked you two girls out for a little treat? Well, that's very kind and friendly of him."

At this date the dinner-party was still an unshaken British institution, a stately serious affair in any circumstances, like matrimony, not to be entered into lightly, and when conducted on the grand scale habitual to Prince's Gate, all preliminaries needed thoughtful care. For the minute of time before the horses pulled up, Mr. and Mrs. Verinder were both turning things over in their minds.

To all of them, as they entered the hall, there came that vague and usually unanalysed sensation which most people experience on returning home from a party; it is a faint shock of surprise caused by the silence and tranquillity after the noise and commotion; as if, because you have been hearing music, chattering, drinking wine, getting warm in a crowd, you expect your house to show that it has also passed through slight agitation and excitement. For a moment you are consciously or unconsciously displeased that it should have been quite unconcerned in anything that concerned you so much; then the solidity of the fact seems to steady your nerves and bring you comfort. Home again!

In the wisely restricted lamp-light turned on for them by the butler, one saw pallid marble nymphs and gods with black caves of shadow behind them, the squat richly carved legs of heavy tables whose further ends were lost in gloom, the gilt balustrade of the staircase glittering, and the stairs themselves rising sharply and as sharply turning till they grew dim and faded out on a level with the first floor. Above that all was dark, and one had an impression of the house stretching upward in the darkness to a fantastic height. The butler moving ahead gave them of a sudden a doorway of yellow flames, so dazzling did it seem as he switched and switched, flooding a large inner room with vivid light. They went in after him.

This room had never been properly named; it was spoken of indifferently as the boudoir, the morning-room, and mother's room—although Mrs. Verinder herself did not put forward any claim to proprietorial rights. Probably her title to it merely rested upon the circumstance that the portrait of her by Millais had been hung above its marble chimney-piece. Like every other room in the house, it displayed evidences of moderate wealth, painstaking care, and a docile adhesion to the prevailing standards of good taste. The walls were cream-coloured, with panels of red satin—two large patches of the satin being hidden by the Millais picture and another picture of similar size but strangely different subject by Leighton. There were more of those massive heavily carved tables, some big chairs with golden legs and tapestry backs, and here and there on the parquetry floor had been placed firmly secured mounds of velvet and brocade cushions, forming the easy backless seats then known as "poufs." These poufs had been chosen by Mrs. Verinder, and, sinking voluminously upon one of them, she gave a sign of fatigue, and stared at Millais' notion of her as she was once. A smaller pouf would have fitted her in that first year of her married life.

Margaret, fairer, shorter, plumper, altogether more bustling than her sister, went to one of the tables, where a silver tray with cut-glass bottles and tumblers waited for them, and poured out soda-water. Mr. Verinder at another table busied himself with the bed-rock detail of his dinner-party, consulting a gold-framed calendar and jotting down names on an ivory tablet. "The Cluttons," he murmured, "and old Sir Timothy—and the Everard-Browns."

"Don't forget some young men for Emmeline," said Mrs. Pratt gaily.

"I never do," said Mr. Verinder. And that was true. Before his time in that respect, he liked to see a few fresh young faces even at his most ceremonious feasts; moreover, as the father of daughters, he knew that one must not think only of oneself. It was at a big dinner that Lionel Pratt first betrayed his inclination towards Margaret. "I am thinking now more of the day than the company," he continued; and he ran his pencil down the calendar. "Seventeen days will bring us to the twelfth, and that's a Thursday. At this time of year you can't expect people to be free unless you give them adequate notice."

"Emmeline," said Mrs. Verinder, yawning, "would you like young What's-his-name—that friend of Mrs. Pryce-Jones—Gerald Something—to be asked?"

Emmeline did not answer. She was standing at the corner of the chimney-piece, one arm stretched along the marble, her cloak thrown open. Her eyes seemed queerly large and black, her cheeks white, her breathing wearily rapid; so that she had the aspect worn by her when, in the maternal phrase, she had been "overdoing it"—playing too many sets at lawn tennis, riding too long in the Row, going to too many theatres in the same week.

"There's no occasion for you to stay up," said Mrs. Verinder, observing this look on her daughter's face. "You go to bed, dear"; and she added the farewell words that she had first begun to utter when Emmeline was a child of fourteen. "Don't read in bed."

"No, I don't want to read to-night," said Emmeline, going out of the room.

No, she did not want to read: she wanted to think.

CHAPTER III

ON the morning after the day on which the two girls watched the polo and drank tea with Mr. Dyke, Margaret went back to her kind husband and two sweet little children at Hindhead, where they lived in a red-brick catastrophe of the largest size that Pratt had brought about among the beeches and pines only a few years previously. On the afternoon of that day Mr. Dyke called in Prince's Gate for the purpose of offering thanks by word of mouth for the invitation which he had already accepted with pen and ink. Mrs. Verinder said that he was amiable but untidy, and a sticker. She thought he would never go.

At dinner a night later—when only Eustace had been claimed by society and the other three remained at home—Mr. Verinder talked again of Anthony Dyke.

It appeared, said Mr. Verinder, that Dyke began his career as a hunter of big game in Africa, where, together with his companion, the eccentric Duke of Ravenna, he had been badly mauled by lions.

"The other night, while we were talking, I noticed some disfiguring marks on both cheekbones, and I should not be surprised if they were the signs of the clawing to which I allude. Whatever they were, he will carry them to his grave." And Mr. Verinder went on to say that Dyke's next scene of operations was Australia, where he had penetrated the unknown desert country in all directions.

Then he told them some more. He did not, of course, know that one of his hearers could have told it to him, had she been willing to display her knowledge.

The fact was that Mr. Verinder, desirous of being well posted by the twelfth of next month, when the man would be here as his guest for dinner, had searched tables and shelves at the Reform Club in order to put things together. That most useful of all volumes, Who's Who, did not as yet exist, but a sort of popular dictionary of biography gave Mr. Verinder all that he wanted, and very much in the modern style. In this compendium he gleaned such essential details as: "Emerged at Shark Bay on the northern coast, sole survivor of the party; Thanked by the Government of Queensland, 1885; Thanked by Governments of South Australia and New South Wales, gold medal of Royal Geographical Society, 1886; First Antarctic cruise, resulting in discovery of the island since named Anthony Dyke Land, and charting of coast-line for five hundred miles, 1888; Establishing Furthest South record"—and so on.

Also Mr. Verinder had been to Mudie's Library and borrowed that book, *A Walk in the Andes*. He read it after dinner.

They sat upstairs in what they called the music-room—the room that comprised the full width of the house, the largest and best room, with the pictures by Long, Poynter, and Alma Tadema. The Leaders were in the room behind; you reached it through those folding doors, now of course closed. Naturally all the light was not turned on, but there was full and sufficient radiance throughout the little camp that the diminished family formed on the stretching desert of parquetry.

Mrs. Verinder, wearing mauve brocade, occupied a sofa and dozed over the newspaper; Mr. Verinder had taken the very easiest chair and settled himself in it with many changes of position, as if determined to perform the impossible task of making it still easier; Emmeline sat upon a lowish stool, her pretty hair darkly lustrous in the soft orange glow of the lamps as she bent her head over a piece of embroidery and made minute stitches slowly and very neatly. From time to time she raised her eyes to glance at the book in her father's hands, noticing how old and shabby it looked with the edge of the cloth binding broken and the librarian's ugly label loose at one corner. She had a lovely clean new copy upstairs in her room—with the portrait-cover intact, and her own name and the author's compliments written in a slap-dash hand on the title page.

"They told me at the club," said Mr. Verinder, half closing his book, "that there's a strong touch of Baron Munchausen about this."

"Did you speak?" said Mrs. Verinder, raising herself and stooping to pick up the newspaper.

Mr. Verinder repeated his words.

"Munchausen," murmured Mrs. Verinder drowsily.

He went on reading and Emmeline watched him while he read.

As she knew or had learned involuntarily, it was not great literature, a modest affair compared with the works of Thackeray, Carlyle, or Ruskin— but why bother about style when you have such a tale to tell? The matter not the manner grips. Was it gripping father? He had assumed a dogged, almost aggressive air, he frowned; but this did not really indicate that he was quarrelling with the book, it only meant that as he was very little used to book-reading as a pastime, he felt that a superior concentration of the intellect was necessary.

Watching him, she had again that odd sense of strangeness; as though he had not been really her father, but somebody that she scarcely knew and did not in the least care for. How strange! Certainly she had never seen him or understood him as now, suddenly, unexpectedly.

She observed his bushy yet straggling grey eyebrows, his inch of close-cropt whisker, his bald head with long strands of hair idiotically plastered across it from the fat neck, his leathery complexion, the creases and furrows of his chin and cheeks. He was well dressed, in a suitable manner—but suitable to what? The well-starched shirt, the black satin tie, the glossy dinner jacket gave him no true dignity, concealed not one of his defects. He was a ruin, a man run to seed; large without being strong, too stout about the middle, too slack about the knees, no steel and whipcord anywhere about this sprawling unimpressive bulk. No force of any sort behind that stupid frown! But he was kindly by nature, well-intentioned, thoroughly good according to his lights; only stupid—stupid, stupid as the Albert Hall is round, as Exhibition Road is wide, as Queen's Gate straight and Kensington Gore flat.

Then she thought how cruel it was that she should thus judge him instead of pitying him—she, with this immense gladness in her heart.

She glanced at her mother, from whose relaxed grasp the newspaper was again slipping, and a yearning compassion for both parents came in response to the call. Poor dears.

The book had gripped father; he read on resolutely, but as yet of course he was only at the beginning, still in Patagonia. Stitching very slowly she thought about it. It was so simple, yet so wonderful, so very wonderful.

He had been "messing about" among the gold-diggings of Cape Horn. "The Gold-diggings of Cape Horn"—inaudibly she re-articulated the words to herself, just to feel them again on her vocal cords. Like all other words that concerned him, they had magic in them. For instance, Tierra del Fuego—the Land of Fire—Tierra del Fuego. And beyond all else, the Andes. The Andes—it seemed to her that the very first time she heard that word when she was a child, she should have thrilled through and through. The word should have taken possession of her by reason of its mystery and might.

Well then, he was moving northward among those islands, trying his luck at the gold-digging, and doing no good. "I don't think I am a lucky man, Miss Verinder. No, I have never been very lucky. How I go on warning you against myself, don't I? But, just as I have been frank to you about important matters, I won't deceive you about small ones. Never mind. Hang it, the luck turns. I shall get my luck one day." Well then—while her father read the book she talked to herself about it: Since he was at a loose end, no big thing on hand, the idea had come to him to land on the mainland, and go along the gigantic spine of the Andes in its entire length from south to north, say four thousand miles. And he had achieved his purpose, alone and on foot—seeing marvellous things, doing marvellous things all the way.

She thought of the lure that danger exercises over the bravest hearts. It is the same to-day as it was hundreds of years ago. It was that—the lure—which drew the brave hearts over the bars of Devon rivers in Elizabeth's time; out, out to the Spanish main. Not the glitter of the gold, but the danger behind the flash and glow—the danger. She quite understood.

The newspaper had fallen with a gentle rustle upon the parquetry. Mrs. Verinder leaned further back, opened her mouth, and, after it had been open for a little while, made the faint sound of a snore. The snoring of Mrs. Verinder was like a terrible family secret, never to be spoken of or even hinted at in any manner to anybody—least of all, to Mrs. Verinder herself. This evening, however, it did not distressfully afflict either her husband or her daughter.

Emmeline ceased to stitch, folded her hands on her lap with a gesture that had become habitual to her even at this distant date, and her eyes grew soft and dreamy. Large as the room was, it was too small for her; with a few dreamlike thoughts she broke the westward wall of it, swept it clean away—the five windows, the rich curtains, the gilded, moulded panels, and all the rest of it—and passed out through the gap, merely leaving behind the graceful external shape of herself to keep her parents company and answer questions, if necessary, during her absence. She went a long way; westward, half across the world. Then she came back again, and was once more in the neighbourhood, although not yet in the house itself. She was walking under the trees, not far from sunlit water, listening to a voice.

The entrance of butler and footmen with the silver tray and the cut glass brought her right home, and she resumed her stitching.

Quite late the book wrung a chuckle and an expostulation from Mr. Verinder. "Oh, I say. Really—upon my word;" and he stood up. "If Dyke actually means what I think! And I don't see what else he can mean. Listen to this. I want to read it to you."

Mrs. Verinder, in the absurd sprightly tone of a person whom sleep has intoxicated, begged him to give them the passage; and Mr. Verinder, standing close to a tall standard lamp, with all available light on the page, read it, after first explaining the context.

Dyke, he said, had accepted a night's hospitality from three savages, who at first appeared friendly, but soon aroused his suspicion. Acting a naïve admiration of the weapon, they had withdrawn his rifle before he lay down to sleep; and now the three of them sat at the fire with their heads close together, planning mischief, as he surmised. At their feet was a great stone axe, and not far from him a horse-hair lasso. "Dyke says that while still pretending to sleep, he moved inch by inch towards the lasso, till he got it and opened the noose. Ah, here we are. Now listen." And Mr. Verinder read slowly, amazedly, fearfully. "'By good fortune I noosed them all three, so that their greased and painted faces crashed together with a nasty bang. Borrowing the stone axe, I used it freely. Then I lay down and slept comfortably, feeling confident that my late hosts would never plot against a visitor again.' He means—doesn't he?—that he killed them. He says his *late* hosts. What! He can't mean anything else?"

"No," said Mrs. Verinder, successfully shaking off the dregs of torpor; "that's what he means, of course."

Mr. Verinder chuckled feebly. "But, upon my word If you think of it, wasn't it—"

"It was in self-defence," said Mrs. Verinder tolerantly.

"Yes, I suppose it was. But doesn't it show—"

Of a truth he scarcely knew what it showed. Unless the obvious fact that there are wide expanses of land and water on this big planet where life does not run as smoothly as it does in Prince's Gate; that when once you go outside the boundaries of civilization, when once you begin to disregard the rules that bind society together—He stood there in the strong lamp-light, with the reluctant confused facial expression of a comfort-loving, peaceable, sheltered person who is confronted with ferocity—legitimate ferocity, perhaps; as when, standing in an hotel balcony during a riot, one sees limbs broken by a baton charge of mounted police. However much one dislikes it, one cannot hinder or interfere. One can do nothing—except to make light of the incident afterwards, and, so to speak, laugh it off.

Mr. Verinder laughed and closed the book. "That's enough for to-night," he said, putting the book down, and feeling the back of his neck.

After this the name of Anthony Dyke faded out of the family conversation, and for a few days at least was mentioned no more. Then Miss Marchant came and made a communication to Mrs. Verinder, saying that she had been sent to do it by Mrs. Pryce-Jones.

Mrs. Jones lived in the large stone house at the western end of Kensington Gore, and Miss Marchant lived with her as a kind of lady companion, assisting her with household management.

Mrs. Jones thought that Mrs. Verinder ought to be told that Miss Marchant, happening to be in Kensington Gardens not long before dinner time, had seen Miss Verinder walking alone with a man there. They were quite alone, without the shadow of a chaperon. Just together—like that. They never saw Miss Marchant, who had observed them until obliged herself to leave the gardens. As Mrs. Verinder knew, they dined rather early at the stone house. As Mrs. Verinder knew also, Mrs. Jones was very fond of Miss Emmeline, and she felt it only right to send Miss Marchant; bearing in mind that the very nicest girls do need a little looking after.

Mrs. Verinder did not at all relish this turn of phrase, and she allowed Miss Marchant to perceive her distaste for it; but Miss Marchant, continuing the narrative after an apology, threw Mrs. Verinder into a state of flabby perturbation which she could ill conceal, by saying that the impression made by Miss Emmeline's male companion had been so very unfavourable. He had seemed altogether a most undesirable person—objectionable even. One did read such dreadful things in the newspapers nowadays—about slight indiscretions of young ladies leading to painful entanglements. Indeed, as she confessed, she had been haunted by the idea of blackmailers—the sort of ruffians who possess themselves of a perhaps quite innocent secret, then distort it and make you pay them to hide it. In these circumstances Mrs. Pryce-Jones and Miss Marchant had both felt that it would be really wicked not to speak about it to Mrs. Verinder.

"Do you imply," asked Mrs. Verinder breathlessly, "that it was a common ragged sort of person?"

Oh, no. The person was adequately, if queerly dressed; a great big tall man, wearing a grey suit and a slouch hat. It was rather his commanding air, the way he brandished his arms, and so on, that had displeased and frightened Miss Marchant.

Then—what was exceedingly rare with her—Mrs. Verinder had an inspiration, or an intuition.

"A bearded man?"

"Yes."

"A man with a red beard, and rather high cheekbones—a great big man?"

"Yes, yes."

It was that Dyke—the explorer. Although no worse, Mrs. Verinder was, of course, very much upset by it; but she displayed a satisfaction that she was very far from feeling.

"Oh, really!" she said, tittering effectively. "You may be quite at ease, Miss Marchant. It is quite all right, thank you. He is a valued friend of the family. No more a friend of Emmeline's than the rest of us. But I don't think I shall tell you his name," she added, acting playful reproachfulness. "I don't think you deserve it—No, I am not in the least offended. I'll at least tell you this—" and for a moment hesitating whether to cloak herself with cold dignity or put on a mask of cordialness, she chose the smiles—"he is dining with us on the twelfth, and although unfortunately, our table is made up, so that I cannot ask you to meet him at dinner, I shall be very glad indeed if you and Mrs. Jones will look in afterwards. That is, if you have nothing better to do."

Miss Marchant withdrew, puzzled and crestfallen.

Immediately Mrs. Verinder despatched a message upstairs requesting Miss Emmeline to come down to the morning-room. She had determined to talk to her daughter without delay, but quite lightly, with a simulation of unconcern. It is always wisest with young people not to show them that you have been fluttered by any act of theirs.

Afternoon tea was done, and trays of cut flowers, the contents of a hamper sent by Margaret from Hindhead, had been brought into the room for Mrs. Verinder to arrange in glass vases and dishes. It was a little task that she liked to do herself—perhaps because she did it with so extraordinary a clumsiness and ineptitude. She seized upon these flowers now—lovely long-stalked roses, pink and red—feeling that they would aid her and keep her in countenance; and as she moved about, dabbing the delicious blooms into obviously improper receptacles, breaking a stalk here or there, and slopping a little water on the choice furniture, she looked like a large over-blown actress playing a part in a highly artificial comedy.

"Ah, Emmeline, is that you?" she cried, with a tone so jarringly spurious that Emmeline stopped short on the threshold and understood at once that the trouble was beginning.

"Shut the door, dear. What was I going to say?" And Mrs. Verinder caused a slop-over and a shower of petals with the same brisk movement of her dimpled hand. "Oh, yes. I could not tell you why, but our friend Mr. Anthony Dyke came into my mind just now; and thinking about him, I thought I'd give you a little hint."

"Yes, mother?"

"To begin with, we scarcely know him."

"We have not known him very long," said Emmeline, gently.

"I say, we don't really know him at all"; and Mrs. Verinder gave a harshly nervous laugh as she mutilated some maidenhair fern. "I mean, nothing *about* him—who he is, or what he is, himself, outside his notoriety. Then the point is this. Because—I don't say so, but I thought it might be—

because he may have interested you as rather striking, a *bizarre* figure, and so forth—" Watching Emmeline's face, she rapidly abandoned a difficult rôle and became more like herself. "I don't want you to indulge in any silliness about him."

"What do you mean by silliness?" said Emmeline quietly.

"Well, I don't want you to fall in love with him."

"I'm afraid I've done that already," said Emmeline, still more quietly.

Her mother flung down a bunch of wet La Frances on the satin seat of the nearest chair, and became entirely natural.

"Oh, what nonsense—what utter nonsense! Emmeline, how can you talk such rubbish? Really—upon my word. A total stranger—and a man old enough to be your father."

"Oh, no. He is considerably under forty."

"Then he doesn't *look* it. And such an untidy creature." Ruffled, bothered, angry, Mrs. Verinder was speaking without plan, uttering scattered thoughts as they presented themselves, and she continued volubly to do so. "I never saw such an untidy man. That night at Mrs. Clutton's. His crumpled shirt— and he kept running his hands through his hair till it was all anywhere." Emmeline was gently shaking her head, as though to imply that she did not mind, that she rather liked the untidy appearance. "You of all people, too— you who've always had such a sense of fitness and niceness. How can you for a moment harbour such silliness? Besides, the *time*! There's been no *time* for it. What night was it, that night at Mrs. Clutton's? Surely not a week ago!" And Mrs. Verinder steadied herself, speaking slower and with weight. "Emmeline, tell me the truth. How many times have you actually seen him?"

"Let me think," said Emmeline, with dreamy introspective eyes, deeply interested by the question and vibrating with anxious care as she answered it. How many times, how few times? Of course, it was so immeasurably more wonderful to her than it could be to her mother. "At Mrs. Clutton's," she said gravely. "At Hurlingham next day. Next morning at Waterloo."

"At Waterloo?" ejaculated Mrs. Verinder loudly. "What's that? Waterloo!"

"When Margaret was going home. He came to see her off."

"See her off! How did he know her train?"

"She told him—or I did. I don't remember."

"More fools, the pair of you."

Emmeline made a deprecating gesture, as of one who pleads not to be interrupted in a difficult mental effort, and for a moment or so looked about her vaguely.

"Then of course he came here that same afternoon," she said, with a brightening face. "And the next afternoon he came again."

"Not two afternoons!" cried Mrs. Verinder. "Not again, behind my back, without my seeing him. Oh, but, Emmeline, that is shameful; that is underhand."

"He is not underhand. How could you see him? You were out."

"Then he oughtn't to have come in. Besides, why didn't he leave his cards? There were no cards on the table. I looked."

"He left cards the day before."

"He should have left them again," said Mrs. Verinder, not really meaning it, only feeling muddled and angry.

Emmeline made another gesture.

"That brings us to Thursday. And the three times in Kensington Gardens. I have met him there, mother, by appointment. That's seven times, isn't it? No, eight—eight!" Her voice faded away as she said the number, as though she was lost in the wonder of it. Could it be possible? Only eight times—all told!

"Well. *Well*," said Mrs. Verinder, pulling herself together. In the midst of her irritation she could not avoid a feeling of pride because of the silly child's absolute truthfulness and candour. "Of course you understand that there must be no more of such meetings."

Emmeline let that remark go, as if it had been a ball at tennis that was not worth moving to—so obviously out of court.

"And your father must be told about it."

"Yes, I suppose he had better know," said Emmeline dreamily.

Left alone, Mrs. Verinder polished off the flowers in a very rough and ready fashion, thinking the while. If Emmeline insisted on making an imprudent marriage, it was doubtful if one could prevent her. No, why not be honest about it? One *couldn't* prevent her. The only way you can keep grown-up girls in check is by holding their purse-strings—and Emmeline had her own money. And she thought that, nice as it is to belong to the third or even fourth generation of families enriched by the highest form of trade, it is perhaps a pity that grandfathers should leave money to female grandchildren—absolutely, on their attaining the age of twenty-one. Wiser and better to leave it in the control of parents—or make the age thirty—or forty. Margaret had gone off so easily and pleasantly with Lionel Pratt. A nice well-dressed rich young fellow, able to build quite a palace for his wife, and send flowers to his mother-in-law.

Leaving out maternal feeling altogether, she could not bear this idea of a quite attractive if rather reserved girl marrying an uncouth stranger—a man who had come from the ends of the earth and would probably want to go back there. Of course if it must be, it must be. "But, oh," she said to herself with a sigh, "it is all too weird; for *I* don't understand what she has seen in him to captivate her."

She determined that she would talk to her husband about it directly after dinner, not before dinner. It was now half-past six o'clock; and, while giving her very last dabs to the flowers, she fancied that she heard the front door open and shut. Going out to the hall presently and seeing one of the footmen, she inquired if it had been Mr. Verinder coming in.

"No, ma'am, it was Miss Verinder going out."

"Oh, yes, quite so."

Mrs. Verinder went slowly up the stairs, feeling seriously perturbed. In spite of all that had been said just now, had Emmeline gone out to meet that man? But Mrs. Verinder held to her determination of postponing her chat with Mr. Verinder till after dinner. If you cannot avoid worry, it is better to take it on a full stomach.

Emmeline gave one glance back at the house, noticed that it too had changed, and hurried on.

Open carriages with a footman as well as a coachman on each box seat were streaming up the road. Quite young ladies in the carriages wore bonnets with strings tied under their chins, daintily small bonnets of delicate colours, primrose, heliotrope, and peach; those that wore hats had them perched in the queerest manner, on the back of the head, sideways, at angles; all of them held up flounced or laced parasols of rich dark tints, and their great sleeves ballooned so widely as almost to conceal gentlemen who were accompanying them—elderly gentlemen, these, like father, in top hats and open frock coats; or comparatively youthful gentlemen, like our brother Eustace, in top hats and buttoned frock coats. A horn sounded joyously, and round the corner from Prince's Gardens there came a four-in-hand—four beautiful grey horses prancing, the whole coach shining in the sunlight, a bevy of ladies, a flower-bed of female elegance, on top; and the two grooms, one standing up to blow the horn and the other sitting down with folded arms. There was another, a plain-clothes groom, concealed within the shuttered doors, but ready to pop out should the gentleman driving meet any difficulties. "So-ho, there. Steady."

The top hat of the gentleman driving shone prodigiously; he wore a button-hole of gardenias and had a light holland cloth round his middle dividing the frock coat from the shepherd's plaid trousers; although his face was red and anxious, he looked very grand. The whole prosperous essentially respectable neighbourhood was rolling through the slanted sunbeams to enjoy its drive of ceremony in Hyde Park.

At Alexandra Gate a mounted policeman held up his white hand and stopped the traffic of the main road, in order to allow all these equipages to roll flashing past unimpeded. The stout plebeian horses of two omnibuses had to be pulled up short with a jerk, the ponies in several tradesmen's carts skidded a little on the macadam; a small squad of lads riding on those new safety bicycles—not the ugly high ones—jumped from the pedals and held their machines sloping to the pavement. Within the rails of the semi-private sanctuary of Hyde Park, Mayfair and Belgravia on wheels at once mingled with and absorbed Kensington on wheels. It was a gay and enchantingly polite spectacle.

But Emmeline turned her back on it and walked swiftly into the cool shadow cast by Albert Hall Mansions—the only edifice in the locality of which Mr. Verinder did not approve. Then, before she reached the Albert Hall, her heart leaped. A tall, excitable man was coming towards her, waving a slouch hat. They should have met on the Broad Walk; she had told him to wait there; but he was not able to wait.

How had he captivated her? She did not know. Was it only because he was the incarnate antithesis of Kensington; because he was individual, unlike the things on each side of him, not arranged on any pattern, not dull, monotonous, or flat; a thing alive in a place where all else was sleeping or dead? Neither then nor at any future time did she attempt mentally to differentiate between the impression he had made upon her as himself all complete, with the dark hair, the penetrating but impenetrable eyes, the record, the fame, and the impression she might have received if any of these attributes had been taken away from him. Say, if he had been an unknown Mr. Tomkins instead of a known Mr. Dyke. Absurd. The man and the name were one. So very much so indeed that yesterday morning when, at the museum, she had asked for a new map of the Antarctic, and was poring over it in order to feast herself with a sight of those magic words Anthony Dyke Land, it was not only that the little black letters of which the names was composed shone like rubies and burned like fire, she felt distinctly the man's hand on her shoulder and heard his voice at her ear, although at this moment he was miles away. He was Anthony Dyke. He was her lord, her prince, her lover.

Yet hitherto she had not been a romantic girl. She had felt nothing irksome in her surroundings, had been content with these broad streets and platitudinous façades; her pulses had not stirred at contact with masculinity; life with the family had seemed pleasant, and the prospect of ultimate union with some good-natured nonentity like Pratt, a well-managed nursery, some humdrum babies, had not appeared repellent. She was not irregular either in thought or conduct. Indeed, she had inherited a fair portion of her father's love of order; showing this characteristic in many ways, keeping her room very neat and tidy, liking, even when she was quite small, to have boxes and convenient places in which to keep her belongings, not leaving books on sofas or dropping her handkerchief on the stairs. Beyond the sensation of possessing latent powers and capabilities upon which there had been no call, there had not come to her herself the slightest indication of the likelihood of what was happening now. It was unexpected, miraculous. As though that Virginia creeper which was so neatly bound upon its wires from the wide area to the top of the ground floor windows of their house had been metamorphosed into an overwhelming growth, with tendrils strong enough to bind a man's limbs, huge pulp-laden leaves, and blazing red tropical passion flowers.

They entered the Gardens by the small gate, and he plunged across the grass with her just at a point where a notice board was imploring people to keep on the paths. They walked away together under the trees, towards the water. It lay all aglow in the mellow sunlight.

When she came home a little more than an hour later she glanced at the outside of the house again. Home. It was not so much that it had changed, it had lost significance.

After dinner she went upstairs to the music-room, while her father was drawn by Mrs. Verinder into the room that they sometimes called her own. In there Mrs. Verinder told him, with a mere expression of regret and no preamble, that Emmeline had fallen in love with Dyke, the explorer.

"But, good heavens," cried Mr. Verinder, "he's a married man."

Mrs. Verinder sat down. As a very broad generalisation, it might be said that there are two classes of people: those who spring to their feet when suddenly confronted with a grave crisis and those who sit down. Mrs. Verinder was of the sitting-down sort.

"Married man!" she echoed, after seating herself. "How do you know?"

"Mrs. Clutton told me so. I asked if his wife was there, and she said no, the wife is never seen."

"Then you ought to have told me."

"I did."

"Never."

"I certainly intended to—although I never thought it could be of the slightest consequence to us. But I meant to warn you for the twelfth—to say nothing to him in conversation about married life or divorce. Oh, but this is ridiculous." Mr. Verinder walked about the room, frowning. "Emmeline! No, no. Whatever fancy—It must be stopped at once. Emmeline must be told the facts of the case, and she must dismiss all thought about him. It can be nothing, so far."

"I fear," said Mrs. Verinder, "that she has been going about with him."

"What makes you think that?"

Mrs. Verinder explained.

"It is very wrong of him," said Mr. Verinder indignantly. "It is very wrong of him in the circumstances." He felt alarm now as well as indignation, and he came to the front of Mrs. Verinder and spoke with frowning emphasis. "That sort of man might be very dangerous—unscrupulous—reckless of consequences. I don't like this at all."

Then he walked about the room again, reflecting upon the manner in which he should break the unpalatable news to Emmeline. He felt that it was a delicate business and one demanding tact; for no sensitive self-respecting young lady can fail to suffer from the sting of wounded pride when she learns that a man with no right to pay specially marked attentions to anybody has been paying them to her. On the other hand, if the attentions have not been special or marked, then in responding by any relaxment of reserve she has made a fool of herself—and she won't like that either. However, he was soon ready for his task, and both of them went upstairs to Emmeline in the music-room.

There, in the music-room, occurred what Mrs. Verinder called "a scene." It was the first real scene that had ever broken the tranquil atmosphere of the house since the family had occupied it; but as many other scenes were soon to follow, one may perhaps indicate the developments of this one by synopsis.

Miss Verinder, coming from the piano where she had been playing, was informed by her father of the fact—Mr. Dyke not in a position to marry, for the simple reason that Mr. Dyke is already married. In these circumstances an obvious necessity to open her eyes; and an equally obvious necessity for her and the rest of the family to drop Mr. Dyke like a hot potato.

All this he had conveyed with delicacy enough; but, observing that Miss Verinder, after her eyes had been opened, showed density, slowness of intelligence, or lack of sufficient recoil, he felt the initial touch of that cumulative irritation with which fate was about to torture him, and he amplified the argument in a heavier and less tactful style. Very, very wrong of Dyke to play the fool with her, and hold this knowledge up his sleeve. Can have so behaved for none other than a caddish motive. Very, very humiliating for her, to find out how worthless he is; but nothing to do except take the thing in proper ladylike style, wash him out, and look pleasant about it—that is, pleasant before company.

Then came the shock.

Miss Verinder, to the horror and amazement of her parents, said she had known it from the beginning. Nothing underhand or caddish about the man; best man in the world; at any rate, the only man in the world for her. As to being talked about, peril to reputation, and so on—it did not, as she implied, matter twopence-half-penny to Miss Verinder. To such questions as, Where had her pride gone? she returned evasive or unsatisfactory replies.

Mr. Verinder, talking now very freely, felt after a little while that he was making too much noise and no real progress. He broke off the interview, saying he would take Mrs. Verinder downstairs with him and go on talking to her alone in the boudoir. Emmeline offered to withdraw from the music-room, leaving them alone there; but Mr. Verinder said he needed pens, ink, and paper, and he would find them on the ground floor. He would return soon to make some final pronouncement to Emmeline; she was therefore to remain where she was.

Downstairs, he used such words as stupid hero-worship, temporary infatuation, passing fancy induced by the plausible cajolements of a man so much older than herself. Of Dyke he said he could not speak with adequate censure—and he added at once that most certainly Dyke's invitation to dinner on the twelfth must be cancelled. But of course there should be no cancellation of the dinner itself. He would write to Dyke to-morrow; he knew exactly what to say to Dyke. That letter, however, could wait till to-morrow. The pressing thing was to decide what to do with Emmeline.

"If," said Mr. Verinder, "she will give me her solemn promise never to see him again, then—"

"She won't," said Mrs. Verinder. "I could detect that, in the expression of her face just now."

Then soon an idea occurred to one or other of them and was immediately adopted by both. They would send Emmeline on a visit to Hindhead, and thus keep her out of the way and give her time to forget this silliness. She would be very happy down there, she was devoted to Margaret's two children, she liked all the sylvan glades that had been left standing after Pratt built his mansion.

It was not too late to despatch a telegram, although it might not be delivered to-night, and they could not expect an answer till the morning. They sent this off, looked in the railway guide to find an early train to Hindhead, gave the necessary instructions about the carriage which would convey Miss Verinder to the station. Then Mr. Verinder stood thinking and frowning, till he asked a question about the maid who would accompany his daughter.

"That girl who looks after her—Louisa Hodson! Can Louisa be trusted?"

"Oh, I hope so," said Mrs. Verinder, already feeling that nobody was to be trusted, that everybody had bothering secrets which one would find out sooner or later. "Oh, yes, I think Louisa is quite trustworthy. She *has* been—so far."

Then they went upstairs once more.

"It is arranged," he said, "that you shall go to Margaret for a few weeks."

Miss Verinder said that she would not go. Her face was white, and she spoke in a quiet but rather breathless manner.

"Oh, yes, it is all settled," said Mr. Verinder curbing himself. Then, as he saw her shake her head negatively, he burst out. "You will do what you are told."

"Oh, no, I assure you, father, I can't be treated like this, as if I was a child."

"It will do you good," said Mrs. Verinder feebly. "You look pale and fagged. The change of air—"

"If I wanted change of air I'd sooner go to the seaside by myself. Yes, I could do that."

"No, you couldn't," shouted Mr. Verinder; and he told her that if she compelled him, he would give orders that would result in total restriction of her movements. Then the servants would all know that there was something wrong in the house; they would talk, and the echo of their talk would be heard outside the house. Nevertheless, facing these risks, he would give his orders. "Understand, I am serious."

"So am I," said Miss Verinder, very quietly.

"The carriage will be at the door at ten minutes to ten, to take you to Waterloo," he said, shouting. "You'll have your things packed, and you'll start—No, don't leave the room." She was going towards the door; but she stopped, and sat down by the piano. "Do you hear? You'll have everything packed to-night, before you go to bed."

"Except her dressing-case," said Mrs. Verinder. "That must be kept open till the morning—to put in her small odds and ends—brush and comb—what she wants for her personal comfort."

Nothing further of a contentious character was said. And presently Mr. Verinder tried to do a little acting in his turn; he essayed a representation of relief of mind, restored confidence, general good humour. He said he had interrupted Emmeline earlier in the evening when she was playing the piano. Would she play something to him now?

She obeyed, playing a selection from the new musical piece at the Savoy Theatre.

Mr. Verinder acted the soothing effect produced by tuneful melody, satisfaction that peace now reigned, and so forth; but, leaning back in the easy chair, he felt unexpectedly tired and shaky.

"Thank you, dear. That is very pretty."

"And didn't she play it prettily?" said Mrs. Verinder.

"Yes. Thank you, dear," said Mr. Verinder again, indicating by his tone that in view of the task which lay before her upstairs he would not ask for an encore. That packing! He tried to express trunks and boxes by his firm but kindly manner; he did not wish to repeat the words themselves.

Emmeline, seeming to accept the hint, rose from the piano and bade them good-night.

"Out of the way for a month at least. That gives one time," said Mr. Verinder, when the door had closed; and he gave his wife an oral sketch of the letter she was to write to Margaret explaining the state of affairs, putting Margaret on her guard, and telling her what precautions should be taken. He thought it ought, if possible, to be in the post-box before one A.M.

Poor Mrs. Verinder sat up late to write it.

Early next morning they received Margaret's reply telegram—just the one word "Delighted." Miss Emmeline had breakfast in her room, and this arrangement appeared to Mr. Verinder both natural and proper. At ten minutes to ten the single brougham with the luggage tray on top stood waiting at the door, and the footman who was to accompany it was in the hall waiting for the odd man to come through the baize doors with the luggage.

"Are Miss Verinder's things down?" asked Mr. Verinder of somebody.

"No, sir," said the butler, "I don't think they are."

"Where's Hodson?"

Louisa Hodson leaned over the gilt balustrade on the first floor.

"Is Miss Verinder packed?"

"No, sir," said Louisa; coming half-way down the stairs to meet him as he came up them, and speaking confidentially when they met. "Miss Verinder told me not to pack, sir. I think she has changed her mind and doesn't intend to go."

It was open rebellion.

CHAPTER IV

MR. VERINDER gave his orders now—foolish ones, as such orders always are. Miss Verinder was not to leave the house except when accompanied by her maid, or her mother. In the case of her issuing forth with Louisa Hodson, she was to account for the time spent while away. Louisa must also account for it. Miss Verinder was to go about with her mother as much as possible; to fulfil all social engagements that had already been made; to do the afternoon drives in Hyde Park, together with both her parents, and so on.

During the course of the morning he called upon his solicitors in Spring Gardens, and saw the head of the firm, Mr. Williams. He desired Mr. Williams to find out all about Anthony Dyke. "Find out everything you can for me. I want the fullest information I can get." Mr. Williams, promising to do so, noticed that his client and old friend looked gloomy and depressed; and the brief interview terminated at once, without passing into the pleasant general chat that was customary when Mr. Verinder came to Spring Gardens.

It has been said that Mr. Verinder had a love of law and order. Truly, he adored them. We are all of us what our antecedent history makes us; and Mr. Verinder, looking backward far beyond his own birth, behind his grandfather's birth even, could see such beneficent factors as open markets, stable rates of exchange, organised means of transport, together with banking and credit systems that are really based on the confidence inspired by a firm government—he could see all this not only as the solid foundation on which the British Empire had been raised, but as the prime cause of the success of those paper mills in the midlands from which he and his family derived their wealth. The mills had long ceased to give any trouble, they just went on; and he merely drew dividends or travelled by train occasionally to attend board meetings. But, of course, except for law and order, the mills could not have maintained their initial impetus so comfortably.

He was proud to think that the mills made paper used by government offices, and that his son Eustace—now aged thirty-three—was actually a government official. Eustace, after taking honours at the venerable long-established institution known as Oxford University, had entered the Board of Trade—not to stay there for ever, but as a step in his career; whereby he would lay up such a store of useful knowledge with regard to the wider aspects of national commerce as should enable him later on, when he went into Parliament, handsomely to assist the government of the day instead of hampering them with unenlightened criticism.

Except in relation to classical music, Mr. Verinder himself was never critical. He was content to bow to acknowledged authority in every form; respecting heads of professions and submitting to expert opinions; believing in the wisdom of judges on the bench, the art of Royal Academicians, the inspired logical faculty of bishops in conclave. Although a stout Anglican, he could not in any circumstances have brought himself to speak disparagingly of the Pope.

Simply but completely he loved his house, taking daily pleasure in its largeness, its unostentatious splendour, its immense comfort. As he lay in bed at night he liked to think of the number of people sleeping under his roof; also their dependence on him the chieftain, who took care of their food and their well-being, who had provided two bath-rooms solely for the servants' use—one under the tiles for the women, one down in the basement for the men. It was a grand, well-managed house. It was his castle, his stronghold. He looked at it with satisfaction every time that he walked or drove up to it.

There was no taint of meanness in this feeling. He remembered with unselfish gladness that several of his friends were almost if not quite as fortunate. Mrs. Bell had one of the largest houses in Queen's Gate, and throughout the whole Cromwell Road there was nothing bigger than Mrs. Clutton's mansion. When speaking of these ladies he rarely omitted to mention the fact.

He loved his neighbourhood too. In imagination he could see it as finally completed, with the College of Music, the Colonial Institute, and all the other fine edifices grouping together—much as it is to-day. The Albert Hall was especially dear to him. He owned a box in it; some of his money went annually towards its maintenance. The vast and noble arena had no traditions earlier than the Prince Consort, but, oh, what glorious traditions since! It would be not too much to say that he derived a subtle kind of intellectual support from the adjacency of the Albert Hall. It stood there so close, unshakable, giving him a sensation directly due to its height above the eye and its stretch to either hand; solid and calm in its triumphant common-sense. For, if you want a building to hold the greatest possible number of people, then make it circular and avoid corners. Add a dome to render it sightly, but do not sacrifice use to ornamentation.

Nor, for the life of him, could he understand why certain folk tried to belittle the merit of the Albert Memorial. To him it seemed a very beautiful monument. He rejoiced even in its accessory groups of sculpture, admiring the taste and judgment that had led the artist to select a camel as symbolic of Africa and an elephant for Asia; often, when alone, he would mount the broad steps and study the reliefs about the square base; with the assistance of the chiselled names, he distinguished certain English Worthies, pausing here and there to gaze reverently at the genial attitude of Barry or the contemplative brow of Wren. English Worthies—the very title was pleasant to him; so honest and unpretentious. English Worthies! He was almost one himself—of course on a small scale, in a humble way.

He thought of Dyke as a subversive agency—an enemy to peace; something unamenable, uncontrollable, that suddenly threatened him, his family, and the whole neighbourhood. He began to hate Dyke, as the best of men begin to hate the thing they dread. It appeared to him now that he had seen through Dyke from the first moment, but that he had refused to be guided or warned by the clear light of his own intuitive intelligence. "I'd like to know that girl over there. Who is she?" when Dyke said something of that sort, he should have resented it as an impertinence and not accepted it as a compliment. Then Dyke had laughed, blatantly—offensively, if you came to think of it. "Pardon me for being a untutored savage." But, no, one cannot pardon savagery—except in savage lands, at a remote distance, beyond the pale. One has to protect oneself against its effects. He wished that somehow he could get the whip-hand of Dyke. And yet even now, so kindly and trustful was he by nature, that at the very moment of dreading and hating Dyke, he could not believe the man really meant mischief.

Within his narrow limits he was always generous-minded. Markedly so with regard to money matters—and perhaps there is still no surer test of a person's magnanimity than that which can be obtained by a record of his consistent attitude towards hard cash. Unlike many men who have all the money that they require, he did not crave for more. No petty gains or economies ever lured him. For instance, although Emmeline had come into the enjoyment of her income, he had never suggested or dreamed of suggesting that she should make any contribution to household expenses. She was freely welcome to bed and board, the attendance of Louisa, the use of the carriages. He had advised her to draw only such a portion of her income as she needed, leaving Mr. Williams of Spring Gardens to reinvest all surplus; and it made him happy to feel that she was doing this, and increasing her modest capital quarter by quarter.

Now, not unnaturally, he thought—as Mrs. Verinder had already thought— that, so far as a whip-hand over Emmeline was concerned, the soundness of her financial position robbed him of much desirable power.

This was Mr. Verinder. Unless one knew him and did him justice, one could not understand his state of mind. He was not in any respects the conventional old-fashioned father that lingered in the comic literature of the period. About him there was nothing either grotesque or preposterous.

After all, it was only 1895; say twenty-seven years ago—yesterday. There are large numbers of people to-day who think as he did then. There are men at his club and at other clubs saying in essence just what he used to say—when, not thinking of Emmeline, but merely generalising, he spoke of fin-de-siècle girls who mistake license for freedom, of regrettable up-to-date ideas, of the danger of abusing the word progress and pulling down before you have learnt to build up;—men who have passed through the devastating experience of the world-war and are less shaken by its rivers of blood, its fiery chaos, its starving millions, than by the social readjustments it has occasioned—"the passing of the old order," as they call it—and the fact that half the members of the club won't even trouble to put on a white shirt and a black tie for dinner.

A week passed, and, to Mr. Verinder's supreme satisfaction, Emmeline showed herself altogether docile and amenable. She attended parties, she drove in the park, she spent afternoons and evenings with their friend Mrs. Bell, at Queen's Gate, and was punctually brought home from these visits by Louisa. Mr. Verinder highly approved of them. Mrs. Bell was devoted to Emmeline, had always admired and made much of the child. Here would be a good influence. But not a hint had been given to Mrs. Bell of any trouble in the air. The only people who knew of the cause of anxiety were Margaret—and presumably Pratt—and, of course, Eustace.

Another week passed. The twelfth of July with its dinner party lay behind them. That feast, although shorn of its guest of honour, had not proved too dismal, all things considered. And in those two weeks not a sign from the enemy. Lulled into a sense of false security, Mr. Verinder began to feel easy in his mind.

Then he discovered that Dyke had been out of London for a fortnight. Dyke was in Scotland, giving lectures at the great Scottish cities. "Taking the hat round," as he had himself described it. A banquet had been given in his honour at Edinburgh, with many notabilities present; the speechifying was recorded by the public press.

After another week or ten days Dyke returned to London. His return was chronicled in all the newspapers. They again began to make a fuss about him. And Mr. Verinder, at his club, had the mortification of hearing his praises sung by certain members of it. He had dined here, at Mr. Verinder's club, last night—a little dinner in his honour, given by Duff-Steele, a personal friend of Mr. Verinder's—with So-and-so, and So-and-so—and a few more. Dyke had kept them there yarning until two or three in the morning. They said, in effect, that he was entirely fascinating; a great irresponsible child, full of the most infectious gaiety. A real tip-topper, madcap, dare-devil—whatever you like—but evidently behind it all, a heart of gold. How he had talked! How he had laughed!

When Mr. Verinder reached home that afternoon Mrs. Verinder at once reported that Emmeline had become restless—very restless indeed. She felt that it would be necessary to watch her closely.

They did it for the next week or so, but Mr. Verinder had the uncomfortable sensation, shared by his wife, that no matter how carefully you watched, more was going on than met the eye. An atmosphere of suspicion permeated all the reception rooms of the house; Mr. Verinder's discomfort and annoyance increased day by day.

Although Mr. Williams of Spring Gardens had long ago written to say he was prepared to communicate the result of his investigations, Mr. Verinder had not yet gone to receive them. He went now, after luncheon one day, and took Eustace from the Board of Trade with him.

There is a candour and unpretentiousness about the very best sort of solicitors that is sometimes almost startling to their clients. If you speak of investments, a really good solicitor will say at once that he is not a business man; if you speak of an attack on your character or a possible career for your children, he will say he is not a man of the world; if you are involved in a wrangle and fancy you have publicly libelled your adversary, he will say that he is not a lawyer. He doesn't in the least mean that he will not carry through to a triumphant conclusion the affair, whatever it is, that you are bringing to him; he only means that he lays no claim to keeping a mass of encyclopædic knowledge on the tip of his tongue, to giving oracular decisions at a moment's notice, or seeing through a brick wall without the aid of a periscope. He will take a little time going into the matter thoroughly, obtaining counsel's opinion, doing everything necessary. Meanwhile and at once, in your presence, he often consults his books of reference; and it must be confessed that this reliance on books and the guileless manner of speaking about them does often disconcert, if it does not shake a client. "You doubt if your bargain is clinched?" says the really eminent solicitor; and he rings the bell for his clerk. "Bring me that book on Contracts, latest edition. And see if we have a directory of county court judges downstairs. I want to ascertain if there is any county court south of the Thames. And, look here, go upstairs and give my compliments to Mr. Cyril and ask him if he knows whether the Stock Exchange is open on Bank Holidays."

Mr. Williams, of Spring Gardens, or his firm, had long conducted the affairs of the Verinder family in a most efficient style. He himself relied greatly on his books, which he kept in handsome book-cases in his own room. This solid old-world room was lighted by narrow windows with reflecting mirrors above them, and had no encumbrances of deed boxes and that sort of thing; a large beautifully neat table for Mr. Williams, a fine comfortable leather-seated chair for visitors, the picture of a marine battle over the chimneypiece, and one or two marble busts on top of the book-cases—that was all; and with these simple surroundings the owner of the room worked in it very happily and contentedly; looking up with a friendly smile as you came in at the door, and showing himself as a shortish, stoutish, fresh-complexioned person of sixty-five or a little more. As his intimates knew, he had only one sorrow in life—the certainty that sooner or later this room, the whole Queen Anne house, and the rest of Spring Gardens, would be swept away by London's unbridled rage for street improvements. But he hoped they would last his time.

He begged Mr. Verinder and Mr. Eustace Verinder to sit down, and with an air of innocent triumph said that he had found out a great deal about Anthony Dyke.

"I may say that directly you mentioned the name, it seemed familiar to me."

"It is familiar to everyone," said old Mr. Verinder rather irritably, and his son sneered. Eustace had a trick of sneering and saying pointed things, in a polite Oxford manner on which he had superimposed a slight veneer of officialness.

"To begin with," said Mr. Williams, "he is a married man."

"Yes, I knew that," said Mr. Verinder.

"Oh, you did? But he is not living with his wife."

"So I understood."

"They have been separated for years—and there is a reason." And Mr. Williams explained how he had found it all in his book. "I have it all here under my hand"; and he laid his hand on the useful volume, lying there on the table. "As soon as you told me the name it aroused associations in my memory—apart from his public performances, you know. There was a law suit—years ago—quite an important case. Mrs. Dyke proved to be out of her mind—immediately after the wedding—and Dyke tried to get the marriage annulled, on the grounds that her people had deceived him. He failed of course."

Mr. Verinder had not known about the madness, and he sat frowning and brooding over it. Then presently he asked what Mr. Williams had discovered about the man himself.

"Yes," said Mr. Williams, "I have his whole record here." And he began to read from a paper of notes, saying that Anthony Dyke left Africa for Australia in such and such a year; was thanked by the government of Queensland for explorations in the interior of the continent in the year 1885; and in 1887 made his first Antarctic cruise, which resulted in the discovery of the island now known as Anthony Dyke Land. It was of course all in the books, and Mr. Verinder, who already knew it by heart, interrupted very irritably.

"Yes, yes, yes. No more than that? Very good." Then, after exchanging a glance with Eustace, he said, "Williams, the fact is—Frankly, our trouble is this. He is paying undesirable attentions to my daughter."

"Oh, really?" Mr. Williams showed suitable distress as well as surprise, and he looked across at the bookcases. "Which of your daughters?"

"My unmarried daughter."

"Oh, really? Miss Emmeline!"

"Yes. What would you advise me to do?"

"Ah, that's somewhat difficult to say. Off-hand, I should scarcely like—"

And another look given by Mr. Williams to the book-shelves was that of a timid swimmer who feels deep water under him and sees the solid shore fast receding. "From what you have let fall—well, so little to go on, from what you *have* let fall."

Mr. Verinder let everything fall, and pressed for counsel.

And then Mr. Williams, bracing himself to the effort and striking out boldly, advised that in his opinion Dyke should be at once tackled.

"Tackled?" said Mr. Verinder. "What do you mean by tackled?"

Mr. Williams meant brought to book, called to account, and so forth; and he said something that Mr. Verinder grasped at because it echoed a hope that he was still glad not to abandon altogether. Mr. Williams considered that, although there had been impropriety in Dyke's attitude, they might be very wrong in assuming that he really entertained bad motives.

"Why jump to the conclusion that he intends harm? Tackle him, and he himself may express regret and discontinue the annoyance. Would you wish me to write him a letter?"

"No," said Mr. Verinder. "But perhaps an interview here, in your presence?"

Mr. Williams, not taking to this idea, suggested that it would be better to get hold of Dyke informally; and after further talk it was decided that Eustace Verinder should go to him not for the real tackling, but for a preliminary skirmish in which an interview with the young lady's father should be arranged.

"You know him personally?" asked Mr. Williams.

"No," said Eustace, sneering slightly. "As yet I have not had the privilege of setting eyes on this gentleman."

"One moment," said Mr. Williams, picking up the notes. "I have his address here. It is care of his bankers—a bank in Fleet Street."

But the Verinders were better informed. Dyke's visiting cards told them that he belonged to a club in Pall Mall—one of the oldest and best clubs in the street.

"When will you go there?" asked Mr. Williams.

"Now," said Eustace resolutely.

He parted with his father in Cockspur Street, and strolled on to Pall Mall by himself.

It was now what journalists of those days called the apotheosis of the London season; what was then considered a flood of traffic came pouring down Waterloo Place; large open carriages with a mother and one daughter on the back seat, and a red book and another daughter on the front seat, swept across to and from Carlton House Terrace, while splendid padded veterans at the corner outside the Senior and sedate members of the Government outside the Athenæum took off their silk hats or even kissed the tips of their gloved fingers. The pavements of Pall Mall were full of gentlemen in black coats and top hats, with here and there a white waistcoat and a button-hole to light up the throng; the sentry in scarlet and bearskin outside the War Office stood presenting arms to the passage of a field officer; and one had a sensation of the further glories at the end of the street—Marlborough House, with the Prince and Princess of Wales perhaps just emerging from the gates, the old palace where a brilliant levée had taken place that morning, the drive shaded by close-standing elms along which people drove to daylight drawing-rooms—an impression of the leisurely pomp, the well-ordered stately calm of the whole realm.

It was 1895, essentially yesterday, and yet, if judged by external aspect alone, another world—the world in which people behaved with dignity, looked pleasant, and never did objectionable things. Eustace Verinder, tall, dark, already bald under his silk hat, looking like the cabinet-minister that he intended later on to be, formed a small but harmonious part of this world; and his blood boiled tepidly at the thought that any intruder should dare at once to violate the governing code of good manners and menace his sister's fair name.

As he approached Dyke's club an amazingly incongruous figure came down its steps. It was a tall big man in a sombrero hat, with a canvas wallet slung over his back and a long staff in his hand; he looked like a pilgrim, like a youthful Tolstoy, like anything strange and odd and absurdly out of place. Eustace noticed the outlandish dun colour of his flannel suit, the huge collar of his flannel shirt flapping over his jacket and all open at the hairy throat, and, feeling shocked at such a moving outrage to convention, stared after him as he stalked across the roadway and disappeared into St. James Square.

The hall porter told Eustace that Mr. Dyke had just left the club. "Just this minute, sir. Shall I send the boy to see if he can catch him?"

Eustace said no, it did not matter. He felt that he ought to have guessed, after all his father had told him. But it was so far worse than one could imagine. He went away feeling profoundly disgusted. To dress like that, in London, at half past three P.M., with the season at its apotheosis!

Anthony Dyke had, in fact, dressed like that only because he was going for a walk. He felt that, yielding to civilization's enticements, he had been for some time sitting too much, eating too much, above all else sleeping too much, and he needed a walk. He had therefore slipped on what seemed to him very suitable attire for the purpose, gone to the club coffee-room to fill his wallet with some fruit and a few rolls of bread—and now was off. Naturally, with the hero of the Andes, a walk meant a walk. He would go straight ahead, over Hampstead Heath into Hertfordshire, round that county and any other counties adjacent; he would walk all night, and probably all day to-morrow; then he would come back, have a bath, and feel thoroughly refreshed—the limbs loosened by gentle exercise, civilization's rust rubbed out of his joints and the mind clarified by avoidance of slumber.

CHAPTER V

RATHER less than a week after this Dyke came to Prince's Gate by appointment. All the preliminaries for the interview had been completed by letters and in the most courteous manner on both sides. Greatly as the Verinders hated him, they felt that there was no other way of doing things. Mr. Verinder, then, politely expressing a wish to see Mr. Dyke for the purpose of discussing "certain matters," Mr. Dyke had replied that he was entirely at Mr. Verinder's service and begged that place and time should be named. Mr. Verinder named his own house and nine o'clock in the evening; choosing an evening on which Emmeline could be conveniently banished from the premises.

Mrs. Verinder had taken her to dine quietly with Mrs. Bell in Queen's Gate, and afterwards they and their hostess were going to a concert given by an elderly widower. The widower had hired the Grosvenor Gallery for his concert; it would be a grand and a late affair; thus Mr. Verinder need not apprehend the return of his ladies until long after midnight. The docility with which Emmeline agreed to these arrangements had made him wonder suspiciously if she had received confirmative instructions from the enemy. He trusted, however, that this was not so.

It was now a quarter to nine, and he and Eustace and Mrs. Verinder's brother, Colonel Gussie Pollard, were seated at the dinner table finishing their dessert. The presence of their brother-in-law and uncle bothered Mr. Verinder, but there had seemed to be no way of avoiding it; for his own convenience he was staying in the house, he now had learned all about their trouble, and his sister said she thought he would add weight to their side of the discussion.

"I should not scruple myself to tell him it isn't cricket," said Colonel Gussie, beginning to peel a second nectarine.

He was one of those very large, radiantly smooth elderly men who take inordinate pains in cleaning, polishing, and decorating their persons. The dress-suit of Colonel Gussie, his white waistcoat, his jewelled buttons, studs, and little chains, suggested that he felt he could never do quite enough for himself; and, as if for this reason, his face was garnished with every small blob of white hair that can be grown on a face—moustache, whisker, imperial, even something under the plump chin, but each sample small and nicely trimmed, and all of it neatly divided. Through the white hair his complexion showed with the silvery pinkness of an uncooked salmon. For the rest, he had a genial yet grand manner, was not disposed to think evil of anybody, and when compelled to censure knew no worse verdict than to say that a thing was not cricket.

If pushed beyond that mark and as it were forced to put on the black cap and pass a final sentence of condemnation, he said the thing was un-English.

Mr. Verinder secretly objected to his insistence on calling himself colonel, since he was not a regular soldier but merely in command of a militia or volunteer battalion attached to one of the city regiments; and he thought it childish of him to like to be addressed as Gussie instead of Augustus.

"Wouldn't be playing the game," said Colonel Gussie, as he finished his nectarine with relish.

Then, after saying he knew that Emmeline was not contaminated with anything of this kind, he spoke in disapproval of these modern notions that were tending to upset the feminine half of humanity—"emancipation," "the new woman," "equal rights," and so on. It was one thing to like advanced education and keep yourself "up-to-date"; but this impressionist art, this Yellow Book, and all these "problem plays"—well, they did no good, did they? There was too much of the spirit of revolt in the air.

Eustace smoked his cigarette and stared at the ceiling. Mr. Verinder allowed his brother-in-law to talk, only saying once, as if to himself, "Freedom, yes, so long as it does not degenerate into license."

Then the butler came in, and informed them that Mr. Dyke was upstairs.

The colonel rose at once, drawing himself to his full height, which was at least six feet three inches, and looking magnificent.

"Come on," he said; and they all three went upstairs to that room behind the music-room—the room that contained the smiling landscapes by Leader. Mr. Verinder had ordered that Dyke should be shown into this room, because he felt it was large enough and yet not too large for their purposes.

In spite of the hatred, the interview opened with extreme propriety and politeness, but Mr. Verinder was at once oppressed by its incredible fantastic nature. It was as though he had not been really Mr. Verinder, here, among these smiling landscapes, in Prince's Gate, but a person wrenched out of a land of probabilities and launched on an ocean of the impossible.

Dyke was in evening clothes, and perhaps recently his hair had been cut and his beard pointed; at any rate, that aspect of Tolstoy or the pilgrim had entirely vanished. He was standing on the hearth-rug when they came in, and he did not move; he stood there, a tall commanding figure; handsome too—with his strong nose and high cheek-bones—in a careless, dare-devil, but not swash-bucklering style; not really taller than the others, certainly less tall and very much less round than the colonel, and yet somehow dominating them and the whole room.

Eustace understood that they had made a mistake in procedure. It was a trifle—no consequence, of course—but it vexed him to think how very obviously they should have had him brought into a room where they were sitting, so that he would have seemed like a person summoned before a tribunal, instead of establishing him here by himself and then coming to him, to be received by him as though they were a deputation.

"Will you smoke?" said Eustace curtly, and he opened the silver cigarette box that he had brought up from the dinner table.

With a gravely courteous gesture and smile—the gesture indeed almost Spanish and antiquated in its courtesy—Dyke indicated that he preferred not to smoke.

"My son—Eustace," said Mr. Verinder. "And my brother-in-law—Colonel Pollard."

"Miss Verinder's godfather too," said the colonel, seating himself.

Dyke ignored the second introduction; not rudely, but as if all that pinkness and whiteness had made no impression on him. He appeared to be quite unaware of them, and throughout this first interview spoke not a single word to their possessor.

"I was admiring that picture," he said with another gesture, and he smiled again. "Mr. Verinder, I don't pretend to be a judge of art, but I must say, that picture took my fancy enormously. So cleverly painted—all the autumn tints of the foliage, and the effect of the sunshine on the lake." He said this as if wishing to put them at their ease and allow them time. "A very charming picture—in my uneducated opinion."

"It is by Leader, R. A.," said Mr. Verinder simply. "I have several of them."

He had sat down at a table on which were blotting pads with tortoise-shell covers, boxes of porcelain, a gold photograph frame, and a massive ivory paper-knife; picking up the knife and toying with it, he conveyed the intimation that he wished Mr. Dyke to sit upon the amber satin sofa which faced the table at about two yards distance.

Dyke, immediately obeying, went to the sofa and sat down.

Eustace had gone to the double doors and he opened one of them, disclosing the music-room as a sombre and empty vault. He closed the door again and turning from it said that, since they were here for a delicate confidential talk, it was just as well to make sure they would not be overheard. This, as he had intended, set the thing going.

Mr. Verinder, balancing the paper-knife, drove at the heart of the matter and spoke of "these attentions and meetings." He said he felt sure that Dyke would himself see that they must cease.

"Mr. Verinder," said Dyke, gravely and very gently, "I hope you will allow me to say that I would sooner die than injure your daughter."

"Just so," said Mr. Verinder. "I was quite prepared to believe so, but—"

Dyke interrupted him. "No, I would rather kill myself many times than harm a hair of her head." As he said this, not only his voice but his face softened in the most extraordinary manner; and Mr. Verinder was pleased with the man for saying it. But Dyke went on, with his blue eyes fixed on Mr. Verinder and his voice becoming a mere whisper. "Not one pretty dark hair of her sweet little head."

The outrageous use of such adjectives made Mr. Verinder tremble from wrath; but, with difficulty controlling himself, he spoke in a firm quiet tone.

"If there is any meaning in what you are saying, Mr. Dyke, you will give me an assurance that no further molestation will occur."

Dyke remained silent for a little while, and during the pause Gussie was heard to mention the national pastime—"Not cricket, what!" Dyke did not seem to hear him; he was now looking at the parquetry. "Mr. Verinder," he said, looking up, "this is not plain-sailing, it is complicated. I suppose you know that Emmie—"

Mr. Verinder flapped with the paper-knife and grew hot and red. The use of his daughter's christian name, the use of a grossly familiar abbreviation of that name! Not a member of the family ever called her anything shorter than Emmeline. But Dyke went on, as if oblivious of his offence.

"Emmie has done me the honour—the very great honour—to become attached to me. Mr. Verinder, you do know that, don't you? Emmie—God bless her—has become very fond of me."

"Nothing of the sort," said Mr. Verinder wrathfully; and both the colonel and Eustace made movements.

Dyke's manner changed, and he spoke with a sudden biting hardness. "Unless," he said, "you admit that, it is useless for us to attempt to discuss the situation."

Mr. Verinder said he would not admit it; certainly not. But, on consideration, he said he would go as far as possible to meet Dyke's argument; he would admit as much as this—that, to some extent, Dyke had unfortunately fascinated the imagination of her; against a young inexperienced girl Dyke had employed the advantage given by age, the glamour of romance, and so forth; and he wound up to the effect that two hundred years ago it would have been said that Dyke had thrown a spell over her.

Dyke answered, sadly, that he had thrown no spell. The first evening he had certainly told her a few of his adventures.

"Oh, yes," said Eustace, sneering. "Othello and Desdemona"; and he quoted a few words of the famous speech. "'Hair-breadth escapes—antres vast and deserts idle.' But then Othello wasn't a married man. Unfortunately you are."

Dyke had now risen from the sofa. He walked about the room and began to make a noise. To Mr. Verinder, in the midst of his anger and distress, the striding up and down of Dyke was a fresh discomfort, a new surface-sting. If anybody walked about rooms in that house, it should be he, the master of the house; it was a habit of his. No one else had the right to take the floor on him.

"Of course I'm married," said Dyke, loudly, almost shouting. "How can I help that? It's my misfortune, not my fault. Besides, I told her so. I told her so at once."

"She doesn't weigh the consequences," said the father.

"She *has* weighed them," Dyke shouted. Then he went on more quietly, but with the incisive hardness that was almost worse than noise. "Besides, she's over twenty-one; she has independent means—why shouldn't she do what she likes? She's her own mistress."

"Exactly. But we don't want her to be your mistress," said the sneering brother. "That's just what it amounts to."

From this point onwards the thing was devoid of hope; and they knew it really. Dyke made more and more noise; he rumpled his hair, brandished his arms, broke his shirt front; and the other three felt their helplessness. How could they tackle this hulking ruffian, this savage in dress clothes who disregarded all rules, who cared nothing for civilization? They were three tame men, and utterly impotent against a wild man. He overwhelmed their minds by his unchecked fierceness; but it should be noted that they had not any unworthy physical fear of him, although Eustace, more particularly, felt that at any moment Dyke might strike him. That odd, hideously vulgar expression, A word and a blow, echoed in the troubled thoughts of Eustace. A blow, a struggle, a disgraceful episode, at any moment now.

They appealed to his better feeling, and he seemed to have none. They spoke of law and decency, and he inveighed against the cursed law. A wife that wasn't a wife, but tied to her irrevocably—a millstone round his neck—"Poor unhappy lady, God forgive me for speaking of her like that. *She's* not to blame. No, no, it's the law's to blame."

As he said all this he was banging on the table in front of Mr. Verinder, so forcibly that the porcelain boxes danced and the gold frame fell over.

"It's fellows like you who make these infernal laws. Why don't you alter them? Why do you allow people to be tormented and bedevilled because that sort of thing pleased a pack of dirty verminous monks hundreds of years ago? Poor little innocent Emmie too! I feel the cruelty of her situation just as much as you do—and a dashed sight more. It's monstrous and iniquitous"; and he strode away from the table waving his arms.

In every lull Mr. Verinder said the same sort of thing—that facts were facts, laws laws, proprieties proprieties. "You must see it, Mr. Dyke. On reflection, you *must* see it. I decline to believe that you yourself will wish to continue—"

Dyke swore that he had no choice; he would continue, he could not stop.

"What do you propose to do then?" asked Mr. Verinder.

"What do you want me to do?" asked Dyke.

Mr. Verinder said he wanted Dyke to give her up altogether.

"*Never!*" Dyke roared at them now.

So the thing went on. Eustace was livid with rage, trembling. The colonel, unnoticed, chattered and fumed. Mr. Verinder felt possessed by that sensation of the dreamlike nature, the sheer fantasticness of it all—this quiet room, with the loud voices in it, servants probably listening on the stairs; yet also the awareness of the framework of society all round them still unbroken; his friends next door enjoying a little music after dinner in one of *their* drawing-rooms, or playing a rubber of whist for moderate points; a small evening-party at Number Ten; above everything, the Albert Hall such a little distance away, with a ballad concert as usual;—only in here this raging lunatic trying to turn the whole world upside down. But perhaps the colonel's agitation and horror were even more painful than what his brother-in-law underwent. To him the thing was so appallingly obnoxious, so immeasurably far from the spirit of the game he worshipped. He continued to say it; and close to his lips, contained but certain to be released if the strain lasted, there hovered the crushing black-cap epithet—un-English.

"I shan't give her up."

Dyke was blustering fiercely as he moved here and there. Once he threatened Eustace, saying that if there was any attempt to bully Emmie, he would break every bone in his body. Finally he left them, mentally shattered.

He was gone, right out of the house.

Then, quite late, after eleven-thirty, there was a tremendous sustained ringing of the front-door bell. What could it be? The house on fire? Mr. Verinder, half unrobed, hurried down from his dressing-room to the first floor, and looked over the gilt balustrade into the hall. It was the man come back again—but altered, strange, in a totally different mood. He forced his way past the butler, past Eustace, past Gussie, and shouted upward.

"Verinder, I must talk to you. Verinder—my dear fellow—I can't sleep to-night, until you and I have settled it."

And he came up the stairs; with Eustace and the colonel following, both of them really scared now.

"Go in there," said Eustace, and, while Dyke entered the darkened room, he whispered to his father: "If he is violent I shall send for the police."

Mr. Verinder ran up for a dressing-jacket, came down and sat at the same table, looking queer without his collar. As Eustace switched on the lamps the Leaders sprang into life, smiling at them all again. Dyke threw his slouch hat and an Inverness cape to the floor, stood with his hair absurdly ruffled; then sank upon the amber satin sofa.

"I have been walking about, feeling half mad," he began in a humble tone, then paused. His face was strangely pale, as though all the blood had gone from it; and they noticed, during the pause, that he seemed suddenly to shiver or gasp for breath. "Look here. I want to apologise to you—Out there, trying to think, I felt that I deserved to be kicked. Anybody would say you're quite right—from your point of view." And he looked at them most piteously. "I'm sorry I made a noise. But please make allowances. This—this entanglement—or whatever you like to call it—is so tragically serious for both of us. I mean for her as well as for me. That's why I beg you to bear with me—to reach an understanding, a solution—to do anything rather than just quarrel about it. If, to begin with, you can only put yourself in my place"; and he seemed to be wringing his hands. "Verinder, I want that girl. I simply can't live without her."

He said these last words in a hoarse whisper that was more disturbing to hear than if it had been a loud cry of pain. It jarred upon the ear, it set one's teeth on edge; and the expression of his haggard face added to the physical commotion he produced, even if one did not think of what he had said. The colonel felt the commotion all through his stout body; Eustace held up an arm, as if calling for invisible cabs.

"Verinder!" He was perceptibly shivering—a tremor that made his limbs jerk. "Verinder—don't you see? This is tearing me to pieces. Surely you can comprehend? You were young once—under forty, full of life. Perhaps you were unhappy too—as I have been—lonely—Didn't you ever feel the longing to make a girl your own?"

Mr. Verinder, once more white with anger, shouted in his turn. "Will you remember that I am her father."

"I know. Forgive me. I express myself badly." And he sat staring at the carpet, and shivering as though some fever of the jungle again had him in its clutch. They watched him; and when he raised his head they saw it for moment convulsed and twitching. He put his hand to his forehead, and then continued to speak. "You and I must have it out, mustn't we? We can't leave it all in doubt. I must settle it before I sail for South America"; and he gave a groan. "I want that girl. I can't live without her. She has become the whole world to me. She wants me, too. And, remember, other people mayn't want her like that—I mean, as I do." As he went on it seemed to them that delirium had set in. He was raving at them now. "We can't do without each other. Well, that's love. Love! What is it? I can't say. But no one's to blame for it. A chance? A fatality? Some day these things will be scientifically ascertained, and then the accident of love will be avoidable—to be guarded against. But it isn't now."

He paused as if for breath, and cast glances round the room before he went on again.

"Verinder, I know you want to do what's right and proper. You're a man of high principle—no one could doubt that. Only don't be hide-bound—or tied down by prejudice. Look the thing in the face. I see the obstacles, plainly, from your point of view—but somehow we *must* get over them. You and your friends are people of the world—you have all sorts of social riddles at your fingers' ends. Can't you find an answer? Can't you cut the knot? If we could only tide over—get round the obstacle—then we should come to daylight one day. No," he cried forcibly. "I mustn't say that—I mustn't hint that my unhappy wife may die and cut the knot herself.

Besides, it isn't true. Her physical health is excellent. She'll probably live to a hundred"; and once more he groaned. "But one thing is certain, Verinder. You can't say we must be left quite without hope—and remain divided for ever. Oh, no, that would be inhuman. Neither of us could submit. Verinder, my dear fellow, it's in your power to make it hard for us or easy. Don't make it hard for us."

All this last part of his appeal had seemed to them worse than delirium, grotesque and terrible in its nearness to a kind of perverted impossible logic. Now he seemed suddenly to collapse on the sofa in a fit of profound dejection. His back stooped, his hands dangled down between his knees, his head subsided almost upon his chest, and he sighed at brief intervals. They watched him, as if spellbound.

He changed his attitude, and sat now with an elbow on the back of the sofa and his head leaning on his hand; and he sighed, as if sick with emotion.

Then there occurred what was perhaps the most astounding incident of the night. The colonel had launched his last word; now he darted round behind the sofa, bent over Dyke, seized his shoulder, and shook him. What was it? Some deep invincible instinct of remote antiquity—the instinct that compels the tame animal to take all risks and fly at and worry the wild beast when it lies prostrate and in pain? Or was it just frenzy and disgust aroused in the colonel by the sight and the sound of something so devastatingly un-English. But Dyke, plainly supposing that the action was prompted by compassionate sympathy, spoke to the colonel for the first time, and in tones of grateful affection.

"Thanks, old boy," said Dyke; and then, as the colonel continued to shake his shoulder, "Don't trouble, dear old chap. I shall be all right directly."

The colonel dropped his hands and tottered away from the sofa. To him the thing had become like the fourth dimension, or the fifth; beyond the range of intellect, brain-destroying. He thought vaguely that if it went on he should faint.

Mr. Verinder was running his fingers round the open neck of his shirt. He felt that his universe had crumbled. He felt that the only sane thing for him to do would be to speak as if to a child, and say, "Mr. Dyke, stop making these afflicted noises; get up, go home to bed, and don't be so ridiculous." He would have said it perhaps, if he could. But strangely, inexplicably, Mr. Dyke was *not* ridiculous; he was still awe-inspiring—dreadful. Yes, that was the word. In the language of the locality, the man had made a dreadful exhibition.

He got up presently, without being told to do so.

"It's not a bit of good my making promises that I can't keep. I've made one promise about it already—to my father—and I'll keep that. My father's a clergyman—in Devonshire."

He shook hands with Mr. Verinder, gave the colonel a wan smile, and went. Eustace let him out, watched by Gussie; the butler standing by, looking very anxious.

When they came upstairs again Mr. Verinder was still sitting at the table.

"Do you think Dyke had been drinking?" he asked, tapping with the paper knife.

"No, I don't think so," said Eustace.

"He didn't smell of alcohol," said Gussie, "when I stooped over him on the sofa."

"That makes it all the worse," said Mr. Verinder, stonily.

"Thank goodness," said Eustace, "that mother and Emmeline didn't come back before we had got rid of him." And he lit a cigarette with fingers that trembled.

After this they had a plain perception of the force they were up against. As Mr. Verinder looked at the imposing façade of the house, he felt that, solid as he had always considered it to be, it afforded a frail protection. He sighed as he drove away from it—his menaced stronghold, his undermined fortress.

He went once again to see Mr. Williams in Spring Gardens, but without any hope that Mr. Williams would be able to help him.

"What can one do?"

Mr. Williams seemed to think that one could do nothing.

"You mean to say," said Mr. Verinder, frowning, "that if I know this man intends to abduct my daughter—"

"Oh, you can hardly call it that, I think," said Mr. Williams; and he moved towards his book-shelves, as if with the intention of taking out the letter A and looking up the article entitled Abduction. But then he was mechanically checked by something already in his mind. "By the way, Miss Verinder herself has been here."

"She has, has she? What for?"

"To ask about her securities. She wants all papers sent to her bank. She said she would discontinue our arrangements, you know, and henceforth manage her affairs herself. She brought her maid with her, and they took some papers I gave her then and there straight on to the bank, I believe."

Mr. Verinder thought that this was very significant. He said it suggested premeditated defiance and rebellion.

The solicitor said, smiling mildly, that she had not the air of "a rebel." No, she had seemed "very quiet and sensible," and he somehow implied that he would like to venture to add "very good-looking, too."

In conclusion, Mr. Verinder asked, "Would you advise me to have her watched by detectives?"

"Oh, surely not? What could be gained by that?"

"It is her mother's suggestion. At least we should then know her movements—and perhaps some of his. He alleges that he means soon to sail for South America. Of course, if one knew for certain that he was out of the country! If we did do it, could you arrange it for us?"

Mr. Williams said yes, if really necessary; but he must own that this class of thing was not in his line, or in the line of the firm.

"Then I will not trouble you further," said Mr. Verinder stiffly.

"Emmeline," he said that afternoon, or on an afternoon very near to it, "come in here, please, I want to speak to you."

Mrs. Verinder had given him a warning; he was flushed, angry, uncomfortable, as he stood at the dining-room door and waited for his daughter. He spoke sternly now, as she appeared at the bottom of the staircase.

"Father, I am going out."

"Going out as late as this? Why, it's nearly seven o'clock. And where's your maid? Where's that girl—where's Louisa?"

"I don't require her. I'm not going far."

"No, so I think." He made her come into the dining-room, and he closed the door behind her.

She was wearing a queer little fashionable hat made of chip straw, with rosebud ornaments, and a white spotted veil neatly drawn under her chin; her dark simple dress was of the kind then known as "tailor-made," fitting close to the waist, but enormously wide at the shoulders; as she stood looking at her father and quivering in anxiety, she had that gentle inoffensive charm of feminine prettiness which du Maurier was at the moment drawing so cleverly.

"Father, I beg you not to detain me. I have an appointment."

"You won't keep it. Do you understand? Sit down. I won't allow you to leave this room."

"Do you mean you'll use force to prevent me?"

"If necessary. Sit down—over there."

She sat down then, meekly, despairingly; but almost immediately she got up again.

"Father, let me go, please. To-morrow he is leaving London for a day or two. I want to see him before that."

Although she had not moved from her chair, he stepped between it and the door; and he angrily told her to be seated. Once or twice more she rose and implored him to let her go. Then she sat still, in agony. She thought of this lost hour, this hour of mellow sunlight beyond the trees, by the water of Kensington Gardens; and of her lover waiting for her.

It was a cruel little scene, and Mr. Verinder felt the cruelty of it. He knew that he was inflicting anguish; worse, much worse than if he had really employed force. Throughout the dragging hour he might have beaten her, thrown her down upon the floor, knelt on her chest, and he would have hurt her less. He walked about the room torturing and tortured; his thoughts on fire, and yet his heart coldly aching.

Once she said words that sounded like an echo of another voice, but in her pathetically pleading tones they stabbed Mr. Verinder with a stiletto thrust.

"I'm not very happy, as it is, father. Please don't make things harder."

"My dear girl," Mr. Verinder groaned, "do you think I'm happy either? Have I been unkind till now? Have I reproached you, even now? How else can I act? I see you drifting"—and he clung to this word—"drifting quite unconsciously to perils that you cannot measure."

She said no more, and she never changed her attitude in her chair until Mr. Verinder, ostentatiously consulting his watch, said it was time to dress for dinner. As he glanced at her it seemed to him that her nose had grown sharp and thin beneath the veil; her eyes were dry and hard, so that the face, instead of being like a young girl's, made him think of a haggard woman who has "knocked about" and "been through a lot."

She herself had thought all the while of the man who was waiting for her, thinking, "He will give me another five minutes; now he won't wait any longer; now he has really abandoned hope."

She had lost the hour with him. It was gone for ever; nothing could bring it back. Out of her life they had taken it; this hour of love they had stolen from her—the hour that should have had love in it; and life is so pitifully short, holding, if you count them, so few hours of any sort.

That morning, quite early, Miss Verinder walked out of the house by herself; and she did not return for three days.

During her absence Mr. and Mrs. Verinder took what seemed perhaps an odd course, and yet it would have been difficult in the circumstances to propose a better one. They wished to maintain "appearances" as far as might be possible, to avoid premature scandal, to keep the talk within the four walls of home; and also they were in this predicament, that they did not really know if Miss Verinder would come back next minute or never. They therefore entered into a conspiracy with their servants, giving orders rather than explanations, and instructing them to tell inquirers that Miss Verinder was ill in bed upstairs—nothing serious, merely indisposition, but bed advisable.

Mrs. Bell, of Queen's Gate, worried them badly by her good-natured solicitude. She was fond of Emmeline; and learning of the indisposition, she came often, brought hot-house grapes, and begged that if reading aloud was out of the question, she might at least be permitted to sit by the bedside and hold the invalid's hand. Except by Mrs. Bell few inquiries were made.

It was just before dinner when Emmeline reappeared. Her mother and father received her alone in the boudoir; directly she came in, her father seized her by the wrist, and Mrs. Verinder sat down on a "pouf" in the middle of the room. Mr. Verinder released his daughter, almost casting her from him, and began walking to and fro; while Mrs. Verinder, sitting in a huddled fashion, following him with her eyes, so that her head moved from side to side exactly as heads move when people are watching the flight of the ball at a lawn-tennis match. Her hands were shaking, her watchful face expressed great distress as well as fear and wonder. Emmeline seemed calm and fearless.

"What's the meaning of this?" said Mr. Verinder tragically, in spite of the commonplace character of the question.

"I am sorry, father, for any trouble and anxiety I have caused—but I couldn't help it."

"Couldn't help it?"

"I mean, you were keeping me a prisoner. Well, I had to break my prison."

"Where have you been?"

Emmeline remained silent.

"Emmeline, why don't you answer?" said her mother. "Can't you see what I'm suffering?"

"Leave her to me," said Mr. Verinder. "You have been with that man?"

"Yes—if by that man you mean Mr. Dyke"; and Emmeline squared her shoulders and looked her father full in the face.

"For—for these three days you have been living with him as if you were his wife?"

"Yes."

Mrs. Verinder uttered a suffocated cry, and it seemed for an instant as if Mr. Verinder was about to hurl himself upon Emmeline and fling her down at his feet; but then he turned his back on her, walked to a window and opened the curtains as if in need of more air.

"And you haven't yet told us where," said Mrs. Verinder, making strange throat sounds as well as speaking.

"Liverpool," said Emmeline quietly.

"Liverpool!" Mrs. Verinder repeated the word, and moaned. "You went that distance—to Liverpool—without even a dressing-bag! No things—not even a brush and comb!"

"I got things there."

"Then where are they? You have come back without anything."

"I left them."

Mrs. Verinder uttered another cry. "So that you could return to him!"

Then there came a tapping on the outer panels of the door.

"Come in," shouted Mr. Verinder furiously.

It was the butler; and Mr. Verinder swore at him roundly. For the first time in his life he swore at a servant, and with ladies present.

"Damn you, you fool, what do you mean by knocking at the door. Why did you do it?"

The butler said he thought they were talking business, and was loth to disturb them. But he wished to know about the dinner.

To Mr. Verinder that tap had been symbolic; it seemed to imply the end of keeping up pretences. It was this thought that made him swear.

"Dinner! Yes, at once"; and he looked at his watch. "Eight-fifteen!"

They sat down to dinner and Emmeline joined them. Sherry was poured out for Mr. Verinder to drink with his soup; he could smell, before it came in, the shrimp sauce that was to go with the turbot; there was general conversation—about the weather and politics, just as usual.

What had happened had happened; yet there they were. In appearance at least, the world was going round at the same pace. The Albert Hall still stood on the old site.

During the course of the evening Emmeline told them that it would be wiser for them to let her go away altogether; and she was unshaken by the storm that both parents launched. She said she was very sorry; she knew they must hate her now; it would be better for everybody if they parted. What amazed them most was her courage. It was as though she drew all this new strength and character from the man. In their distress and confusion they told her so.

"I don't recognize you"; "You are changed"; "I simply do not recognize you"; and so on.

CHAPTER VI

THROUGHOUT the month of August, while drawn blinds in all the handsome windows of Prince's Gate announced that Kensington was at the seaside or on the continent, Miss Verinder enjoyed the absolute freedom of a sitting-room and a bedroom at the Langham Hotel. Mr. Dyke did not lodge in Portland Place, and the hotel porters scarcely knew him by sight. He and his Emmie were never seen together at the west-end of the town. If he appeared anywhere in public he was alone. Although Emmie might not be very far off, she never disclosed herself. She retired into the modest ill-lit background—as on the occasion of his lecture at the hall in Wigmore Street, where she sat in her dim corner shooting arrows of love from misty eyes as she watched him step upon the platform, and trembling with pride and joy as she listened to what the noble chairman said about him. He belonged to her, "this wonderful explorer, this man of resource as limitless as his courage, this man who, alone and unaided, has gone into the dark places of the world, tearing the veil from nature's face and making foot-paths through the unknown,"—he belonged to her, but fate had ordained that she must possess her property in secret and not openly claim it as her very own. He too understood that the wide public need not be told everything, and he showed a delicate reserve in spite of his passion. As was said by one of the very few people who knew anything about them: on the whole they were decent in their indecency.

To use a phrase much favoured and commonly used at this epoch, life had become a fairy tale to Miss Verinder. It seemed to her that the first sight of Anthony Dyke had awakened her from a sleep of death; that then he had breathed fire into her, and that now he was filling her with purpose and power. He was moreover the key to all enigmas and the magical expounder of the commonplace. Nothing tired her, nothing bored her; everything, however drab and cold till now, had light and warmth and colour in it. Also nearly everything was new. She rode with him in hansom cabs, was hugged by him in delightful smoky compartments of the underground railway, spent whole days with him on the eastern side of the Mansion House; seeing in flashes the Monument, the Tower and the new Bridge, the Commercial Road, the docks—the places she had heard about but never seen before. These, with glimpses of the river, the rattle of the city traffic, the roar of trains rolling through iron bridges above crowded streets, made a new forceful world for her after the dignified repose of her old universe.

All this while he was making preparations for his departure, which could not be delayed after the middle of September, and his business in the city and beyond the city concerned the ship that was to take him to South America and the cargo it would carry. She felt elation, pride, and overwhelming interest as she trotted by his side, or a little behind him; dodging through the thronged streets, dashing down dark little courts, and in and out of such queer offices, where among dust and gloom one seemed to smell sea breezes and have visions of distance and adventure. He walked so fast that she was always out of breath, but even this discomfort was pleasant since it came from him; she felt that romance and poetry were making her breathless, and not merely muscular effort. He left her sitting in outer rooms, and if the truth must be told, he sometimes forgot her, so absorbed did he become in the negotiations he was conducting. Once, after waiting for an incredible time, she looked down through a dirt-stained window into a narrow street near Tower Hill and saw him going away engrossed and gesticulating with two other men; and her heart almost ceased to beat as she thought it would be like this when he went from her for ever. He came back exultant, apologetic, her lover again now that the business had been completed, and swept her away with him for a belated three o'clock luncheon, a ravenously hungry meal in a strange tavern—the first of those queer repasts in queer places of which destiny decreed she was to eat so many. He drank her health, he touched her hand beneath the table, he looked sudden death at inoffensive strangers that he suspected of glancing at her with an admiration too patent to be respectful; he praised and thanked her for granting him her companionship and counsel, for giving him—as he said without the slightest intention of flippancy—her "moral support."

His praise was music to her, sweet as the singing of birds, grand and voluminous as a cathedral organ; but she reproved him for the murder glare at those always well-meaning and now terrified young men.

"Because you like me," she said, smiling at him, "you mustn't fall into the mistake of supposing that other people see me with your eyes. Except you, no one has ever thought me worth looking at—or in any way out of the ordinary."

"Emmie, why do you say that?" He stared at her in surprise, and his face grew troubled. "It's not like you—not worthy. You should be above all that. You must know quite well"—and he said this softly but very firmly, with a kind of grateful solemn reverence—"that you are the most beautiful thing God ever created."

"Oh, no," she said, with one of her swift blushes, and in a voice of frightened confusion. "That's utterly absurd—even for *you* to think. But, dear Tony, I am quite content if, as I say, in your eyes—"

"In *all* eyes," he said loudly and almost angrily, administering a sharp slap to the table with his open hand. "Why pretend—why try to spoil my rapture? Emmie, my dearest, don't do it. My lovely priceless girl, it—it hurts me"; and there was real pain in his tone.

She vowed both to herself and to him that she would not do it again. His illusion was ecstasy to her. Why should she try to shatter it in the name of dull stupid truth? Rather pray to heaven that he might continue thus divinely deluded.

Miss Verinder, then, was happy as well as entranced. She averted her gaze from the cloud represented by that ominous date of September Fifteen. She refused to look at it in her diary at the hotel or to notice its advancing shadow out of doors. Four more weeks, three more weeks—and then the end. She would not think of it, she could not think of it. Does the busy little gnat as it moves with a whir of tiny wings in the sunlight brood on the ephemeral nature of its joy or feel premonitions of the darkness and the frost which will close its brief day?

She knew that his plans were finally settled—cut-and-dried, as he said himself—and that nothing would change them. He was going to the Argentine Republic with a cargo in which, as she soon learned, he owned the largest share; he hoped that this venture might prove exceedingly profitable; and, immediately on its completion, he intended to make some mysterious kind of excursion to his old friends, the Andes—"a picnic," as he described it; "a little trip on spec"; "just a lark." Then, after this, he would be off to Australia and its deserts again. One of those governments wanted him. Then, when he had finished the governmental job, he would turn once more to big work—the noble work that, as he had hinted to Mr. Verinder, requires solid cash behind it.

Speaking of the preliminary commercial venture, he touched on this point.

"Emmie, my grave little judge, you mustn't think me sordid and grasping when I chatter about pots and pans, and gas about fleecing the honest Argentinos. If I'm keen—and I am desperately keen—to get money, it isn't for myself—it's for what I feel my life-work"; and he laughed gaily. "Look here, old lady, you can't make an omelette without breaking eggs. I'd stick at nothing to put myself in funds. The end justifies the means." And he laughed again. "Don't look frightened, you innocent angel. All I wish to imply is this: If Dyke is desired to find the South Pole on one of these long evenings—as Dyke intends to do, mark you, Emmeline of the dusky locks—well, he must have a bob or two in the bank."

Immediately Miss Verinder offered him her own money, all of it, or as much of it as he felt he could make use of; but he told her that acceptance was quite impossible. He could never take a penny of her. Besides, as he explained, it was a duty of the public to support him, and he proposed to make them fulfil their duty. "If our little gamble turns up trumps, it may keep me going for two or three years. But the public must put up the stuff for the big thing. Emmie dear, I confess it's a matter of pride with me. Dyke has done enough already to establish his title to public support. Why shouldn't they back Dyke—as well as the other fellows? Ah, here we are. I shan't keep you ten minutes here."

They had been hurrying down a lane not far from Liverpool Street Station. Taking her by the elbow, he guided her through the doorway of a warehouse and up a narrow flight of stairs. The warehouse belonged to a Birmingham firm of gunmakers; and soon she was following Dyke and his business friends down more and more stairs, till she found herself in a cellar deep below the level of the roadway, where a shooting-gallery, perhaps twenty-five yards long, had been contrived for testing fire-arms. Dyke, very gay and jovial, chaffing black-coated managers or partners and slapping on the back a stout workman in an apron, selected from hundreds of rifles about a dozen, and took up position at the opening of the gallery. An assistant with black hands and oil-stained face began to load the weapons, and the man in the apron handed them one after another to Dyke. The whole cellar was well lit with electric light, which its whitewashed walls reflected harshly. One saw the vaulted entrance in front of Dyke, and a white target against a brown bank at the far-end.

"How much earth have you got there behind the disc?"

"Three feet—quite three feet."

"All right"; and Dyke loosed off.

The noise was appalling. In that confined space each discharge made a crash and roar as of a thunder-storm; the walls seemed to be shaking as well as echoing; one felt that the building overhead must fall and one would be buried alive. They were repeating rifles—clumsy and poor machines if compared with the magazine rifle of to-day; but Dyke fired them so rapidly that he might have been working a mitrailleuse. Miss Verinder felt that the top of her head had gone, that the drums of her ears had split, that she was suffocating by the sulphurous fumes of the exploded powder; but all the while she was proudly watching, proudly admiring him.

He was a younger Anthony now, the shooter of big game, out in Africa; bringing his gun to his shoulder in one motion so swift that it was there before you saw it begin to come up; standing firmly planted on his legs, with his hat on the back of his head, his eye intent, blazing away under conditions where a miss means death.

"There. Thank you"; and handing back his smoking rifle, he began very carefully to examine each one that he had fired.

"Well," said the stout assistant, with a complaisant grin, "I never see anything like it. You don't fiddle about—you don't shilly-shally, sir. No, my word, you don't."

Dyke gave him another slap on the back, laughed, and spoke in the frank exulting tone of a schoolboy who brags so simply that what he says does not sound vain-glorious. "I was taught to be nippy, old chap, by shooting at elephants on the charge. I never had any lessons at the rifle-butts—with a marker and a flag. But I was hurrying now because I have another appointment"; and he turned to one of the gentlemen in black coats. "Yes, they're all right. Yes, I pass that lot. Two hundred and fifty, aren't they? Come along."

"That was a very noisy performance," said Emmeline, when they were out in the street again.

"Was it?" he said carelessly. "I suppose it was. I say, I'm behind time. We must leg it, darling."

He did not apologize for having nearly deafened her; it never occurred to him that anybody could be upset by the pleasantly familiar racket of fire-arms. Nor did he ever notice that he walked much too fast for her—although he bowed like a Spanish hidalgo as he stood aside for her to pass through chop-house doors, handed her into hansom cabs as if she were a princess, and often looked at her across soiled tablecloths with the eyes of a mediæval knight kneeling before the shrine of his patron saint. And perhaps Miss Verinder's most exquisite bliss lay in her recognition of the fact that, beyond thinking her the loveliest of created things, beyond thinking her his counsellor and moral supporter, he instinctively regarded her as a comrade and a pal. Merely for dashing about the city, there was not a man in the world—and, scattered about the earth, there were, as she knew, many men for whom he had a great tenderness—there was not one that he would have preferred as companion to his staunchly trotting breathless little Emmie.

One day she met the captain of the ship on which Dyke was to sail, and the three of them had a delightful intimate luncheon in a remarkable eating-house with low beamed ceilings, panelled walls, and partitions surrounding each of the tables—a place, it was said, exactly the same as it had been in the time of Mr. Pickwick and little changed since the time of Dr. Johnson. It was hot, full of loud voices and oppressive kitchen smells; but Miss Verinder ate with appetite, being astonished to discover the charm afforded by grilled steak, tomatoes, and Worcestershire sauce, when you happen to be very hungry as well as very much in love. She liked Captain Cairns, a short but enormously strong man of fifty, with grizzled beard, and face and hands the colour of the woodwork that perhaps had seen Dr. Johnson and faithful Boswell. Captain Cairns inspired confidence; her Anthony would be safe with him. She was pleased, moreover, to observe his profound regard and admiration, when he spoke of Dyke's famous deeds.

"One of my oldest and loyalest friends," Dyke himself had said of him.

"Oh, Miss Verinder," said the captain, "it does make me that angry when folks cast doubt on his discoveries. Pack o' silly stay-at-home fools. I saw a bit in the newspaper the other day actually sneering at what he'd seen with his own eyes—those pigmies at Patagonia, Tony—you know—and the remnants of them temples in the Andes. Has he ever said what isn't true? Oh, it makes me fair mad, when they go on like that—in print, too"; and Captain Cairns grew warm in his genuine disgust and indignation. "Not fit to clean his boots, they aren't."

Miss Verinder said that the incredulity of Mr. Dyke's critics had made her very angry also.

"What does it matter?" said Dyke grandly. "Wasn't Columbus doubted? We're prepared for that sort of thing. It all comes right—we get our due at long last. Calumny and suspicion, perhaps, as long as we're alive, but a piece of sculpture and a brass plate, a tomb in St. Paul's or the Abbey, when the last cruise is done."

"Oh, don't speak like that"; and Miss Verinder shivered.

The industrious city clerks did not linger over their meal; the room grew nearly empty; but Dyke and the captain sat smoking cigars and talking of the cargo. She listened with unabated interest and puffed at a cigarette— one of the queer Spanish cigarettes given to her by Dyke. To smoke was a new accomplishment, and she was not yet very good at it, coughing occasionally, and blowing out when she meant to suck in. But she gloried in it, because it seemed to bring her closer still to him.

Captain Cairns, it appeared, had himself a share in the cargo; and it appeared further that a small portion of the cargo was for Uruguay and not for the Argentine. This consisted of bicycles and bicycle parts.

Miss Verinder, deeply interested, asked if the fashionable craze for bicycling had really reached that distant land. She said she was amused by the thought of a fashion spreading so swiftly.

"Captain Cairns was amused too." He laughed until he rolled about on his bench.

"Yes, miss," he spluttered, "no mistake about it. Them Uruguayans want bicycles—mad for 'em—ready to give any money for 'em."

"Then what a splendid idea—how clever to have thought of bicycles."

"Yes, yes," said the captain, still laughing immoderately. "*His* idea. It was you, Tony, as thought of it first. Yes—bicycles. Why, bless me, Miss Verinder, the Uruguayans will be bang in the fashion—like so many monkeys on wheels." Then he slowly recovered composure. "You set me off, miss. Forgive me. I'm one who will have his joke."

It was a little difficult to understand of what this particular joke consisted and she saw that her sweetheart, although he had smiled to begin with, now seemed troubled if not annoyed by the captain's sense of humour. For a moment he looked contritely at his Emmie, as though about to apologize for something or explain something. But then he seemed to change his mind, and he soon broke up the little party and took her away.

They walked westward along Cheapside and Newgate Street, and on to Holborn Viaduct; and, as always, their progress was enlivened by occurrences, incidents, excitements, emotions. Whether starting from Cape Horn or the Bank of England, he could not take a walk without things happening. At the corner of a side street a young woman selling flowers offered him roses. He bought a bunch for his companion, gave the woman half-a-crown, and told her to keep the change. The woman, overwhelmed by this largesse, huskily asked heaven to bless him, and then burst into tears saying she had been there since seven in the morning and those were the very first flowers she had sold. Dyke, almost weeping himself, implored her to be calm, made her tell more of her circumstances, gave her a couple of sovereigns with some loose silver, and took off his hat in the most respectfully courteous of farewells.

As he walked on—very slowly for him—he spoke with sadness of the cruelly hard fate of many women at great centres of civilization, like this enormous labyrinth of London—women, who ought to be cared for and loved in the shelter of happy homes, out in the open street, snatching a doubtful livelihood from the caprices of the crowd. He said it broke his heart when he thought about it.

Soon ceasing to think about it, he talked of those detractors of his—the people who, like Mr. Verinder and fellow members at the club, spoke of "travellers' tales," "Baron Munchausen," and so on.

"It's all true, Emmie dear; every word that I have ever uttered or put down on paper. What dolts! Because they read at school that Patagonians are a large race of men, if you tell them of an older smaller race not quite extinct—And those temples, too! Huge masses of masonry welded to the cliffs and rocks"; and he waved his hand above his head, as if to indicate the vastness and grandeur of these sacred remains. "Well, I couldn't bring them away with me, could I? I couldn't prove their existence by carting them home to the Geographical Society in Saville Row. No, believe me, the Andes still holds marvellous secrets. Yes," he added triumphantly. "One little secret I have here, in my pocket," and he tapped his chest. Then he stopped suddenly. "By the way, we've done our work. Why shouldn't I go there now?" And he smiled at her fondly while he brought out a notebook. "I spoke of the labyrinth of London. But you, as a born Londoner, ought to know your way about. Where's Hatton Garden?"

Miss Verinder had to confess that she did not know.

"There's a merchant there I want to see." After consulting his notebook, he hailed a hansom cab, with the usual ceremony handed her into it, and followed her.

"Hatton Garden," he called to the driver, and gave the number of the house he wished to visit.

"Hatton Garden! Did you say Hatton Garden?" asked the driver, in surprised tones, through the roof trap.

"Yes. Drive on," said Dyke authoritatively.

The man drove on for perhaps fifty yards, and then pulled up his horse.

"Drive on," said Dyke, again, opening the trap-door. "What have you stopped for?"

"You've arrived," said the man.

"Is this Hatton Garden?" shouted Dyke, as he sprang out of the cab.

The man said yes, and Dyke exploded with terrible force.

"Then, you infernal scoundrel, what do you mean by luring me into your cab and defrauding me of a fare when I was in Hatton Garden already and I had only a few steps to walk?"

"You *wasn't* in Hatton Garden," said the man. "You was facing it. I did ask you and you yelled I was to get on. I thought you knew."

"No, you didn't. You thought I was a stranger—you thought, because I didn't know all the twists and turns of your senseless town you'd fleece me and make a fool of me—" And continuing the explosion, increasing it even, he said he would not pay the fare, not one penny of it, and he had a great mind to pull the driver off his seat and break every bone in his body.

Miss Verinder begged that the man might be paid. Gasping bystanders distressed her, the wrath of Dyke had thrown her into a flutter. "For my sake, Tony, pay him and be done with it."

"For your sake? But the principle of the thing, Emmie. Oh, very well"; and he spoke now calmly and grandly to the cab-driver. "Because this lady wishes it, because this lady has interceded for you, you shall have your shilling. You shall have your—" He was feeling in his trousers pockets. But there was nothing there. He had given all his money to the flower-seller.

Miss Verinder opened her purse, and paid the cab-driver—a little more than his exact fare, in order to remove a perhaps unfavourable impression. Of course the cabdriver could not be expected to understand Anthony's noble but explosive nature as she did.

"Thank you, dear," she said, linking her arm in that of her hero and giving it an affectionate pressure. "Please dismiss all that from your mind—for my sake."

Thus, arm in arm, they crossed the threshold of "Cunlip and Company, dealers in precious stones."

Dyke in a moment was smiling, like a child who in the midst of fearful tantrums is soothed by a magic word from the lips of governess or nursemaid.

"Now this will be fun," he said, beaming at her. "You listen to everything that he says. Where's Mr. Cunlip? I want to see him at once, if he can make it convenient."

Mr. Cunlip, a small, dark, old man, received them in a dingy office behind his show-rooms on the ground floor. He seemed a little taken aback by Dyke's breezy self-introduction and cordial greetings.

"Well, here I am at last—Dyke—Anthony Dyke, you know. That doesn't impress you, eh?" And Mr. Dyke laughed good-humouredly. "Well, I'll give you a name that will mean something to you. Pedro del Sarto! Ever heard of Pedro del Sarto? Of Buenos Ayres, you know."

But, to Dyke's slight discomfiture, the name aroused no immediate memories in Mr. Cunlip. It became necessary to give further details—such as that old Pedro was a tip-topper, a white man, one of Dyke's best friends, that he had been over here in 1880 and had done business with Mr. Cunlip.

Then the dealer in precious stones at last remembered. "Oh, yes, to be sure. But I see so many gentlemen from Argentina. A Spanish gentleman, wasn't he? Headquarters at Buenos Ayres, but connected with those gold mines at

Cape Horn? Yes, I've placed him now. I hadn't much business with him. I passed him on to the assay people over the road."

"*That's* the man," said Dyke, beaming. "Well, you'll recollect now that he wrote to you two years ago to say I'd call on you at the first opportunity."

"Two years ago! First opportunity, what!"

"This *is* the first opportunity. I have been occupied in other parts of the world," said Dyke, with a very modest air.

Mr. Cunlip then wished to know how he could avail himself of the opportunity, now that it had come, by being of service to Mr. Dyke.

"Something to show you," said Dyke modestly.

He had brought from his waistcoat pocket a small envelope; he opened this, extracted a tiny packet of tissue paper, and after unfolding the paper, rolled out upon the top of a glass case what looked like five or six greenish pebbles, each about the size of a pea. Then he spoke in a tone that had changed from extreme modesty to almost aggressive triumph.

"What do you call those?"

Mr. Cunlip put a magnifying glass in his eye, and examined a stone carefully before he answered.

"I call this one an emerald. What do *you* call it?"

"I call it the same," said Dyke jovially. "And the others too. Emeralds, my dear Cunlip—and beauties, eh? The real article."

"Do you want me to weigh 'em up and name a price?" asked Mr. Cunlip.

"No. That'll come later. What I want now is just your opinion—expert advice. Suppose—I say suppose, later on, I began to dribble them across to you! How many could you do with like that?"

"Why, as many as you could send. May I ask where they come from?"

"No, you mustn't ask that—not just at present. I know where I got them, and Pedro del Sarto knows—and we're the only two men alive who do know. But we think there's more there in the same place—and I'm soon going to have a look."

Then Mr. Cunlip spoke rather disparagingly of the specimens before him; he had his doubts as to colour; they were not very big either; he said that to judge actual merits before cutting was almost impossible, even to the greatest expert in the trade—and he delicately implied that between that gifted person and himself there was little if any difference. But, urged to do so, he gave a rough estimate of the value of a particular stone, if after cutting it proved as good as it looked now.

"Splendid! As much as that? Then I may take it that emeralds are keeping up their price, and it isn't likely to drop?"

"Their price *can't* drop—so far as I can see."

"They're as fashionable as ever?"

"They're just as fashionable as they were in the time of the Incas."

"Ah. Glorious?" Dyke gave an exultant laugh. "The Incas! *Rem acu tetigisti.*"

"I beg your pardon—what's that?"

"Nothing," said Dyke gaily. "I liked your way of putting it. The Incas! They covered themselves with emeralds, didn't they? Very apt—your historical allusion. Emmie, did you hear what Mr. Cunlip said?"

While he spoke he was packing up his specimens in their tissue paper. He put the envelope in his waistcoat pocket, and, with compliments to Mr. Cunlip, he hurried away.

"Let's walk, Emmie. No more cabs. Besides, all this has excited me. The days of the Incas! Ha, ha."

And as they walked on, through Holborn and New Oxford Street, he told her the story of how he had found those emeralds quite by chance, high up in the mountains. As he sat resting in the fierce sunshine, he had seen one of them on the edge of a small basin of sand among black rocks, and had scratched for the others with his hands. He described the place—oh, yes, he could find his way back all right; he had mapped it very carefully, and given the corrected map to his partner, Pedro del Sarto. But he himself needed no maps; he could take you there blindfolded—a valley narrowing to and shut in by a perpendicular cliff a thousand feet high, down the face of which the melted snow had made deep channels—a valley where no white man had ever stood, where perhaps no man of any colour had even been since the Spanish Conquest four hundred years ago, till he, Dyke, came to tear the secret out of its lonely heart and profit by the discovery.

As she listened, she fancied that she could see it all in imagination. People on the crowded pavements jostled them, they passed close to the noses of van horses in crossing the Tottenham Court Road, and they noticed nothing of these surrounding sights, sounds, or pressures. They were both of them thousands of miles away.

The time of the Incas! Yes, he honestly believed that he had stumbled upon the trace of workings of emerald mines that were in use before the advent of the Spaniard. He might prove wrong, of course. He had been in a hurry, with no time for close investigations. Perhaps what he fancied had been wrought by human beings labouring was really made by nature using such of her tools as lay handy—storm, frost, sunshine, and the upheaving forces that had built the whole mountain backbone of the continent. In any case, the real point was—How many emeralds had man or nature left there?

At any rate, Dyke would go now and see for himself. It would be a lark. Let us leave it at that.

"Not a word to anybody, Emmie. You and I and old Pedro. No one else—till the day when I give my queen a tiara of green stones all as big as filberts, with a few Brazilian diamonds to flash among the greenness. Then when you go to the Opera—on one of the grand nights—you lovely Emmie, like a high priestess of the sun—then—But I say, let's have tea. That is, if you don't mind paying for it"; and, laughing, he grasped her elbow and led her into a crowded tea-shop.

They sat there, on a seat against the wall, at the end of a table that was occupied by other people; and Dyke while waiting for their tea and while eating two crumbly currant scones, continued to talk to her, but in a voice so low that no one else could hear. His eyes flashed sometimes, he raised his head and shook his hair; he was talking enthusiastically, with a freedom that he could only use to her, and in the midst of it quite automatically he pushed his cup across the marble table for more tea and picked up and began to eat another cake.

"You don't know me yet. Above all, you don't understand the impetus—the added drive—that your love has given to me. Listen. I can't say it too often. You have lifted me up—you have placed me on high—you have *saved* me. For your sake—oh, how I worship you when you say those words—for your sake, Emmie, I must and I shall keep on the summits of endeavour—and never yield to the powers of darkness or the cowardice of shameful compromises. I'm all out now—to the last ounce—for my good angel's sake. Yes, two lumps, please. These buns are stale."

He went on, in his vibrating heart-stirring whisper, to speak of the South Pole. She had divined—as it seemed, long ago—that this was his ultimate goal, the glorious hope of his life's work. Dyke meant, had always meant, to capture the South Pole, and all other tasks were but a filling or wasting of time. He had marked it down as his own. He spoke of it as if it had been some dangerous yet timid animal of the chase, round which he had made narrowing circles till it crouched fascinated, unable any more to flee from its pursuer; it knew that it could not escape and that when Dyke ceased to circle and dashed in, it must fall into his hands.

"Remember, Emmie, I'm not all talk; I'm do as well. Yes, Dyke will do things"; and his blue eyes flashed at her, and the colour came to those high cheek-bones as if the tea was beginning not only to cheer but to intoxicate. "If they won't support me—if they won't fit me out in the style I ask for— if they won't give me the ship I want—Then in a sieve I'll thither sail, and like a rat without a tail, I'll do, I'll do, I'll do. No, you don't know me yet, Emmie. You don't know me yet."

But already how well she knew him! Better perhaps than he knew himself. She knew that behind all the courage which for so long had made him hold his life at a pin's fee; behind the insatiable curiosity, the love of adventure, the fiery challenge to the universe that form the very substance of a true explorer's mental constitution;—behind all that there was the unslumbering desire for personal fame. If only by his little individual trick of speaking of himself in the third person—"That's not good enough for Dyke"; "Anthony Dyke has other plans"; and so on—she would have known so much as this. Habitually, during all those enforced silences that had made up his active career, he had listened to the imagined voices of the world thinking about him; and now he could not think of himself in relation to fame without, as it were, standing for a moment outside himself. Dyke wanted the South Pole; but Dyke wanted the undying fame of getting it. Why not? The labourer is worthy of his hire. She felt that she need not class his ambition—the last infirmity of noble minds—as even one slight defect of his innumerable glorious qualities.

Nevertheless, she thought sagely that it was the thing she must always reckon with—the factor never to be omitted from her calculations when making plans for his assistance, moral or immoral.

She knew him—he need not fear her lack of knowledge. She knew that he was noble to the core; simple only as everything fine and great will always be; at his own trade as resourceful as Pizarro, in all other things as grand a gentleman as Cortes; gentle with women, splendid with men—familiar, as people who live their whole lives in Kensington cannot be, calling sea-captains old boy, slapping underlings on the back, and yet being a leader and a chieftain all the while. Yes—even when exploding under a misapprehension with cab-drivers.

Before paying the bill for tea, she picked up the bunch of roses that he had bought from the beggar. She attached exactly the same value to it as if it had been that tiara of emeralds. It had been given to her by him. And with deep penetrating joy she remembered how he had called her his queen, wishing for an instant perhaps that she was really and truly some splendid historical queen or empress. But, no, even then she would have been just as unworthy of such a lover.

CHAPTER VII

THE last days had come. They were staying at Liverpool at the North Western Hotel: and Dyke, although as sweet to her as ever, was preoccupied with final business. He hurried to and fro about this new strange city unaccompanied by her now, talked in her presence of such abstruse matters as the charter-party, bills of lading, the ship's clearance papers, and had no time to teach her what it all meant. In some mysterious manner the agent of the owners of the ship had "got upon his nerves," as he said; but he was long-suffering and indulgent towards this gentleman, permitting himself no explosions; even asking him to dine at the hotel with Captain Cairns, the first mate, and other men. They had a round table in a corner of the big room, drank a great deal of champagne, and talked rather too loudly for the comfort of their neighbours.

Miss Verinder's table was at a distance, right on the other side of the room, where she sat quite alone and ate her dinner with little appetite. Dyke came over to her once, bowed to her, and stood by the table; outwardly just a friend or an hotel acquaintance, a person upon whom she had no claims of any kind. But he looked down at her with eloquent eyes, and whisperingly told her how terrible it was to be separated from her for one of their last three evenings.

She understood. He was constant and loyal as ever; the only change in him was what every woman must fatally see in the man she loves when he begins to take up again a man's job. She understood—only it made her heart ache; and while telling the waiter that she did not require any more of the dinner but would like a cup of coffee, she thought of the essential force of those two hackneyed and inexact words. A heartache! Of course her heart was not really aching, and yet it *felt* like that; the pain was mental, yet it seemed physical—this dull oppressive discomfort that had taken the taste away from the food, the colour from surrounding objects, the brilliancy from the electric light, suggested something primitive and instinctive that might be shared by dumb animals quite low down the scale; say the young sheep driven into a different gate from that through which its companion passed as they both approached the shambles; or, at highest, the sensations of a dog when it loses its master.

Separation. Anthony's own word echoed itself as she sipped her coffee and glanced across the room to the corner where he was being jolly with an unexplained purpose to that agent of the shipowners. She was losing him by inches; every moment those men, that ship, the breezes of the wide estuary, the trackless ocean, and the call of plains and hills that she had never seen were taking him bit by bit even while he was still here. It was not like the end of a dance; or the falling of a curtain at the end of a play, or the blowing out of candles when the feast is over; it was like night slowly creeping into a lampless room, where you have to sit and wait, watching the walls fade and the window frames grow fainter, until it is quite dark. Her world would be such a room to her when the slow separation had been completed and she was finally alone.

Her brain and not her heart ached now, as for a few moments she allowed herself to think of what separation would really mean to her. Her eyes smarted, her throat grew hot, her head was full of the dully throbbing anguish. She could scarcely breathe. Then she drove thought away again, beating it from her with the verbal weapons she had prepared against this emergency; saying to herself, "It is wrong of me. I must not be selfish. I must look at everything from his point of view. I know very well that if it were in my power to keep him, I would urge him to go."

And beneath the words and the thoughts and the pain, she had now the sense of unreality or impossibility. They could not be separated in this manner. Some chance would intervene; by no action of her own but by some eleventh hour leniency of fate, the consummation of the catastrophe would be prevented or at least retarded; nature itself would recoil from adding this one more to its tale of endless cruelties. It was with Miss Verinder, finishing her coffee, as with children when they think of death, believing that death is something that will certainly happen, and yet, owing to some failure of the thought-machine at their disposal, being unable to believe in its possibility.

It could not be that if on the fourth night from now she entered this great dining-hall, she would find apparently the same crowd of travellers, the swing-doors opening and shutting, the waiters going round asking people whether they wanted any liqueur with their coffee—and yet no Anthony Dyke to be seen or heard anywhere. It could not be that she should creep back to London, a broken useless thing wanted by nobody, and that her lover would have gone from her for years if not for ever. It *must* be impossible that so strong, so overwhelmingly real a thing as he, should fade out of her life and take his place among such weak impalpable things as ghosts or dreams or haunting memories; that he for whom she had forsaken and renounced her home, her parents, her friends, every precept of education, every habit of the mind, should become again scarcely more to her than he had been three months ago—a name in a newspaper.

She went out of the room, and a party of travellers at the nearest table to hers thought her a good-looking but hard sort of young woman—too proud and defiantly British for their taste—and, considering her youthfulness, too self-possessed and self-satisfied. Did you hear how she spoke to the waiter? "No, no liqueur, thank you." Just like that—so off-hand.

Miss Verinder had the same air of hardness and resolution, together with a new and metallic form of gaiety, next morning when Dyke took her with him to visit the ship. The *Mercedaria*—a steamer of about three thousand tons—had come out into the river now, and she lay moored in the bright but soft sunlight towards the Birkenhead shore. With her one tall funnel and two raking masts, she looked, not only small, but a battered and rather disreputable kind of tramp, when compared with the lofty shining mass of a big liner a little higher up the river. But she loomed up high and solid, as their boat passed under her stern.

Dyke took the honoured visitor here and there about the vessel, showing her first the saloon, and what they pompously called the state rooms. This accommodation, although originally planned for a few passengers as well as the ship's officers, seemed to Miss Verinder's untutored eye appallingly inadequate and restricted for so long a voyage. The state rooms were but dark and stuffy cupboards, with a bunk in each. A rough partition of woodwork, left plain and unvarnished, had been erected athwartship at the back of the saloon, which itself was a dull malodorous den, with a table surrounded by seven permanently fixed swivel chairs. A large oil lamp hung beneath a skylight above the table, and really, this was all of furniture or decoration. It was a relief to emerge on the upper deck, and feel again the air and warmth. Here Dyke showed her the chart-room—quite a comfortable retreat—immediately below the bridge, with leather cushions to its benches and printed certificates in frames against the wall.

An unshaved but smiling steward or cook followed them up, to say that by the orders of Captain Cairns he had put out a bottle of champagne and some biscuits down below, for the lady. Captain Cairns himself, immensely improved in appearance now that he was wearing uniform, welcomed her very courteously, and said he only wished that she was going with them across the sea. He was busy, Captain Cairns, making these kindly civilities brief and to the point, and then at once resuming his task. There were lighters alongside, and the last of the cargo was being hoisted on board by the noisy rattling steam winches.

On this pleasant sunny morning the very air seemed full of bustling activity; the whole stream was alive with traffic; crowded steam ferry-boats shot diagonally across it, and made their practised curves, as they glided to the huge landing-stages. Tugs whistling insistently went up and down, together with strings of barges; and farther off, one saw the long forest of masts that told of unceasing trade. It was as though everybody was hurrying to get away, and the great city itself, seen from here with diminished eminence and towers and domes brought together by the distance, seemed to be sitting on the waters, calmly meditating in the midst of a foolish tumult.

Miss Verinder stood near a boat that hung inboard on its davits, with her gloved hand on the rail and her gauze scarf gently stirring in the friendly breeze, while she talked and smiled, gaily and cheerfully. This is the woman's portion. One must not say anything, or do anything, to bother one's man or to lower his spirits when he is taking up his own burden of care and anxiety.

She watched, with intelligent interest, the toil of the sailors and the winches, as the wooden cases one after another came up from the hidden barge, swung round, and disappeared in their proper hold. This part of the cargo, as Dyke explained, was coming in last because it would go out first. The sailors, he assured her, although they certainly looked a shabby untrimmed gang, apparently of all nationalities too, were a real good lot. Oh, yes, one could trust old Cairns for that, and everything else.

With her heart aching rather worse than last night, Miss Verinder laughed and showed most intelligent interest.

Some of the big cases had on them, marked roughly in black paint, the words, "Bicycles" and "Bicycle accessories." Oh, yes, of course, this was that consignment of which Dyke had spoken. The bicycles for the people of Uruguay, all bitten with the fashionable craze—the bicycles, of which the mere notion had caused Mr. Cairns to laugh so uproariously. Making conversation, she reminded Dyke of the Captain's humour.

But Dyke looked at her doubtfully. Indeed his whole face clouded and he answered with a strange glumness. Then abruptly he took her by the arm, drawing her across the deck to the corresponding boat on the other side. There he told her firmly that he could not allow the continuance of a deception, however trifling. He could not leave her in the dark about anything in any way concerning him. Between him and her there must not be a secret, even though the secret was devoid of all importance. Well then, he had to confess, or rather to inform her, that all these bicycles—and he looked round to be sure that they were not overheard—those bicycles, don't you know, were not really bicycles. No, they were, in fact, rifles, and so forth, technically known as small arms.

"But, Anthony," said Miss Verinder, looking at him timidly but intently, "isn't that what you call gun-running?"

"Oh, no, I don't call it that. I shouldn't think of calling it that, Emmie," and he laughed. With a very uncharacteristic confusion, even sheepishness, he answered her further questions. He had released her arm, and he stood there really like a naughty boy answering a governess. He could only try to laugh it off. He had no excuses.

"But, Anthony, isn't it dangerous?"

His eyes gave a flash, and sheepishness vanished.

"Oh, I know *that* wouldn't deter you, Tony. But, I mean, isn't it against the law?"

"Well, there's no revolution in Uruguay—not at this minute, anyhow. I don't pretend to any blind respect for the law; but I don't see why the law should object. No," and he laughed now with unembarrassed cheerfulness. "If they don't stop us here, they won't stop us out there. So don't you worry, darling. If we get safe out of the Mersey, I promise we'll get safe into Rio Grande."

It was their last day. After a misty morning there had been a little rain, then the dark sky fought the sunlight, and now a settled gloom lay on the town and the river, with presages of more rain. Smoke was rolling languidly from the *Mercedaria's* ugly yellow funnel. She was to sail before night. She was to sail in five hours.

Miss Verinder wandered about her disconsolately, and talked to Dyke from time to time. He was very busy. Down below Reynolds, the steward or cook, was busy too; in his shirt sleeves, packing away all kinds of light consumable stores in the narrow compartment that was his whole realm. She gave money to Reynolds, begged him to take care of Mr. Dyke as well as he could. Reynolds promised. She sat for a long while alone on the bunk in Dyke's cabin, staring at trunks that were like old friends to her, trunks that had been in his room at the hotel such a little while ago; and she fingered many parcels all thrown down there on the bunk, the things she had bought for him yesterday and the day before—comforts, contrivances, and books. That small square parcel contained the poems of Tennyson. He loved them—especially the *Idylls of the King*. Both head and heart were aching so intolerably that she had to clench her hands sometimes; and her breathing was affected. She felt that she might suffocate if she did not have more air, and yet she did not like to go up to the deck where Dyke and Cairns were busy with some one in the chart-room. Down here, in this small buried cabin, she had a feeling that the ship was enormous, a monster of the deep now gathering energy, angrily shivering, like the men on the upper deck panting to get to work.

Then she heard Dyke's voice calling to her, and she went up with him. He said that he had been looking for her everywhere. As she came out into the daylight he noticed her whiteness, and saw that sharpened, hardened aspect of the face that had once impressed itself on the attention of her father. Her nose seemed much too thin, her chin much too pointed and the almost colourless lips were drawn inward by an ugly contraction; seeing her thus, no sane person could have described her as a pretty girl, indeed it would have been kind not to call her plain; but this marring of her beauty, this swift disfigurement, for one who not only knew the cause but was himself the cause stirred deeper wells of love and made admiration more poignantly sincere. He took her twitching fingers, and in a husky whisper muttered words of encouragement and hope.

"It—it's quite all right, Tony. I—I'll not disgrace you."

"You see, Emmie dear. The time will pass," he mumbled. "Back soon as I can."

"Yes—I know. But not too soon—not—not till you've done your work."

For perhaps seventy seconds they stood holding hands, and looking at each other.

"Anthony."

"Oh, Emmie. It's awful, isn't it?"

Then some one shouted to him. Some one had just come up the side.

"You'll let me stay to the last moment, won't you?" she said, with a spasmodic clutch of her fingers. "You won't send me ashore, till you need?"

"No, no," he said, hurrying away.

It was now about three in the afternoon, and during the next hour she had but flying sentences from him at long intervals. Worrying, annoying things, as she gathered, occupied all his thoughts. Men came and went. There were gusts of loud swearing in the chart-room and confidential irritable exchanges as Captain Cairns appeared and disappeared. Then there was talk of the pilot. Something was very much on Anthony's nerves, obviously; she learned from his snatches of explanation that this concerned certain formalities that should have been completed but were not—the ship's papers not yet absolutely in order, clearances still required, the port or custom-house authorities rubbed the wrong way by sheer stupidness and now becoming troublesome when there was no leisure to soothe them? She did not know. She only knew that Anthony was angry, using strong language and saying he would go and attend to it himself since he could trust nobody else.

There was a second cause for annoyance. Four or five of the crew were on shore instead of on board—five, perhaps six of Cairns's international mob absent, playing the fool, getting drunk, what not, just as their services were urgently required. Cairns was as angry as Dyke about this. The second mate must go off in a boat at once and bring those men aboard dead or alive, with or without their kit; and Dyke exploded, roaring threats—advising the captain to put them in irons after breaking their bones. And then, with more talk of another boat, a boat for Mr. Dyke; with more talk about the pilot, the tide, those papers—then, after all this, suddenly, Miss Verinder understood. The ship was going to sail before its time. The ship was going to sail as soon as it possibly could.

"Yes, my darling, yes. No, you can't stay now. I'm going ashore myself. I haven't a minute to spare. Come along."

As they were rowed away from the ship the other boat parted from them, and Dyke shouted further menaces across the water. He was worried, irritated, answering his Emmie's questions automatically. She sat bolt upright, rigid, so that her slim body jerked all in one piece as the rowers plunged their oars faster and faster, but she still showed a sympathetic intelligent interest. Replying to her quite sensible inquiries, Dyke told her at which landing-place the mate's boat would lie waiting for those men; also that if the mate failed to find the absentees he would return to the ship without them. If Dyke could polish off his rather ticklish bit of business, he intended that the ship should leave her moorings in two hours.

"So it's good-bye, Emmie"—they were close to the shore now—"Good-bye, my best—my dearest—my only love."

She did not reply, she could not reply. This manner of parting with him was too bitter. It was too bitter.

He hurried her across the landing-stage and through the crowd on the sloped bridge, put her into a cab, and told the driver to take her to the hotel. One more squeeze of the hand, and he had vanished. She could not see if he jumped into another cab himself or crossed the wide roadway towards lofty buildings on the other side. Anyhow he was about his business. It had begun to rain, a gust of cold wind swept through the cab windows.

At the hotel, as she passed his room, the door stood open, and she saw the chambermaid with brush and broom making its emptiness neat and clean for another lodger. There was a litter of crumpled newspapers on the tiled hearth; the low table on which he packed his last valise had been pushed away from the foot of the bed; and the window curtains were looped up high, to keep them out of the dust that the broom was making.

Miss Verinder went into her own room, and remained for a minute motionless, with clenched hands, struggling for breath. This parting was too bitter—much too bitter. It was more than she could bear. She rang the bell, and continued to ring it until the chambermaid came to help her. Then she began to pack, with feverish haste.

Dusk was falling rapidly and the port light of the *Mercedaria* made a red reflection in the grey stream when, after less than two hours, Dyke got back on board. He had achieved his object, but he roared in anger again at hearing that the mate had not returned with those men.

They came while he was still shouting. Their boat was alongside. They were coming up the ladder. Captain Cairns, on the bridge with the pilot, looked down at the vague clambering forms and cursed them one by one and all together. They were in tarpaulin coats, clutching at their bundles or chests and seeming to have an absurd amount of baggage; one at least of them—if not every one of them, as the Captain said—appeared to be drunk. The others had to aid him as he sprang weakly and clumsily from the boat to the ladder.

Then soon the *Mercedaria* began to glide down the river, emitting a melancholy siren blast to demand her rights of way. They were off. The dusk was deepening, the rain swept along with them; all was greyness, mistiness, and smoke, and the city towers and pinnacles seemed to sink lower and to fade behind banks of cloud, below which hundreds of lights began to twinkle feebly. The wretchedness and misery of departure enveloped the whole broad estuary.

Dyke had put on a waterproof and a sou'wester, and he prowled to and fro below the bridge gazing across the water, now on this side, now on that. He was quiet now, and yet not altogether easy in his mind. The fretfulness caused by dread of delay and interruption could not immediately be subdued, and perhaps certain doubts still lingered. He went down to the lower deck, made his way aft and stood for a while right at the stern, looking out intently. One might have supposed that he was now silently brooding on his love, sadly thinking of the girl he had left behind him; but in truth he thought only of the voyage and the venture. Watching and waiting, as the low land slid away and the darkness fell, he was wondering if a steam pinnace with those confounded custom-house people would come racing after him, and feeling that he would like to sink them if they came. But nothing happened. It was all right.

He went up again to the chart-room and stood there, cheerful, rubbing his hands. He slapped jolly old Cairns on the back and the two sat there for a bit, drinking whisky and water, and gaily chatting, like two schoolboys glorying in the success of their latest prank.

The pilot had been dropped. It was black night now and the *Mercedaria* was safely out at sea; rain and wind drove at her as she ploughed across the pleasant heave and swell, rolling scarcely at all, but filled with throbbings and vibrations—with delightful sounds too, of orders repeated through the darkness, the scurry of footsteps, of the rudder chains clanking in their grooves, the work of her screw, the splash of water against her bows: sounds that are so stimulating and seductive to those who delight in journeys by sea, but so insidiously distressing, so suggestive of augmented woe, to those unpractised in the ways of the unsteady deep.

Every throb and murmur rejoiced the heart of Dyke; the very smells of the ship were refreshing to him. Some of them rose, to welcome and cheer, as he went down the companion-way towards the comfortable lamp-light of the saloon. There was the peculiar characteristic stuffiness, with odours of leather, stale salt water, and dead fish, enriched at the moment by the efforts of Reynolds the steward frying meat and onions in grease, and that oil lamp burning cheerily but with a smoky flame.

Dyke stood in the saloon doorway, his face all wet, his beard glistening, and the water falling from his coat to the floor. He stood there, dripping but full of enjoyment, for one moment; then Reynolds in the cuddy heard him shout.

"Great heavens! Emmie!"

She was calmly sitting at the table, with the lamp-light on her white face; and she spoke to him in gentle pleading tones.

"Don't be angry with me."

But he was angry, terribly angry; with himself or fate, rather than with her. He did not speak harshly or unkindly to her herself, but he addressed the woodwork, the skylight, and all inanimate things with dreadful severity. He waved his arms, he pulled at his hair; never had she seen him so agitated, so perturbed.

"Tony dear, what does it matter?"

He said that her presence there had put him in a hideously false position. He said that he must not of course blame her; what she had done was noble, heroic, angelic; only he ought to have warned her of the disastrous effect of such an act. "Emmie, you reckless self-sacrificing saint, you really have carted me. You've made me break my solemn promise. In all my life

I've never gone back on my word. My old father foresaw, he feared—and I gave him my word of honour that I wouldn't take you out of England."

Poor Miss Verinder said forlornly, "You must tell your father the fault is mine. It is I who have run away with you, not you with me."

But Dyke then said they must stop the ship and land her as soon as possible. He would go and consult with Captain Cairns. Miss Verinder said no, she begged him not to think of doing that; she would go with him to their port of destination and then quietly return to England. Deprecatingly she explained that she had not planned this treacherous act, she had never meant to do anything at all on her own initiative or without his explicit approval; but the accelerated departure, that hasty good-bye, the bundling her into a cab and disappearing, had been too much for her. Then the thought had come of the mate's boat lying there waiting—and then "Tony, I had to do it. I couldn't, I *couldn't* help it." And she concluded with urgent entreaties that Mr. O'Donnell, the second mate, should not be made to suffer for her imprudence. Mr. O'Donnell, she said, had at first strongly objected to bring her off, but she had not been quite truthful to Mr. O'Donnell. She had "over-persuaded" Mr. O'Donnell. After that he had been kindness itself; lending her one of the men's coats, helping her out of the boat, troubling about her luggage.

"Tony!" and she stretched out her hand.

She was deadly pale, trembling a little, and her dark hair hung down loosely about her pleading eyes. Dyke stooped over her and kissed her cold forehead.

"Emmie!"

Reynolds came in with a tray of plates, and was followed by heavy waves of that odour of fried steak and onions; he fixed the tray to the table in some ingenious manner, and every time the *Mercedaria* softly heaved the plates made a musical clatter. Those invisible chains rumbled behind Miss Verinder's head, and before her eyes two scuttles with brass bolts slowly sank a few feet and as slowly rose. She shivered, but went on talking; her gentle voice a little shaky, but very sweet still.

"And I meant—dear Tony—not to give anybody any trouble—not to get in anybody's way. But now I fear—that I may not be quite well on the voyage—at least at first. Tony!" And she looked at him despairingly. "I do feel so ill. Can I go and lie down anywhere?"

CHAPTER VIII

MISS VERINDER suffered from sea-sickness in a more or less acute form throughout the interminable voyage. The ship touched at Lisbon and Dyke wanted to put her ashore, but she refused to stir. They encountered terrible weather in the long trudge to St. Vincent; and there, in a spell of stifling heat while the ship coaled, she seemed so desperately ill that he tried again, with the aid of a German physician. She refused to move; she might be dying, but she certainly would not leave the ship. She faintly declared that of course she was not dying; very soon now she would be quite well.

With the ship in motion again, and a cool head wind in their faces, she seemed to revive a little; but she relapsed as they worked southwards towards the equator—a relapse not occasioned but perhaps intensified by the well-meant efforts of Reynolds to tempt her appetite with pork and beans, and kindred dainties. She lived on tea and biscuits—and on the sound of Dyke's voice. He was her steward, lady's maid, and nurse. At meal-time she liked to have the door of her cabin wide open, so that through the narrow passage she could hear him laugh and talk. Along with the sound of his voice, came perfumes of hot coarse food that made her writhe in sudden spasms of nausea; yet she never closed the door. She took what gave her joy at the cost of all that gave her torment. Indeed she never counted the cost in regard to this or any other matter that concerned her love. Not for an hour, not for a minute, did she regret that she had come with him. She merely apologized for causing him such dreadful trouble.

"Tony dear, I shall wear out even your patience. How can you forgive me?"

He used to tell her that each trifling service he had the honour to perform was like a tiny piece of flax, and that out of such pieces she had made a rope so strong as to bind him to her invincibly. He could never break loose now if he wanted to be free. And he wouldn't want. He became husky when he spoke of her courage, and then he would laugh to cheer her; promising that she should have three happy weeks at Buenos Ayres while he and that staunch old sportsman Pedro del Sarto were preparing their jaunt to the Andes—weeks to make up for all this. "Our honey-moon, Emmie!"

Truly he served her and waited upon her with a surpassing tenderness. He had a trick of kneeling by the berth, making one arm her pillow, and with his other hand softly playing with her hair. That rough muscular hand grew light as a rose leaf while it swept back the hair and touched her face. And once, while in this attitude, perhaps because of noticing her debility and frailness, or because of thinking of what she had done for his sake, he began to weep. Then, till he recovered composure, she did really believe she might die; it seemed that in her weak state the mingled sweetness and pain of their love must surely kill her; and she thought that, for bringing tears to those eyes, she deserved death.

"There. You musn't let me get too sentimental, Emmie. Check me. It's a fault of mine. Now here's cheerful news. Cairns says we may see land in four days. So the worst is over. Down the Brazilian coast it's nothing at all."

They got her up on deck, after they had entered the glorious harbour of Rio de Janeiro. And she sat, wrapped with shawls, languidly surveying the broad smooth waters, the vast semi-circle of mountains, and the garden-like beauty of town and shore. It was a vague dream-panorama, so far as she was concerned.

Here the ship was joined by two Italians from the southernmost province of Brazil. These, it seemed, were the consignees of those bicycles and accessories. They were citizens of Brazil—adventurous merchants—dealers in bicycles, and a variety of other things—anything, in fact, likely to prove quickly marketable. As Dyke informed her, confidentially, it was at their option where they would accept delivery of his merchandise. They had made all arrangements for landing the goods, and they would pop them over the border into Uruguay, as appeared best and most convenient. It was all going to be as easy as falling off a house.

As soon as the ship steamed out of the placid bay Miss Verinder went below again. She remained there, listening day after day to the gaiety of the saloon, a gaiety largely increased by the addition to their party.

She was once more very unwell—at her worst almost during forty-eight hours when, as Dyke explained, they were standing on and off by the lagoon in front of Porto Alegre. They were waiting for a river steamer of shallow draught that was coming out to meet them. This steamer, as Miss Verinder gathered, duly arrived alongside, and, before the dawn of another day, the most delicate part of their cargo was transferred to her. Miss Verinder listened with anxious interest to gentle bumps and jarrings, produced by their temporary consort—to the noisy racket of steam winches, the shouted orders, the general hubbub that continued during the lengthy task of transshipment.

Then they were under way again, and Dyke came down to her joyous and smiling, snapping his fingers in innocent glee. Those Italians and their perhaps slightly compromising bicycles had gone for ever. The deed was done. All the cargo now on board was good honest domestic stuff for the

Argentine, and, as Dyke said, laughing, "the Pope himself might come and look at it, if he cared to."

They steamed steadily southward, and although Miss Verinder felt relief of mind, and delighted in the thought that Dyke's cleverness and resource had met with a prosperous issue, she still remained far from well. Then at last they were on the brown mud-stained bosom of the River Plate. They were between the black stretching arms of the Ensenada Canal. They were on shore. Emmie stood upon a stone pier that did not undulate beneath her feet, and leant against a post that yielded no vibration to her shoulder. She was better, even as she staggered through the Custom House on Dyke's arm; she was convalescent when she entered the train, able to take pleasure in looking at the flat low land and herds of cattle, in catching glimpses of a huge two-wheeled country cart, and fantastic, brightly-coloured figures on horseback; she was almost well when Dyke helped her out of the train, in the fine noisy station at Buenos Ayres.

He kept his promise. He gave her the happy weeks. Flush of money, joyous after the successful voyage, he had only one slight care or disappointment, and he did not allow this to trouble him long. He insisted on buying for her wonderful, gay-coloured dresses that had come to the street called Florida direct from the Rue de la Paix; like a debonair honey-moon husband with a runaway bride, he could not buy enough for her; and himself, with hair cropped and beard trimmed, faultlessly attired, too, in white flannels, was now a not unworthy companion to those enticing Paris frocks. In the sunshine and the warmth, lulled by all the charms of exotic novelty, revelling in the strangeness and freedom of her environment, Miss Verinder blossomed with beauty and health.

She drank deep of the brimming cup of life. As a favourite poet expressed the thought that was often in her mind—whatever happened now, she would have had her day.

She felt that this Buenos Ayres, although the biggest city in the world if judged by extent, was not large enough to hold her joy. It flowed out from her beyond the vast chess-board of houses and far over the dusty plains; it danced with the sunlight on the water that she saw in flashes as they drove in their two-horse fly along the incredibly uneven pavement of the streets; it filled the whole summer night as they sat drinking their coffee under the palm-trees of Palermo's park.

They were staying at one of the lesser hotels—a place built in the Spanish style about a garden-courtyard that was full of sweet-smelling flowers and shrubs; with the very modern addition of a wooden hall in which was set forth the one long table at which the guests assembled twice a day. There were fifty or sixty of them often at the table d'hôte dinner, a gathering of many races with representatives of many trades; German commercial travellers, Argentine farmers come from their estancias to pass a few days in the city; comfortable Chilian families en route for Europe, sea captains and their mates like Cairns and O'Donnell, Frenchmen travelling for pleasure; and generally some of the engineers and surveyors whose work related to the construction of the trans-Andine railway. The talk frequently ran on this wonderful railway that was soon to pierce the great mountain barrier and enable you to travel from one ocean to the other as easily as if you were going from London to Brighton. A Frenchman said that although the railway would be marvellous and admirable as an engineering feat, he regretted it as something which attacked one of nature's last remaining strongholds, which would rob you of romance and mystery; but Dyke jovially laughed away this notion, vowing that the Andes were big enough and strong enough to withstand a hundred such inroads, and referring them to a certain book on the subject which it might not become him to particularise more fully.

Those of the hotel guests who did not know him already made his ripe acquaintance during the progress of a single meal; and they rarely failed to felicitate Emmie on her good fortune in having such a man to act as escort and guide.

"Yes, yes, Mrs. Fleming. Vairy well-known man throughout the Argentine Republic. Vairy well respected man to the populace and the government."

Dyke had given out that she was Mrs. Fleming, a lady journalist, visiting South America for the purpose of gathering literary materials, and that it was his task to show her things of interest; but these chance friends drew their own conclusions as to the bond that subsisted between the two. Dyke was not really good at deception; after making those hidalgo bows when they met for dinner and ceremoniously standing by the door as she passed out, he would allow his far-reaching voice to be heard in the gardens as he called up to her in her room: "Emmie, my darling, come down for a stroll. It's a perfect night."

Moreover, they could not do otherwise than notice the meek adoration in her face as she looked at him. But this crowd did not mind. They liked her; they felt sure that Fleming, her husband, was a blackguard, and that she had been driven by his ill usage to place herself under the protection of the illustrious Don Antonio Dyke.

On the other hand the official people, with their wives, daughters, and young lady visitors, fought shy of Mrs. Fleming, dodging introduction to her and ignoring it afterwards if undodgable—more especially at the Lawn Tennis Club, where nothing could prevent him from taking her. Indeed one might say that just as he had been "that man" in Prince's Gate, so she had become "that woman" in Buenos Ayres.

When he left her in the hired victoria outside consulates, ministries, or government offices—and necessarily he did thus leave her now and then,—frivolous clerks and minor officials peeped at her from behind sunblinds or even came forth to get a good stare at her. Aware both of this curiosity and its cause, she did not at all suffer because of them. The swarthy coachman drew the carriage into the shade of some gum trees, mounted the box seat again, and immediately fell asleep; and Emmie brought out her grammar or conversation book, and unconcernedly pursued her study of that Spanish tongue which Dyke lisped so fluently. She would not trouble to change the position of her flaming parasol when the silly young men passed to and fro, staring. Let them say what they pleased. She could not now bother even to think of such trivial matters as conventional etiquette or orthodox relationships. She was in another hemisphere—too far from the Albert Hall for it to be worth while.

From the Argentine government—a government that has always proved the most liberal in the world towards colonists and travellers—Dyke was obtaining every facility and authorisation that he required for his new journey to the Andes. Emeralds had not been mentioned, but it was understood that he would explore in search of mineral deposits, and if he found anything worth finding a full share of the value of the discovery would be secured to him. For the best of all reasons, he was going to make the trip alone and not in company with his associate, del Sarto.

To his great disappointment Pedro del Sarto had totally vanished. It seemed that his varied business had gone wrong, he himself was obviously dropping into low water, and then, of a sudden, more than a year and a half ago, he had left Buenos Ayres without a word to anybody. Dyke hunted throughout the city for a faithful underling of Pedro's, a man called Juan Pombal. But this man had also disappeared. Then, after more hunting, he found an Indian woman who had been Pedro's cook, housekeeper, and perhaps other things as well; but beyond confirming the fact of the departure she could supply no information. She expected to see her master again one of these days, and meantime she bore his absence philosophically.

The loss of the expected comrade and partner was a blow to Dyke; but, as has been indicated, it was temperamentally impossible to him to permit any disappointment either to weigh upon his spirits or to turn him from his purpose. He must go by himself—that was all about it. Nevertheless, during his first surprise at so strange a failure to keep a business appointment, he confessed to Mrs. Fleming that he felt "flummuxed" by dear old Pedro's conduct.

"I told him I would be back here in two years—at the very latest. And you see, Emmie, he *believed* in my discovery. He believed we had got a fortune in it. He believed, even before I gave him the map I had made. He trusted my judgment—just as I trusted his fidelity. We were *fond* of each other. Emmie, I don't pretend that Pedro is really a gentleman, but he is a clinking good sort all the same. He and I met first at Punta Arenas—when I was messing about after the beach gold—and we became like brothers. Well then, if he was down on his luck, why didn't he write to me? And since he knew I was coming back, why couldn't he wait? The very fact of his losses would have made him all the keener for such a chance as this. It beats me, his going without letting me know. I can only explain it by a guess. More than eighteen months ago. Well, I expect it was the gold again down south that tempted him—and he and Pombal lit out for it, thinking they'd make a bit down there and be back here again in time for me."

Once more Emmie was taking intelligent interest in Dyke's preparations, and the three happy weeks glided into four and five before everything was completed. A contractor at Mendoza was supplying the mules and their equipment, with an excellent muleteer as chief; seven other men, of whom four were Indians, stout hefty fellows inured to hardship and capable of using picks to good effect, had been engaged by Dyke himself; light mining tools, shelter tents, suitable garments, and a tremendous provision of food in the most conveniently compressed form, made up the outfit of the expedition. It would assemble at Mendoza, and make its real start higher in the hills, at the existing end of the railway. The month of December had now begun, with settled summer weather. As Emmie understood, any further delay would be unwise if not inexcusable.

And so once more their parting drew very near. These were the last days. One lovely night when after driving about the park they had left their carriage in order to saunter among the crowd and listen to the band, she spoke to him quietly but very seriously concerning the risks that he would run on his mountain trip.

"Risks!" he said gaily. "There are no risks of any sort or kind." There was only one word that could adequately describe this amusing little jaunt, the word that he had used all along. It would be a picnic—a picnic, neither more nor less. And searching for similes, he assured her that he would be as absolutely safe up there as he could be on his native Devon cliffs, or Richmond Hill, or Hampstead Heath.

But apparently not satisfied, she suggested dangers one after another. Hostile Indians? Storms and mists? Ice crevasses? Snow avalanches? Excessive cold?

"No, no—of course not." He laughed at her suggestions. Hostile Indians no longer existed, it was summer time, the only snow likely to interfere with him would all be melted. She also laughed, but then continued her serious talk, linking her arm in his and pressing it to her side as they strolled away from the music, the lamps, and the crowd.

"Tony dear, you make light of things because you yourself are so wonderful. You don't feel cold or fatigue. Danger is nothing to you."

"Oh, isn't it, by Jove? Emmie, I'm the most cautious old bird alive. It's been my maxim and watchword never to take an avoidable risk. No, that's a fool's game. And—see here—if I've been careful in the past, how much more careful shall I be in the future—now that I own the universe? I swear it's true, Emmie. No chances henceforth for Anthony Dyke."·

But she did not yet seem satisfied.

"I wasn't thinking of your real work," she said quietly. "Only about this one little expedition. Supposing it wasn't yourself—suppose it was somebody else, not trained and clever like you—suppose it was just an ordinary person—would you still say there was no risk?"

"Yes, I would," said Dyke, after a slight hesitation. "None worth considering. No, any ordinary healthy person could do it as easily as falling off a house."

"Do you say that on your honour, Tony?"

"Yes, on my honour."

"Very well," said Miss Verinder firmly. "Then I'll go with you."

Throughout the drive back to the hotel, he was explaining that he had spoken of ordinary men, not of women; that not for a moment could he consent; that it was quite splendid of her to entertain such a wild idea, but she must dismiss it at once and for ever.

"Oh, no, Tony," she said, smiling in the darkness as she took his hand and got out of the carriage. "We'll consider it quite settled, please. Of course I mean for the trip only. Directly you are ready to go to Australia I'll say good-bye—and no more nonsense." And she squeezed against him as they passed through the fragrance of the hotel garden. "I'm too proud of you to be selfish. I'd never, never try to come between you and your real work."

CHAPTER IX

A RAILWAY journey of something under seven hundred miles, during each mile of which the train and everything in it became enveloped in a deeper and deeper mantle of dust, brought them to the town of Mendoza at the foot of the Andes. They stayed here for two nights and a day; then they went on again, climbing now, in the narrow-gauge railway, as far as it could take them. They slept the following night at a still comparatively decent inn, and next day mounted their mules and began to ride.

It was at this point that Miss Verinder, or Mrs. Fleming, or whatever one liked to call her, temporarily disappeared; her place being taken by a person in breeches, with boots big enough to contain a fur lining and at least three pairs of stockings—a person who might readily have been mistaken for a bright-eyed, eager, excited lad, until for a moment she took off her immense straw hat and disclosed an unexpected profusion of dark wavy hair.

Thus she rode out, bestriding her large mule jauntily, with Dyke on one side of her and the capataz or chief muleteer on the other side, the keen thin air fanning her, the fiery sun blazing at her—through such scenery as till now she had seen only in dreams, along the edge of precipices, past ravines through the hidden depths of which torrents went raging, beneath stupendous overhanging cliffs—she rode out into brain-reeling wonder and heart-folding enchantment.

"Isn't it a lark, Emmie? What?"

"O pig, O laziest of swine," said their capataz, smiling at her ingratiatingly, but addressing her mule. "Will you move when a lady rides you or will you not?" And, dropping back, he belaboured the hindquarters of Emmie's mule with a substantial stick.

This highly praised muleteer—Manuel Balda by name—was ferocious enough of aspect; dressed in the usual gaucho style, with slouch hat, poncho, and knife at belt; rolling his sloe-like eyes and showing yellow teeth in a weather-stained face. But his manner had been quite magnificent when Dyke ceremoniously presented him to Emmie a few minutes ago, and since then he had taken off his hat and bowed to her at least five times. His voice, too, grew gentle and caressing whenever he addressed her directly. He spoke English well, and one understood at once that he was inordinately proud of his knowledge of the language. He called her Missis, not Señora or Donna. "Now he moves for Missis," said Manuel, satisfied with her mule's accelerated pace. "And I, Manuel Balda, myself would die for Missis"; and he doffed his hat and bowed. "That is comprehended, is it not? Don Antonio has said me to be the guard of Missis all time our journey shall last. Be it so, to the last drop of my blood." Then, with the most graceful ceremony, he gave his cudgel to her, vowing that he had trimmed it for this express purpose, and begging her not to spare its use. Then with another profound bow he galloped ahead, and they saw him no more till the evening. He had gone on to overtake their train of pack-mules, which had been slowly plodding forward for the last three days.

Emmie, although amused by Manuel's words and manners, did not take to the man himself. In her first swift impression there was something vaguely disconcerting, as of weakness or shiftiness detected behind the outward show of loyalty and strength—the quite vague feeling that decides one during one's first interview with a servant. It did not in any way perturb her, but it was just sufficient to make her ask Dyke if he trusted Manuel implicitly.

"I don't trust him an inch further than I see him," said Dyke cheerily. "But he knows his job. That's the great thing. Presently I'll let him see—and the others too—that there'll be trouble for anybody who attempts to play the fool."

They rode on, and the imagination almost fainted in presence of reality. It made one turn dizzy to look down, it set one trembling to look back. Each sharp turn or twist of their path revealed things more tremendous. The heights and depths, the chaotic masses, the savage grandeur of it all, made the fantastic impossible pictures drawn by that popular artist Gustave Doré seem, in one's memory of them, pale and insipid.

Yet they were still on the beaten track. This was the high road, through the pass, from one civilized country to another; and plainly its frequenters treated it as a quite ordinary affair. Single horsemen came galloping down at them with loose reins; a four-horse coach swept round one of the bends in the granite ledge at break-neck speed; long files of laden mules made clouds of dust, and twice the path was blocked by droves of cattle in the midst of which gauchos, apparently gone mad, were shouting and cursing.

Emmie's excursion had but begun, she was merely doing what every tourist did, although the romance and grandeur of it kept her pulses racing. "I am in the Andes," she murmured to herself. "I am with *him*—on the road to the Uspallata Pass—getting higher and higher in the Andes."

They spent that night at the last of the mountain inns to be encountered by them for a long while. Next morning the true fun would begin.

The inn was a wretched little assemblage of low sheds standing on flat ground a few hundred yards away from the track; but it had a large walled corral in which the baggage of dozens of mules lay stacked or tumbled in loose confusion. The mules themselves—Dyke's lot among them—were picketed or tied to the walls. Muleteers, the railway people, itinerant dealers, and so forth crowded the place. The living-room had more dreadful odours than the cabin of the *Mercedaria*. The sordidness and dirt of the boarded compartment in which she and Dyke were to sleep surpassed belief; one glance at the two beds—the two lairs—caused the flesh to creep in anticipation of the attack of an insect horde. Dyke, on their arrival, immediately became occupied with his men, and Emmie fell into the charge of the landlady, a dirty but kindly matron, and of Manuel Balda.

"A bit rough," said Dyke; "but Manuel will help to make you comfortable."

No one of course could do that; although Manuel, who was torn in opposite directions by his desire to be outside with Dyke examining the equipment and to be here waiting upon his lady, gallantly attempted the impossible task.

She wanted water to wash with; but both he and the landlady implored her to abandon this desire. Already the glare of the fierce sun had scorched her delicate complexion. She might rub her cheeks with vaseline or any procurable grease; but, for the love of heaven, no water! No more washing, Señora, for the future, if you are still to mount.

And now let us chat of these insects which "Missis" dreads in the beds and elsewhere. Well, it is so; and so unhappily it will continue. Perhaps Missis has not thought to meet lice in profusion at these big altitudes?

Miss Verinder confessed that she had not indeed thought of such a meeting; and, before an hour had passed, accepting the strong advice both of Manuel and the landlady, she decided to have her hair cut. Manuel did it for her—using a pair of shears generally employed on the manes of mules, after he had carefully cleansed the blades with oil.

"Yes, I'm sure you're right," she kept murmuring, as she sat upon a wooden box and the long dark tresses fell about her on the dirty floor. "Yes, I feel more comfortable already—much more comfortable."

Dyke, coming in just when the operation was finished, gave a yell of horror and fury at sight of her sitting there brutally bobbed, changed while his back was turned from his glorious dusky-locked princess into a travesty of du Maurier's popular heroine, Trilby. He beat his breast, he waved his arms, he roared. And then, as Emmie pacified and explained, he picked up fallen meshes, ran them through his fingers, and almost wept.

"Your greatest loveliness. Oh, Emmie, I can't bear it. It has broken my heart."

"Don't be silly, Tony. My hair will grow again. There will be plenty of time—when you are gone"; and again she explained her reasons.

Ah, yes. Well, it must be admitted, lice are lice. Dyke muttered and moaned, but gradually submitted to the cruel stroke. Yes, perhaps, after all, it was the wisest thing to do. "But mark you. This"—after winding a long mesh round his fingers he was putting it in his pocket-book—"this I shall keep for remembrance to my dying day."

She did not mind the loss of her pretty hair. She did not mind anything— not the foul odours, the greasy food, the bitter cold, the inability to sleep. She feared nothing, she regretted nothing. She was with him still, postponing the inevitable, sharing life with him high in the Andes.

She slept a little towards dawn, and was awakened by Dyke, who for two hours had been working with his men in the darkness outside, loading the pack saddles, seeing that everything was in its place. Now the cavalcade was ready to move. They drank some hot coffee, and started.

It was wonderful to her, most wonderful, that departure in the grey mists of morning. Near a broken gap in the wall of the compound, Dyke, sitting high beside her, held the rein of her mule, and they remained there while one after another the mounted men and the laden mules flitted past, silent, ghostly; vague shapes seen for a moment and immediately lost in the mist. Then, with his hand still on the rein, they trotted boldly on, as if through a white sea, until he had reached the head of the column.

The ground was apparently level and there seemed to be few impediments, but as yet nothing of the way was visible. When Dyke spoke to her his voice seemed to come to her from a distance and to roll from her in the moving waves of white vapour; strange murmurs swept above her head; the rattle of hoofs as they struck upon stone made echoing sounds behind her; and she had what she supposed to be an illusion of a bell that chimed and tinkled, now near, now far away, but never ceasing.

Then swiftly yet gradually the mists broke and the light came flooding down upon them. First the tall peaks caught fire, vast rock buttresses thousands of feet high flamed with orange and crimson, black ragged cliffs shone and glittered, fields of dazzling white snow hung like islands in the air till dark brown mountains rose to carry them; then the whole brightly coloured masses of the hills seemed to spring forth, to steady themselves, to grow less fantastic of shape, more solid of texture; and in a few moments it was broad daylight, with a translucid blue sky, every object far or near sharply defined and the mighty crests of Aconcagua, monarch of the wilds, highest mountain of the southern continent, towering majestic in the blue.

The strong, clear picture given to her by the sunlight was one that would remain with her until memory itself should fade and grow dark. The ground was not as she had supposed, level and free from obstacles; they were winding their way along a rock-strewn valley and mounting fast. The pack-mules, twenty or more of them, with lowered heads climbed patiently each in the footsteps of another; at intervals rode the eight mounted men; and Dyke now pushing ahead, riding alone, seemed an enormous figure in his huge mushroom hat and hung round with wallets. He was happy and joyous, beginning to sing scraps of song; so that his music floated back to them pleasantly, and after a while caught the riders with its pleasant contagion and made them sing too. But queerly there mingled with the song or its pauses that other music of the bell, which she had fancied an evocation of tricked senses. It was with them still, faintly chiming, gently tinkling, as if a cadence of the march itself.

Manuel Balda, most attentive of guardians, riding by her bridle since Dyke had left her, explained the matter. Pointing to a small grey pony that plodded unladen in advance of the pack-mules, he told her that this little mare was the "madrina" or adopted mother of the troop. With the bell strapped round her neck, she and not any of the riders was really leading the mules. Wherever she went they would follow. If they strayed, the sound of the madrina's bell would bring them back. They would be miserable, despairing, if they lost it.

Emmie liked Manuel better to-day; indeed that first faint distrust or questioning doubt of him recurred no more to her contented mind. Every hour he proved himself more useful and valuable. Moreover, though no less respectful, he was less ceremonious now that they had entered the wilderness and left the beaten track far behind them. He laughed and joked, told her travellers' tales, and showed her how he could swing down from his saddle and pick up a stone from the ground as he cantered past.

He told her, amongst other things, that there had been much talk last night at the inn concerning Ruy Chaves, the notorious bandit of the mountains. This bloodthirsty ruffian and his gang were still at large—a disgrace, as Manuel opined, both to the Chilian and the Argentine frontier forces—and quite recently they had seized a pack train rich with merchandise and murdered the inoffensive merchants and muleteers. "It is a shame, Missis." And amplifying his narrative, Manuel related how travellers in small parties feared to move freely because of Chaves, how the poor defenceless little innkeepers were forced to pay him tribute; and how, impelled by the cruel humour that is traditionally common with such pirate-dogs, he "teased" as well as killed his victims—for instance, making them dance and caper on the edge of precipices, till to the prick of his knife they jumped into eternity.

Miss Verinder wished to know if Mr. Dyke had heard this talk about Ruy Chaves the bandit; and Manuel said yes, he had heard it all, and he "had laughed and done so." And Manuel snapped his fingers, and then looked very fierce; implying that bandits would be wise to give him, Manuel, as well as his friend and patron Don Antonio, the widest of wide berths. "You not fear, Missis?"

And he laughed gaily, assuring her that bandit gangs worked frequented highways, and never came up here where there was nothing to prey upon; and that in any circumstances they would not for a moment dream of attacking a strong armed party such as this. Missis need not fear it or anything else. Starvation, thirst, snow—those were the true enemies. And there was much food on the mules, there would be water nearly all the way, the full summer season was propitious.

"So we hope Don Antonio will find what he seeks. It is treasure, is it not, Missis? Ah, ha"; and Manuel laughed cheerfully. "You must not say me. But *he*—Don Antonio—has allow the boys to guess. You can see in the boys' eyes—so happy and hoping. The Indians most. They will not grow tired— our Indians—now they know what they hunt."

"Which are the Indians?" asked Emmie. "They all seem just alike."

In fact, except to a practised eye, there was little that could enable one to distinguish between the descendants of the men who had once owned the land and the descendants of the men who had stolen it from them. Spanish or Indian, these muleteers were dressed in the same manner, spoke the same tongue, and had the same wild cut-throat look except when they were singing or laughing. There was not even a difference of complexion visible. But, as Manuel said, these good boys, although of unadulterated Indian blood, had long enjoyed the advantages of civilization. They were gauchos; they had abandoned the savage hills for the prosperous plains. Yet they could be more useful here than anybody else, because this was their ancient home; they would be able to work well in the air that their ancestors had breathed.

Dyke, far ahead, had reached the top of the valley, and, dismounted, was leading his mule up a steep ridge. This was the first taste of difficulty. They climbed the ridge, scrambled down a long slope, and emerged into another valley, more rock-strewn, more chaotic than the first, with a deep-cut stream running a serpentine course towards them.

They made a long halt by this stream during the intense mid-day heat; and then moved on again till dusk. Their camping-place was on a wide ledge above the stream, where the admirable Manuel made them extraordinarily snug. Dyke was well pleased. Although going so easily, they had made a long march, he said—and not a mule galled, not a pack shifted. Before crawling under the tilt of their little tent, he stood for an hour talking to the men round the camp fire—"jollying them," as he called it.

Emmie, already asleep, warm and snug in the nest of blankets and furs, murmured a welcome as he crept into it; changing her attitude when he had settled down, dreaming a little, and then sinking back to those depths of slumber in which memory itself lies still and no gleam from the surface of life pierces the darkness.

And so it was day after day, as they moved steadily northwards. It seemed to her that she had never been doing anything else. Climbing, scrambling, fording; eating tinned meat and hard biscuits, sleeping on the ground, smearing oneself with vaseline—all this seemed perfectly natural, the easy routine of the glorious nomad life that she had been leading for many years.

In these early days of the pilgrimage they were not yet entirely out of touch with the rest of mankind. The distant roar of an explosion, with the long rolls of thunder that followed it, told them of the operations of those railway engineers, blasting the rock barrier where they could not pierce or evade it. Through a cleft that gave an unexpected view of lower slopes and foot-hills, they saw roofs and smoke that belonged to a camp made by other engineers, who were busy with the underground telegraph cable. Once they saw a string of mules carrying provisions to a military post, and twice they met solitary riders searching for lost mules.

For the rest, all things were exhilarating, charming, amusing. Dyke, always now in the high spirits of a schoolboy, rode by her side whenever possible; made her sing with him snatches from Gilbert and Sullivan's operas—"The flowers that bloom in the spring, tra-la"—gave her his revolver and made her fire it.

"Aim at that white-topped boulder, Emmie. Now then—let go! No—don't shut your eyes when you pull the trigger. Go on."

He loaded the weapon again, and she practised its use in a business-like way, with open eyes. She certainly hit boulders, but perhaps not those that he had selected for her target. Whatever she did, and however she did it, he laughed and praised her. He made her strain her eyes to see black spots in the sky that were condors, hovering, waiting, at an immense height, for the chance of a meal.

It seemed once that their chance had come.

Manuel was leading the column, and she and Dyke had dropped back to the rear. It was easy going, judged by the higher standards of her experience, and yet still most tremendous. They were following what might be almost called a path, half way up the brown hillside. Rolling stones and débris shifted and slid beneath their feet, and every now and then they came to horrible narrow scrambling corners on top of almost perpendicular cliffs, where a stumble would have been as dangerous as the "teasing" knife of that atrocious brigand. Emmie, having got round the worst of these corners, was admiring the cautious and yet fearless progress of the pack mules, and thinking that travellers might well describe the sure-footedness of these animals as miraculous. They never made a mistake. Then, that moment, the pack mule immediately in front of her fell. She saw its hindquarters rise, and its laden back disappear; then there was a flash of its four feet, upturned, and the weight of the saddle and burden carried it head over heels into the void. It was dreadful to see—and to hear too. One heard it crash down the precipitous slope, the loosened stones tumbling with it. Down there at the bottom, far below, it lay stretched—perfectly still.

Then, before the men had done shouting, it got up; it staggered to its feet, shook itself, and attempted to struggle upwards. They all watched. To give aid was impossible. Wildly and desperately it began to work its way along the bottom of the ravine, with head lifted and ears pricked, listening for the tinkle of the bell, as the bell-mare plodded onward, unconcerned. They could see that its pack was hampering it terribly. Then, in its scrambles and leaps, the surcingle broke. The whole thing was under its belly now, and it bucked and kicked, till it fell again. When it rose this time, the pack was round its hocks, and plunging, jumping, springing like a chamois from rock to rock, it kicked itself free. Then, lightly and easily, it sprang along the slope, clambered up, and rejoined the head of the column, where it curvetted playfully to the sound of the bell, and rubbed its wounds against the ribs of the beloved grey pony, which was still plodding on, and still quite unconcerned.

Little incidents like this, ending so happily, served but to enliven the days.

Indeed, so far, the whole jaunt was, as Dyke had said, a picnic—a picnic on a large scale; a "lark" of antediluvian dimensions.

Imperceptibly, but most completely when one perceived it, the character of their pilgrimage had changed. The way was harder, the obstacles were greater, the heat and the cold became more difficult to support. Each day's march seemed unending, yet the distance traversed in a day was comparatively small. They moved still from valley to valley, fighting the walls that intervened, laboriously working round insurmountable barricades. But hitherto the line of their march had been falling as well as rising; now always the valley they entered was at a higher level than the one they had left.

Dyke was systematically jolly with the men at the now frequent halts. He allowed a magic word to be spoken in order to keep up their spirits—the word that for hundreds of years has controlled the destiny of the land and signified life and death to the races of men that inhabited it. Gold. Yes, why not? If we can dig or scratch some to the surface at the end of our journey, or wash it out of its dirt in those bowls that we have brought with us on that saddle, well, we shall be able to make presents all round, beyond the handsome amount of the promised pay. So come along, my lads.

One whole day they were stopped by wind and storm. That was a day of wretchedness, and next morning Dyke did something that appeared utterly fantastic to Emmie watching and shivering before she mounted her mule. He gathered the men together, jollied them, and then solemnly paid them the money that they had so far earned. Truly it was astounding to watch this solemn handing over of the paper dollars to men who were hundreds of miles away from shops and drinking saloons and any other of the joys that money would bring them. But Dyke knew that they liked the feel of the notes in their fingers, the comfortable glow which came when they had bestowed them in recesses of their garments, the certainty that this the price of so much accomplished toil could never be forfeited or taken away. Understanding that one should not travel on credit even in the remotest places, he had brought much money with him.

They all started merrily, and the burning sun soon dried their wet garments. Emmie ceased to shiver, and could smile when Dyke praised her courage and good humour. He said they had a bit of a ridge to get over in the next few days, but *after* that it would be downhill again—all easy going, plain sailing, what you could do on your head.

They crossed the ridge.

It was an exhausting episode. The scene had become Dantesque, terrible; they were amidst a ruin and devastation that had been wrought by countless ages, and still the work of destruction was continuing. These gigantic hills were slowly crumbling to dust; their sides, torn and split, poured down together with torrents of melting ice the very fabric of which they were composed, so that their foundation lay buried beneath a vast, ever accumulating rubbish heap. And over and through this débris the little party laboured upward; through twisting lanes of detached rocks as large as churches, under high jutting crags that looked like fortresses shattered by a titan artillery, upon shifting beaches of smooth pebbles, in refuse that time had pulverised so finely that it was here a layer of sand and there a quagmire of mud. Riding was no longer possible. One led one's mule, one panted and gasped for breath in the increasing thinness of the air. One stopped and rested every moment that one might.

On the first and the second night of the climb Emmie suffered a little and a great deal. The cold was almost unbearable; it numbed, it stabbed, it seemed to gnaw away the envelope of flesh and then play havoc with one's bones. Dyke took the most tender care of her, but neither wraps nor solicitude could keep her warm. Towards morning of that second night he took alarm, scared by thoughts of frost-bite, when she confessed that after considerable pain all sensation seemed to have gone from her feet. He took off her boots, woollen socks, and stockings, and for a couple of hours rubbed her bare legs and feet. She was all right; the suspended circulation restored itself; and daylight showed him the white flesh stained with dirt, but not discoloured, and quite unswollen. He put grease on her feet; and Manuel brought them a breakfast of condensed milk, some ground sugar, and a biscuit. The lamps refused to boil water for tea, and only by much coaxing had they consented to give out heat sufficient to thaw the milk. It froze again before Emmie finished her portion.

"Now let's be off," said Dyke; and looking at her attentively, he asked if she felt sick. "No? Well, that's grand of you. Now, listen. The worst is really done. To-day's climb will bring us over the top."

They climbed long slopes of pebbles in which they sank to their ankles. At each footstep they slipped back; if they trod upon a slab of rock it slid from beneath their feet; the mules floundered and sent down cascades of loose stones upon those behind. Between the slopes came stretches of nearly bare ground. They skirted glistening fields of snow, made an immense detour above the neck of a glacier that had plunged into and been held by the gorge furrowed out by preceding torrents. And all this time the sun beat upon them with hammering strength.

Sometimes an hour was spent in climbing, with many halts, a hundred yards. One halted now without orders because one must, mules lay down and let the sound of the bell grow faint, all along the line the men were coughing. If one made a false step and stumbled, one immediately caught one's breath and had a fit of semi-suffocation. Then, as soon as one was able to breathe again, a sort of despairing drowsiness possessed one; a weak recoil both of mind and body urged one to move no more, to escape at all hazards the anguish of further effort, to close one's eyes, lie down, and forget the odious impossible task. On the last and longest slope Manuel Balda abruptly gave in. He was seized with mountain sickness. Two of the

Indians tried to pull him to his feet, to help him on, but he went down again.

Thus all were suffering—except Dyke. Just as he had not seemed to feel any real annoyance from the cold, he appeared to find no trouble in keeping his lungs comfortably at work without a sufficient supply of air. With his arm about her waist he pulled Emmie, almost carried her, along with him till they reached the naked and nearly level table-ground that was the summit of their climb. Now he went back, leaping and sliding down the slope to the rescue of Manuel. He brought him up, and went down again to drag up the mules. He wrestled with them, pulled them, pushed them, somehow set them going, and one heard his cheery shouts from far down below while he still expended his super-human energy.

Then at last they were all up—the men lying on the ground, the poor mules side by side, their heads all one way, their nostrils widely distended as they vainly sought more air, their legs shaking, and the sweat pouring in rivers from their heaving flanks—and Dyke stood there laughing, snapping his fingers, chaffing, "jollying" his too feeble crowd. He also praised them, swearing that they had done grandly, and that they might feel proud of themselves. But it would not do to linger, he added; for the afternoon was getting far advanced, and the lower they could get before pitching their camp the better it would be. A few more minutes, and then down we go.

For these minutes he sat beside his Emmie's prostrate form, and "jollied" her in her turn.

"You angel, you have been magnificent. You have set us all an example." And laughingly he confessed that, after her performance on board ship, he had dreaded lest she might be sick again in the mountains. He confessed, too, that until they were fairly started and "things began to come back" to him, he had forgotten that there was this little high bit to negotiate. "We are at an elevation of sixteen thousand feet. Do you realize it? We are well above the summit of Mont Blanc. In Europe people would say we had made a remarkable ascent."—and he laughed. "Yes, quite an ascent— something to write about to the newspapers. It is only out here, in this glorious atmosphere, that it seems such a trifle. No, I oughtn't to have said that. It was very wrong of me. For of course I know that it must have tired you. You dear girl, you are so splendid and brave that I forget. But all easy going now—as I promised you. And, Emmie, I want you to have a good look at the view. You'll say it's worth all the trouble. Sit up, dear."

She obeyed him, and looked about her with dazed eyes at the incredibly superb panorama. Truly, if one had been able to breathe painlessly, if one's head had not seemed to be bursting, if the murderous sun had not been melting one's spine and battering at one's shoulders, it was a view to compensate one for the trouble of attaining it.

One seemed to be lying on the roof of the world, and the nearer peaks, which still rose above them, were its towers and cupolas; across its parapet one gazed at a vast semi-circle of sunlit space. Looked at from here, the great brilliantly-coloured hills through which they had fought their way appeared smooth, gently curved and rounded, dull of tone; northward one saw, as if painted on a map in sepia, with streaks and patches untouched by the brush, a perspective of almost parallel ridges that one guessed were the outlines of unending valleys; while eastward beyond a range of lower summits, one had a glimpse of the plains themselves and a true horizon, a flat, faintly golden sea meeting the sky at a distance of eighty, a hundred, or perhaps more miles away. Closer to one's eyes, if one looked directly downward, there were strong colours, forceful shapes. Spires of red rock glowed fiercely beside a profound gorge filled with purple shadow; and an immense unbroken cloak of snow that stretched from the crest to the base of one neighbouring hill gave off a white smoke in the sun's rays and made rainbow shafts hover amidst the smoke. But the prevailing impression was of colourless distance, measureless space, and light so strong that it destroyed the substance and form of all that it shone upon.

They began the descent. Two thousand feet lower down one felt an immense relief, after another thousand one was breathing in comfort; all the heads had ceased to ache; Manuel Balda was cracking jokes, laughing at sickness, vowing that he had stopped that time merely because of a slight stitch in the side of him.

Next day they rode on, through a valley wider and easier than any they had yet entered. Dyke set the men singing, made Manuel the leader of the march, and kept by Emmie's side. She saw condors at close range. Four or five of them rose from the dry bed of a torrent, and, coal-black in the sunshine, swept upward on extended wings. They looked enormous, as sinister and evil as their ugly reputation had led her to imagine. One of the men fired his rifle, but without effect. They soared into space, vanished.

Dyke spoke to her of the emeralds, telling her how he meant to set about the work of exploration. Without his telling her, she understood that he felt excited as they drew nearer to the goal.

He talked to her also of "the sense of direction." This was after she had paid him compliments upon the unwavering confidence with which he had led them through the labyrinth of hills and vales.

"It is too wonderful, Tony. I can't think how you do it."

"Well," he said modestly, but much gratified, "of course, there's the compass—and the sun. Besides, I can always go to any place where I have once been. Then I have my landmarks. If you want to know, I'm looking for one of them now. It's about due. Yes," and he smiled complacently, "I suppose I *am* rather good at finding my way. The gods, Emmie, gave me something beyond the usual European outfit—they gave me the *sense of direction*." And he held forth about this instinctive faculty, saying it was being investigated and that much more would be known concerning it later on. There had been some good research work with homing pigeons, migratory birds, and wild as well as domesticated dogs. "I don't attempt to explain it myself. If you've got it, you've got it—and you know you've got it. It was that and nothing else which saved my life in North Australia in the year 1884. I was temporarily blinded, by the sand, you know—so that I couldn't see five yards ahead—but I knew. I didn't go in circles—I didn't falter—I didn't have to calculate or think. I knew. Yes, that's my trump card—and except for it, I wouldn't be so bumptious. I might consent to take a back seat to others—the gentlemen that the press eulogise for their scientific training—and their learning—and culture. But Anthony Dyke beats them *there*. That's why I say, put your money on old A. D. What?"

He broke off, laughing. "How I do gas about myself! But you lead me on, Emmie; you spoil me. You should check me instead of encouraging me. All those Indian fellows behind us have the gift I speak of—but perhaps less fully developed. You remember where we lost that pack—the place where the mule went down. If I told one of them to go back there, he'd find his way unerringly—even, mark you, if he didn't actually retrace his steps. He'd get there."

They rode on. And Emmie felt as if her past had gone from her utterly; it was not now that she had grown so accustomed to this new life that she felt she had been leading it for years. There had never been another life.

And certainly, could they have seen her, no old friends of Queen's Gate or Prince's Gardens could have helped to recall her to herself. They would not have recognised her. Although she still spoke so gently and smiled so dreamily, she sat her mule with the nonchalant ease of a gaucho; her whole aspect was wild and fierce; the remnants of her stout straw hat, battered out of its original shape, were tied beneath her chin and bound about her neck; her dusty smeared face was almost black, with yellow lines that had been scored by perspiration. She might have been an Indian boy—as Dyke had told her. He said he must hit upon a good man's name and rechristen her.

Soon after the mid-day halt there came into view the landmark for which he had been watching. With a grunt of satisfaction he pointed it out to her—the white dome of a mountain that had shown itself above the nearer summits. "That's my guide now." The sight of it made Dyke pleasurably excited. He talked of his emeralds again. They must push on steadily now and waste no time. He galloped off to tell Manuel that the goal was drawing nearer, and then returned to her.

They rode on—on into silence. That day Emmie was conscious of it, in this manner, for the first time. Yet it must have been with them, one would think, for a long while. The silence seemed to have become a property of space. It could no more be broken by the slight sounds they made—such as the note of the bell, the shuffle of so many iron-shod feet, the shouts of the muleteers, the song of Dyke—than you can break the ice of a frozen lake by throwing a small stone at it. The stone slides across the surface till it comes to rest. She remembered the noise of explosions heard during the early days, when they were still in touch with the fretful ambitious labours of humanity—those engineers on the new railway blasting the rocks that opposed them. Here it was as if the mountains could permit no noises, not even echoes of noises, that they did not themselves create. They commanded a universal hush, in which, after breathless listening pauses, they sucked the roaring wind through their jagged teeth, threw a garment of snow from their shoulders, or with earthquake groans let their sides gape open and a vast new ravine appear in the raw wound. Then one might hear their reverberating voice high in the air and low in the ground. But otherwise all must be still. Silence and solitude—the sense of loneliness undisturbed since the world began grew deeper as the shadows of the hills began to creep across one's path. It seemed then to be a valley into which man had never been, into which no man should ever go.

But that was an illusion, mere nonsense. As Dyke told her, in the dim past many men had been here. These valleys, all of them running north and south, had formed a great trade route that stretched nearly from one end of the continent to the other. During the dominion of the Incas, perhaps earlier still, perhaps ages and ages ago, before the Pharaohs reigned and pyramids were built in Egypt, this was a busy crowded highway of commerce and government; with troops of soldiers passing and repassing, tax collectors going south, great nobles being carried in gilded litters, priests of the sun, long trains of llamas instead of mules carrying tribute northward from remote provinces or conquered territories. Doubtless, if one dug away the dust of time, or could remove the layers of fallen rocks, one would find traces of the great highway—its buried pavement, the foundation masonry of ruined bridges, fragments of wall that had belonged to rest-houses.

Yes, if all the ghosts of antiquity should appear, they would form a multitude to fill the valley floor from hillside to hillside.

Talking of these things led him naturally to speak once more of the emeralds. Of course, it stood to reason that they mined as far south as this. In those days the mineral wealth of the hills was searched with untiring vigour; there were mines everywhere—for gold, for silver, for the precious stones—above all, one must suppose, for emeralds. The word was on his lips continually. Emeralds!

He was eager to push on, but with all his urging, the march had grown slow and languid. The men seemed tired and stupid; they would not respond to his cheering holloas. They let the mules string out. And two or three times Manuel Balda came and asked him if they might not halt for the night. At last he gave the order.

The night fell swiftly, and it was very dark until the moon rose. Emmie, after lying down, lifted the flap of their tent, and saw the bare ground silvered and the rocky slopes greyly shining, and she felt as if far and near, all round her, to the ends of the earth, there were solitude, silences, mysteries. The sensation—for it was no more—had not the smallest importance to her mind. She was very happy, supremely contented.

She looked at the tiny camp-fire, dying down now, to red embers, so that the group of men who were crouched upon the ground about it showed in the pale moonlight with no glow of flame upon their faces. Dyke was standing by them, still talking to them. It was a lengthy jollying to-night.

There stood her man. She had got him now, for her very own. These hired followers did not count; he and she were alone now, with no human being to come between them. They had travelled far in their great love—away from etiquette books, beyond the reach of laws—backward through the ages to forgotten codes and outworn ceremonies—back, almost, to the elements of life and the rule of nature. She was half dreaming; and she thought, as she dropped her curtain and lay down beneath the rugs, that Aconcagua had married them; these mountains had confirmed the bond, making them one under the cold stars, mingling their limbs by the pressure of iron frosts, moulding their embrace to the uneven surface of their bed of stone; and now the shadowy stately ghosts of the Incas had gathered round the nuptial tent, to put a mystic seal upon their union.

"Emmie, are you asleep?"

She was asleep, but she woke to the murmur of his voice at her ear. Lying beside her, he continued to whisper.

"Emmie, there's something wrong with the men."

"Something wrong? How do you mean?"

"I can't understand, myself. I've been at them for hours, and I can't make anything of them. It's as though they had become suspicious—or as though they were all sickening for some infernal disease."

"What does Manuel say? Is he all right?"

"No. I believe he's been somehow upset too, but he won't own it. He was helping me with them, seeming to back me up, and yet I had the feeling that he would let me down if he dared. It struck me they might have taken alarm because I made them fill the water skins yesterday. You know—they might have supposed we were going where there'd be no water. But it wasn't that. Emmie, I had to tell you this. Don't worry about it."

"No—only because you are worried yourself, Tony."

"Well, it would be too damnably disappointing if they lost heart now, or shirked the work I have to give them. But I don't believe they will. No, it is some ridiculous and absurd fancy that has taken possession of them. One must be prepared for anything—in the Andes. Whatever it is, I'll put it right to-morrow."

At daybreak they went on.

There was something wrong with the men—you could not observe them and retain any doubt as to the fact. They moved slowly, silently, often with downcast eyes; the whole march was languishing. Dyke rode up and down the straggled column talking to the riders one after another; he was very jolly with them, full of fun and good fellowship, but resolutely determined to get to the bottom of the queer paralysing trouble.

At last one of them told him. The explanation was more fantastically absurd than anything he could have divined. They told him they were disturbed because they had heard him using a word—a bad word—an ominously bad word to use in these regions. Gold was a good word—a word to set one's mind on fire, brace one's muscles, and make one's blood dance. But that other word, emeralds—oh, no. Merely to hear it, in the mountains, took the heart out of one. Surely everybody knew that the quest of emeralds was forbidden.

"Yes, that is the silly belief of these Indian boys," and Manual Balda, voluble and discursive now that the secret was out. "It is their legends—how can I say how old? Oh yes, Missis, vairy silly. But an Indian is a child always. Not Christian-believing. Su-per-sti-tious!" And he indicated that he and the other three Spaniards held such nonsense in proper contempt.

"Then why didn't you tell me the truth about it yesterday?" asked Dyke.

Why? Ah, that was difficult to answer. Manuel had felt timid, had not liked to carry tales, had feared that Don Antonio, instead of laughing and snapping his fingers, might be angry.

"Has he think I was su-per-sti-tious also, like those boys?" he inquired of Emmie. "See here, Missis. Why should I, Manuel Balda, fear the evil spirits? I am good Christian. I carry my charm." He had pulled out of his clothes a little silver crucifix tied to a dirty string, and he held it up reverently. "No evil spirit will dare touch him who carries that."

Dyke called an immediate halt, and gathering the men together he thrashed out the matter with them in jovial friendly style. First he made the Indians talk, encouraging them to say all that was in their minds; with much wisdom patiently listened to the long involved stories that they soon began to tell him. For a considerable time he denied nothing. Yet it was very difficult not to make mock. To stand there, at this late period of the world's history, and hear such legends from the lips of strong grown men, no matter what their race or position in the social scale! But for the setting of the scene itself, it would have been impossible. The primeval ramparts, the forlorn grandeurs, the lonely unvisited pomp, that surrounded them, made what is real and what is incredible seem almost to join hands.

They told him stories as old as that of the famous River of Emeralds and its guarding dragon, who demolished with thunder and lightning every intruder that sought to steal the hidden richness. They told him stories as recent as that of the five travellers from Santiago, who were changed into five round stones only a few years ago. Then when Dyke thought the time had come to argue with them and jolly them, they said that perhaps they did not implicitly believe such tales; but this they did indeed believe—that a curse or ban had been laid on emerald-hunting, and that for their part they were averse from defying it. They vowed that at least this much was true: for hundreds of years no one had done any good by looking for emeralds, and many had come to grief at the game. The Spaniards nodded their heads in grave affirmation.

Dyke said that, accepting for argument's sake the notion of a ban, or curse or bad luck, then anything of that sort would fall upon him, the leader of the expedition, and not on them his honest followers. It was he who made the defiance and wanted emeralds, not they. And on his head be all the consequences. He said this loudly and solemnly, looking about him with a majestic sweep of the eyes; and it had a great effect upon them. They cheered up visibly.

At the mid-day halt he tackled them again, enforcing his successful argument; telling them he merely wanted them to dig for him. There would almost certainly be gold. And if emeralds were found, they need not even touch them. He Dyke would do that. They were not likely to find so many that he could not carry them all away himself. He made them laugh, and after that all seemed well. He snapped his fingers and told Emmie that he had done the trick. They were now "as merry as grigs."

All seemed well; the afternoon march progressed rapidly.

At night he sat with them, sang to them; told them how nearly their destination was reached. Early to-morrow, he said, they would come to a break in the hills on both sides, and the narrow valley that opened on their right hand would bring them to the final halt. They need have no apprehensions about water. There would be no difficulties.

Next day they started betimes. All was well; the men seemed alert again, just as they had been when they first brightened to the sound of the "good word." Manuel, who was nearly as excited as Dyke and far more exuberant, obtained leave to go ahead and signal to them as soon as the promised fateful valley came into view.

There was a cry of satisfaction when they saw him, far ahead, standing in his stirrups and waving his hat above his head. They waved to him in return, to show they had got the signal, and he disappeared. All pushed on to follow him. Dyke shouted and sang, as they swept into the entrance of this the last of the valleys, his own valley.

Plainly it was the ancient bed of a torrent that once used to pour down into the wide valley they had left; strewn with rocks large and small, it looked even now so much like a water-course that one could scarcely believe it was dry. The hour was still so early that the high frowning cliffs filled it with grey shadow, and made the sunlight overhead seem trebly vivid.

Then they saw Manuel riding back towards them with breathless haste. They could see him belabour the galloping mule, urging it to its full speed, oblivious of all obstacles. He pulled the poor brute almost upon its haunches when he reached Dyke, and spoke in wild excitement.

"Don Antonio, we are forestalled. There are men there already."

Dyke would not believe. He laughed. "Manuel, old chap, you have been dreaming."

But Manuel, gesticulating, swore that he was very wide awake—happily so, perhaps, for everybody's sake. He had seen. He could trust the evidence of his eyes.

"How many men did you see?"

"Two only. But there may be more, many more, hidden there among the rocks."

"What sort of men are they?"

"How can I say? Brigands! A gang perhaps? Not Indians."

"What were they doing?"

"Watching—those two—as if on guard—as if they certainly knew we were coming—and so watched and waited for us."

"I don't believe it," said Dyke quietly. "I can't believe it. It's impossible. Emmie, fall back a bit, and keep with the others." And he ordered the men to unsling their rifles and to follow him slowly, leaving the pack-mules behind. "Now, Manuel, old boy, come along with me."

The thing was a fact, no day-dream, no optical delusion.

Dyke saw them plainly, unmistakably, when Manuel drew rein and pointed with outstretched hand. At perhaps five hundred yards distance the sun's rays, pouring down through a break in the cliff top, had invaded the lower ground and made a bright patch of coloured rock and sand; and here, apparently crouched beneath a huge boulder, but in the full sunlight, the two men were sharply visible, although one had an impression that they themselves were perhaps not aware of how conspicuous they had become. Dyke rode boldly on and Manuel reluctantly for another four hundred yards; and the men, though seeming to watch them, did not once stir.

Dyke dismounted, gave his mule to Manuel, and walking on slowly, with his revolver in his hand, called to the two watchers. They did not answer, they did not move. They were seated side by side, but at a few yards one from the other; their hats were drawn down upon the brow, so that Dyke could not see the eyes which seemed to be watching him with such intentness; their attitude was identical, backs slightly bowed, hands clasped about their knees.

When he got within fifty yards of them, he put the revolver in his pocket, turned round, and beckoned to Manuel and the others to come on.

He knew now why these men remained so strangely motionless. They were dead. They had been dead for a long time, possibly for years; the cold and the rarefied air had preserved their bodies, their mummified hands were intact, all the flesh of their faces that one could see beneath the broad-brimmed hats was free from any sign of decomposition. Dyke, looking sadly down at one of them, judged him, by the grizzled hair upon his chin and the deep wrinkles at each side of the mouth, to have been a man of over fifty years of age, and noticed how the sun had obliterated the colour of the once scarlet shawl that was bound about his waist, and faded the brown leather of his belt and pouches. With gentle reverent hands he raised the soft brim of the hat, and looked at the whole face.

Then he started back in horror and disgust. Not the faintest suspicion of the truth had come to him till the lifted hat disclosed the nose, the eyes, the forehead; and all the features, swiftly assembled, flashed into a long familiar mask. It was his old comrade, Pedro del Sarto.

He sprang to the other body, and took it roughly by the shoulder. It fell over sideways, queerly and lightly, like a thing made of basket-work and hooped steel, and lay there with its hands still clasping its knees, in the frozen attitude that could not change. But the hat had rolled away, and Dyke saw the face that he had expected to see. It was Juan Pombal, del Sarto's underling and constant associate.

Dyke went back to the other body, knelt by it, and searched it. There was no weapon of any kind; there was no food in a wallet on the ground; but in the belt pouches he found dollar notes, a small pocket book, and some papers—amongst them, tattered and stained, the map that he himself had given to Pedro at Buenos Ayres over two years ago.

Manuel and his fellow Argentines had gathered round; they were gesticulating, chattering, asking each other questions; while they feasted their curiosity in scrutinising the dead men. How had they come here, whence, why? The four Indians stood where the mules had been left and would approach no nearer.

Dyke, going to Emmie, told her the nature of the discovery he had made. He understood at once all that it implied. His comrade, his friend, the man he trusted as a brother, had played him false, had tried to cheat him, and in making the attempt had thus miserably met with disaster. No other explanation was possible. Pedro, falling into low water, as people reported at Buenos Ayres, had yielded to the temptation offered by a chance. He knew that the friend he was betraying would not return for a year and a half at least; there would be plenty of time to come up here, put his dirty hands in the pocket of treasure, and get safely away. As to facing Dyke afterwards, he probably made no plans; he left the future to take care of itself.

"And I loved him, Emmie," said Dyke bitterly. "I loved that man."

But Pedro and Pombal did not venture to come here alone. No, obviously, they must have brought mules and muleteers with them; they fitted themselves out much as Dyke had done, although in more meagre style, before they risked themselves in the wilderness. What had happened to their hireling followers?

The bitterness passed from Dyke's tone, as little by little he reconstructed the horrible details of the tragedy. Their muleteers had deserted them. But why? Perhaps Pedro bullied the men, drove them too hard, or fed them badly. Or the men took fright, thinking their provisions might give out.

Something had frightened them, and they had consummated the hideous deed. The betrayers had themselves been betrayed.

Working backwards to the date of Pedro's disappearance from Buenos Ayres, he hit upon the most probable cause of the men's fright. It was the menacing state of the weather that struck fear into their craven hearts. Dark snow-laden clouds banking up from the south, a spatter of rain and sleet, a wind with ice needles in its breath—and they had thought that the winter was upon them. Pedro had started too late; he himself must have known it by then. But he would not give in. Perhaps the men urged him to turn back, pleaded with him; but dogged, and resolute even to ferocity, he drove them on. Then waiting for an occasion, they fell upon him and his fellow slave-driver, disarmed them, and left them to perish. The doomed pair wandered hither and thither, lost themselves in a gathering darkness of sluggish death. Storms of snow hid the faint light. The wind cut them. They sat down in the shelter of these rocks to wait till the wind dropped. It was a bad place, the worst possible place, if the wind changed its quarter and the snow began to drift. They slept, and woke no more. The snow covered them; the sun melted the snow. Twice they had been covered and uncovered.

Rancour against a treacherous friend had vanished, and a fierce impersonal indignation moved Dyke as he thought of the treachery of those half-bred dogs. The damnable curs—to leave their leaders, taking food, arms, everything. It made one sick. But, as he knew, things like this happen in the Andes—have always been happening.

Philosophising presently, he spoke of fear, and of what a horrible force it is. The most degrading of all passions, it would seem also the most powerful. Half the wickedness of the world can be traced to it. When it binds five or six people together in its loathsome clutch, there is no enormity that they may not commit, because—and this is so terrible—fear felt in common by five or six men is not five or six separate fears added together, but multiplied together many times.

And Emmie, looking round her, thought that this place might well be the primeval home of fear; in this overwhelming loneliness, among these dark cliffs, the stealthy grey shadows, and the sunlight that seemed to make the solid rock tremble, fear was originally engendered; so that the first live matter, waking to life here, was afraid—afraid of all things, even of itself. It was only her transient thought. She herself had no fear. Why should she? She was with Anthony Dyke.

They resumed the march. There was a question of burying the corpses, but in view of the evident reluctance of Manuel and the others, Dyke gave up this intention. The pious task would have entailed a considerable labour and waste of time. "Leave them there as a warning," said Manuel, not to

Dyke but to the empty air. He had fished out his crucifix, and looking back, he crossed himself and shivered. "Leave them to the condors," said one Indian to another. "The condors left them so long without touching them. Let no one touch them now." All were eager to get away from the sinister spot.

A profound depression of the spirits had fallen upon them. Again they moved languidly and needed frequent rallying. They spoke apathetically, if not sullenly. Dyke dealt gently with them, and pleased them by making the day's march shorter than he had wished. At night, when they had eaten their food and Dyke as usual went and talked to them, they seemed contented enough.

They camped at a point where one enormous rock—a monster carried by ice and stranded here thousands of years ago—stood isolated in the middle of the way. Manuel Balda pitched Dyke's tent and made the sleeping-place behind this rock, out of sight of the camp-fire and the men, very neatly and snugly. More silent than was his wont, but as efficient as ever, he carried out his customary duties, boiled their tea, gave them their supper.

The moon had risen high and was shedding its gentle radiance far and near, as Emmie and Dyke came round the broken angles of the big rock, and standing side by side, looked down at their little camp. All was peaceful; the familiar aspect of the nightly assemblage gave one a sense of comfort and security. The men lay huddled on the ground with saddles for pillows; the mules, some with shining moonlit coats, some dark and shadowy, were ranged behind their deposited burdens. In the profound silence one could hear the slightest movement, and a note of the bell as the madrina raised her head startled one by the sharpness of the sound. Beyond this one spot of animated existence the moonlight showed them the valley stretching away tenantless through its stone walls, like an unused passage in a dead world. There was no need to post sentries on guard; there were no living foes that could attack the camp. Dyke and Emmie went back behind their rock, and they too lay down to sleep.

Dyke woke at dawn, and mechanically groped for the revolver that from habit he kept within reach of his hand while sleeping. His hand did not encounter it. No doubt it lay buried in the blankets and the rugs. He crept from the tent, got upon his feet, stretched himself, and went yawning round the rock. Then he uttered a roar of anger.

The place was empty. The camp had vanished. Not a sign of man or beast was anywhere visible. Like Pedro del Sarto, he had been abandoned by his cowardly followers. As far as the eye could reach—and that was for many miles—the valley lay grey and void. Those scoundrels already had made good their escape from it; their resented intrusion no longer troubled its blackened heights and barren flats; it had swept them away with the deadly impalpable force that it contained. They were gone again, by the path on which they had dared to come; and Fear triumphant laughed in the sunlight above the deserted valley and lay down to rest in its shadowed depths.

Presently Dyke found a small pile of tinned meat neatly arranged near the ashes of the fire. The deserters had left him food, then? Not a great deal, but some. He stood looking at the piled tins and thinking. The germ of panic had entered the blood of those Indians when they first heard what they called the bad word, and hence onwards they were diseased, sickening creatures able to spread contagion to the rest of his crowd; the sight of the dead men, scaring them, seeming to confirm their notion of a curse upon an impious quest, had made it almost certain that they would try to do what they had now done. All of them together had become resolved to go no further. The Spaniards, little less superstitious than themselves, agreed to their plan. And Manuel? He too was afraid, and yet perhaps he endeavoured to be faithful and staunch; but if those others stood round him with their knives at his breast, his fidelity would not avail. They would simply tell him what they had resolved; they would give him orders, and he must obey. They had no grudge against the chieftain. Dyke knew that they liked him—until they began to fear him. Thus, if Manuel asked them to leave that food, they would be willing to do so. They took the riding mules because, if left, these would have provided the means of pursuit. Dismounted, he could never catch them. When one of the Indians crawled on his belly like a snake, and with careful hand beneath the flap of the tent abstracted his revolver, it was a necessary precaution, nothing more. They disarmed him merely to prevent any dangerous interference should he chance to wake. Then, their precautions taken, the madrina's bell muffled, and all being ready, they stole off in the moonlight—with Manuel Balda, perhaps looking back, trembling, crossing himself, feeling pity and regret. What must be must be.

Dyke shook his fist in the direction the runaways had taken. Every bone in their bodies should eventually be broken; but meanwhile old A. D. had allowed them to put him in a very tight place. He did not doubt that he could get out of it easily, on his head, if—It would be almost amusing, a sprightly continuation of the lark, if—Yes, if he had been alone.

An immense remorse seized him, and he stood for a few moments with bowed head, staring at the stony pitiless ground. Why had he brought her here? Wrong—very wrong. But it was not in his nature to remain brooding on past mistakes when the future demanded prompt activity. He roused himself, shrugged his shoulders and gave a grunt.

Those blackguards had left tins of meat but no tin-opener. He smashed a tin against the rock, and he and Miss Verinder had their meagre breakfast. He offered her his apologies before sitting down.

"I blame myself—I should have forseen—guarded against it. Of course," and he laughed ruefully, "my emeralds have gone up the chimney. And for ever probably—for goodness knows if I can find time to come back here again later on. A disappointment, I admit. But I am not thinking of *that*. Certainly not. I'm only thinking of you. Emmie—you plucky, jolly little Emmie—it's going to be difficult—for *you*"; and he looked at her wistfully. "On foot, you know! Without our furs we're going to feel cold at night. We're going to miss our nice hot tea, too. Yes, we're ill provided with comforts now." And he laughed again, but gaily this time. "I have plenty of money—my pockets are full of money. That's rather funny, isn't it? An object lesson, what! No grocer's shops—or Army and Navy Stores handy.

"But, of course, you understand, Emmie, my pretty one, that there's not the least cause for anxiety. It will be absolutely all right if we go slow and don't fuss. That's the one great thing on these occasions—never fuss yourself."

While he talked he was thinking hard. He decided to strike for Chile and hit off one of the hill roads at its nearest accessible point. That way they would have nothing to climb; it would be all down hill. And he calculated the distance and the number of days that would be required. Could she do as much as twenty miles a day, on an average? Then he calculated the amount of nourishment contained in the tins. How long would it last her? He saw plainly that it was going to be a desperate race against starvation.

He took two blankets for her; he dared not cumber himself with more.

"Now, Emmie, my lad," he said, smiling at her, just before they started. "Left foot foremost. And don't hurry."

CHAPTER X

IT was nine days later before they met their first chance of aid. They had emerged from the labyrinth and were coming down the seaward slopes, along a flat gulley between two low ridges of granite. Before them at a great distance lay the surface of the ocean, placid as its name, majestic as death, like a vast enveloping obliviousness on the confines of man's brief futile life; between this and them, but still invisible, stretched a broad land of hope and plenty, the grazing grounds of Chile, woods as pretty as gardens, little nestling hamlets, and then thriving towns, splendid cities, the noise and bustle of prosperous ports;—but as yet nothing of all this in sight, not one stunted shrub, not a trace left by human kind. Behind them lay those nine pitiless days and the eight unendurable nights; a plodding delirium of cold, hunger, and toil. For more than forty-eight hours he had not been able to give her anything to eat. How long it was since he himself had eaten he did not count. He was carrying her on his back, his arms about her thighs, her arms about his neck, her blackened shrunken face close against his hairy dust-begrimed cheek. At intervals he had carried her in this manner throughout the ordeal, but now his burden was becoming pitifully light.

"It's all right, darling," he whispered as he stalked along. "Keep up your spirits. On my honour I see daylight at last. We have come out just where I wanted. Sense of direction, what! Trust A. D."

"Put me down, Tony. You *must* be tired. Let me walk again."

"Yes, directly. There's another steep bit ahead."

He set her upon her feet soon, and helped her to scramble with him from the gulley down into a sort of plateau or wide terrace running north and south upon the hillside. At the southern end of this terrace they stopped to rest.

They were a pair that might well arouse swift pity in all but the hardest of hearts. Their thinness alone sufficed to tell their story and to urge their immediate need. The manifold print of famine was upon them. Dyke, ragged and dirty, had mysteriously preserved his strength; while Emmie rested he examined the ground, peered over the edge of the plateau at the precipitous but not impossible cliff, went forward to find a better way; moving to and fro, he looked gaunt, dingy, dangerous as a famished wolf. Emmie, with lips that the sun had split for want of grease, with blood rusty and dry upon her chin, with matted hair plastered to her forehead, looked like an emaciated boy who had been huddled into the worn-out garments of a grown man. She seemed weak to the verge of complete exhaustion; her eyes in the enlarged orbits seemed enormous, spheres of dull glass without flash or glow. Yet her faith in her companion was quite undaunted, her love for him quite untouched.

He came and stood by her, snapped his bony fingers and produced a chuckle in his hollow throat. He said that there was an unmistakable track straight through this ledge and at the end descending in zig-zags as far as he could see. It most certainly would lead them to habitations and the road.

It was at this moment that they heard the sound of a human voice. Dyke looked round eagerly. As if from nowhere, as if he and his mule had dropped out of the sky, a man was riding towards them. He sat high upon a padded and peaked saddle, and as well as himself, the mule carried a couple of large sacks of forage and various wallets and bags; till he drew considerably nearer he had the aspect of a Chilian farmer, who on a business journey had somehow attempted a short cut along the face of the hills. He shouted to them in Spanish, telling them to stand still; and even before noticing that he had drawn a pistol, Dyke whispered a warning.

"Emmie, I don't like the look of him. Take everything quietly. Don't interfere, whatever I say or do. And, Emmie, this fellow mustn't know your sex."

Indeed, one could not like the look of him, now that he drew close. He was a thick-set man of about forty, with small blood-shot eyes in a swarthy scarred face; his whole air, suggesting sullen fierceness, stupid cruelty, unreasoned suspicion, was very distasteful to Dyke. This peremptory stranger seemed far from being the friend in need for whom one had hoped.

Dyke, obeying his order and the menace of his levelled revolver, stood now with raised hands; and Emmie had to rise too and assume the same attitude.

"We are neither of us armed," said Dyke, meekly. "But my boy there is very tired. Please don't trouble him."

The man told them to pull up their outer garments, in order to see if there was anything concealed about their waists. They obeyed him. And he then told them to turn round, so that he could look at the backs of their breeches. Then, satisfied that they were weaponless, he allowed Dyke to drop his hands and the boy to lie down again. With an oath he asked what they were doing here, and what they wanted.

Dyke said they were doing nothing, and they wanted food.

"Food?" the man echoed. "Food?" And bringing his mule still nearer, he stared at Dyke's high cheekbones and bearded mouth. "Have you any money to buy food?"

Dyke said he had no money.

"That's a silly lie," said the man. "People don't come up here without money."

"No more did I," said Dyke. "But I've been robbed."

"By whom?"

"By bandits," said Dyke. "There are many of them about."

The man grinned, as if amused, and said something to the effect that such a great hulking rascal ought to be able to defend himself. To this Dyke replied that he might have tried to do so, but he was so completely exhausted by hunger. "My boy and I are almost at our last gasp. You can see that for yourself." Then humbly and plaintively he begged for food, saying that the man assuredly had food stowed away in those wallets, and imploring him to spare a few morsels of it. "Have pity on us. Please have pity on us."

The man sat upon his mule, staring stupidly; hardly seeming to listen to these piteous appeals, but to meditate. With his eyes still on Dyke's face, he dropped his rein round his saddle-peak, passed the revolver from his right to his left hand, drew from his belt-sheath a formidable knife, and then replaced the revolver in its holster.

"You are lying," he said, with some more oaths, but with no sign of real anger. "You may have money concealed about you, as surely as I have food in my bags. Perhaps if I searched your filthy carcase, I should find it." Then he began to grin again, as if an idea had come into his sluggish mind. "Where do you think you're going?"

Dyke said he was going down the hillside towards the high road.

"And further, perhaps," said the man. "To hell, if I choose to send you there. Eh?"

Dyke gave a little groan, and began to tremble very perceptibly. He gazed at the man in mute despairing entreaty.

It was horrible. One could see the man's mind dully working; these poor wretches were utterly in his power, and he was cudgelling his slow wits for a means of gratifying himself by making them suffer. Merciless as a tiger, stupid as a wild hog, he meant to torment them; their helpless condition afforded the chance of inflicting pain, and pain must be inflicted. To run his knife into them would be pleasurable, but too tame a jest. Here was the chance of real fun. He wished, if he could, to work the thing up into a huge side-splitting joke that he could brag about afterwards.

And presently he got upon what he felt to be the right line. Grinning, and with the conscious effort of one who forces himself to appear as a wit although nature has not given him an original sense of humour, he said it was true that he had food, but he did not feel disposed to part with it for nothing. Yes, he had good food—bread and meat—wine too; and telling Dyke to keep his distance, he opened a wallet and turned its gaping mouth so that the food could be seen.

"There, that's what you want? Eh?"

Dyke, trembling from head to foot, stared at the food and groaned, as if in the agony of his craving.

"Ha, ha." The man laughed. Then he said, with the same pompous and straining effort, that he was quite willing to trade his food. If they had no money, they at least had clothes. He would give them a little food in exchange for their garments—say a bit of bread as big as his finger for their boots; another such mouthful for their breeches; another for their socks; and so on. Then, having satisfied their hunger, they could continue the journey in their shirts. That would keep them cool after their repast. It would also be very amusing to him, and make a merry tale. He said he loved a bit of fun. He and his friends were famous for their jokes: good fellows all, liking to make the rocks echo to their laughter.

In vain Dyke pleaded. The man said those were his terms. If Dyke and the boy accepted them, they would all three sit down quietly and make the exchanges; and he laughed at the gaunt starving creature who shivered and quailed and at last consented. Emmie had risen to her feet, and, silent and intent, was watching.

They had no choice but to agree, said Dyke, tremblingly.

Then the man dismounted. He suffered Dyke humbly to hold the mule's rein as he did so; not turning his back as he got out of the saddle, but swinging his right leg high over its peak so that he came down facing his victim. But in the very moment that his feet touched the ground he fell. In that brief fraction of time Dyke had slipped his left arm through the rein and struck with his right fist.

The man went down exactly after the style of the prize ring, when something nearly if not quite as good as a knock-out blow lands upon the jaw; and his attitude on the ground was similarly characteristic—face downwards as he struggled to rise.

Dyke sprang upon his back, frustrating the attempt; with the terrified mule rearing above them, nearly wrenching out the shoulder of Dyke, he nevertheless kept his place. He was battering the man's face upon the stony earth because of his reluctance to let go the knife; he was throttling him as well, working hard at his windpipe; he was giving the man no respite or ease.

He got up presently with the knife in his own hand. He patted and soothed the mule, led it a few paces away, gave it some hay to nibble from one of the forage bags. Tranquil and composed at once, in the manner of mules, it allowed Emmie to take charge of it. The man lay quietly where he had been left, emitting groans—real ones, not sham ones.

Dyke went to him, kicked him, and told him to get up. He obeyed at once, staggering to his feet and moving his hands vaguely. He was dazed, but could understand all that was said to him.

Dyke had a very ugly smile as he looked at his bleeding face, but he spoke quietly and with a great affectation of politeness. He told him that he might go now. They would retain the mule, but they did not require his company any further.

The man obeyed, beginning to move stumblingly in the direction of the zig-zag path, but Dyke barred his progress.

"No, not that way," he said. "That's the way we're going ourselves. You would taint the air for us. You smell of garlic. That way, please"; and he pointed with the knife to the cliff.

The man, as if waking from his stupor, pleaded anxiously; the cliff was too steep, to attempt it meant certain death. But Dyke said no, he had examined it; any agile, fearless person could easily manage it.

"Besides, this is my fun. You fellows can't have all the fun to yourself. I, too, like a joke—even a stale joke—the joke you've seen so often. Please tell your master how well I've learnt the trick of it"; and he pricked him lightly with the knife. "Now, skip—spring like a guanaco, dance like a mountain goat. Let the rocks echo to our laughter."

It was dreadful to see. With clumsy antics, in a sullen rage and despair, the man retreated from the goading knife. Driven nearer and nearer to the edge of the cliff, he made strange abrupt pauses and capered heavily before moving nearer still; then, shrinking, recoiling, on the very brink he really danced.

Emmie called to Dyke—"Tony, don't. Tony, don't"; but at first he did not seem to hear her.

"Tony, stop," she called again. "You are making me feel faint. I shall lose the mule."

"Oh, all right," said Dyke, grumblingly.

And he ceased to use the knife, and used his boot instead. The man crouched on all fours, lowered himself over the brink, hung by his hands, disappeared. Dyke stood there watching him, laughing at him, as he scrambled, fell, and rolled. About a hundred feet down he seemed to stick fast; or fear prevented him from launching himself further. Dyke went to the mule, came back with the revolver. "Go on, you clumsy fool. Go on, or I'll shoot." The man looked upward, but disobeyed the order. "Go on, I tell you. Very well"; and Dyke fired—not at the man but near him. Immediately he went on again, fell, rolled, scrambled, and at last was gone.

Then Dyke and Emmie dined. It was a never-to-be-forgotten meal. They ate sparingly, feeling their internal cramps and pains melted by the warmth of a divinely gentle fire, and yet almost dreading that what gave back their lives might take them away again if they were not careful. Above all else, the wine seemed to restore their forces and set the blood flowing in their veins.

Dyke, dangling his legs over the abyss, talked gaily but philosophically.

"I oughtn't to have let him go with his life. No, I really ought to have killed him, Emmie. But, then, I knew you wouldn't like—And I never like to myself, either—if it can be avoided. Of course, I spotted at once that so poor a specimen as that couldn't work alone—that he was just an understrapper." And Dyke explained and apologized for the slight untruths that he had felt compelled to tell in regard to the money. "You can't call that lying, Emmie. I never lie. I hate lies. That was mere poker talk. If he had known I had it, and I hadn't been nippy enough to down him first, he'd have sent a bullet through me and you too. I thought it all out while he was riding up to us—in fact, the moment I guessed he was one of the gang. If I was to spare his life, I must conceal the money, or he'd tell the others. He hasn't anything to tell them now." Dyke chuckled as he said this. "And it'll take him some time to get home."

It was past noon. Emmie mounted, and Dyke led the mule. Thus they proceeded very comfortably, encountering no difficulties, on a track that grew plainer and more easy all the way. Before long they stopped and ate again. After another two hours they took another snack. Before the sun went down, they came in sight of what Dyke had been seeking. "There," he said, pointing downward, "do you know what that means, Emmie? It means safety. Yes, safety at last."

It was a base camp of the engineers—not the engineers of the railway, but those employed in relaying the underground telegraph cable. One saw two rows of sheds where the men slept, and, close by, something that might almost be called a house. This, as Dyke knew, was an inn that had been established there four years ago when the cable people first appeared in the hills. All round and about these buildings were scattered heaps of material, broken implements, balks of timber.

Dyke said that on the other side of it they would find the open road, only a mile away.

"So we shan't want the mule any more. And in any case it's just as well to leave him here, and save ourselves the bother of answering questions. But we'll keep this"; and he took the revolver from the holster. "It might come in useful—even yet. One never knows. Where did our friend keep his cartridges? Ah, here we are." He refilled the empty chamber of the revolver after extracting the spent case, and, laughing, drew Emmie's attention to the fact that the weapon was of English make and Army Service pattern. "Where did the blackguard get it, Emmie? Between you and me and the post, people ought to be a lot more careful than they are in bringing fire-arms into these South American republics. It *pays*, but I begin to think it isn't really right."

He stripped the mule of saddle and everything else, shook out a heap of hay for it to munch, and left it.

Some prowling dogs barked at them in timid fury as they stood at the inn door, but no watchful attendant came out to welcome them. The door was locked, and none of the engineering folk showed themselves in response to Dyke's shouting. Then after a little while a man came round from the back of the house. He was a shambling, hang-dog sort of fellow, and he seemed afraid of his visitors. He said he could not possibly take them in; although it was true that the place had once been an inn, it was an inn no longer. The engineers had gone a week ago, taking all possible custom with them. He and his wife were ruined. Dyke said that he and the boy must spend the night there, and they would pay for their accommodation. Fearfully and unwillingly, the man opened the door, saying that they should settle the matter with his wife. Dyke followed him into the house. The wife proved to be a small, alert, brown woman, and obviously very much the better half of the firm. Of uncertain nationality, she jabbered French and Spanish alternately, sprinkling her discourse with a few English words also. She showed no fear, but she was as reluctant as her husband to perform an innkeeper's task. She said there was no food, no drink, nothing. She urged the visitors to proceed on their journey. But Dyke made short work of her scruples, and ignoring her inhospitable manner, promised to pay her well.

She said then that if they insisted, they must have their way. "We are all alone here, my husband and I. We are very helpless. Often we are forced to do what we are told, whether we like it or not." As to food, she could give them coffee, bread, perhaps some cheese. Dyke said that this was enough.

The building consisted of three rooms: in the middle a public room, that they had already entered, and on each side a smaller room; one the guest-chamber, and the other used by the innkeepers as their kitchen and bed-room. Dyke took possession of the guest-chamber. For furniture it had a low truckle-bed, a small table, and some three-legged stools. The woman, bustling in and out, brought coffee cups, hung a metal lamp to a hook on the wall, and asked them innumerable questions, looking at them curiously with her quick little eyes.

While waiting for their coffee, Emmie lay down upon the bed, and immediately slept. Dyke strolled out of the house, walked all about, and presently went into the kitchen and talked to the man as well as to the woman. In his turn he asked questions. He asked if by chance they were expecting any other visitors. The woman said no, certainly not. Who should ever come here now that the engineers had gone? Then he asked if, since the engineers left a week ago, anybody at all had been there. They both said no, not a soul. Had there been any passers-by? No. Were they sure that they had not seen any horsemen—one horseman—or a farmer on a mule? No.

He went then and stood at the open doorway, looking across at the vacated sheds and the refuse of timber and iron. The night had now fallen, thinly and greyly, more than dusk, and yet much less than darkness, so that one could see all salient objects, even at a little distance away. Dyke stood there, noticing everything, thinking about everything. He did not feel easy in his mind. There was something very suspicious, if not quite inexplicable, about this inn and its landlords. He did not want to make any more mistakes. Emmie was in sore need of a night's rest. He was keenly anxious that she should get it. But he thought now that perhaps it might be wiser to forsake the comfort of a bed, and, pushing on farther, sleep in the open by the roadside. Should they drink their coffee and go?

The woman came out of the kitchen, and passing through the room behind him, said that the coffee was ready. She took it in to the guest-chamber, but he did not follow her. He remained in the doorway. He was doing more than looking out now; he was listening.

In the guest-chamber, the landlady set down the steaming pot of coffee, and, bright-eyed, jabbering, quick-moving, called to Emmie on the bed. Emmie raised herself, sat up, stretched her arms; and the woman, who had sidled close, with an action as quick and sudden as that of an animal, slid a brown hand into the opening of Emmie's coat, and felt her bosom. Then swiftly she stepped back and laughed. "Yes, a woman! I thought so"; and as Emmie rose, angry and disgusted, she laughed again, and with darting hand gave her a playful pat behind. "Yes, a woman all over." And roguishly nodding her head, she bustled from the room.

Dyke at the doorway, listening intently, had fancied that he heard a sound of horses' hoofs, but it was gone again, and he thought, "Yes, but the ground looked almost like a meadow beyond those sheds—smooth and stoneless." Then he heard the sound close and near, and almost immediately saw two horsemen riding towards the door. They came on until he could see them distinctly—two men in cloaks and sombrero hats, riding small mettlesome horses. He drew back and watched them. It was too late for him and Emmie to get away now; and, as he guessed, they were in a peril greater than any they had met in the mountains.

The two men did not immediately enter the house. The innkeeper came from the kitchen with a lantern, and, after tying their horses to posts near the door, they walked away with him talking. They seemed to be waiting for something. Then more men arrived, perhaps ten or a dozen, all mounted, but on mules, not horses. These bestowed themselves and their animals in the empty sheds. The light from the lantern, carried now by one of the horsemen, showed them fitfully—as an ugly lot. Orders were asked for by some of them and instructions given by the man with the lantern. He said they would move from here at two in the morning, and they could sleep till then.

Who were they? Dyke without difficulty guessed; and he wondered if one of their crowd, a man with torn clothes and a broken face, had yet joined them. The nature of their attitude to himself might be affected by the presence of that stupid swine. Why were they here and upon what errand were they engaged? Planning to pounce at daybreak on some carefully tracked booty—a pack train, a government consignment of gold mail bearers, something weak and defenceless that they could surprise and overpower? Dyke did not tax his brain. They were here. That was what concerned him.

He went back to the inner room. Emmie had drunk her coffee and was again sleeping on the bed. He did not disturb her. The oil lamp burning on the wall showed him the disconsolate bareness of the room; the one window high against the ceiling was too small for anybody to get through, even at a pinch; there was no way of leaving the room except by passing through the public room. He picked up one of the clumsy three-legged stools, and looked at it reflectively. Then he put it down, sat on it, and continued to meditate. Yes, let Emmie sleep. There was not anything to be done—certainly not anything until those fellows in the sheds had had time to settle down to their slumbers. They were to move on at two—that was the order. At two they would begin to stalk their game; after two they would be busy; till two they were free. Then the longer one let them sleep, the nearer it came to two o'clock, the better chance one would have in any attempt to slip out of this undesirable company. He decided to postpone personal effort as long as he possibly could.

Those two horsemen came into the house, and were welcomed and made much of by the landlady. One had a gruff loud voice, the other spoke quietly, drawlingly. The drawling man called the other Martinez. The landlady was finding various food for them, although she had an empty larder for ordinary travellers, and there was talk of wine, their own wine, the wine that she had in keeping for them. They talked freely; but Dyke, listening with his door ajar, knew instinctively that they were aware that the inner room was occupied. The landlord, of course, had told them about his unexpected guests. Then all at once the drawling man spoke of these wanderers, saying he would go in and see them presently. There was laughter—the man called Martinez laughing gruffly and the woman shrilly. Then the voices ceased, and Dyke understood that all three of them had gone into the kitchen and that they were still talking of him out there.

They returned, and the woman came to the inner room to fetch the coffee-pot and cups.

"Good trade to-night," said Dyke, smiling at her. "Plenty of custom all of a sudden. That's fine for you."

"One never knows," she said, darting her eyes here and there. "People come and they go. Strange people sometimes—like you two"; and glancing at the recumbent figure on the bed, she gave a short shrill laugh. Then she stooped towards him and spoke in a low voice. "Don't trouble them until they trouble you. Perhaps they will leave you alone."

"Yes, but one must be civil," said Dyke, sufficiently loud to be heard in the other room; "one can't ignore the claims of courtesy."

And he followed her through the door and closed it behind him.

"Good evening, gentlemen."

They were seated at the long table where the innocent laborious engineers used to eat their well-earned food. The man called Martinez, a brutal-looking ruffian, stared at Dyke, but took no notice of his bow or greeting. The other man rose immediately, took off his hat, and sat down again. He was the person of importance, and Dyke concerned himself with him and paid little regard to the uncourteous lieutenant.

As well as a lamp on the dresser, there were two candles stuck in bottles on the table, so that one had him fairly illumined and easy to study. He was tall and thin, so sallow of complexion as to seem like a sick man; every tint of him was vague and unnatural, from the sunken yellowish eyes, the blue mistiness of his shaved cheeks, the umber-coloured lips and blackened teeth, to the undyed shaggy cloth of his coat and the tarnished velvet of his broad belt; for the rest, there was about him the air of something that must necessarily cause fear and shrinking in all that looks at it—as of a pallid ghost in a graveyard, or the body of a hanged murderer brought into a dissecting room and there come to life again—an arrogance of sheer repulsiveness that seemed to defy one to look at it a second time. Dyke observed the mark of a sword cut on his forehead, the saliva at the corners of the brown lips, and the spasmodic flicker of his hairless eyelids. He wore two unusually long knives in a leather belt above the velvet.

"A pleasant calm night," Dyke said carelessly, as he crossed the room and opened the door of egress. He stood there looking out, taking the air. The two horses were in the same place; all was dark now at the sheds; the landlord had left his lantern on the ground by the corner of the house. Overhead the stars shone brightly from a purple sky.

Dyke strolled back to the door of his own room, and, leaning against its jamb, talked to the pallid man. He spoke politely enough, but with the careless, indefinably contemptuous tone that he might have employed to a stranger at his club, somebody who ought to be a gentleman and yet isn't.

"You are moving on soon, I hear—before to-morrow."

"Yes," said the man, drawling and blinking his eyes, "I do not stay long anywhere. So I may go soon from here. With me it is always uncertain. And you?"

"As soon as I can. I have a boy here with me, and he's very tired. I want him to get a good night's rest, and then—"

"Ah, yes." The man interrupted him. "There is a boy. You are not alone. There is your boy"; and he turned his eyes from Dyke and blinked at the ceiling.

"Moving as I do," he murmured, after a pause, "now here, now there, not sure myself where next I may be, I do not care to account for myself. In truth—as is generally known—I prefer not to be met with or observed, even involuntarily."

Then he asked Dyke how it was that he, who appeared to be an Englishman, had so reduced himself in baggage and belongings, when visiting a neighbourhood as unfrequented as this. In the same careless tone as before, Dyke gave him a brief but entirely truthful outline of his trip: describing how he had gone far north in search of an ancient mine, and how his followers had decamped, leaving him and his young servant to get out of the scrape as best they could.

"And you succeeded in getting out of that scrape. It was well done. And the boy, too." As the man said this, a flutter seemed to pass from his eyelids downward through the flesh of his cheeks till it played about his moist lips as a sickening deadly sort of smile. "Yes, you and your boy!" And, his face rigid again, he showed for a moment the underpart of his tongue obtruding through his opened teeth.

He asked a few more languid questions, but not one in regard to Dyke's possible possession of any money; and Dyke knew that this apparent lack of curiosity on the point was a bad sign.

While they talked the woman brought in the food—an omelette, some cold chicken, and a flask of wine. She hummed a few notes of a song as she bustled in and out. Acting as waitress, she moved swiftly round and about the table, and every now and then darted at Dyke a glance that seemed to have meaning in it. The man called Martinez ate greedily, but his leader scarcely at all. He sat staring at the wine in his glass, held the glass up to the flame of the nearest candle, and slobbered its edge as he took an occasional sip.

Then abruptly he asked Dyke to leave them alone now, adding that he would join him later.

"By all means," said Dyke; and he went back into the other room and closed the door.

"Emmie, wake." He was shaking her by the shoulder, but holding his hand firmly over her mouth lest in waking she should cry out. "Listen," he whispered, "and don't speak. We have got to do a bolt. Not yet, but soon. First, hide this for me. Put it right under you and lie on it." And he pushed the revolver into her hands. "Now can you keep awake? Emmie, you must. Somehow keep awake and listen to what goes on—but pretend to be asleep. Then, when I call to you, come straight to me and give me the revolver—as quick as possible. Lie still, darling—and for God's sake keep awake."

Then he moved hastily to the table and sat on one of the stools. He looked back towards the bed and saw that Emmie was lying motionless, sprawled in an attitude of deep sleep; then he turned again to the door. Without the slightest sound it had been opened wide, and the pallid man stood on the threshold looking at him.

"We will not keep you waiting long," he drawled. "Only a few minutes."

"Don't apologize," said Dyke. "My time's your time."

"Thank you"; and the man half closed the door and withdrew. He could be heard speaking to Martinez, and for a little while Martinez growled and muttered to him. Then they moved about the outer room, and there was silence. Dyke sat quietly waiting and Emmie did not stir.

Then he heard the woman humming and the chink of crockery as she began to clear the table. Next moment she had slipped through the doorway and was at his side. She touched his forehead with her fingers and spoke cautiously. "They have gone to their horses—and to fetch something. They will come back."

"Are you a friend?" said Dyke, looking up at her and smiling gravely.

"Yes, I'll be your friend now."

"So I guessed. That was what you meant when you made those signs?"

"Yes." And nodding her head she went on rapidly. "Because you are so brave; and because I am sorry. Very sorry since I told him"; and she pointed to the bed. "I should not if I had thought. You must risk everything to get away."

"That seems the idea," said Dyke, still smiling at her.

"See." She stooped suddenly, pulled up her skirts, and whipped a knife from the clip that held it to her girdle. "I bring you this."

Dyke shook his head negatively.

"Not? Why? You have a gun?"

"Not, so to speak, about me."

"Then take this. It is something. Why not?"

"Because directly they come in here they'll search me. Put it away, please."

She did so, talking fast. "I will help you. I will watch. And you will take your chance—you are very brave. If you could once get out. There are the horses."

"Exactly. It had occurred to me. If I could get the horses."

"I'll try my best. I'll watch. Hush."

Swift as a lizard she glided into the outer room, and begun to hum merrily as she picked up the plates.

They had come back. Dyke heard them lock the outer door and drop a cross-bar into its socket. Then, obedient to an order, the woman entered the inner room carrying the two candles in the bottles. The pale captain of the revels followed her, pointed with his hand, and she set the candles on the table. Martinez had come in too. He dropped some sacking and a coil of rope upon the floor-boards near the door, and stood there. The woman went out, glancing back at Dyke. The captain called after, telling her to get wine ready.

"Now we will talk," he said, "and perhaps drink. But first of all—if you permit—"

"Oh, that's all right," said Dyke. "I have no weapon about me of any sort or kind."

"If you will be good enough to prove that, we can talk comfortably."

Dyke, with a contemptuous smile, stood up, opened his garments, slapped his large breeches pockets, showed them the tops of his boots, and satisfied them that he was without means of defence.

"That is quite satisfactory."

"But I notice," said Dyke, "that you don't return the compliment."

"Ah, no. With us it is different," said the captain, and he picked up one of the candles, and sauntered towards the bed.

Dyke was there before him and stood in his way.

"What do you want?"

"Only another peep at the boy—the wonderful boy. No, I will not wake him—not yet. I will attend to him later. But soon." Mistily and vaguely, the man moved his disengaged hand as though sketching in the air the shape of the recumbent form. Then he went back to the table and invited Dyke to sit down again. He himself sat down, drew one of his long knives from its sheath, and laid it across his knees.

"Martinez, the wine. Get some wine ready"; and he sat looking at Dyke over the table until, after a minute or two, Martinez returned with a small tray, three glasses, and two flasks of wine. "No, not on the table. Put it on that stool."

"Well," said Dyke, "I am at your service. What do you want with me?"

"With you not much"; and once more there was the muscular flicker about the brown lips. "But for myself I would like, if possible, to have a little fun."

"Oh, damn your fun, Ruy Chaves," said Dyke forcibly. "You are Chaves himself, aren't you? But of course you are. There couldn't be two such jokers knocking about at the same time."

"Martinez."

Martinez was growling. He picked up the coil of rope; but at a sign from the chieftain dropped it again.

"Well then, Chaves, I'm tired of your fun," Dyke went on quietly. "Get to business. What's the game?"

"So you don't like fun. But your boy? Is not all this funny? Oh, that boy!" And for the first time he laughed. It was a rasping, whistling snigger. "Suppose now I ask you to spare me your boy."

"I can't do that."

"Oh, ho. You speak resolutely. Suppose then the fancy comes to take him without your permission."

"I should be sorry for you to try to do that, Chaves."

"If it amused me! To keep him with me in the mountains. Ho, ho. You flush. Be calm. I said, to keep him in the mountains, make of him my pet and my toy, as you seem to have done."

"Ruy Chaves."

"Yes, perhaps to put him in girl's frocks—and when I have played with him so—dressing and undressing him—then hand him on to my men for their doll."

"Chaves," said Dyke, raising his voice, "that's enough. I am asking myself if it can possibly be true—what people say—that you were once a soldier—consorting with other soldiers—fighting fair, as they fight. When did they find you out? When were you first flogged, or branded—or whatever they did to you, to show what they thought of you?" He went on speaking, grimly and defiantly, scarcely knowing and not really caring what he said. From the bed he had heard the sound of Emmie's breathing, quickened and sharpened by fear; and he wanted to drown the sound.

"I think," said Chaves, "you had better have a drink now."

"No, thank you, I am not thirsty."

"Martinez, pour out wine for him. From his own bottle. Let him have a bottle to himself. There. Toss it off."

"Thanks, no."

"Then I think you had better go to sleep."

"I am not sleepy."

"Drink. Then you may feel ready to sleep. Sleep is so good, so comfortable. And remember, I have yet to attend to the boy. When one sleeps one sees nothing, one knows nothing. Whereas to a wakeful man, bound fast with cords, and compelled to watch, while—"

Once more Dyke talked loud. Again he had heard the terrified breathing from the bed. But he chose his words now, such word as might possibly relieve the strain of the listener.

"Chaves, drop all this rubbish and rot. Stop chattering. Talk sense. There's nothing in what you're saying to frighten anybody. It's ridiculous."

"Be it so. Then drink. We'll drink together; and happily you may sleep. Take your glass."

Behind the bulky frowning Martinez, the innkeeper's wife showed for a moment in the doorway, and Dyke saw her sign to him not to drink. The warning was of course unnecessary. Indeed, the bandit had himself plainly indicated that he was offering a drugged beverage.

"I am obliged to you—but no."

"Take the glass."

Dyke took it then, and, looking steadily at Chaves, he poured the wine on the floor and replaced the glass on the table.

"Martinez."

Martinez displayed a cutlass, and taking a step forward from the wall, felt the blade with his nail.

"Keep where you are, but be ready," said Chaves; and he refilled the glass. "Drink. I have told you to drink—and I don't like to be refused. Drink this to the dregs."

For the second time Dyke took the glass. He held it high in the candlelight, sniffed at it, and again held it poised.

"Drink. It is good stuff for you. It will save you pain. Drink and forget."

"Emmie!" Dyke called the name loudly, as he drove the rim of the glass against the bandit's sunken eyes and flooded them full.

Chaves gave a yell of pain, and, blinded, spluttering, sprang up with his knife. But already Dyke had the wooden stool high in the air; he crashed it down, broke it on Chaves's head, and sent him senseless to the floor.

Turning, he tried to ward off Martinez with the fragments of the stool; but his foot slipped on the wet boards. Martinez cut at him, closed with him, and both went down together, Dyke underneath.

It was all in a moment, this sudden tumult and struggle. Emmie had leaped to the signal, and, half mad with terror, she screamed aloud as Dyke fell. Twice she screamed, in her agony of dread, as the two men fought at her feet. Then some one fired. One after another, three shots were fired, filling the room with smoke, seeming to split the walls with the force of the explosions. And then in the cloud of smoke Dyke was up, gripping her hand, dragging her through the doorway.

"Be quick now. Not that way. Here." The woman was there. She took Dyke by the arm, led him through the middle room, through her kitchen-bedroom, and out into the cold clean air. Dyke looked round the corner of the house. The horses were no longer there. There were shoutings in the sheds, the men all stirring, roused by the noise.

"Come quick," said the woman, hurrying them away, chattering as she went. "My husband has the horses ready. My husband is good too. He was set to guard the other door, but he opened it for me."

They came to the man meekly holding the horses. But pursuit was too close at hand. Some one—Chaves possibly, certainly not Martinez—had recovered sufficiently to unbolt the main door and yell frenzied orders to the gang. One could hear the mules coming out of the sheds. Then the men began to fire their rifles, blindly, down the path towards the high road. It seemed to Dyke that it was too dangerous to use the horses as he had intended. Emmie was in no state to mount and run the gauntlet in the dark. Yet the horses might be useful in another way.

He took them from the man, set their heads towards the road, loosed them. Then he kicked the stomach of each in turn, and they galloped away. As he guessed, they knew the road and would surely make for it.

As he and Emmie ran off in the opposite direction, he heard the men firing. Then evidently they mounted their mules and started on a stern chase of the galloping hoofs.

Presently he dived with her down a sharp slope until they lodged themselves in a horizontal ravine. They waited there for sunrise, and then worked their way back along the hillside, far below the now silent camp, and onward till they came to the high road. Trudging down the road, they met almost immediately a Chilian officer with a couple of gendarmes. Their troubles were over.

The officer, courteously turning, took them to a place that was at once post-house and barracks, and there provided them with a two-horse wheeled conveyance which he grandiloquently called a carriage. He told Dyke that two troops of cavalry had gone up to the hills, and spoke hopefully of those pests, those disgraces to civilization, being sooner or later cornered and caught. He said that they had been too long permitted. He promised that within a few hours the innkeeper and his wife should be rescued from their precarious situation, that they should suffer no reproaches for any indiscreetness of which they might have been guilty as compelled accomplices of the gang, and that he would hold as a sacred charge the money that Dyke gave him for their future use.

The travellers drove away then, after breakfast, in their carriage—jolting, bumping, making the dust and the stones fly, as they whirled downward side by side; downward, with feathery tree-tops rising to enchant their eyes, green meadows, sparkling streams, brilliant many-coloured flowers— downward into the kindly smiling paradise that nature has spread out between the foot-hills and the sea.

"Oh, for a bath, Emmie! And what price a bed with sheets? That's what I always tell people. If you want to enjoy—But, by Jove, I've forgotten something. The revolver! I must make quite sure." And he opened the breech of the weapon and emptied the six chambers. "Yes," he said, "just as I thought." Three of the cartridges were intact, the other three had been fired. "You saved my life! You killed Martinez."

And suddenly he burst into tears. The tears ran down in rivulets, melting the dirt, whitening his cheekbones, bringing out the red here and there on his dusty beard. "You killed him," he sobbed, "dead as mutton. How the devil you missed me in doing it, I don't know. All—all the more to your credit. Oh, Emmie—my little fragile, delicate girl—the, the bravest creature that ever lived, as well as the most divinely precious. Oh, Emmie, Emmie."

Miss Verinder, herself affected by emotion with her arm round his neck soothed and quieted him.

"Don't, Tony, don't."

She said that she did not really know what happened in that horrible room, except that she was crazy with fear. She never wanted to think of the place again, and it would be unkind of him if he did not help her to forget the agony she felt during the moment when he was rolling about the floor and she was trying to get the revolver into his hand. She knew that, despairing, she had pulled the trigger once. But surely not more than once? It had seemed to her then that all the people in the room and in the house were firing together—not merely revolvers but large cannon. It was hot, too, as if the house was on fire. She remembered no other sensations of any kind whatever, until the choking smoke lifted and she felt cold air upon her face and Dyke's hand dragging her along.

They left the carriage at the nearest railway town, and went on by train to Santiago. Here, in perhaps the most beautiful city of the world, they stayed three days, washing themselves, sleeping, eating. Here too they bought clothes, and became once more Mrs. Fleming the journalist and Mr. Dyke her guide.

At Santiago he learned, in telegraphic communication with his agent at Buenos Ayres, that Australia was clamouring for him as much overdue. Important work awaited him; and he was at once in a fever to be off, willing to forgo or indefinitely postpone bone-breaking vengeance on muleteers, thinking only of the new adventure. He flushed with delight when he found that a steamer was on the point of sailing from Valparaiso for Brisbane. Since Emmie showed a strong disinclination to recross the mountains by herself and go home the shortest way via Buenos Ayres, he said she must travel in one steamer to Panama, in another to San Francisco; and thence in a train to New York, where she would have a choice of Atlantic liners.

They parted at Valparaiso; and six weeks later she was sitting at breakfast in the coffee-room of a private hotel in the Cromwell Road, Kensington.

CHAPTER XI

OTHER people having breakfast in the room glanced from time to time at the lady with the short hair who was sitting all alone at a table near the window. Gently stirred by the vapid curiosity that would seem to be the atmosphere itself in private hotels, they had already put themselves to the trouble of ascertaining that she was a Miss Verinder who had arrived last night from foreign parts, and they wondered if the oddly shortened hair meant that she had suffered from a fever while abroad. One or two of the old ladies determined, since she was obviously quite proper and genteel, to make her acquaintance before luncheon—by rolling a ball of crochet silk across the floor at her, by inquiring if they had inadvertently taken her chair, or by some other polite method usual in such places.

A large proportion of the visitors were old ladies, some of them very old indeed, and each had a comparatively young lady as attendant or companion—a granddaughter or great-niece, or merely a nice girl glad to see London under any conditions—who readjusted the white woollen shawl, cut bread into convenient slices, and made herself generally serviceable. There was talk about the inclemency of the weather, the unusualness of it so late in the year; and these juvenile aids were sympathetic and thoughtful, saying "Auntie, you won't venture out, of course." At a table larger than the others there was a family group, father, mother, governess, and well-grown children, visitors from the northern provinces. The father stood in the window to eat his porridge, and without searching for pretexts, spoke genially to the solitary breakfaster; telling her that his way of eating porridge was the only correct one, and advising her to adopt the method. "At hoam 'tis always served to us on the sideboard, never on the table." Then he jerked his head towards the windowpanes. "Give it an hour, an' all that snow will have turned to fair sloosh. I've ben watching those la'ads shoovel away wi' it off the steps and the footway."

It was Sunday morning; and Miss Verinder, automatically resuming one of her old customs, set forth an hour later to attend divine services at Brompton parish church. The hotel manageress insisted upon lending her a pair of indiarubber goloshes, and praised her for her temerity while the page-boy knelt and put them on her feet. "Yes, I do call you brave," said the manageress, "to face the elements on such a morning as this. *I* wouldn't have the courage"; and she shivered. "No, I wouldn't. And walking too! Why don't you let me send Charles to fetch you a cab?... Oh, shut that door, Charles. I declare the cold comes in enough to cut you in half."

Miss Verinder did not feel the cold—she was inured to cold. In fact, the air out of doors seemed to her only remarkable for its flatness and heaviness. She observed the snow—if one must honour with the name of snow that niggardly smoke-stained deposit which men with tools had scraped from the pavement into mean little banks and defiled with a crust of mud as they swept it here and there. Changing already to "sloosh" in the roadway, with wet tracks made by cart wheels, and pools of primrose-coloured water where the faint wintry sunlight touched it, any approximate whiteness that it still retained served only to make the house fronts seem darker, more offensively drab, more overwhelmingly dismal. Out of the porches and down the steps came people who seemed to be in some queer manner parasitic to the houses, rather than their owners or leaseholders; as if the architect's incessantly repeated design, the builder's profuse stucco, and the plumber's leaden pipes, had mysteriously engendered human tenants. Born of the Cromwell Road, they closely resembled it; they were uniform, drab of complexion, with a dingy respectability that took the last fading lustre out of the trodden snow and obliterated every spiritless effort of the sunlight. All similar, but of both sexes, well wrapped in coats and furs, with prayer-books in their hands, they moved slowly and cautiously, begging one another to beware of slipping, to avoid puddles, and to step back and stand still when a passing carriage splashed the mud dangerously. They seemed to Miss Verinder strange, small, pitiful. Moreover the roadway that she used to think so wide had constricted, the lofty line of the house cornices came crushing down upon her, a narrowing vista of plate glass and window curtains seemed to close any chance of escape into freedom and open spaces. Even the terra-cotta mass of the Natural History Museum shrank to nothing as she approached it, and offered to her, instead of the dignity of soaring towers and vaulted vastness, a fantastic little toy, or that picture of a toy that is pasted on the lid of a child's box of bricks.

Why had she returned to this particular neighbourhood—like the wounded animal creeping back to the place it used to haunt before, largely straying, it received its wounds? As though exhausted by rebellious originality she seemed meekly to have surrendered to the force of habit. Or perhaps when the cab-driver asked where he should take her she had said Kensington as the only name of a locality belonging to this hemisphere that she could remember in her great weariness. Because the effort required for thinking hard was just now impossible, because nothing that concerned herself personally was any longer of the least consequence; because one place was the same to her as another, since more than half of the world had become quite empty and she was condemned to live alone in it?

She mingled with the small stream of worshippers passing beneath the drip of the trees by the blank wall of the Oratory, threaded her way past two or three broughams regretfully brought there by devout masters or mistresses who could not walk but hated troubling their stable on the day of rest, and then just outside the church door she came almost face to face with her parents.

Sweeping into the sacred edifice, they both cut her—Mr. Verinder in the manner known as dead; Mrs. Verinder with a vacillation of gait, a fluttering of furs and feathers, the first rough sketch of a gesture, and a look. It was in its essence a look that Emmie had often seen at home; the look that came when servants had committed an accident with valuable glass or rare porcelain, angry but not really inexorable, seeming to say: "I *cannot* ignore it. You have broken our hearts, and we are very much annoyed."

In spite of the disastrous turn of events that occurred last August, Mr. and Mrs. Verinder throughout the month and during half of September were still sustained by a modified form of hope, and still making strenuous efforts to conceal the disgrace that had befallen them. They felt that they were engaged in a contest with time. If they could "hush things up" until their enemy went back to the wilds no one need know of this truly *fin-de-siècle* escapade, and Emmeline need not be given that horrible up-to-date label of "The woman who did." Dyke was leaving England about the middle of September—really going—no doubt of it. Not only the newspapers said so, but Mr. Verinder—without the aid of detectives—had assured himself of the truth. When once Dyke was gone all would be over; Emmeline would come to her senses, rub her eyes as one awakening from an ugly delirium, and be very grateful to find her reputation still intact. They could then do anything they liked with her—for instance, marry her to that old widower who hired the Grosvenor Gallery for his concert, and thus, as Mr. Verinder put it, "save her from her temperament."

Straining therefore towards these ends, they for the moment gave their daughter what she had already taken, absolute freedom; they frustrated the desire of Eustace to get Dyke out on the sands of Boulogne; and they officially intimated to their servants, through the housekeeper and butler, that a very slight tiff recently existing between Mr. Verinder and Miss Verinder had now been completely smoothed away, leaving father and daughter the very best of friends as in the past. The faithful servants were glad to hear this; they knew they had a good master, and never meaning to quarrel with him themselves, they could not understand why anybody else should fall foul of him. They thought that the girl Louisa Hodson had acted like a rare fool in forfeiting her situation—for it should be mentioned that Louisa had been despatched with a month's board wages as well as salary, in lieu of notice. She was dismissed not because her complicity had been established, but because Mrs. Verinder could no longer bear the sight of her.

Then came the middle, the end of September, and the total vanishment of Louisa's late charge. The enemy had gone and his victim with him. Nothing more could now be done by her tormented father. In the whole circle of the family acquaintance the dreadful affair became more or less known. Within those limits it was a very solid scandal—a scandal that could only have been allayed by the production of Emmeline herself, and Mr. Verinder was unable to produce her. He abandoned fictional enterprise, clothed himself in a garment of silence, and suffered. Conscious that the local society was talking about him, he had the illusion that it was talking of nothing else; when old friends like Sir Timothy shook hands with him he seemed to feel an added pressure on his fingers and winced beneath this contact with sorrowful sympathy; if people spoke of such matters as public morality or licentious domestic habits and then broke off the conversation, he believed they had all at once remembered his misfortune. Doubtless, he thought, they condemned him for failing to bring up a family in the way it should go, for being unable to govern his own household, for letting things drift until they came to a pretty pass indeed. If now it had been necessary to issue debentures of those paper mills, he felt that the terms would be less favourable than in the past and the response not so large, because confidence was withdrawn from one of the principal directors of the company. If a man can't look after his own daughter, you don't trust him to look after anything.

In this winter of 1895-96, he suffered, feeling as he walked to the house and away from it that invisible eyes were looking at him from all the neighbours' windows and that he was not holding up his head as he used to do. Only in the spacious tranquillity, the well-warmed atmosphere of egoism, the nicely arranged comfortable total indifference to all things except oneself, that permeates and makes up the charm of a really good London club—only there could he shake off his depression and feel sure that nobody was sympathising with him, pitying him, or blaming him; that if members laughed at the story of his fugitive child, they immediately forgot what had set them laughing; that if, going into the coffee-room, they connected the names of Anthony Dyke and Emmeline, they disconnected them again, and probably for ever, in the moment of asking for red currant jelly with the hot mutton or mixed pickles with the cold beef.

At Kensington these names had been fatally connected. Kensington knew that Dyke, the famous Anthony Dyke, was at the bottom of everything, at the side of it too, and all round it. The most faithful servants will chatter, even at the risk of losing the best of places. If people are quick at putting two and two together to make four, they are quicker still at putting one and one together to make two. Perhaps Miss Marchant, emissary to Mrs. Pryce-Jones, not really hoodwinked by Mrs. Verinder's explanation, had continued to keep a watchful eye. Perhaps as well as Miss Marchant, the mournful angels on top of the Albert Memorial had seen the infatuated couple walking side by side, and had told the summer wind while begging it not to carry the news any further. Such things always leaked out somehow—more or less. Thus rumour, busy with both names, had enlivened drawing-rooms, by swift amplification; and in the protracted absence of Miss Verinder there had been reports that somebody or other had met her and Mr. Dyke at Monte Carlo, had lodged next door to them at Folkestone, had bumped into them at Tunbridge Wells.

During the church service she meditated, without emotion, upon her new social status. Glancing at one or two familiar faces she thought she could observe a rigidity of feature, a marble restraint of expression, that was something more than should be produced by absorbed interest in a religious exercise. They could not of course, at such a time and in such a place, even faintly nod or smile at an old friend; but their devotion was not surely quite so profound in past days; this statuesque aspect of the praying saint was surely new and significant. She felt a numb grief at having caused pain to her parents; but she cared nothing for the mental perturbation of these other people.

Except perhaps Mrs. Bell! She felt a sting of regret, a sudden realisation of forlornness, as she noticed that, far from assuming that air of sculptured oblivion, Mrs. Bell from time to time looked at her in a most distressful manner. Mrs. Bell had always shown strong regard for her. Emmie was fond of Mrs. Bell.

As has been mentioned, Mrs. Bell owned one of the largest houses in Queen's Gate, and it may now be added that her heart was as large as her house. She was a childless widow of forty-two who had earned a widowhood in which she frankly delighted by assiduous care of an elderly invalid husband; loquacious but devoid of malice, indeed exuberantly good-natured, she loved to clothe her pleasant expansive figure with grand garments; fair of complexion, gracious, smiling, when dressed at her grandest she looked blondly opulent like the queen of diamonds in the very best and most expensive packs of cards. She was waiting on the porch steps, when Emmie, after allowing the congregation to depart, herself left the church.

"Now, my dear girl—my dearest Emmeline—you are coming home to lunch with me. *That* goes without saying."

She would take no refusal. Her brougham, the last of the carriages remaining on the wet gravel, stood with its door open; she pushed Miss

Verinder into it and the footman smothered them with a fur rug. As they drove away Miss Verinder's eyes for a moment filled with not easily repressible tears. She was touched by the warmth of her friend's greeting.

"Now I want to tell you," said Mrs. Bell, with affectionate impressiveness, when she and Emmie had crossed the hospitable threshold and were alone together, "I want to tell you at once that nothing that has happened makes the least difference to *me*."

"Thank you, dear Mrs. Bell," said Emmie gratefully.

"I am not even going to ask you what *has* happened."

Miss Verinder thanked her again.

"I shall not ask a single question; and I want you to know that you will be welcomed in this house precisely as before—at all times and seasons, do you understand? If any of my friends object, then," said Mrs. Bell firmly and grandly, "they can stay outside. Yes, they shall soon find I will not stand anything of *that* sort. You see, I am perfectly frank with you, Emmeline. I should be less than a friend if I attempted to conceal the truth from you. You have the whole world against you. So far as worldly opinion is concerned, your only chance is to live it down—just *to live it down*. And, as I say, by *me* you will be asked *no* questions of any kind. But, oh, my dear child, what on earth have you done with your hair?"

"I had it cut," said Miss Verinder meekly.

"But *why*?"

"I mean to let it grow again," said Miss Verinder, evading an answer.

"I hope so indeed. Now we will go into the other room and have lunch." But before opening the door good Mrs. Bell put her hands on the visitor's shoulders and administered a warmly affectionate kiss. Then she looked at Miss Verinder doubtfully, distressfully, and with a slight piteousness of appeal. "As I have promised you, I shall not ask questions—unless, my dearest Emmeline, you yourself would like to tell me every single little thing. If you feel it would be a relief to you for me to know exactly where you have been and exactly what you have been doing since you left England—but, no, I see you would rather not. Then come along."

And with that tremendous adventure for ever locked in her heart, Miss Verinder sat down to luncheon.

She remained in the neighbourhood. Cut by her friends and cast off by her family, she calmly settled in the flat at the corner of Oratory Gardens and went about just as if she had been anybody else instead of the disgraced Miss Verinder. The arrangement of the flat pleased her; she liked the narrow steep staircase with its private street-door beside the auctioneer's office; when she closed that door behind her she felt safe, and when she passed through the door at the top of the stairs she felt that she was in an impenetrable stronghold. She furnished the flat charmingly, with antique things that as yet were not valued by everyone. Mrs. Bell said she had made it "too pretty and comfy for words." Louisa Hodson, discovered without much trouble, came to the flat as factotum, and added to Miss Verinder's sensation of being finally established in a shelter and retreat that was quite unassailable. No one on earth could interfere with her here. Even when the street door stood wide and an invader mounted the stairs, there was Louisa at the top of them to bar further progress and send him down again. In these days visitors were of the kind that wish to sell tea or dispose of tickets for a benevolent concert; but neither then nor at a later period could anyone get past Louisa when her mistress desired brief or lengthy seclusion; no one—not even Mrs. Bell of Queen's Gate.

At once Miss Verinder began to occupy herself in the pursuit of knowledge, as though attempting a sort of higher or secondary education. She read scientific treatises and learned to draw maps. She studied such impossible things as logic, rhetoric, and English composition. She joined a literary society, attended lectures and classes; wrote essays on subjects chosen by a severe young professor, and humbly carried them back to him for sharp censure or faint praise. She was in many ways busy.

Almost at once too there fell upon her that air of self-reliance which, whether proudly deprecating or gently defiant, is observable in all women who are for any length of time compelled to manage without assistance both their outward and their inward lives. All people knowing her story must see in her appearance as well as her manner a confirmation of their own way of interpreting it. Even her cheerful resignation was suspicious; they looked for the sadness in her face when she thought herself unnoticed. To such critics she was in every detail precisely what might be expected in one who has forfeited all chances of respectful attention, who is left to herself because she deserves to be left to herself. To those who knew nothing about her she was merely old-maidish. Her hair grew again, long and thick, but the brightness of youth had irrevocably gone from her. Her complexion slowly faded, the tints of the frail blush rose giving place to the waxen permanence of the lily. At twenty-eight she looked at least thirty-five.

And the long years began to glide away. Colourless, without salient features, swift in their cold monotony, the years were like ghosts of years flitting across a half-lit room into the endless dark passages that leads to the eternal. Mrs. Bell had said that she must live down the past, but it seemed that her real task was to live down the future.

At least thus it all appeared to external observers. Events of one sort or another were truly happening in the flat all the while. For instance—as observed by Mrs. Bell—after a time a parrot arrived, to be petted and fed and cared for. Then Louisa, the maid-housekeeper, asked permission to keep a cat. Louisa did not intend to marry; she had established herself in the flat as firmly as her mistress; she and Miss Verinder understood each other—they played with the cat in its kitten stage, they made much of the solemn and probably very aged parrot. Seemingly they were just two old maids together.

During this period the illustrious name that had been whispered in Kensington drawing-rooms sounded at intervals loud and clear on the public tongue. As hitherto in the career of Dyke, he was alternately lost to view for long stretches of time and lit up by a blaze of publicity for brief spaces. Throughout the year 1897 those deserts of Australia hid him completely. Then early in 1898 he was very much before the world again. His book *Sunshine and Sand* gave the history of his most recent vicissitudes and successes, and appearing at a moment when the ultimate confederation of the Australian Colonies was being widely discussed, the book, as critics said, was not only more entrancing than any novel, it took its place as an indispensable volume of reference for all students of imperial history. Also at some time early in this year 1898 he was in London, being interviewed by newspapers and delivering a lecture before the Royal Geographical Society. Then the dark curtain promptly descended upon him once more. He had been sent to examine the interior of British New Guinea and to explore any unvisited islands to the east of it; and the newspapers had not much to say about him for two or three years, except that he was alive in spite of the insatiable craving of the cannibals with whom he now consorted. Then came the publication of *Among the Papuans* in two bulky volumes, which the press welcomed with compliments similar to those showered upon his previous work. Critics said that since there could be little doubt that the Crown would cede its interests in New Guinea to the Commonwealth of Australia as soon as that federation should be finally constituted, these two illuminating and compendious volumes of Mr. Dyke's appeared at a most opportune hour. Then soon one heard that Mr. Dyke was in the United States lecturing, and trying to collect money for another Antarctic voyage, which should start, as he hoped, in 1902, or at latest in 1903. The lecture tour closed stormily in a pitched battle with American critics who had thrown doubt on his records of the Patagonian pigmies and the Andine temples. The noise of this contest echoed loudly even on our side of the Atlantic.

Thus Miss Verinder was not allowed any true chance to forget the man who had been so much to her. For her, one must suppose, even the occasional mention of his name, a mere newspaper reference to him, should prove stirring to the memory, if not absolutely upsetting to her peace of mind. And above all, those books of his—always running into a new edition or being advertised by the publisher as about to appear in a cheaper form! The earlier ones, too, got themselves reissued—*First Antarctic Cruise* (1888); *The Second Cruise* (1890); "At all booksellers, uniform with *A Walk in the Andes*"; and so forth! Perhaps she was reading one or other of these works and suffering in consequence, when she lay indisposed behind her shut doors, or suddenly and abruptly disappeared from the flat altogether on one of her strange lonely excursions. Louisa, growing older and sterner every year, merely reported that Miss Verinder was unwell and could see no one; or that Miss Verinder had left London and it was quite uncertain when she would return.

Moreover, had Miss Verinder been in any danger of forgetting the man himself and his more intimate characteristics, she received at least one sharp reminder.

On a certain winter afternoon his father came to call upon her, by appointment.

"I was so glad to get your note giving me permission," said the elder Mr. Dyke. "It is very kind of you."

"Oh, not at all," said Emmie; using, as so often happens when we feel that an occasion is momentous, the tritest and most simple form of words. "Do please sit down"; and she indicated that she wished him to choose the sofa as his seat. Her nerves were fluttered and her thoughts in some disorder during these first civilities.

"It is a great pleasure, Miss Verinder, to make your acquaintance."

"And I," said Emmie earnestly, "have wanted to know you, Mr. Dyke. I have wanted it so much—so very much."

"Thank you. It is good indeed of you to say that. I should have wished to come long ago—but, well, somehow I did not venture"; and he had a smile that seemed to shoot like an arrow into Emmie's gentle breast and set it throbbing with exquisite pain. Almost, for that instant, Anthony might have been there smiling at her. "No, I wished to do so—but one is always afraid of seeming intrusive. Only when he wrote to me—"

Mr. Dyke sat then upon the sofa, and they began to talk about his son.

He was a much smaller man than Anthony, very thin and spare, and yet obviously possessing something of Anthony's iron strength; so that, although sixty-four or sixty-five years of age, he gave one an impression of a person who will go on living for a great while without ever growing really old. He too had blue eyes and a straight nose, but one could not imagine this face becoming hawklike or fierce. He was quite dignified, yet devoid of all commanding or majestic attributes. His manner, reminding her of Anthony's now and then in its deferential courtliness, more particularly as expressed by bowing the head, was quite that of a man of the world. And Emmie noticed that his sacred calling was not indicated by the slightest sign in the clothes he wore. Then as her nerves steadied themselves, while he went on talking and she listening, she thought of nothing beyond the one fact that he was Anthony's father.

He was telling her about Anthony's birthplace, their home in Devonshire, and the time of Anthony's boyhood. "Endells—that is the name of our house, you know—quite a small place, but in a way very charming—to *us*, at least—we all love it. Close to the sea, you know. Endells—so many places in our part of the world have a plural name. Abertors—that's the big place, the show-place. An old house, ours, you know—and the most delightful old church close by, on our own ground. I am, you know, what they used to call 'a squarson,'" and he smiled again. She could bear it now; and it was not really Anthony's smile. It was full of goodness and kindness, but it had not that warm flood of light as of the sunshine bursting through splendid dark clouds and making the whole world happy. "At the time I speak of, I was still doing my clerical duties. I hadn't then turned lazy and handed everything over to a curate. And will you believe it, Miss Verinder? I then thought that Anthony, when he grew up, would be ordained and follow in my footsteps. His mother thought so. Poor dear"; and he sighed. "We lost her before he was fourteen. As a boy he was religious—unusually religious. But now, I fear—well, you know his inmost thoughts a great deal better than I do. We won't speak of that."

Then, continuing, he said he felt it would interest her to hear that as a boy Anthony showed no sign of the adventurous spirit. "Isn't it strange, Miss Verinder? But so it is." He was a dreamy boy, loving mystical books, with a hankering after magic, astrology, and spiritualism. He had never been seen to read tales of travel. Nor was he fond of athletic sports. He did not care for riding. "You know, there are hounds of course within reach of us. And sometimes he would follow them on foot, but never on horseback. Always a prodigious walker." Then Mr. Dyke laughed gently. "He would not come in to meals. It worried his poor mother, and our housekeeper—who had been his nurse—used to say nature never put a clock or dinner bell inside Master Anthony's stomach as it does with other children. He would climb along the cliffs and lie on his back on some ledge or other, looking at the sky or watching the seagulls, and dreaming—dreaming hour after hour; the whole day often, in summer. All one can imagine is that during these long reveries great purposes were slowly shaping—unknown to himself perhaps.

At any rate not one single word about it did he utter to me—and we were *friends*, Miss Verinder—a very real affection, thank God, remained always between us two—I fancy, something more than is common with fathers and sons." And Mr. Dyke paused to blow his nose. "Not one word until he was approaching his nineteenth birthday. Then he said to me—I was never more astonished in my life—he said, 'Father, I can't stand this any longer. I am starting for Africa to-morrow.' Just like that. And he went, you know.

"The rest—if a father may say so—is history. It is, isn't it, Miss Verinder? Now I musn't tire you by too long a visitation. But I felt that these little early details would interest you. They are so little and yet so much. And they should certainly come into his life when it is written. I think it is a mistake in biographies to omit all the slight and seemingly trivial details and give one only the big events. Nothing is trivial in the lives of really great men."

Miss Verinder assured him that she had been enthrallingly interested; and, taking leave, he detained her hand in his for a moment while he asked if he might call again in a few days' time before he returned to Devonshire. She was conscious during these moments of a constraint or uneasiness that he had seemed to feel even when he was talking to her so gently and kindly. It had been as if the talk was merely superficial, and that beneath it there was a communication that he desired to make but could not. Now it seemed that this had risen close to the surface, and with her hand in his, she braced herself to meet it. Perhaps that mental preparation on her side, detected and misunderstood, was sufficient to check him again; for, without saying anything further, he went away.

Thinking about this afterwards, Emmie felt that it had spoilt everything. It was not difficult to find interpretations of a reticence or shrinking that would check Mr. Dyke's flow of words and make him hesitate each time that he approached a fuller confidence; yet if such thoughts, however natural they might be, were really in his mind, she did not wish ever to see him again. If they were not there, then she wished, without doubts or self-questionings, to enjoy the immense comfort and support that the sight of his face and the sound of his voice gave to her. She determined at once to lay the doubt at rest, and when, fulfilling his promise, he reappeared at the flat, she asked him a very simple question.

"Mr. Dyke, do you blame me for what I have done?"

"*Blame* you? Oh, how *could* I? How can I? Oh, my goodness, no," said Mr. Dyke, in visible agitation, and he sprang up from the sofa and stood looking down at Emmie, who was seated on one of her lowest chairs. "But I see what you mean. A clergyman? I feared you might think—That is why I have been so anxious to see you. That is what I wanted to say—but it was so difficult." He was stooping, and he took her hand and raised it to his lips. "To tell you my gratitude to you for your love of my son. And that I, just as much as he, can measure the extent of your sacrifice—its nobility and its completeness."

The barrier between them falling thus, she was free to take such comfort from him as he could convey. They sat on the sofa together now, and patting her hand and calling her his dear Emmeline, he talked again of Anthony.

That afternoon he told her among other things the story of Dyke's miserable, fatal marriage. Although the mother of Dyke's wife and her other relations were dreadfully common people, the girl herself was decently educated and showed a certain refinement inherited from her father, who had been both a gentleman and a scholar. Unhappily, she inherited from him also the strain of madness that in his case had led to violent mania and suicide. Before Dyke ever saw her, incipient insanity at least had declared itself in the daughter, and, as was discovered afterwards, her wretched relatives had been warned by doctors that it would be a monstrous wickedness to allow her to marry anybody at all. But when the ardent, impetuous Anthony fell into their hands they made remorselessly short work of him. He was then only twenty-one, just back from his first visit to Africa, full of chivalry and altogether devoid of caution; and to such people as these he would naturally seem a grand prize. The girl—Mr. Dyke believed—practised no deception, and indeed was wholeheartedly in love with her splendid wooer.

Three weeks after the wedding she entered an asylum in the Midlands, and she had remained there ever since. She was incurably insane—with a sort of dull religious melancholia that flickered up into mildly homicidal tendencies at intervals. Dyke from the beginning had taken every possible measure for her comfort and security. It was a good asylum, and the annual charges were not light. In order to insure the payment of these, Dyke had invested money left to him by his mother; so that, whatever happened to him, the asylum would continue to receive the half-yearly amounts. For a considerable number of years he had not been allowed to see his wife—or rather, she had not been allowed to see him; for the sight of him threw her into a dangerous kind of excitement. But Dyke was never in England without paying a visit to the asylum. He went down there, to make certain that she was being properly treated; after an interview with the doctors, one of the attendants guided him to some part of the grounds where he could stand unobserved and watch her as she passed by in charge of her nurse. In this manner he had seen her many times.

Her mother and the other relations had more or less blackmailed him as long as they lived, and he had been generous to them in spite of the wrong they had done him. Now they were all of them dead, except an aunt—a horrible old woman who from time to time wrote abusive letters to Anthony and his father.

"A sad case, my dear Emmeline. And I must say I find it difficult not to condemn the cruelty of a law that refuses to annul such marriages. I should tell you that my boy tried to obtain release by appealing to the law courts. Yes, he brought a case—but without success."

One after another the years glided past. In 1904 Anthony Dyke, the explorer, was about to do his third Antarctic cruise in command of an expedition that had been organized for purely scientific purposes, and with no intention of pushing far south. But newspapers said that it would be strange if Dyke did not make some sort of dash and attempt to lower the record that he himself still held.

Long before this year of 1904 the number of people who condescended to be aware of Miss Verinder's existence had largely increased. After the tea-sellers there had come in due course clergymen or church lay-helpers; for, however much you may disapprove of a lady's former way of life, you cannot be so uncharitable as to preclude her from herself exercising the virtue of charity; and, moreover, the acceptance of a donation or subscription commits you to no real friendliness. Then came a chance acquaintance who had been warned against her but could not bother about the warning, or thought that in regard to scandal there ought to be a statute of limitations; and, adopting this broad-minded view, they even asked her to dine with them quietly and at short notice—more especially when they were at their wit's ends to find a fourth for bridge. Then she began to be "taken up again," as they termed it, by a few of her old friends—the few still remaining in the locality. Staggered by the countenance given to her by Mrs. Bell, or moved to pity by their own reflections on her lonely blameless life, they essayed a smile and nod when they passed her in the street, and, encouraged by her unresentful courtesy, a little later attacked Louisa with a packet of their visiting cards.

So the legend of Miss Verinder's wickedness slowly tended, if not yet to fade and die, at least to lose its strength and high colour. Young people yawned and refused to learn when elderly people narrated the legend for their benefit. "Hot stuff," was she, when she was young? But all that must have been a mighty long time ago. It was as if the house walls absorbed whispers concerning her past, instead of echoing them as they used to do. It was as if the varnished front doors and plate glass windows of the straight, correct roads, conspiring with iron rails and neat rectangles of grass and gravel in the gardens of the squares, had now determined, if they could, slowly to obliterate all vivid recollection of a glaring irregularity. It was as if the whole monotonously respectable neighbourhood had said to its parasitic inhabitants, "We never experienced anything of the sort till then. Let us now try to forget that it ever happened."

At last her family forgave her, and for form's sake insisted that there should be some slight intercourse, although Miss Verinder herself declined or evaded any resumption of real intimacy. To her relatives it had become so very awkward to go on cutting her, and with all the children growing up, to have an aunt that mustn't be mentioned. It was far more convenient to know her and name her again. Margaret Pratt was now the mother of five and putting on flesh rapidly. But, because of her shortness, she could never hope to be as big round as Mrs. Verinder. Eustace had married with the utmost propriety, and his wife in an equally becoming manner had given him first a female and then a male infant. It was Eustace who advised a reconciliation with his erring sister, and Mr. Verinder at once agreed.

Mr. Verinder had been badly shaken by the South African War—a rebellion, a defiance of authority, that should not have been called a war at all; during the early reverses he could not sleep at night, although he doggedly declared at the breakfast table that he was not anxious and that everything would could right in the end. He sincerely mourned the death of Queen Victoria, that august lady who had been as fond of the Albert Hall as he was himself. He described this great loss as "the breaking of a link."

Already, in Mr. Verinder's opinion, his beloved neighbourhood was changing. He could not disguise from himself that it was not all that it used to be. That old closely-bound society was breaking up. The war had shaken things as well as people. New ideas were creeping in, with a new monarch on the throne; that grand old British institution, the dinner-party, was threatened by the new fashion of entertaining at restaurants.

Then soon he began to suffer in health, and submitting to the most terrific of all possible upheavals, he consented to sell his house and go to live with Mrs. Verinder at Brighton. Mrs. Verinder had fallen in love with Brighton, having there found a row of houses almost exactly like Prince's Gate— same colour, same porches, cornice, everything; only smaller, and therefore requiring a less ample and more easily managed style of household.

From Brighton Mr. Verinder wrote to Emmeline inviting her to spend Easter with them, saying that Eustace, Margaret, and the little people would be there, and *all* of them glad to see her. He underlined that word *all*; but Emmeline could not accept the invitation.

It was a comfort to the kindly feeble old man to be able to write to Emmeline now and then, or to talk about her once in a way at dinner; and it was an immensely greater comfort, a comfort always with him, to know that the ancient dreadful affair was so completely over and done with. To his mind, Emmeline had finally lived it down. He knew that Dyke had been in England during these years at least twice, and—again without the aid of detectives—he had ascertained that Emmeline had not renewed relations with the man; indeed, had not even attempted to see him. All the time Dyke was in London the last time, Emmeline had been away somewhere in the country. She did not return to that little flat of hers until the man had gone once more. All this Mr. Verinder had learned from Mrs. Bell, who vouched for the truth; and he admired his daughter's fortitude and strength of mind in thus running away to avoid any possibility of temptation.

A closed chapter. Yes, thank goodness, over and done with.

CHAPTER XII

IT was about half-past nine o'clock on a bright crisp morning in early Spring; the sun shone gaily into Miss Verinder's drawing-room, eclipsing the genial red glow of the fire; the leafless branches of the plane tree tapped against the window panes; and, although one could not see it, one had a feeling of there being a blue wind-swept sky with little white clouds racing giddily above the highest chimney pots. Miss Verinder herself, seeming if not quite as sunny and bright as the weather, at least strangely gay and alert, had been in and out of the room two or three times; while Louisa bustled hither and thither, giving last touches to the breakfast table that she had set forth between the sofa and the fire.

Louisa was indeed laying out a lovely breakfast, and her mistress glanced with pleasure at the honey, the various jams, and the hot-plate and the kettle, under both of which a lamp burned cheerfully. Over the back of the sofa were about half-a-dozen different newspapers. With a smile upon her unusually carmine lips, Miss Verinder unfolded one of these and read the account of how Mr. Anthony Dyke had arrived in London yesterday afternoon. This particular journal stated that the famous explorer appeared to be in the most robust health and the highest spirits. He would say little about the ill-fated expedition or the series of mishaps that had led to the return of the ship and the postponement of her voyage to another season; but he explained that he would give the fullest details of results so far achieved in the lecture that he proposed to deliver shortly. "He left at once for Devonshire, to pass a few days in complete quiet with his relatives."

Louisa brought in three silver dishes, a glass jar of marmalade, a china basket full of apples; but Miss Verinder was thrown into slight agitation by the discovery that there was still something wanting to perfect the breakfast. The hot rolls had not arrived. Louisa, even more distressed and worried by this failure, said the baker had faithfully promised. "It's that wretched boy of his who has played us false"; and Louisa used an odd expression, and using it laughed in spite of her annoyance. "I'd like to break his bones for him, I would."

She had left the hall door ajar at the top of the flight of stairs, and for about the fifth time she pushed it open and looked down. There was not a sign either of the boy or the rolls. She went into her neat little pantry, fuming. Then after a minute she heard a footstep on the stairs, and, rejoiced that the rolls had come at last, she called gaily, "Put them down, you imp. And shut the door."

"What is that?" said a totally unexpected voice.

Next moment Mrs. Bell of Queen's Gate had passed through the hall and entered the drawing-room. Miss Verinder, turning, was really much agitated by the sight of the visitor with Louisa behind her in the doorway showing a scared face. She made desperate signs to Louisa, who precipitately sprang away; and kind Mrs. Bell in her astonishment nearly let fall the large parcel of hot-house grapes that she was carrying.

Yesterday Mrs. Bell had been refused admittance because of an indisposition that had overtaken Miss Verinder. This morning, being out earlier than was customary, she had come to bring the grapes and to inquire after the state of her cherished invalid. Naturally she was now amazed to find Miss Verinder up and about, and, as she said at once, "looking better than I've seen you for years."

Miss Verinder said that she was indeed quite well again. Her slight illness had entirely passed off.

Then Mrs. Bell noticed the breakfast table, so nicely prepared, here, in the drawing-room, with silver dishes and cups and plates for at least two people—yes, with two chairs, one on each side of it.

Miss Verinder explained that she had a friend staying with her.

"Now that's very wrong of you," said Mrs. Bell in good-natured reproof. "You have struggled up to entertain your friend when you ought to have remained in bed. I can see now that you are not at all well, really. You are feverish, I believe—yes, feverish and shaky. Why did you allow her to come at such a time? Why didn't you put her off? You should not have studied her convenience. Who is she? Do I know her?"

Miss Verinder said "No."

"Take care of yourself," said Mrs. Bell, going. Then she paused, one of her usual kindly ideas having come into her mind. "Listen, dear. If your friend is on your nerves—you didn't mention her name—send her round to me. I'll take her off your hands for the day."

"You are too good, dear Mrs. Bell. But really I wouldn't think of it."

Miss Verinder saw her safely out of the hall, and bolted the door behind her—that door at the top of the stairs that had been left open in such a reckless, dangerous, unheard-of fashion by Louisa, merely because it was early in the morning with nobody about.

"You old goose," said Miss Verinder to the culprit, as she returned to the drawing-room. "It's all right. Mrs. Bell has gone. But that was a narrow squeak."

"All right," said Louisa, loudly repeating the words of her mistress. "She's gone."

And next moment a great big laughing man came into the drawing-room.

"Anthony," said Miss Verinder, "you're a very naughty boy to be so late. Your breakfast is getting cold."

"Oh, this room," he cried ecstatically. "This room! Let me look at it."

"You saw it last night."

"But by lamp-light. It's by daylight that I always see it in my dreams. I want to feel that I am really in it—awake and not dreaming. Let me touch things." And he moved about, putting his hands softly on pieces of furniture, cautiously picking up delicate fragile bits of china, admiring them, and putting them down again.

"Tony, your breakfast."

"Oh, damn the breakfast. Don't you understand what these moments are to me?" And he told her for the hundredth time how he carried with him always the whole of this room in his thoughts—a picture of it and its minutest details so indelible that thought instantaneously recreated it. He was verifying the picture now. If there was anything changed, anything missing, he would certainly know. "And now let me look at *you*." He said this with infinite pride and love. "My girl—my own little girl." He was holding her hands apart, as he always did, while these first transports lasted, so that her arms were opened and she could not push him from her. "Emmie—my darling." Emmie, under this attack, was vainly struggling to maintain her dignified primness of manner; she uttered bashful remonstrances, hanging her head, laughing and blushing, but was in rapturous joy all the while. "Angel of my life"; and suddenly he took possession of her, hugged her, and smothered her warm face with kisses.

Louisa brought in the tardy rolls while he was doing it, and as if blind and preoccupied went out again.

"You're too silly—really too silly," said Miss Verinder. She had withdrawn to the bevelled looking-glass in the front of the Queen Anne bureau and was arranging her hair.

They sat down to breakfast, and she made the tea for him exactly as she would have made it for Mrs. Bell or the vicar of the parish, had either been visiting her; but her eyes were bright, and the colour still glowed in her cheeks. Dyke watched each precise little movement with a sort of swooning ecstasy. First she warmed the tea-pot, then she began to load her tiny shovel from the silver tea-caddy, and as she transferred each shovelfull she demurely recited the habitual incantation. "One for me; one for you, Tony; one for the pot—and one for luck. Shall we have one more? Yes, I think one more for luck. Now the kettle, please."

"Go on," cried Dyke, with a roar of delighted laughter. "Say it." He wanted the rhymed couplet to finish the unchanging rite, that foolish rhyme that he himself had taught her. "Say it, Emmie."

And she said it, quietly and gravely, as if there was nothing ridiculous about it. "'For if the water not boiling be, filling the tea-pot spoils the tea.' Push back that little bolt under the kettle. Thank you, dear."

They spent four or five heavenly days together in the flat, never issuing from it till after dark, and not then without a preliminary reconnaissance by Louisa and her report that the coast was clear. All day long they were perfectly blissful, making up to each other in endless talk for the vast tracts of time during which neither could hear the other's voice. It was during one of these secret visits that Dyke taught the parrot to say "Look sharp, Louisa." Emmie could never have done it without aid.

Under the friendly cloak of darkness they used to take long walks about the huge town. They had jolly little treats too. Dyke loved the "moving pictures" from their very first introduction, and Emmie was devoted to this form of entertainment for the reason that it afforded her an opportunity of holding Dyke's hand and squeezing it while the lights were down. They also attended representations of the legitimate drama, going to the cheaper seats of unfashionable theatres on or beyond the four-mile circle; and they found and cherished the strangest sort of restaurants or cafés far from the more frequented haunts of well-to-do mankind, where they dined and supped with the utmost enjoyment. Some of these eating-places were almost too humble and doubtful, scarcely better than cabmen's shelters; for Dyke, fresh from New Guinea or an uninhabited island, was almost incapable of differentiation. To him, at any rate for a while, the Ritz Hotel and a refreshment room at an Underground railway station seemed equally magnificent and luxurious.

Emmie's favourite restaurant was at least clean and respectable, a little place kept by Italians in a side street near Hammersmith Broadway; and thither she guided her illustrious traveller when he wished to invite a guest to join them at dinner. These guests were always of the same class, rough simple fellows, generally colonials, with whom Dyke had sailed the seas or plodded the earth at some time or other in the past. He had promised to have an evening with them when the chance came and was anxious not to break his word. So, Emmie consenting, he sent off a slap-dash line inviting them to meet him at Spinetti's.

One night dear old Captain Cairns of the *Mercedaria* dined with them there.

"Well, upon my life, Tony, it's a sight for sore eyes to see you again," said Cairns. "And you too, miss."

He was just as he had been when she first saw him at that Johnsonian chop-house in the City; wearing a pea-jacket with a blue shirt collar, and, although so short, seeming excessively broad and powerful. His stubby beard was perhaps a little greyer, his big round head balder, and the network of wrinkles on his sun-burnt cheeks had become more intricate. His weight and solidity inspired confidence in her just as they had done at their very first meeting; but Emmie had a premonition that he would certainly break the fragile cane chair on which he had seated himself, and gracefully vacating her own place, she manœuvred him to the more substantial foundations of the velvet-covered bench against the wall. He sat there, beside Dyke, and beamed at her across the table.

"Oh, how he did make me laugh about them Papuans. Yes, I can see the old chap's going as strong as ever. Meanin' to have another bang at the South Pole, isn't he, miss?" And Captain Cairns's sense of humour induced a fit of chuckling. "Him and that Pole! I wrote and told him he's like the baby with the cake of soap. He won't be happy till he gets it."

They had a jolly evening.

"Ah well." Captain Cairns sighed when taking leave. "Here's my address, Miss Verinder, if you should have news you'd like to send me at any time— for he doesn't answer *my* letters. Good-night, and thank you. Those were happy days on the poor old *Mercedaria*."

"What is she doing now?" asked Emmie.

"She's broke up"; and Captain Cairns sighed again. "She was a good ship, she was—in her time. But her time was mostly over, when you honoured us, miss."

Then Dyke, laughing, said he had a little tale to tell; and he insisted that Cairns should sit down again and have another whisky and soda.

"If so, it must be a small one," said Cairns. "Really only a spot."

They sat down and Dyke gleefully narrated how, after saying good-bye to the *Mercedaria*, they got into a tight place—and Miss Verinder saved his life by killing a man.

In vain Emmie protested; he would go on.

"It's too bad of you, Tony. I asked you never to remind me of all that— never to speak of it to anybody."

"Only to Cairns. Such a real true pal as old Cairns!"

"Well, I'm blessed," said Cairns, when he had heard the story; and he looked at her with the deepest admiration. "That was grit, and no mistake. Whips out a revolver, and—"

"Mr. Cairns," said Miss Verinder, pulling on her black suède gloves and speaking rather primly, "please forget this nonsense. You know Tony's way. In order to make out that I did something remarkable, he is led into exaggerations. Good-night. It has been so pleasant to see you, and I hope we shall meet again before very long."

After five or six days spent in this manner Dyke would disappear from the flat and give himself to the public. There were interviews in the newspapers; he delivered his lecture, asked for financial support, visited his publisher, was seen at his club, attended one or two public dinners. Some time was spent with his father at that old house called Endells. Then perhaps he was secreted at the flat again. Then once more he was gone from England; and Miss Verinder, shopping with Mrs. Bell at Knightsbridge, or taking a walk by herself in Kensington Gardens, felt that she herself, all that was real and solid in her, had gone too.

It was she who had decided on the necessity of this long-sustained concealment of their love, and not he. Truly she was not a woman to shirk consequences—she had proved that handsomely; but not for nothing had she been born at Prince's Gate and reared in the Verinder tradition. She knew her England, which never really changes, however much people talk of change. She knew that to this day, just as in the time of Parnell, no public man is allowed to have an unauthorized intimacy with a person of different sex—in other words, if he cannot show his wife, he must not show anybody else. And more especially would this be so in the case of a man appealing to the public for money to carry on his public work. Had the fact been discovered, it would have meant an extinguishing cap (of the requisite size—very big) over the head of Anthony Dyke.

It had been necessary to hide him, and she had hidden him. With regard to this achievement one may perhaps for a moment consider how excessively difficult it is for a woman to hide a man in a life that to all appearances is being conducted on a conventional pattern, a life that seems open to observation by every curious person; and one may further remark that of all men Anthony Dyke was obviously the most difficult to hide, because of his large proportions, his loud voice, his terrific explosiveness—not to mention the fact that he was, if not yet as famous as he desired, at any rate sufficiently so to be a well-known, closely-marked public character; some one worth following by newspaper reporters, always remunerative for a chatty interview, and of market value as a snap-shot, take him how or where you would.

Nevertheless she had done it. If the truth must be owned, since there was but a single aim to her existence, she had welcomed as likely to aid her, the very hardships under which she was supposed to be suffering acutely; such as, the loss of reputation, ostracism by near relatives, coldness at the hands of friends.

Louisa, the tried and faithful servant, had also been a heaven-sent gift. But perhaps the real key to the triumphant deception had been her own unflinching audacity—the bold idea carried out with a boldness that never faltered. For at the beginning, when people were naturally most suspicious and keeping a sharp watch for the man Dyke, not the most suspicious of them all could suspect that the place to look for him was so outrageously near home as Oratory Gardens.

She was successful, then, and as time went on the thing grew easier. At those queer haunts of theirs they scarcely ever met anybody who knew him, and never anybody who knew her. They had no accidents; that narrow shave with her solicitous kind-hearted Mrs. Bell was the closest approach to catastrophe. But on the last evening of this same visit of Dyke to his native land they had a really unfortunate encounter.

They were coming along the Brompton Road, past the top of Thurloe Square, when a small elderly woman caught sight of Dyke in the full light beneath a lamp-post, and accosted him. He told Miss Verinder to go on, and stopped to talk to the woman. Miss Verinder, obeying him, went by herself slowly to the corner of Oratory Gardens and round it. Then, turning, she strolled back again to meet him. He was hurrying towards her, waving his arm as if as some kind of signal, and the woman was following him and calling after him angrily.

"Straight on, Emmie," he whispered, taking Miss Verinder's arm, "and step out."

He led her rapidly past the two corners that would have taken them home, round into Ovington Square, Pont Street, Sloane Street, and thence by devious twists back to Oratory Gardens; explaining while they took their sharp bit of exercise that he wished "to shake off that old devil," who was by no means to learn where Miss Verinder resided. When they were safe in the flat he further explained that the old devil was an aunt of his wife, a dangerous objectionable person with whom Emmie must never come into

- 158 -

contact. He was sorry that Emmie had made that rather significant turn towards the flat, but he hoped that it had not been noticed.

But next day, after Dyke had gone, the woman called at the flat, and, as reported by Louisa, asked who lived there. Louisa refused to say, and shut the street door in the woman's face. Then, after a little while, opening it, she saw the woman come out of the auctioneer's office. Either from the auctioneer or somebody else the woman obtained the information she desired. She was in fact that connection by marriage whom the elder Mr. Dyke had described as a pertinacious writer of abusive or blackmailing letters to him and his son. Soon now she wrote a letter to Miss Verinder.

The last post brought it one night when Emmie was sitting by the fire and thinking of the man who had gone. Louisa, looking stately in her black silk dress and apron, laid it on the small table beside her mistress; and there for a little while it remained unopened.

The evening had begun with desperate sadness as Emmie lived again in memory those perfect days, and thought that once more the joy had fled and life for another merciless stretch of time could be summed up by the two words, waiting and hoping. She must get through it somehow, as she had hitherto got through these dreadful empty intervals, and fortunately he had left her work to do. Work was always a comfort. Then she thought of his recent disappointment—the first failure of the scientific expedition— and of his anxiety that the second attempt should be a complete success. She felt, although he had not said so, that he was dissatisfied with the reception given to him in England. Some of the newspapers had annoyed him by taking the wrong side of the quarrel with that French explorer Saint-Bertin, had condemned him for hastiness and overbearingness. She remembered with burning indignation something really rude that had been said about him by one newspaper. None of them, as it now seemed to her, had been as eulogistic as they used to be; they did not recapitulate sufficiently the magnificent achievements of the past; they dwelt too much on a temporary set-back.

As much as he himself, she was eager that he should ultimately attain undying fame. She knew too that he would never settle down and be quiet until he had reached the goal. And, alas, he was growing older; the years, however lightly they dealt with him, left some marks. The time available was not infinite. He himself asked for luck; and the luck was always against him.

Sitting by the fire, and feeling the natural depression of spirits caused by the sense of loneliness after companionship, she was attacked again by a horrible doubt with which more than once she had been compelled to fight. Was bad luck the only explanation? It was most horrible to her when, as now for a few moments, she seemed to hear mocking questions which she disdained to answer, but which she could not silence. Why always the bad luck? That little trip of his to the Andes was typical; representing on a small scale the big adventures of his life. Again and again, if not always, the tale had been the same. He fitted himself out for an expedition, plunged into the wilderness, and was heard of no more, until he emerged starving, with nothing but the shirt on his back. Should not this make one doubt his powers, and admit that, splendid as he is, there may be some flaw in his mental equipment—some clumsiness of thought that, in spite of his brilliant qualities, makes him less than the truly great; so that he will never really achieve what he desires? As on previous occasions, she fought with all her strength against this disloyal and treacherous doubt, and drove it away to-night perhaps for ever.

It is love that kills doubt of every kind. She thought of the love, and of that only. These seemingly interminable absences must be supported with joy and pride as a part of the love itself; far from spoiling it, they made it what it was, unique and glorious; they lifted it high above the common bond of any ordinary marriage. She need not envy any woman who ever lived or think any more fortunate than she.

There was a smile on her lips now; she folded her hands and half closed her eyes, as she thought with an immense pride that no woman ever made a man more completely hers or gave herself to a man so utterly. He was her lover, whom she loved with a flaming passionate strength; he was her faithful mate, her partner, so that, as much as in any business partnership, any *firm*, all that struck at him struck her also; he was her child too, over whom she yearned with more than a mother's tenderness—her wayward noble boy, who sometimes acted with rashness from sheer nobility of spirit; who must be thought for, cherished as well as encouraged; who must be subtly guarded and secretly aided by the poor weak half of him that watched, waited, hoped at this fireside while his other splendid half battled magnificently in the frozen darkness twelve thousand miles away. Still preserving that characteristic attitude, with meekly folded hands, she thought thus rhapsodically of her love, and the glory of it—yes, the wonder and the glory of it.

Then she opened the letter, which tried to put everything in a different light. Cruelly abusive, it produced the effect upon her of something vile and incongruous and stupid, seen suddenly in a beautiful or sacred place—as, shall one say? mud-stained feet upon a marble floor or a bundle of filthy rags dropped by a passer-by on the steps of a cathedral altar. The writer signed herself "Mrs. Janet Kent"; she headed the letter with the name of a midland town; and she began by saying that she had just paid a visit to "the Assylam" and seen her niece, Mrs. Dyke.

"...the lawful wife of the man who keaps you. And I say it is a shame for a wicked kept woman to keap my niece in prison as she is. Miss Verinder, she is no more mad than I am, and would not be if proparly treated with a house of her own, and those who love her to take the care as I have told him I am ready to do. But no he says. Notwithstanding I say for a miss like you he can spend all the money required to make his own wife comfatable with me. You ought to be exposed for what you are."

And lapsing from the abusive to the blackmailing habit, the writer threw out a not ambiguous hint that it would be wise to avoid exposure by prompt generosity.

"Miss Verinder, waiting your answer, I am, Yours truely, Mrs. Janet Kent."

This letter remaining unanswered, Emmie soon received another of the same sort; and after that more letters until at last one came with very direct threats in it. Writing to Dyke, Miss Verinder refrained from speaking of the annoyance to which she was subjected. Why worry him? It would be time enough to tell him when she had him safe home again. But she went now for advice to a solicitor—not to Messrs. Williams, the family solicitors, but to some one whose name she had chanced to read of in a newspaper as connected with criminal proceedings.

This gentleman appeared to be as clever as he was sympathetic; surprisingly few words enabled him to grasp the whole matter, but he told Emmie that hers was one of those cases in which the law unfortunately could be of little assistance to the injured party. He pointed out that the only way of bringing the horrid old woman to book would be by police court proceedings, and it did not seem to him they could very well face the publicity that such action would entail. Indeed there could be little doubt that the old woman understood this quite well. It was probably her perfect understanding of it that made her so bold and impudent. He thought that perhaps the best chance would be for him to write her a "frightening" letter.

He wrote his letter, but Mrs. Janet Kent was not frightened; and his final regretful advice was that in his opinion it would be worth while giving her a little money "to shut her mouth." He said he would do it for his client, adding that of course if the abominable old wretch were paid once she would probably have to be paid again. The pride of Miss Verinder revolted from the advice; but she saw no escape from following it.

In this manner the last living relative of Dyke's wife became a humble pensioner on the bounty of the lady whom he was precluded from marrying.

He knew nothing about it, and perhaps would never know. He was busy. The good ship *Commonwealth* with all the scientific gentlemen on board was skirting the northernmost fringe of the pack-ice. The last letter that Emmie received from him for many many months contained a photograph taken on deck just before they left New Zealand—Anthony, looking enormous, in the middle, Mr. Wedgwood, the physicist, on his right; Mr. Cleeve, the biologist, and Mr. Hamilton, the geologist, on his left; Lieutenant Barry and the rest of the officers with their names written underneath them, and the crew unnamed. She put it away carefully with her collection of similar pictures.

And she went on with her work. He had left her all the materials for the short volume that was to appear later on under the title of *The Third Cruise*. All those studies of hers, the classes in logic and rhetoric and composition, at which Mrs. Bell and others smiled indulgently or contemptuously, had been undertaken in order to render herself capable of helping him with his books. Dyke, as often happens with authors of his character, had no notion of style or of construction. When he first honoured her with the task of knocking his stuff into shape for publication and she found herself confronted with the mass of manuscript, the muddle and tangle of it threw her into such despair that she, the assistant, called for assistance, and the publisher sent her a real literary person to put the opening chapters into literary form. It was the book called *Sand and Sunshine*, and the expert strongly objected to Dyke's initial sentences, condemning them as naïve and childish. "Sand and sunshine," Dyke had begun, "are very nice things in their way, but you can't eat them." She herself did not much care for this turn of phrase, and she connived at very large modifications. But when the proofs of those early chapters were sent out to Dyke, then eleven thousand miles away, he almost went mad with indignation; so that the explosion of his wrath, even at that great distance, made the flat in Oratory Gardens tremble and shake. He said he would break the bones of the literary man. He cursed his impertinence, for tampering with "a document." She finished the book herself; and then, and afterwards, Dyke allowed her to take any liberties she pleased. He would accept anything from that hand—in fact he never appeared to observe that she had changed things; and she always, with great tact, minimised what she had done. "A word here and there, Anthony, and of course the punctuation; but my effort is simply to make your meaning clear—never to alter it in the slightest degree."

Each year becoming more skilled, she altered just as she chose, anything or everything—except the titles of the books. Those she dared not touch. They were idiosyncratic. A certain arrogance or assumption in the sound of them had meaning for her, although the rest of the world might not understand. They linked themselves in her mind with that other mannerism, the habit of speaking of himself in the third person—"Dyke will be heard of again; Anthony Dyke is not conscious of failure," and so on; speaking as he wished the universe to speak of him. Thus the bare simplicity of these titles—The First Cruise, The Second Cruise, The Third Cruise—meant that they were chosen for posterity rather than for the passing hour. In future generations when people saw these words, The First Cruise, they would be in no doubt as to whose cruise it was. They would all know that the cruises made by Dyke were the only ones that had really counted in the century-long siege of the South Pole.

So skilled was she now that she saw *The Third Cruise* through the press without submitting the proofs to anybody, but not without those fears and agonies from which all very conscientious people suffer when they feel that they are engaged upon a task of supreme importance. She had nightmare dreams about the maps and the illustrations, dreaming once that three photographs of herself and Dyke, taken years ago at Buenos Ayres, had crept into the binding; and she woke early in the morning after she passed the last revise with a cold certainty that she herself had made some such abominable slip as saying seven hundred degrees South Latitude instead of seventy degrees. But everything was correct. She had done her work well, and the book was so favourably received that she soon had a fine batch of press-cuttings laid by for Dyke's gratification on his return.

That fourth cruise was a long business. Throughout one year she thought he was coming home, and waited full of hope. In that year she did not see him; he never came. Then during the next year she saw him once—for half an hour.

In a letter despatched from New Zealand he told her what she had already learnt by reading the telegraphic news. The fourth cruise had not been very successful. Those scientific gentlemen had squabbled among themselves and Dyke had squabbled with all of them; at a certain point he wanted to let science go hang and push boldly south, while each of the others wanted special facilities for his own line of research—ocean-sounding, magnetic observation, dredging, scraping, altitude-measuring, or whatever it might be. Dyke, making his southern dash, soon got the ship tight-locked; provisions ran scarce, scurvy appeared, one of the scientists died; then when the ice set them free and he reluctantly turned northward, they encountered terrible weather. Moss scraped off rocks, stuff dredged up from the bottom of the sea, and other treasures, were lost; the dead man's diary was destroyed by salt water; the homeward voyage of the battered ship became a chapter of accidents.

Dyke wrote with the best attempt at cheerfulness that can be made by a sick man who is heavily bruised in spirit. He was ill—he had to confess it—and as soon as the ship reached Brisbane they would put him into a hospital. He said he knew he would get well again directly, but, oh, how he wished that he had his little Emmie there to console him.

Of course he had not meant that she was to go to him; but she sent off a cable message and started next day. At Marseilles she overtook and caught a steamer of the Orient Line. Many people on the vessel noticed her and several talked with her—that old maid who used to sit out on deck knitting, always knitting, looking up with a pensive smile sometimes while her fingers continued to move the needles busily.

At Brisbane she found him strong and well, entirely recovered, but in the very act of departing for New Guinea, whither he was being sent again on government work. Delay was impossible. They had thirty minutes together in an hotel drawing-room.

Half-an-hour. It was enough—if there could be no more. It was worth all the trouble. She came back to England at once, by a steamer of the P. & O. Line—sitting on deck, knitting, the old maid to whom people spoke because of her loneliness and her gentle smile.

CHAPTER XIII

THE two books *New Guinea Revisited* and *A Further Investigation* give the three years narrative of Dyke's exploratory work in the mountains, with his study of the various native races, and his adventures among the lesser islands. These matters, as his father said, belong to history; and there is also historical record of his having been at home, or very near home, in the year 1908. It was in this year that the lingering quarrel between him and Saint-Bertin, the French explorer, found its culmination in a duel *"à outrance,"* which took place somewhere on the outskirts of Paris. Saint-Bertin was the challenger and in regard to the combat itself there were many stories afloat in both countries; the accepted English version being that four shots were exchanged and that Dyke fired his two straight into the air, although he had received a scrape on the thigh from the enemy's first round. The Frenchmen were undecided whether to take this as a further insult or a *beau geste*, until, as it was alleged, Dyke said the whole thing was damned nonsense and he would continue to shoot at the sky all the afternoon, since, however much he disliked Monsieur de Saint-Bertin personally, he refused to risk injuring France by incapacitating one of her bravest sons. If indeed he said anything of the sort, one may suppose that he did so in his grandest manner, with a Spanish bow or two and with all sincerity of spirit. For, whatever accusations might be justly levelled against Anthony Dyke for arrogance or overbearingness, no one could charge him with a lack of magnanimity. At any rate his late foe was satisfied by his demeanour—a satisfaction proved by Saint-Bertin's dedicating his next book to Dyke.

Emmie was satisfied too, when the packet arrived at the flat, forwarded by Dyke's publishers, and she read the dedication: "I offer myself the signal honour"—all in the most beautiful French—"of inscribing on this page the name of a good comrade, a courteous gentleman, a knight who has wandered from the age of chivalry to teach in this epoch of low ambitions and sordid concurrences the lesson that men may be rivals, and yet friends, of different fatherland but one brotherhood, united to death and beyond it by mutual admiration, esteem, respect, homage"; and so on and so forth. Miss Verinder, thrilling to the lavish praise of her knight errant, liked the beginning of the inscription better than the end. It seemed to her that the Frenchman, winding up, put himself too much on a level with Dyke.

She was doing more and more for him. All his correspondence was sent to her by the bank or the publishers and she dealt with it as best she could. Among these business people she was known as his authorised representative, his "attorney." She had long ago bought a tin deed box for the safe keeping of his papers, and in course of time she bought another of the same shape and size. These boxes stood in her bedroom, disguised by brocade covers that she had made and embroidered with her own patient hands; and she was never happier than when they were pulled forward from the wall, uncovered, showing the white letters of the name on the shining black enamel—"Anthony Dyke, Esq., C.M.G., etc., etc." On her knees before them, tidying their always tidy contents, docketing and stringing the various packets, she had wonderful sensations of power and importance—as if she had been rearranging Dyke's life itself instead of its scribbled records, setting it in order for him, making it easier and more comfortable.

Amongst the neatly folded packets there was one with the label, "Mrs. Anthony Dyke"; and to this Emmie added every six months a receipted account from the asylum in the midlands—Upperslade Park, as they called it. The sight of that address on the stamped piece of paper always gave her a little shock of pain or discomfort; she hated that particular bundle in the box, and used to shrink involuntarily from the task of opening it and retying it. Her hands grew slow as she touched it, and she lapsed into a waking dream while she thought of the great irrevocable fact, and of what his life, their life, might have been if the fact had not been there.

Since his banking account came entirely into her charge and duty compelled her to examine the passbook with close attention, she had made the discovery that another person beyond herself was taking liberties. As well as subscribing rather large sums anonymously to the funds of those various expeditions and thereby to a certain extent "dipping her capital," as her old friend and adviser, the late Mr. Williams, would have described it, she had also paid smaller sums directly to Anthony's account at the bank. She began this practise in fear and trembling. But Anthony never detected that he was being thus mysteriously aided. He never counted his money, knowing always that he had not enough, and devoting always every penny he possessed to the needs of a work insufficiently supported by the State and the people. Now she discovered that old Mr. Dyke also fed balances or reduced overdrafts from time to time by unacknowledged contributions.

Her own father was now dead, but in old Dyke she had found another father—a father who understood her. There was nothing that she need keep back from him, nothing that she might not discuss with him. She knew the house called Endells better than she had known her home in Prince's Gate, and felt more truly at home there. Everything about it was old, settled, full of time-honoured repose; when she and Louisa arrived upon a visit, the old servants, the old walls, the dear quaint old furniture itself welcomed them. Neighbours thought she was a relative of the house; the people of the village smiled at her, and remembered her as somehow belonging to Endells although not regularly living there. She might have lived there, had she wished, in all the time of Anthony's absences, but she continued to be merely a frequent visitor. And not once did she go there with the son and future owner of the house. A delicacy that all three felt but never spoke of debarred her from that joy. The precious days that Anthony gave to Endells were lost to her entirely.

At the side of the house there was a bit of walled garden where she used to sit with Mr. Dyke. The ground sloped down slightly, so that the tops of the side walls were not horizontal but slanting, and you looked upward to the house with its modest terrace, broad eaves, and latticed windows; sheltered from the wind, the little place was such a sun-trap that you could sit there even on winter days. But it was prettiest and most delightful in early summer. If Emmie, walking along the ugly Brompton Road, cared to shut her eyes and think of it, she could always see it—those flint walls with the odd pent-house roof to protect the blossoming peach trees, the borders of bright flowers, the trim grass path and stone steps; dark green ilex trees against a blue sky, and a glimpse of one of the old servants moving to and fro behind the open casements. Over her head the sweet sea breeze was blowing, bees were humming in the fragrant lavender, and perhaps the bells of the church began to sound behind the pointed gables and huge chimney stacks at the end of the house. Seeing and feeling it thus imaginatively, she had a consciousness always of comfort and rest; the kindly friendly little spot of earth had sunshine in it that filled and warmed her heart. Its walls were buttresses against which she could lean when she felt her weakness and longed for supporting strength.

Here, during her last visit, she had unburdened her mind of the distress caused by the treatment of Dyke in newspapers and reviews. As his publicity agent as well as his man of business, she was pained by a change of tone that she found it difficult to define; it was not that press writers—at any rate those of the better sort—were ever disrespectful, but they were too often oblivious. Mr. Dyke, sitting beside her on the garden bench, patted her hand and told her not to fret.

The fact was there had come to Anthony Dyke what comes to all who have built a reputation by startling the public, as soon as they cease to startle. Moreover, people were busy saying about others all that for so long they had said about him. The many new names demanded loud-voiced recognition—Nansen, Jackson, Scott, Shackleton, and others.

Reeling off the new names, writers merely touched on the old names in parentheses—"nor must we forget the pioneer work done by Anthony Dyke"—or "such men as Bruce, de Gerlache, and Dyke." They spoke of him as "the veteran explorer"; "still active, unless we are mistaken," and so on. One hateful rag, using the newly introduced phrase, even spoke of him as "a back number." And several times the list-makers forgot him altogether; his name was omitted from their roll of honour. Then Emmie, with her facile pen, was compelled herself to write "A Correction," indignantly asking for space to point out that Mr. Anthony Dyke by piercing the vale of mystery in the year 1888 had opened the southern path which all others had since then followed; or that it appeared strangely ungrateful when speaking of Antarctic explorers not to mention that Mr. Anthony Dyke had held the Farthest South record for fourteen years.

But his father said all this was of no consequence. It was an experience through which the greatest men invariably passed. Matters would right themselves. And he reminded Emmie of the splendid solidification of Anthony's earlier work, of the proof during recent years of all that had aroused question or doubt—those pigmies, the sacred remains, everything. Each year the foundations of his fame were being rendered firmer by the continually enhancing value of his discoveries, and the edifice raised thereon would stand lofty and secure ages after all these scribbling worms had returned to the dust from which they came.

"Dear Mr. Dyke," said Emmie, "you are always so wise. You always are able to make me see things again in their proper proportions. Yes, I remember what Tony once said. Justice is done in the end."

They were fond of each other, these two, bound close by their fondness for that other one. The friendly village folk liked to see them in church together using the same hymn-book; or on the cliff path, the old gentleman leaning on the lady's arm.

He was glad of this assistance sometimes; for he had not borne out that promise of the man who will never grow older. After his seventy-third birthday he began to age rapidly; and although he still preserved an outward aspect of alertness and carried his thin frame erectly, he had become frail. His walks were restricted; at each visit Emmie noticed a diminution of their range. A certain bench on the cliff path that they used to pass swingingly was now his farthest goal, and he was glad to sit and rest before turning homeward. They sat there one Sunday morning, high above the many-coloured sea and the dark rocks, and he spoke to her of religion.

"Emmie dear, it is good of you to go to church with me."

"I love it," she said. And this was true.

"Tell me," he said. "Was it Anthony who took your religious faith from you?"

"Oh, Mr. Dyke!" She gave a little cry of surprise and distress. "Of course not. Tony and I haven't discussed sacred matters for ever so long."

"But you don't believe—I mean, as we church people—do you, dear?"

Emmie made a fluttering movement of her gloved hands, then folded them on her lap, and with puckered brows looked across the sea to the faint silver line of the horizon. "It would be wicked of me to pretend. I'll tell you what I believe." But what did she believe? It was not easy to say, although she spoke with absolute sincerity. She told him that all her faith in the orthodox Christian doctrine had gone from her so gradually—and she must add so easily—that she scarce knew how it went or when it was gone finally. She thought—now that she considered it—that association with a mind as bold as his son's had perhaps had its part in rendering her old submissive faith impossible. But the loss of orthodoxy had not made her a materialist—oh, far from that. She firmly believed in some supreme and beneficent force that ruled the spiritual universe. That, she thought, was his son's belief also. And she wound up with words to the effect that it would be most terrible to her if she might not go on hoping there would be some kind of after life in which she and Anthony could clasp impalpable hands and exchange the phantom equivalent of kisses.

"I see—I understand," said Mr. Dyke gently; and he got up from the bench. "Perhaps very few people could say more nowadays. I don't know. I never judge. It is all a mystery—but I am too old to change, myself. Shall we toddle back to our roast beef? If we're late Hannah will scold us again. Thank you, dear"; and he took her arm.

He said he was old, and he looked old; she noticed then, more clearly than before, the uncertain footsteps, the violent yet feeble effort, the moving fragility of age.

Why should she be surprised? Time was standing still for nobody. The blondness of comfortable Mrs. Bell of Queen's Gate had gone. She had lost that appearance of an expensive court card, she had been shuffled from the pack or had become a queen dowager; she was out of breath when she got to the top of Emmie's steep staircase, and she went regularly to Homburg or Harrogate for the waters. When she gave parties her fine big rooms were thronged with another generation, who asked leave to push the valuable furniture on one side in order to dance, and then didn't dance, but romped in a thing they called "the Boston."

Wherever Emmie turned her large mild eyes, she could see the changes wrought by unstationary time. It was becoming dangerous to cross the Brompton Road because of the buzzing motor cars, which travelled faster than the motor 'buses. The tube railway had been opened. Men were flying in the air and going in boats below the surface of the water; members of the female aristocracy were dining in low necks at the Carlton Hotel; Mr. Lloyd George was a responsible cabinet minister. What would Mr. Verinder have thought and said? In Exhibition Road one met well-to-do young men smoking pipes, wearing preposterous knickerbockers, and carrying golf clubs; young ladies rode astride past the windows of Prince's Gate; only the will of Queen Alexandra kept mechanically propelled traffic out of Hyde Park itself.

In the golden summer of 1909 she had the wanderer with her for a long while.

She knew that he was coming, but had not been prepared for his actual advent. It was after luncheon, the room full of sunlight, and she sat in a corner busily typewriting; with a tray of papers on a table at her elbow and slips of printers' proofs lying on the floor by her feet. Louisa shouted in the passage, and when Emmie heard his voice she jumped up, knocking down the tray and its papers as she did so. She nearly sent the typewriting machine after the tray as she sprang forward to meet him at the opened door. Then something brought her to a dead stop.

He was grey. His beautiful dark hair had lost its black lustrousness; it was the dull colour of a grey silk dress. She gave a little shiver, and then took his hand and looked into his face as if not noticing any difference.

"Emmie! Let me look at you."

As always, he held her arms apart before drawing her to him, studied her with adoring eyes; and she knew without the possibility of doubt that he could not or would not see the slightest change in her. So far as she was concerned, she need never fear the years or their marks; always he would see not what she was really, but the girl that she had once been.

Soon they laughed together at the new colour of his hair, and Emmie said it was an improvement. It gave him greater dignity. He would look very handsome in the portrait that a famous artist was going to paint. Truly the grey hair did not make him look any older; although now fifty-one he was wonderfully, almost incredibly, young; sometimes making her and Louisa feel, as they had felt long ago, that they were hiding in the flat an overgrown schoolboy and not a middle-aged public character. He chaffed and teased Louisa; he took the parrot out of its cage and could not get it back again; he spent one whole day in teaching the new white cat to jump from between his knees over his clasped hands.

He was cheerful and gay; yet beneath the high spirits Emmie detected his occasional sadness. After running down to Devonshire for a few days he returned to her; and never had he been so entirely sweet or more absolutely devoted; and yet, nevertheless, she understood that he was restless in mind and, except for the comfort of their love, unhappy. It would pass—as all signs of weakness passed from him—but she knew that he was feeling the smart of disappointment. It was more than his own failure in the fourth cruise, it was the knowledge that his province had been invaded. That ocean which he had come to consider as belonging to Anthony Dyke had been attacked by so many others. The hidden mystery of its continent was imminently threatened not by him, Dyke, but by the new men.

He was still generous in his praise, trying hard to conceal the touch of bitterness caused by personal considerations. "Nansen is a splendid fellow. Take it from me, Emmie, he deserves all that is said of him—and they have made a deuce of a fuss, haven't they? He has been lucky, of course—devilish lucky. Mark my words; the North Pole will be reached"; and walking about the room, he paused to make a widely magnanimous gesture, as though giving away the North Pole. After all, the North Pole was nothing to him; he had never marked it down; anybody might have it—that is, anybody who deserved it. "They are wonderful people, the Norwegians, Emmie. I suppose you know they are fitting out the Fram for a third voyage. Yes, Roald Amundsen will be in command—topping chap, Amundsen—he'll get there." Then she saw him wince as he went on to speak again of things relating to the other Pole, the South Pole, *his* Pole. "That was a tremendous performance of Shackleton's, Emmie. Great. Lucky beggar, Shackleton. Scott too. I take off my hat to Scott." And he sighed. "Scott ought to be invincible—sent out as they mean to send him—with all that money behind him. You remember what Sir Clements Markham said about Antarctic exploration—he wanted a hundred and fifty thousand pounds to send a man in proper style." Then, after looking ruefully at Emmie, he laughed and snapped his fingers. "Poor old Dyke never scraped together a tenth part of that sum, did he?"

When she suggested that they should hire a motor-car, cross the channel, and go for a tour in Brittany, he eagerly embraced her idea, vowing that it was an inspiration. Those three weeks on wheels were idyllic—rest in motion, quiet introspective joy with a changing outward panorama of pleasant images. He seemed perfectly happy, scarcely once mentioning the South Pole; and she, watching him as a mother watches a son who has been crossed in love, hoped that he was not secretly grieving.

As soon as they were back in London he grew restless. He would sit looking at her, pretending to listen to her, and then suddenly go and ask Louisa to see if the coast was clear, because he wanted a walk. He walked by himself on these occasions, fast and furiously, "blowing off steam," as he explained to Emmie. At other times he would stand by the window, with his hands in his pockets, motionless for an hour and more, staring down through the foliage of the plane tree as if trying to look through the whole globe and see what was happening down there at the antipodes.

The news had come of the Japanese Antarctic expedition; the newspapers were always talking of Captain Scott's preparations; there were vague rumours of other carefully planned attacks. It seemed that all the world was "chipping in," and that poor old Dyke's white garden was to have its ice flowers snatched, as if by marauding gangs of mischievous children.

There was talk also, well maintained, of Amundsen and the Fram; and again Emmie observed that Dyke could speak of the gallant Norwegian without wincing. Amundsen—topping fellow—was for the North. More power to him. Only, confound these Japanese, and the rest of them, southward bound.

Beyond the restlessness there was irritability. Often he was irritable with his Emmie, rudely impatient at least once when she was not quick enough to grasp the point of intricate explanations concerning the various plans of these other adventurers; and he snapped at faithful Louisa—a thing he had never done till now. Miss Verinder bore with him, showed always an infinite patience. She could interpret all his emotions; even if she got muddled now and then in latitudes and longitudes. He was suffering in its acutest form the nostalgic longing that is felt by the disabled fox-hunting squire when he has to lie in bed and listen to the huntsman's voice and horn while hounds are drawing the home coverts. "Oh, damn the doctor. Get my boots, and saddle any old crock that's left in the stable. I'm going."

He began to tell her of what he would do if he "made a bid for it" himself, at this eleventh hour. "Do you follow me, Emmie? There are more ways of killing a dog than by choking him with butter." He said that if he could put his hands on so small a sum as ten thousand pounds, he would join the race—even now. "Listen, Emmie. These are my notions of a chance to get ahead of them all—even now." She listened meekly and attentively to his interminable harangues; she watched him as he paced to and fro, still talking, quite late at night sometimes, long after they ought to have been asleep; and she never blinked an eye. Nor did she demur, unless conscience obliged her to question his too sanguine calculations.

Then at last he said some words that wounded her most dreadfully.

"Upon my soul, Emmie, you seem as if you could never understand anything."

She uttered one of her faint little cries; but he went on, not seeing that he had caused her pain. He went on until, pausing for breath, he noticed that her lips were quivering, while her hands agitated themselves queerly; and she said in a strained voice that she knew very well how she failed him for want of intelligence, but she was always trying to improve herself.

"*You* fail me, what!" He gave a roar as of a stricken beast, and dropped on his knees, with his arms round her, imploring forgiveness. "My darling little Emmie—my guardian angel. Oh, I ought to be kicked from here to Penzance. I didn't mean it. On my honour I never meant it. Yet, clumsy lout that I am, I said it. Forgive me, oh, forgive me."

And she, stroking his bowed head, her face shining, said that it was "quite all right"; never could she really doubt his indulgence towards her, his loving kindness.

But it was long before she was able to comfort him or make him forget the offence of which he had been guilty; remaining on his knees he continued to apologise.

"Emmie, you're such an angel—you can make allowances and find excuses. It's only that I am so cursedly miserable about all this. If you think, it is devilish bad luck, isn't it? To be kicked up to the equator as I've been—to be cooked in that damned Turkish bath of a New Guinea—to be kept there these years—how many?—with the very colour bleached out of my hair and the marrow grilling to nothing in my bones—while your Newnesses and your Harmsworths, your admirals and cabinet ministers, your lords and fine ladies, have all been putting their heads together and opening their purse strings—yes, and your kings and mikados too—to fit out and give carte blanche to any one who has the cheek to tell 'em he knows the way to the South Pole! And I'm not as young as I used to be, Emmie. I don't feel it myself, but the others say it; they throw it in my face. I'd show them, if I had the chance—now. In another ten years it may be too late and I may be really done for then."

A few days after this she told him that the balance of his banking account would very soon amount to half the sum he had mentioned; he could rely on there being five thousand pounds to his credit. He would scarcely believe it possible. Had the money fallen out of the sky? She said that the cheap editions of his books had been selling marvellously well, and reminded him that royalties for six months were due from the publishers.

He asked no more questions. He was frowningly absorbed, he rumpled his grey hair and cogitated; then he laughed gaily. "Five thousand! It's a nucleus. If only I could add to it somehow."

It was of course futile for him to think of taking the hat round here in England; the public had thrown their very last threepenny bits into the hats of those other beggars. Then suddenly he said he would try America. "Emmie, there's a fellow out there who believes in me—a prince of good fellows—I stayed with him at his house on Long Island—lovely place, like Hampton Court Palace on a small scale—and he's rolling in money. What the devil's his name? Porter? Potter? James—yes, James L. Porter! That's it. By Jove, I'll see if I can touch him."

Immediately he cabled to Mr. Porter of New York, asking him to put up five thousand pounds. He made the message as eloquent as possible, not sparing words or considering rates, and he grinned while he read it with mock emphasis to Emmie. He was a schoolboy again, full of life and impudence; the gun-running Dyke of ancient days. "Now, old girl, if my pal's a sportsman—as I think he is—he'll do it."

He despatched his cablegram early in the morning and fidgeted all day, calculating the difference of time between London and New York, walking about the rooms of the flat.

At six in the evening the reply came. Mr. James L. Porter had cabled the money.

Dyke was almost delirious. He kissed Louisa on both cheeks, he waltzed with Miss Verinder, he executed a *pas seul* and made the cat do a record jump. Then he sang pæans in honour of the Yanks—those sportsmen over the pond—with a chorus of disparagement for the citizens of his native land. "Is there an Englishman alive who would have sent that answer? They don't waste time *talking* over there, they do. What was it Tennyson said? Our old England will go down in twaddle—or was it babble?—at last. And I scarcely knew the fellow. Any obligation was on my side, not his. He entertained me royally. Bravo, Porter. What's the matter with James L. P.? *He's* all right."

At once he sketched his plan. There could be no difficulty in collecting staunch comrades; he knew dozens of likely men. Of course everything must be done cheaply. He would go to Greenland at once to get dogs; he would buy a whaler, fit her out as best he could, and go down light—a scratch lot, certainly. "But with luck, Emmie"; and his eyes flashed. "Get there before Captain Scott, eh? Why not?"

They went out to dinner, after he had sent a dozen telegrams, and he was on fire with happy excitement.

"I shall write to Scott and tell him I'm chipping in. That's only common courtesy. Although, hang it, no one asks *my* permission when *they* chip in."

He had gone. She knew that the thing was hopeless, and yet she hoped. The letters that he sent her were not reassuring; with his scratch lot he would run dreadful risks and have no real chance of success, but still she went on hoping. It is too hard merely to wait and not to hope at all.

Although her financial position would have been described by the late Mr. Verinder as distinctly unsound and she was drifting from the smooth waters of safe investment towards the maelstrom of sheer speculation, she sometimes blamed herself for not having encroached on her already reduced capital to a greater extent. It was horrible to her to think for a moment or two that if she and J. L. Porter had given him more money, his perils might have been less and his prospects brighter. But, no, if she had put her contribution at a higher figure than five thousand pounds it would have aroused his suspicion, and then he would have refused to take anything at all. Moreover, as she consoled herself by reflecting, it would not have been *right* to give him more; she *must* think of the future; she *must* be decently provided against the day when his travels would be over. When that day came he would not of course have a shilling of his own; for whatever he possessed or earned or inherited he would certainly spend on his work before he ceased working. Then, if they were both poor, what would happen to them?

The time passed very slowly. Although he wrote to her she had lost touch with him; after the beginning of 1910 no exchange of letters was possible. In March he had begun to work his way southwards, and later he wrote to her from South American ports. She sent all her letters to Tasmania. At Hobart, as he said, he would do a lot of refitting and much valuable time would be consumed. His letters showed that he was happy and hopeful; and she too hoped.

Then in September of this year strange news burst upon the world and threw her into a state of white-hot indignation. Amundsen with the Fram had arrived at Madeira; instead of going north Amundsen was going south. He was going to the Antarctic. It seemed to Miss Verinder, quite unreasonably, a piece of dreadful treachery. This commander, all the while that his preparations are being made has permitted every civilized country to suppose that his aim is northward; he sails amid their good wishes; people stand with their eyes turned northward, thinking of him, peering after him. And suddenly they are told to turn round and look the other way. He has gone in the opposite direction, secretly stealing a march on innocent trustful rivals.

Miss Verinder held forth on the subject at an afternoon party given by Mrs. Bell in Queen's Gate that same day. It was a quiet informal party, because people still wore mourning for King Edward and many of Mrs. Bell's acquaintance had not yet returned to London. Emmie, standing by the buffet and being assisted to tea and cake by two attentive clergymen, looked very nice in her black dress, with a large picture hat, and some ermine round her slim neck. Unusually animated, a spot of wrathful pink on each cheek, she spoke in scathing terms, and almost choked once as she bit the rather dry cake. Indeed she was throbbing with anger, although her voice, while it emitted bitterness, was still modulated and gentle of tone. She said in effect that it was disgraceful of Mr. Amundsen to chip. Captain Scott must be utterly disgusted.

"Who is Captain Scott?" asked Mrs. Bell. "Do I know him, Emmeline?"

Other ladies gathered round, telling each other that Miss Verinder was speaking of the South Pole and all these explorers. "She is always so well informed."

And Emmie, firm and explanatory, said that such a "chip-in" as Amundsen's simply isn't done. She knew as a fact that in such cases warning was always given. And continuing, she boldly named the name. It was not only Captain Scott who would be upset, there were the Japanese to think of—and the private expedition that was being conducted by Mr. Anthony Dyke.

"Oh, yes," said somebody. "Dyke. Yes, to be sure. Dyke's one of the most famous of them all, isn't he?"

Mrs. Bell had moved on and was talking to a middle-aged couple who had just arrived at the party; but if she had heard Dyke's name mentioned, it would scarcely have aroused any recollection of the annoyance and trouble that he had once caused. That old scandal was so completely dead that the most vindictive enemy could not now have revived it, and nothing perhaps better proved the esteem in which Miss Verinder was held by all these people than Mrs. Bell's manner when presently introducing two of them to her. They were the late arrivals, a Mr. and Mrs. Parker, of Ennismore Gardens. They themselves had craved the introduction, and they said their nurse had told them of the very charming way in which Miss Verinder had spoken one morning to their little girl Mildred on her pony outside the front door. They thanked Miss Verinder for her kindness.

Miss Verinder said she deserved no thanks; she was very fond of children; and she thought their daughter such an intelligent, pretty little thing.

"Well, she really is," said Mrs. Parker, enormously gratified; and she and Mr. Parker together related that the child was good as well as attractive; a quite extraordinarily obedient child—"so different from her brothers"—

seeming to take the sweetest kind of pleasure in doing exactly as she was bid.

Miss Verinder said that was very nice indeed, and then she rather startled both Parkers by asking, "What will you do with her when she is grown up? I suppose you mean to give her some sort of profession?"

"Oh, come," said Mr. Parker, with a foolish chuckle, "I shouldn't have expected you of all people, Miss Verinder, to say that."

"No," said Mrs. Parker. "Surely *you're* not modern? You don't believe in letting girls leave home, and make careers for themselves, and all that?"

"No, no, Miss Verinder is not serious," said Mr. Parker, smiling and nodding his head. "In spite of all the talk nowadays, the best career for young ladies is just what it always was—*marriage*! Unless, of course," he added hastily, "a young lady, to the surprise of her friends and admirers, declines—ah, refuses—herself deciding that she prefers—possessing the cultivated and informed type of mind that does not seek—or perhaps I should say, does not brook—domestic ties"; and he embarrassed himself badly in his efforts to convey the polite opinion that, although Miss Verinder was an old maid, she might have married many, many times had she wished to do so. Then he wound up in regard to his own daughter by indicating that when Mildred was old enough, say, in ten years time, he would select for her a suitable husband, somebody that her parents both trusted and liked, and the docile, obedient Mildred would take him and say thank-you.

"It has been such a pleasure to make your acquaintance," said Mrs. Parker; "and we should be so very glad if you would visit us. Ennismore Gardens, you know."

Miss Verinder, in a somewhat absent-minded style, said she would be pleased to avail herself of this invitation some time or other.

"*Any* time," said Mrs. Parker. "Of course, we know how much you are sought after."

The year 1911 was the longest that Emmie had as yet experienced. The last of Dyke's letters told her that he expected to cross the Antarctic Circle in January, and then the immense silence began. She spent a couple of months at least at Endells with his father, who had been ill; and she and the old man encouraged each other to hope for almost impossible things. Notwithstanding insufficiency of preparation, unsuitability of vessel, doubtful allegiance of subordinates, "Why should not Tony pull it off this time?" Heavily handicapped, yes, but with such inexhaustible power in him himself. Emmie, hoping more and more, was ready to abandon painfully acquired knowledge, and to believe that only luck was needed. All luck really. The luck must turn in his favour—he had always said so. Moreover, who should venture to assign any limit to the probable in the case of such a man? He was so miraculous.

Having no literary work on hand, she went about among her neighbours much more than in the past. She liked and sympathised with the youthful generation. She listened to music with Mrs. Bell, and was always ready to join a bridge table even at the shortest notice. She played the game accurately and boldly; and one evening, when she dined at the Parkers and the young people prevailed on Mr. Parker to countenance poker, she astonished everybody by her manner of sharing in this more reckless amusement. There was a gentle inscrutability about Miss Verinder at poker that proved deadly to ardent and excited adolescence. One of the young men, cleaned out, stood dolefully behind her chair and afterwards reported that he saw her do a bluff big enough to lift the roof. He said it had given him palpitations of the heart to watch her.

But all these slight interests, the concerts, the cards, the tea-parties, as it were dancing and flickering on the surface of her existence, were as nothing; the true Miss Verinder was far otherwise engaged. The world of Parkers and Bells, and tradesmen and cabdrivers, never once met her. Or if for a moment anyone caught a glimpse of her, she had flown away next moment and was back with her wandering man. So that one may truly say of her that often, as she passed along the broad smooth pavement round the corner into Prince Consort Road, she was in reality breathlessly clambering over hummocks of ice; or that when in the quiet flat she put down a saucer of milk for Bijou the cat, that small useless creature had swelled for her into the largest kind of Weddell seal.

The silence remained unbroken, over Christmas and on into the new year of 1912. One morning in March, Mrs. Bell asked her to come to tea next day, the eighth of the month. It was a date that Emmie never afterwards forgot.

She said she was sorry; she had an engagement.

"Oh, what a pity. I'm expecting the Alderleys and I wanted you to know them. Can't you come in afterwards?"

"No, I'm afraid not," said Miss Verinder. "I'm going out of town to-morrow for the whole day."

"How annoying! Well then, the day after?"

"Yes, I shall be delighted."

"Good," said Mrs. Bell. "I shall put off the Alderleys. Hope you'll have an enjoyable day."

Miss Verinder's engagement was to visit a certain town in the Midlands, and truly she looked forward to it with no pleasurable anticipations, but rather with a sinking of the heart. She was going to Upperslade Park only because she felt that it was her duty to go there. The asylum authorities had sent a very troublesome letter to Dyke, and she as his representative must attend to it properly. They asked for a large increase of the annual payment, on the ground of the enhancement of cost of everything since the time long ago when the bargain was made. They said that a bargain was a bargain, and they "would not go back on it"; but they could not possibly continue to maintain Mrs. Dyke as well as in the past, giving her the greatest comfort, the best food, and the closest attendance, at a dead loss. If, then, it was impossible to adopt their suggestion, they would go on taking care of her quite adequately, but much less luxuriously. There was a possibility, of course, that her health would suffer from the deprivation of comforts to which she had grown accustomed. Farther, they pointed out that although the asylum was to some extent a public institution enjoying an endowment, they had no power to devote a penny of these funds to the benefit of the private paying patients.

Emmie travelled by the North-Western Railway, and it was one of those days with which March can surprise and disgust even those who remember the evil notoriety of the month. Dark skies, rain, and wind travelled with her all the way. She drove through the ugly town, seeing nothing but wet pavements and tramcars; through outskirts of factories and smoking chimneys, and on to a broad long road skirted on either side by villas and gardens. Her cabman stopped at an iron gateway in a high brick wall. This was Upperslade Park. A man came out of a lodge and spoke to her at the cab window. Then he unlocked the gate, and the cab drove in.

Beneath leafless dripping trees, across wide lawns, she saw the place itself vaguely, a mass of buildings with wet slate roofs and towers that stretched and sprawled gigantic. It was like a workhouse, a gaol, like anything sinister and dark that depresses the mind, at the mere sight of it, with painful associations and impotent regrets.

She was received by a doctor in an office that opened from a large and totally bare hall, and she said that she wished to have her interview with the patient before entering into any discussion of business matters.

"All right," said the doctor. "Yes, she'll have had her dinner"; and he called for an attendant. "I'll tell Dr. Wenham that you'd like a chat with him afterwards."

Emmie was ushered then to a waiting-room or parlour, where, they said, Mrs. Dyke would presently be sent to her. It was a lofty room, with high windows through which one had a view of the driving rain, the sodden lawns, and a broad smoke-stained gravel path. Some of those unreadable richly-bound books that used to be displayed years ago in hotel sitting-rooms lay on highly-polished circular tables. Instead of a fireplace there was a large white earthenware stove. Some horsehair and walnut chairs stood in a row against one wall, and on each side of the stove there was a straight-backed early-Victorian sofa covered with faded green rep.

Emmie waited for what seemed a long time. She was looking out of a window when the patient and a woman nurse entered the room.

"How do you do, Mrs. Dyke?" And they shook hands.

Immediately after this conventional greeting, Mrs. Dyke seated herself on one of the rep-covered sofas and laid upon her knees a largish Bible that she had been carrying under her arm. Emmie went and sat beside her on the sofa. She was a little middle-aged woman, dressed very neatly in a blue serge gown of no particular fashion; her hair, parted in the middle, was drawn to the back of the head and there rolled into a compact ball; her manner was precise and formal, and she spoke in measured tones, as if weighing her words and attaching importance, even finality, to some of them. It seemed to Emmie that only her eyes were insane. Their colour was brown, with little specks of amber, and they had the sort of shining intensity that is to be observed in the eyes of children during high fever. Then Emmie noticed that there was something strange about her hands. The left one, the one with the wedding ring, had marks of severe wounds on the knuckles, and it appeared to be stiffened. Emmie thought at once—with a queer feeling of already having heard of this—that it had been banged through a window pane during a fit of violence.

"Insufficient organisation and want of method is usually to blame," Mrs. Dyke was saying, in her precise way. She had begun talking as soon as she sat down, as if resuming a conversation with Emmie that had just been interrupted. "Then praying time is naturally forgotten. Prayers get omitted at the appointed moment, and one rarely if ever squares the account and gets the tally right. But in this book," and she softly patted the Bible, "all such things are noted. Did I say *this* book? Pardon me—in a very much larger book, kept by the recording angel, who neither sleeps nor accepts drugs to make him sleep."

The nurse was standing at a little distance, smiling good-naturedly; and she now asked Emmie if she should remain or go outside the door.

Emmie said she would like to be left alone with Mrs. Dyke.

"All right," said the nurse, and she nodded significantly. "I shall be just outside the door—and I'll leave it ajar. Call, if you want me, Miss Verinder."

"Nurse Gale," said Mrs. Dyke, quietly but authoritatively, "keep an eye on the clock. Don't let the proper moment slip by."

"Oh, do drop your rubbish," said the nurse, laughing good-humouredly, as she went out into the corridor.

Mrs. Dyke continued to speak of religious matters, until, in a pause, Emmie tried to change the subject.

"Now shall we talk a little about yourself? I want to know if you are comfortable here."

Mrs. Dyke, after a meditative silence, said, "No, I'm always hungry."

Emmie, shocked and pained, asked: "Don't they give you enough to eat?"

"Too much," said Mrs. Dyke mysteriously. "But I daren't eat it. They want to poison me"; and she added after another pause that, having defeated this plot for a considerable number of years, she hoped still to get the better of them.

Then it was as if of a sudden she had been moved by some strange glimmer of intelligence or intuition with regard to Emmie. She looked at her searchingly with a changed expression in the eyes, and shrinking from her on the sofa, spoke loudly. "Are you an enemy or a friend?"

"A friend," said Emmie.

"Of course she is," said the nurse briskly. At the sound of the raised voice she had immediately come into the room. "And a very kind friend, too—to have come all the way from London to see you."

"Who is it that has done me a great wrong?" said Mrs. Dyke, still scrutinising Emmie. "Aunt Janet told me. Is it you? Have you wronged me?"

"Oh, what stuff and nonsense," said the nurse. "Wronged you indeed! That's the silly way she goes on."

Emmie, perturbed but brave, got Nurse Gale to leave them alone once more. Then she took the injured hand and very gently held it between both her hands.

"Mrs. Dyke, don't fear me; don't suspect me of evil intentions. I mean well."

"So be it," said Mrs. Dyke, drawing nearer on the sofa and allowing her stiff cold hand to lie passive and imprisoned. "In the fullest confidence." That evanescent aspect of normality had gone; she looked at Emmie with mad eyes, and spoke in a tone that was vibratingly intense. "I want my husband—dead or alive. If he is dead, I wish the body embalmed and put in a glass case. If he is alive—send him to the devil and choke him. Look here. A stitch in time saves nine. I put my husband in the bed—a colossal bed that I had built to hold him. Room for five or six other people—of ordinary size. So it's quite absurd to pretend that there wasn't room in it for me. Very well. When I woke he wasn't there. I hunted for him high and low. He was under the bed laughing at me, or up the chimney. 'Be calm,' they all said. 'That is the watchword henceforth—Be calm.' 'Well, I am calm, Aunt Janet,' I said. 'Could anyone be calmer? I am quite reasonable and obeying orders. But I simply say I want my husband.'

"But not a bit—they dragged me into the carriage. They flogged those poor horses—" And suddenly her manner changed to a sort of exalted fervour. "Glory be to the Father, and to the Son, and to the Holy Ghost. Awake—throw off the chains. For on that day there shall be a great light shining from the high mountains. I am the resurrection and the life. Whoso believeth in Me—If you don't mind, I'll say my prayers. I forgot them again"; and she sank to her knees and laid her face upon the seat of the sofa. "Please ask them not to disturb me." And she began to murmur monotonously.

Miss Verinder waited a little while, and then went to the door and beckoned the nurse. She asked her not to disturb Mrs. Dyke.

"But she'll go on like that till midnight."

"As a favour to me. Give her a quarter of an hour." Emmie tipped the nurse. "You promise, don't you?"

Emmie, wrung with pity, stood at the door looking back into the room. That was the last sight and sound—the poor creature kneeling in the unchanged attitude and the toneless murmur of the prayer.

Miss Verinder during her interview with the head of the asylum was very business-like. She arranged to pay what was necessary now and whatever might be necessary in the future, should a further increase be required.

Thus oddly she began to contribute to the comfort and maintenance of the unhappy soul whose place in the outer world she had taken. She had not hesitated to answer the call. Nor did there for a moment pass through her mind even the vaguely formulated thought that she was taking every possible means to keep Mrs. Dyke alive, when the death of Mrs. Dyke might have relieved her of an embarrassment which, although it had grown slight, still existed.

She was very tired when she reached Euston about seven in the evening, and, since she was alone and without luggage, the porters neglected her in the scramble on the arrival platform, and she was unable to get a cab. Advised to try for one on the departure side, she went through a subway, up into the great hall among hurrying people; and suddenly heard two men saying words that made her heart leap and sent the blood rushing to her head. Hastily turning, she moved towards the bookstall; and there in bright strong light, she saw the same words that she had just heard. All round the front of the stall they were repeated in enormous lettering, on the bills of the evening papers; for to-night no other item of news was worth displaying—"South Pole Reached"; "Discovery of South Pole"; "South Pole."

In those few moments, while she bought a paper and opened it, she believed that it was her man. Her man—the blood beat at her temples, her lungs were full of fire, and a wild passionate joy possessed her. It seemed as if the station walls were falling, the lofty roof bursting open and floating away; vistas showed themselves, filled with vast pressing throngs; triumphant music swelled in her ears, and the voice of whole nations shouting echoed and re-echoed the loved name. Dyke, Dyke, Dyke! He had done it. Nothing could stop him, he had beaten them all—her man. She held the paper high to read the message.

It was Amundsen.

She refolded the paper and looked at the large clock above the door. Ten minutes past seven. When she got safely into her bedroom at the flat the pretty little Sèvres clock on the chimney-piece showed that it was now twenty minutes to eleven; and, except that she had been walking, she never knew why it had taken her so long to get home from Euston.

"What's the matter with you?" asked Louisa, helping to put her to bed. And she spoke again, in the grumblingly affectionate tone that trusted faithful old servants often permit to themselves. "You don't take proper care. You overdo it—and then you make yourself ill, like this."

"I am quite all right," said Emmie. "But I have had a rather agitating day"; and she turned her face to the wall.

CHAPTER XIV

IN due course the stories of the various expeditions arrived. Each had done nobly good work, but in the splendour of the achievement of Amundsen and Scott all else paled to insignificance. National sorrow for the death of its glorious representative made England at first almost impatient of listening to the voices of those who remained alive. Dyke, it seemed, had performed valuable services to science—he had cleared up a good deal; although behind the illustrious two, he had crossed their tracks, and he had also struck into the Japanese and the Germans. But who now could care about discoveries of mountain ranges, charting of coast-lines, or correction of surmises as to land and water? The praise he received in the British press was pitifully small; and one American paper was cruel enough to say that "Comic relief had been given to the tragic drama by the antics of elderly Dyke, who had been fooling around all the time like the clown of the Antarctic Circus."

He was in England during the summer of 1914; a man forgotten, not given a single newspaper interview, not once bidden to a public dinner. The birthday list of honours was announced in advance as including recognition of all who of late years had served the state usefully or ornamentally; yet neither in forecasts of those to be thus honoured nor in the list itself was the name of Dyke mentioned. He did not say a word to indicate that he even noticed this neglect. Emmie, however, thinking she understood what he must necessarily feel, took him away from London into the country, where he could no longer hear the noise and fuss about recognition and national gratitude.

They stayed at a farmhouse on Dartmoor, and they were very happy; but she had wronged him when she supposed that there was now any bitterness of disappointment in his mind. Alone with him between the sky and the heather, she became aware of a subtle inward change. He was never by any chance irritable. He was calmer, more dignified, whether he spoke of the past or the future.

Yes, as she knew, he had irrevocably lost what had been the hope of his life. Dimly she began to guess that it was the very completeness of the loss that, after the first shock, had brought a new tranquillity of spirit. The game with all its excitements was over, and he experienced a sensation of enforced rest. But truly it was something more and better than this. It was perhaps as near to obliteration of self as the most magnanimous men may reach when they see good work accomplished and measure the extent of the good work that still remains to be done.

She did not really understand until she heard him paying tribute to the memory of Captain Scott; and in her admiration and delight there went from her then the last twinges of the pain that had been caused by her own disappointment. This Anthony that she worshipped and reverenced for every word he said was a nobler and a bigger man than the Dyke who might have been—the Dyke who might have come home amid the plaudits of the world, to drop his laurel wreaths at her feet.

He was lying among the heather, his head resting on his elbow, and a hand playing with the tiny crimson bells; while Emmie with her holland parasol made a screen to keep the sun off them both. An injury to the head inflicted by a tumble on shipboard had left a slight deafness, and because of it he sometimes unconsciously spoke louder than was necessary. Now his voice rang out very strong in the light, pure air; but they were quite alone, and indeed Emmie would not have minded if all the world had heard what he said.

"You will see it written—it is being written already—that Scott's noble gallant heart was broken by his failure to get there first—that it was the sight of the Norwegian flag flying over the tent that really killed him, and not the hardship and fatigues. Emmie, that's a wicked thing to write. It's a wicked poor-spirited thing for anyone to believe. Scott was far, far above all that. You remember I wrote to him to say I was going?"

"Yes."

"Well, I never had an answer to my letter. I'm sure he sent me an answer, only it missed me. I never got it. Amundsen telegraphed to him too."

"Did Mr. Amundsen telegraph to him?" said Emmie, flushing. "I was not aware of it. I fear I—"

"Scott's answer would have been the same to both of us. I know it as surely as if I had heard him say it or had read it in his hand. Scott would have said, 'You or I or the other fellow, what does it matter, so that the thing is done?' I am so sure that, when I was rather down in the dumps about myself, I took it as a message from the dead, and it steadied me, Emmie—it steadied me at once. As soon as I can, I shall go back there to carry on the work. I consider it a sacred duty that we Englishmen owe to his memory; and while there's a kick left in me I'll be true to it. If I can't get anyone to trust me with the command, I'm ready to serve under anybody else—any Englishman—as second in command, if they think me good enough;—as third mate, or cook, if that's the best job they think I'm worth."

For some reason or other he was going to North China when the outbreak of war stopped him. The four-years agony had begun. He served first as a sailor, then as a soldier; and it may be said at once that Emmie was never less anxious about him than at this time, for, although the war of course had its risks, they seemed so much smaller than those of his ordinary life.

But she had anxieties of another kind—about money. Fortunately, with exploration at a standstill, she was given a breathing space; in fact, she was in such a mess financially that she could not anyhow have assisted the good cause by secret donations. For some while she had been gambling. There was no other word for it—and her very respectable stockbrokers used the word freely.

"My dear Miss Verinder," said Mr. Burnett, the stockbroker. "I must really warn you against this sort of thing. It is not investment at all; it is speculation. It is sheer gambling."

Ignoring his advice, she bought some oil shares and lost her money. She had been impelled to make this venture by a hint concerning the future of oil that had fallen casually from the lips of Anthony. Another philosophic reflection of his led her into copper; and this commodity also played her false.

"What did I tell you?" said Mr. Burnett. "Why *will* you jeopardise your position in this manner. It isn't as if you were not well-off."

Miss Verinder demurely replied that, although originally well-off, her expenses had increased, and for certain reasons she would be pleased to add to her income.

"Oh dear, oh dear," cried Mr. Burnett, almost writhing in his altruistic despair. "How often have I heard people like you say exactly what you have just said! In this very room, Miss Verinder—clients who really ought to know better"; and he gave her a severe little lecture on her recent speech, which, he said, was absolutely typical in the foolishness of its underlying ideas. Widows and spinsters, living out of the world, knowing nothing of business, with no man to control them, invariably talk in that silly manner before they fall into the most frightful pitfalls.

But this incorrigible spinster went on with her bad practices, buying this and that queer thing, and once, to the astonishment and annoyance of Mr. Burnett, securing a little profit. That made her worse than ever, and she soon went right down all among the pitfalls.

"Now what do you intend?" said the stockbroker, speaking very gravely of the catastrophe. "Are you going on, or are you going to stop?"

"I scarcely know how to answer," said Emmie, after a silence. "I have dropped so much that it almost seems as if I couldn't *afford* to stop."

Mr. Burnett writhed despairingly. Then nodding his head, and pointed his finger at her, he said, "Miss Verinder, may I tell you a story?"

"Oh, please do," said Emmie. "I should be so glad if you would."

"A client of ours was bitten with this mania—for mania it is; although, mind you, there was more excuse for her, because it was in peace-time, and not when the whole world has gone upside down and from day to day one cannot make the wildest guess as to what the value of anything will be to-morrow. She was not only a client but a relative—my own cousin—Adela Burnett—so I knew all her circumstances. She too was an old—Suffice it to say that she was the unmarried daughter of my uncle John, who had left her quite a good little property. Really a jolly little place in Sussex—perhaps three hundred acres, not more—and I don't know how many feet above the sea—*The Mount*, they called it—not that the name matters. But there she was—don't you see?—surrounded with comfort—quite able to play the lady bountiful in a small way—respected by everybody. The first doubtful order she brought to me—the very first, Miss Verinder"—and he shook his finger impressively—"I said, 'Adela, stop it.' But did she listen to me? No. It was nothing to her that my firm is one of the oldest in the City of London and that her own cousin is its senior partner. She would sooner act on the advice of the local doctor, or the curate, or the wife of the master of hounds, than listen to anything our firm could tell her. Well, I warned her for the second time. And what do you think she did? What, Miss Verinder, do you think she did?"

"I can't imagine," said Miss Verinder, feebly.

"She removed her business to another firm."

"Oh, what a shame!" said Emmie, with sympathetic indignation. "Oh, I think that was mean of her. I promise never to do anything like that."

Mr. Burnett writhed again. It seemed that Miss Verinder was missing the whole point of the story. As he hastened to explain, it was not the loss of his commission but the ruin of his cousin that he deplored.

"Yes, she ruined herself. And where is she now? Where, Miss Verinder, is she now?"

"Where is she, Mr. Burnett?"

"Living in one room—in a wretched road not far from Clapham Common. Pigging it in one single room—subsisting as best she may on a voluntary allowance made to her by—her blood relations"; and for a moment Mr.

Burnett looked modest, as though imploring that no compliments should be paid with regard to the generosity of Adela's family. Then he became more impressive than ever. "To this she has reduced herself by Stock Exchange gambling. Think of it. Here you have a delicately nurtured lady, no longer young, accustomed to be waited on by a highly-trained domestic staff, now cooking her own meals in a bed-sitting-room. One room, Miss Verinder. Just think of it."

Miss Verinder thought of it. The accommodation would be hopelessly inadequate in her case. Three rooms was the very least she could do with— one for herself, one for Louisa, and a spare one for Tony.

Should she go on or stop? With the cost of life leaping upward, with a humble invalid pensioner called Aunt Janet still on her hands, with further obligations to an unhappy prisoner in the midlands whose expenses had again risen, with an income tax threatening to absorb half her diminished dividends, she looked at the future in trepidation and saw it full of difficulties and dangers. She shook with dread as she thought that the time might come when she would not be able to maintain this beloved flat just as it had always been. Oh, for a *coup*, for a stroke of luck that would bring security! During long hours of feverish wakeful nights she asked herself that question. Should she go on or stop?

She went on. Perhaps it is impossible to consort for a number of years with an adventurer and yet not catch the adventurous spirit; or to force oneself to think boldly in regard to a few matters without acquiring the habit of bold thinking in regard to all matters. And her pulses had been stirred by what seemed to be another hint from her oracle. Although the submarine menace was as yet nothing more than a menace, Dyke foretold the ultimate scarcity of shipping; and writing to her from a mine-sweeper in the Mediterranean, he said he believed that anybody now could make a certain fortune by getting hold of ships, no matter how old they were, and selling them again later. "No doubt," he added, "a lot of artful dodgers are doing it already."

A fortnight after receiving this letter, Miss Verinder was established at the Adelphi Hotel, Liverpool. She had with her as travelling companion Mr. Cairns, late captain of the *Mercedaria*; and he and she, passing here and there unnoticed among the war crowd at the big hotel, were exceedingly busy— so busy, in fact, that she had no spare moments for reviving sentimental memories of her only previous visit to this great maritime city.

Cairns, although so much older now than then, still gave one the same impression of solidity and trustworthiness. He still loved his joke, but the years had made him a little asthmatic and his laughter was apt to end in a fit of coughing. Emmie, taking tender care of him, made him give another turn of the muffler round his neck as they rowed up the river one morning and met the sharp winter's breeze on their faces. In the rowboat with them were two shabby-looking elderly men that Cairns had produced after searching among his seafaring and commercial acquaintance. These queer associates were Mr. Gann, a tall, mournful man, and Mr. Rice, who was stout and jovial; and by Cairns's arrangement they and Emmie had entered into a little partnership for the purpose of buying an iron steamer named the *Marian II.*, this vessel being one of three that a panic-stricken owner desired to shuffle off his hands. To-day they were going over her for a last look round, before taking the plunge.

"I don't like being mixed up in business with a woman," Mr. Gann had said sadly, after his first introduction to Emmie's pale face, charming graceful manner, and fashionable London costume. "Always lands you in more than you bargained for."

"My experience too," said Rice.

But Cairns had reassured them, and, as it were, thrown them into Emmie's arms.

"My lads," said Cairns, "don't you worry about her being a woman. Take it from me, she has more grit than half a dozen ordinary men."

Now they were beginning to think that Cairns was right.

Truly she was wonderful, ducking under a wet hawser that caught one of her partners as the boat approached the wharf alongside which lay *Marian II.*, climbing slippery steps, and crossing a rickety gangway to get on board. Yet it would have been impossible to imagine anybody who appeared more incongruous to the business and the scene. In the bright cold sunshine the ship seemed a melancholy ruin, full of rust and grime, with the air of forlorn abandonment proper to a thing created for men's use but deserted by all mankind; and Emmie, dressed in her fur coat, with her veil neatly tied under her narrow chin and her chamois leather gloves being blackened by each bit of wood or metal that they touched, was like a lady going over a house that she thinks of taking for a term of years. As she walked about with Cairns and the caretaker, now on the rusting decks, now in the gloomy depths, she asked a multitude of questions, all charmingly unprofessional and yet all full of common-sense.

"Can the machinery be put in working order? Are there no leaks? Is she *sound*, Captain Cairns? I think nothing of appearances—no one cares now;—but is she really watertight and seaworthy?"

"Yes, miss," said Captain Cairns. "The three ships are all right. You may take my word for it."

"But this *is* the best of the three, isn't she?"

"Yes, I think she is. She's the best-looking, anyhow."

Nothing tired Miss Verinder, and she took nothing for granted. Although they were only concerned with the *Marian II.*, she insisted on being rowed up the river a little further, to see the other two steamers that belonged to the same owner. One of these, the *Osprey*, was out in the stream, black and forbidding, with the water racing past the faded paint beneath her load-line. The third one, the *Anemone*, was literally on the mud.

"Is her back broken?" asked Emmie.

"Good Lord, no," said Cairns. "She's right enough. Get her reconditioned, and no one would recognize her."

Mr. Gann and Mr. Rice were both suffering from the cold, and both weary of the excursion. At their request the boat was turned and the party made its way back to Liverpool.

Miss Verinder was more wonderful still at the final meeting with the timorous owner and his agent. They all sat round a carved oak table in a luxurious private sitting-room at the hotel; but, as the manager had not been able to allow them a fire, Miss Verinder retained her fur wraps and the gentlemen their overcoats. She took no part in a lengthy struggle with regard to the price they were to pay. Cairns and the agent grew heated in a contest of praise and disparagement. Mr. Gann became sadder and more sad. Mr. Rice at last told Mr. Jones, the owner, that to ask twelve thousand pounds for a rotten old tub like the *Marian II.* was high-seas piracy; and Mr. Jones said that unless this word was immediately withdrawn he would break off the negotiation. To show that he was in earnest, he pushed back his chair and put on his hat.

"Ladies present, kindly remember," said Cairns.

"Oh, please don't mind me," said Miss Verinder, sweetly. Then she went and rang an electric bell while the others continued to wrangle.

A waiter brought, not inopportunely, a tray with sandwiches, biscuits, whisky, soda water; and, at Miss Verinder's request, the gentlemen consented to take light refreshment.

Then she sat at the table again, and smiled deprecatingly at Mr. Jones.

"Will you allow me to speak quite frankly, Mr. Jones?"

Mr. Jones, with his mouth full of biscuit, signified assent; and Emmie startled him and her allies by a quiet but entirely damaging attack upon the *Marian II.* She said that if Mr. Jones was fond of *Marian II.* and wanted to keep her, there was no more to be said. But if he really wished to sell the ship, she must confess that the price he was asking struck her as quite ridiculous. She admitted that *Marian II.* was the best of the bunch. "Oh, yes, certainly. As to the other two—" and she gave a little shiver, as if upset by the mere recollection of their state. One of them, she went on demurely, was to her mind little better than a derelict, and the other one gave her an impression of being about to sink at its moorings.

"Nothing of the sort," said Mr. Jones.

"Well, that was my impression," said Emmie. "I don't profess to be an expert. But I can assure you, Mr. Jones, we are here to do business. We *want* to do business. Can't we make a deal of it, anyhow?"

"Not on your terms. I'd sooner go to government. You forget there's government always ready to buy."

"Oh, Mr. Jones!" said Emmie, as if shocked by this pretence. "I understand that the government officials have inspected your ships at least a dozen times."

"They may change their minds."

"Never. If the government had wanted them they would have taken them long ago."

"That's so," said Cairns, firmly.

"Nevertheless, Mr. Jones," said Emmie, resuming a gentle argumentative tone, "suppose we were to make you a sporting bid for the three vessels?"

"No, no," said her partners, astounded; and Mr. Cairns touched her arm and began to cough. But Miss Verinder quietly went on with it.

"A bird in the hand is worth two in the bush. Every day your ships are deteriorating in value. Now a *firm* offer, Mr. Jones. *Cash!* Twenty-seven thousand for the three!"

"No, no."

Mr. Gann and Mr. Rice both turned upon her; Captain Cairns, choking, took her by the arm and led her to the recess of the furthest window. There her partners expostulated with her, declaring that they could not plunge in this manner. One ship was all they were good for.

"Very well," she immediately replied; "then I'll do the other two ships on my own."

"And let us stand or fall on number one?"

"Yes, unless you think better of it. Don't, please, suppose I'm trying to squeeze you out. At equal stakes we were to have a third share, weren't we? Now divide it into twenty-sevenths. You see how simple it is, don't you, Captain Cairns? Instead of one-third each of these gentlemen will have four and a half twenty-sevenths—or whatever the correct fraction is. That can easily be settled at leisure. But, please, let me get back to Mr. Jones now. I want to strike while the iron's hot."

Then she returned to the table, and with a slightly ostentatious flourish produced a cheque book.

"Now, Mr. Jones, I'm ready to write you a cheque for a ten per cent. deposit. Is the deal going through?"

The deal went through. Perhaps because of his naturally timid nature, perhaps because of the obvious reluctance shown by the lady's partners, Mr. Jones said "Done."

"And done," Emmie echoed brightly.

She seemed mildly excited and no more. As she bowed to the company and withdrew, she still had that air of a well-preserved middle-aged lady conducting some little affair of ordinary well-to-do life—such as taking a furnished house or buying a motor-car.

"Well, I'm blowed," said Mr. Rice, when the vendor and his agent had in turn gone away. "She *is* a card, and no mistake. But confound her arithmetic. Here, give me a drop more whisky. I don't know whether I'm on my head or my heels."

"That's always the outcome, with a woman," said Mr. Gann sadly.

"Look here," said old Cairns enthusiastically. "You stick it through with her. For, take it from me—although I was staggered a moment—she's done a big thing, and she's *right*. It'll turn up trumps." And Mr. Cairns began to laugh and cough at the same time. "What gets me," he spluttered, "is the comic side of it. All our faces, when she said—firm offer! Didn't I tell you she had grit? Listen half a minute. As an example—in strict confidence—a thing she did when she was quite a girl!" And, splutteringly, he narrated how once when Miss Verinder was travelling with a friend in foreign parts, they were captured and set upon by bravos; "and just as it seemed they were going to be down and out, she whips in with a revolver and—"

At this moment Miss Verinder herself interrupted the narration by reappearing at the door.

"Captain Cairns, can I have one word with you?"

Outside in the corridor she spoke to him tremulously. She was very pale, and she betrayed a nervousness and agitation strangely out of character with the melodramatic heroine of the Captain's interrupted tale.

"Oh, Captain Cairns, do you think"—and after hesitating she used a phrase that on several occasions he had used himself—"do you think I have bitten off more than I can chew?"

"No," said Mr. Cairns stoutly. "You've done a good morning's work, and I, well, I'm proud of you."

The venture turned up trumps. After three months of painful hope and fear they sold *Marian II.* and got back all their money. Then four months later they sold the last ship and wound up the modest syndicate with a profit of fifty thousand pounds. Meanwhile, operating alone, Miss Verinder had bought and sold two larger vessels and thereby gained nearly seventy thousand pounds. Then she bought ordinary shares in shipping companies, received fabulous dividends, and got out again. Then, as a last flutter, returning to an old fancy, she did something really big in oil. And then, literally and metaphorically, she folded her hands.

Long before this time Mr. Burnett, the stockbroker, had ceased to talk to her about his cousin Adela, or to lecture her in general terms on the foolishness of lonely widows and spinsters. He understood now that in a world which has gone upside down wise saws and ancient instances are out of place. He hung upon her words, he treated her with the deference due to an important client; as his clerks would have said, "he wished he had half her complaint."

She herself was frightened by her success. In the inevitable reaction after so much nervous strain and excitement, she felt an almost superstitious fear of the flood of new capital that was rolling in upon her. She had dreaded poverty, and now it was as if some instinct warned her that she might have a greater cause to dread the consequences of wealth. She told no one anything about it—no, not even Tony. She guarded all knowledge of it as though it had been a guilty secret. She flushed and felt ashamed when affluent Mrs. Bell emitted groans under the war taxation, or when people spoke with scathing contempt of war profiteers. She longed for peace.

But the war went on. "Will it ever stop?" wrote Mr. Dyke from Endells. "It is very cruel to us old people."

Yes, it was cruel to old people. It shook them, it weakened them, it killed them. Emmie thought of this—when old Mr. Dyke fell ill again; and when her mother died. Mrs. Verinder, shrunk to half her past size, for many years had been an old lady in a Bath chair gliding slowly along the sea-shore at Brighton with her head a little on one side; sometimes speaking of Mr. Verinder as though he was still alive; rather doubtful about the identity of Emmeline when she visited her, and always prone to confound Margaret Pratt with Margaret's eldest daughter. Now she subsided in the chair, and vanished. Then one day Emmie's clever solicitor wrote to inform her that her pensioner, old Mrs. Kent, was no more.

Still the war went on. It had reached that point when one felt and said that civilization was doomed, that this planet was lapsing into irremediable chaos, and that the whole universe might crash to fire and dust. When Emmie read the obituary advertisements in *The Times*, she felt now that, young or middle-aged or old, the war spared none. As many people were dying of it here in England as out there at the front. Only that unfortunate life-sentence prisoner in the prison called Upperslade Park remained quite undisturbed by the war, and, as her guardians told Emmie, enjoyed excellent health.

It was unending. Dyke had served in the Mediterranean, in East Africa, in Mesopotamia; and all the while he had been getting more and more angry, first because the Germans took such a lot of beating, and, secondly, because, although they knew themselves beaten, they wouldn't own it. "Do you realize," he wrote now, "that I am fifty-eight? If it goes on much longer I shall be fit for nothing but to settle down with my old governor in Devonshire, and hoe potatoes and carry the muck pail to the pigs. Well, perhaps it might be the best thing that could happen to me. I should be happy there if my Emmie was with me."

Oh, if only that could come true! His Emmie sat dreaming with the letter in her hand, giving herself to the mental vision that his words had evoked— the tranquil perfect life down there in the house that she loved, the unbroken companionship; Anthony satisfied, with his roving spirit finally at rest; he and she as the squire and the squire's lady, being kind to everybody, doing a little good with her money.

Then she remembered the real Mrs. Anthony Dyke. Even if he consented to remain in England, that peaceful dual life would be as impossible as it had always been. And thinking again of all this money of hers and of the power that money brings, she grew cold and sad. It was as if already she knew that the money would draw her irresistibly to a supreme sacrifice.

CHAPTER XV

IT had come to an end; and that first Christmas after the Armistice was spent by Emmie at Endells.

On Christmas eve they had an afternoon party for the children of the village; with the curate, a schoolmistress, Mr. Sturgess the doctor, and a few friendly neighbours to assist Miss Verinder in entertaining the guests. She acted as hostess for old Mr. Dyke, and was indeed treated by all as though she had been a daughter of the house. Everybody there knew her and liked her.

After a plenteous tea she led the company to a hall or annexe that had been used as parish-room and general meeting-place in the days when the house was the rectory as well as the residence of the squire.

"Keep down here, please," said Emmie. "I have something to say to you all."

The children, surging into the big room, had made at once towards a screen of curtains at the far end; from behind which came the sound of whispers and busy movements, suggesting that some mystery was in preparation there. Now they obediently flocked back towards the wide hearth, and formed a dense half circle of eager shining faces.

"That's right. Thank you," said Emmie.

It was a pretty old-fashioned little scene; very pleasant, in its homelike character, to eyes that for so long had been gazing towards the smoke-clouds of foreign lands. The electric light burning gaily brought out the cheerful colours of flags, paper festoons, and holly berries, with which Miss Verinder had decorated the walls and ceiling beams. The boys, smooth and oily of pate, were still rather shy; the bigger girls, in their very best frocks, looked dignified but self-conscious; and some tiny little girls, large-eyed and fluffy-haired, like dolls, hopped excitedly and clapped their small hands. One of these animated dolls had attached herself to Miss Verinder, and moved with her while a chair was fetched from the wall and placed in the middle of the room.

Miss Verinder made Mr. Dyke sit on the chair. He had carried plates of cake, waiting on the children at their tea; he was so happy, and so much pleased with the party, that he would not spare his old legs or think for a moment of the danger of overtiring himself.

"Now," said Emmie, with her hand on the back of his chair, beginning the expected oration. At the same moment the curate went to the door, and stationed himself by the switches that controlled the electric light. In the background there was a delighted whispering and giggling of the servants. "Now, first I think you ought all to thank Mr. Dyke for giving us this treat."

"Thank you, sir. Thank you, sir." Prompted by the schoolmistress, a noisy chorus of thanks burst from the attentive audience.

"Don't thank me. Thank Miss Verinder," said old Dyke, beaming. "It's she who has taken the trouble."

"Thank you, miss. Thank you, miss."

Miss Verinder smiled, blushed, and then continued her speech. "I want to speak about Father Christmas. It is Father Christmas, is it not? who comes down the chimney at night and puts things in your stockings. It is he who goes into the dark woods and grubs up the lovely Christmas trees and drags them over the fields to the village. You like those trees of his, don't you? Yes, and Father Christmas carries a great sack over his shoulder full of toys to hang on the tree—or perhaps the sack is a bran *pie*! And he has a staff in his hand. You've seen heaps of pictures of him, haven't you? But you've never seen him himself. Oh, how nice it would be to see him! Perhaps"— and Miss Verinder smiled archly—"I say perhaps, he is really close by— only afraid to show himself. I believe he is afraid of the lights. He always moves about in the dark. Shall we turn down the lights?"

"No," cried the little child at Emmie's skirts, "don't turn down the lights. I'm more afraid of the dark zan Fazer Kissmuss is of anysing"; and she clung to Emmie.

"Only for a moment, dear. And you've got my hand. There, I'll keep my arm round you. Now you don't mind. Mr. Vincent!" And the curate by the switches received his signal.

The room was in darkness, except for the glow of the fire and certain gleams that came through those curtains. One could hear everybody breathing hard. Then out burst the lamp-light again, dazzling one.

"Oh, oh, oh!" The children, recoiling, stared in awe and ecstasy. Father Christmas was in their midst.

He was enormous, overwhelming; a magnificent apparition, all in red, with immense white beard, cotton-wool eyebrows, high reddened cheek-bones, and a great beak of a nose. He stalked towards the curtains, the enraptured children following him.

He drew the curtains wide open; and exhibited a most splendid Christmas tree as high as the ceiling covered with fairy lamps and glittering ornaments, its branches hanging low under the rich burden of toys. He began at once, under the direction of Miss Verinder, and aided by Hannah the housekeeper, to pluck the fruit of the tree and to distribute it.

And very soon the children lost their awe of Father Christmas, hustling him, pulling his skirts; thinking only of the toys, and saying, "Gi' me that gun—oh, please. Hi, mister, let me have this box o' dom'nos. I'm older than what she is.... Sir, play fair, sir. My turn, sir."

The little girl alone still believed in his supernatural attributes, still clung to Emmie and shrank from him.

"Send him away," she implored. "I don't like him."

"He's only a man, really," said Emmie.

"No, he isn't. He's Fazer Kissmus."

Then Emmie issued a command.

"Tony, pull off your beard."

Father Christmas, willingly obeying, divested himself of beard and cotton wool, and thus brought into view the rumpled grey hair and reddened cheeks of that well-known and respected local personage, Mr. Anthony Dyke.

He went away to get the paint off his face, and was soon back again, capering gaily about in an ordinary blue serge suit that could frighten nobody. He played with the boys, he danced with the girls, and he kissed Hannah under the mistletoe. Hannah, resisting, called him "Master Anthony," and told him that he ought to be ashamed of himself.

Shyness and constraint had long since left the young guests; after an orgy of cracker pulling and the loot of the tree, the party became a romp.

At dinner, when they talked it over, all agreed that it had been a great success. They had with them for dinner the curate and his wife and Mr. Sturgess, the doctor, kindly simple people of whom Emmie was fond. Comfort and peace presided over the friendly meal, and in this old room, sitting beside the old, old man, Emmie looked quite young. She could see Anthony casting glances of admiration at her throughout some very long anecdotes with which Mr. Sturgess always loved to refresh himself when he dined at Endells.

It was the first time that she and the younger Mr. Dyke had ever been here together. The war, destroying so much else, had blown away that delicacy which used to separate them during Anthony's visits to his home. All over the world—as Emmie thought, sending back glance for glance—this first Christmas of peace had reunited those who loved one another. Oh, what a peace it would have been if it could have brought with it a law that there were never again to be any more good-byes and partings! In the midst of the warmth, the joy, and the contentment, sadness coldly touched her heart.

They spent the evening in an oaken parlour, where the polished floor reflected things as in black water, and round mirrors gave one small framed pictures of the whole room and its occupants. Emmie, seated at the immensely ancient cottage piano, played pretty old-fashioned melodies that she used to play in Prince's Gate as a girl; the curate sang; and the doctor, regardless of the music, told more anecdotes. Old Mr. Dyke, although obviously tired, would not allow the guests to leave early. Then when they had at last said Good-night and he himself had gone upstairs to bed, Emmie and his son lingered, sitting together before the fire.

Hannah came in to tell them that it was nearly twelve o'clock and she, too, was retiring.

"I've seen to the shutters," she said severely. "But now can I trust you, Mr. Anthony, to turn out all the lights, and make sure the fires are safe in here and the dining-room?"

Mr. Anthony promised to do his duty.

Then Hannah turned to Emmie. "Your hot-water bottle, miss! Louisa took them up an hour ago or more."

"Thank you, Hannah."

Just before midnight Dyke went and undid some of Hannah's shutters in order to open the front door. He wrapped Emmie in one of his overcoats, and they stood side by side on the gravel outside the house. The night was fine and still with the stars very bright in a dark but cloudless sky. Above the black mass of the ilex trees they could see vaguely the church tower.

"Will the bells be rung?" asked Dyke.

"Oh, no," said Emmie. "That's the new year, you're thinking of. They don't ring in Christmas."

Presently the church clock began to strike the midnight hour. Dyke counted the strokes, and when the twelfth came he stooped and kissed her forehead.

"A happy Christmas, Emmie."

"And to you, Tony dear. But *are* you happy, I wonder?"

"As happy as several birds"; and he put his arm round her waist. "How could I be otherwise?"

They came in again, and barred the door. As she went upstairs she looked down at him and saw him looking up at her, his face all gay and bright.

"Good-night. Good-night."

From the landing at the top of the stairs she looked down again, and saw his whole attitude relax. His head drooped, his shoulders hunched themselves; and with his hands in his pockets he went slowly back to the room they had left.

In spite of his eighty-five years and bodily weakness, the old man got up long before daylight and attended the early celebration. They went with him to the ordinary service at eleven o'clock; he leaning on Emmie's arm as they walked through the garden, and Anthony solemnly following. Anthony looked fantastic as well as solemn in an astounding top-hat and a skimpy black coat, at least thirty years old, that he had unearthed from a wardrobe of his dressing-room. At certain of the sacred words that they presently heard Emmie turned her eyes towards him with unutterable love in them, and she felt a great tenderness and compassion as she held the hymn-book for his father and listened to his thin quavering voice as he piped the sweet Christmas songs; but during most of the service there was rather a far-away look on her face. She was in truth thinking very deeply.

The sun shone on them as they came out of the church, and after all the greetings and interchange of good wishes with neighbours on the church path, Emmie and the old man went to sit in that small walled garden that they both loved. It was really warm here. The sunshine made strong dark shadows as well as bright patches among the stalks and branches of the flowerless borders. Mr. Dyke said he could feel it on his hands. She had wrapped a rug about his knees and under his feet; and she turned up his coat collar and muffled his neck with a big scarf. Here, sitting comfortably in the sun and out of the wind, they had a long serious talk.

Anthony, having cast his ancient finery and clothed himself in a loose Norfolk jacket, was on the little terrace and busily engaged with the man who worked the electric light engine. They were mending a kitchen box for the cook. Anthony, thoroughly enjoying this carpenter's job, only ceased his chat with the electrician to fling a cheery word from time to time towards the sunlit pair on the bench down below.

"Mr. Dyke, we must face the fact," Emmie was saying. "He is *not* happy. It is all pretence. Ever since he came home he has been trying hard not to let me see what he feels. But I can see always—knowing him as I do. He wants to go back there once more."

"Go back there!" And she saw the sun-warmed hands begin to shake upon the shrunken knees. "Not—not to the Antarctic?"

Emmie nodded her head. "Yes, he can't deceive me. It is more than a wish—he feels that it is a duty."

"Oh, no, he has other duties."

"But he feels that this duty is sacred—a sort of charge upon him. Unless he fulfils it—or at least tries to fulfil it—I know that he will never be really happy or at peace."

"Oh, no"; and the poor weak hands were shaking very visibly. "He mustn't do it. He is too old."

"Well, that is what I want us to consider carefully," Emmie said in a quiet business-like tone. "*Is* he too old? He is fifty-nine. That of course would be too old for any one else; but then he is not like other men."

Instinctively they both looked upward to the terrace. Anthony, after stooping over the box, was standing at his fullest height and stretching his arms. He stooped a little even now, as if the weight of his big shoulders was not quite so easy to carry as it had once been; but his head and neck were magnificent, with the sunlight on the thick grey hair, the strong bold features, and the close-cropped beard. If you judged him merely by the indefinable impression that age itself produces, and at this slight distance, you would have said that he was a man of forty-five whose hair had become prematurely grey.

"He says himself that he feels all right—ready for anything. He is not conscious of the smallest diminution of his strength. Mr. Dyke, his health *is* wonderful"; and as Emmie said this, she was like a sensible unemotional mother speaking about a grown-up son. "Have you noticed, too, that he is less deaf—scarcely deaf at all?" And Emmie's tone changed, and her face grew sad. "No, I'm afraid we can't in justice rule him out on the score of health and age. Three or four years hence perhaps. But not now."

She looked up to the terrace again, and then spoke with great firmness. "Of course, if he does go, it must be his very last voyage. There must be no nonsense about that. He must solemnly promise us both."

"Emmie, he musn't go"; and the old fellow put a trembling hand on her arm. "Don't encourage him."

"You shall advise me, dear Mr. Dyke. But let me tell you everything first."

"Yes; but he mustn't go," he said eagerly. "He *can't* go—if you consider it. We needn't frighten ourselves. You and I may think he is still young—not yet too old for it. But he'll never persuade other people to think that. He'll never get anyone to give him another chance."

"Ah!" Emmie winced, and moved her hands swiftly. "When I remember what has always happened, I believe that he will go anyhow—*somehow*. The real question is the *how*."

Then she told Mr. Dyke all about her money.

"My dear Emmie, what an astounding affair! It sounds like a fairy tale."

"I wish it was a fairy tale," she said; "but unfortunately it is sober truth. No, I ought not to say that. It's very wrong of me. Only, now you see the position in which I am placed—with all this money—so much more than I want or could possibly use—with this *power* in my hands. Oh, Mr. Dyke, what am I to do? You see what I mean? He need not persuade other people to give him a last chance. I myself can give it to him."

"Oh, no, he would never take money from you."

"I think he would. I'm *sure* he would. To begin with, I could show him that I should still have enough, even after he'd taken all that he needed—all that he needed to do things in such a style as has never been possible to him till now. So there would be no question of leaving me impoverished."

"That would make no difference. He'd never consent."

"Dear Mr. Dyke, you may trust my instinct. He would refuse at first; then, after a little while, he would consent. He is eating his heart out—so that the mere personal temptation would be more than he could resist. But, beyond that, there is this idea of his that has grown so very strong. He feels that it is not only his own duty, but the duty of all English people to complete the work of that brave Englishman who gave his life down there to bring honour to England. He would feel that I could not spend my money in a better way—We'll say no more for a moment."

Anthony was coming down the brick steps from the terrace.

"I am having a confidential talk with your father," said Miss Verinder, in the primly crushing manner of a grown-up person interrupted by a troublesome child.

"Secrets, what?" He laughed, and went away again.

"That is the position," she said quietly, when he was back on the terrace and busy with his carpentering. "I feel that I *ought* to help him to his heart's desire—I feel now that I have no choice really. But I want you to advise me—to tell me what you think."

"He oughtn't to go," said Mr. Dyke, once more touching, her arm. "It wouldn't be fair to you."

"Oh, *me!*" Her lips twitched, and for a moment her whole face seemed to be distorted, as if with a spasm of violent pain. "I mustn't be allowed to count for a moment. No, leave me out of it altogether."

"Emmie, dear. Emmie"; and Mr. Dyke kept his hand on her arm.

Quite quietly, without any convulsive movements of her throat or bosom, she had begun to cry. The tears flooded her eyes, rolled down her pale cheeks, and she looked through them towards the terrace while remaining absolutely still; so that no one up there who saw her rigid attitude could possibly guess what was happening. Presently, with furtive caution, she got out a handkerchief and dried her eyes.

"I have tried not to be selfish, dear Mr. Dyke—all along, you know. I claim no merit. For how could I be selfish, in such a case? Indeed his work and what the world says of him make up my life really. They *are* my life—that is, my pride and my joy. But one is weak. He himself is so much to me—so dreadfully much—so incredibly more, it always seems, than at the very beginning, when I was young—when we were both young. This time, it seems as if his going will be almost more than I can bear. It will seem like suicide if I bring it about, myself. In these last weeks I have been struggling with myself. Oh, dear Mr. Dyke, I have struggled in such terrible agony. I want him with me so dreadfully, and yet he wants to go away from me. And if he could do something big and splendid to wind up his career—well, I could never, never forgive myself if it was I who prevented him."

Mr. Dyke was greatly perturbed.

"I said I wasn't selfish," she went on. "It is selfish, what I am doing now, pushing my burden on to you. But you are always so brave and so wise— and there is no one else that I can ask for counsel. Besides, you are his father. You have the right to be consulted—to decide. A much greater right than I—everybody would say."

"If he goes," said the old man, in a low voice, "I shall never see him again."

"Oh, no, don't say that—don't think it."

"I know it. I shan't be here to welcome him home."

Then Emmie shed tears again, and again succeeded in wiping them away without being observed by either of the box-menders on the terrace.

"We have to bear in mind, dear Mr. Dyke, that it is very doubtful if either of us could prevent him from going sooner or later. And certainly, if he is to go, it should be as soon as possible. But my most dreadful thought is this. If I don't give him the money he will start as usual, poorly equipped— he will be defeated by difficulties and turn back. Yet that perhaps may mean his eventual safety. Whereas, if he is really well fitted out for once, if he has every possible chance in his favour, then he will be able to push right on—and that may mean his doom. It's a horrible responsibility. Think of it. It would be *I* who had sent him to his death."

"No." Old Mr. Dyke raised himself on the bench and looked at her. "No, Emmie, no," he said; and in his dim eyes she saw a faint flash that made him seem like a thin small ghost of Anthony. "No. If he is to do it, let him go for the big prize. Give him his full chance and don't count the risks. Let it be all or nothing."

She jumped up from the bench and stood looking down at him.

"I can't decide," he said. "You only can do that. The sacrifice will be yours, not mine. Only, as I venture to say, don't spoil it by half measures."

Then she called to Anthony. She had decided.

Anthony Dyke refused her offer, and stood firm to his refusal for two days. Then on the morning of the third day he accepted. He was of course enraptured. He echoed Mr. Dyke's words in saying that her acquisition of comparative wealth was like a fairy tale.

"All this time I never knew I had a fairy godmother—I who have groused about my bad luck. At the fateful moment you suddenly show the shining crown on your dear head, you wave your magic wand, you give me the enchanted key. Oh, Emmie, what can I say? What can I ever do?"

"You can come back safe and sound," said Emmie. "And you can give me your sacred word that you'll never leave me again."

Kissing her with frenzied warmth, he made his vow. But this first ecstasy being over, he began at once to treat her with a new and strange deference. He said that she had become the patron and chieftain of the glorious project.

"Oh, yes, it's your show entirely. You trust me, you honour me with your instructions."

Before that evening everything was settled between them. She made a proviso that he should arrange for a relief expedition to follow after him at a certain date. This must be an integral part of the plan. And the whole thing must be organised in its smallest details before he himself started southward. She was very firm as to all this.

He agreed, saying she was quite right and he knew the very man to put in command of the relief ship—"Twining, who was my navigating officer in 1910."

He bowed deferentially to her decision with regard to other matters; saying, "Oh, your word would be law. You would be the real head, and I shouldn't forget it." Then he smiled. "You pay the piper, Emmie, and you call the tune."

She said that there must be no departure from plans.

"No, no. But you'd give me a free hand when I get down there?"

"Yes, but only within specified limits."

"Very good," he said humbly.

Then, in reply to her questions, he said he intended to follow Captain Scott's line. The fact that it was sixty miles longer than the other one was of no consequence. He proposed to go to America and get his ship and everything else there.

"The Yanks will pull themselves together quicker than we can hope to do over here. America's the shop to buy our little bag of tricks in." And he had a bright idea. "I say, old J. L. Porter might be willing to stand some of the racket. I let him down rather badly last time; but he's a real sportsman— and I may as well try to touch him again."

"No," said Miss Verinder firmly. "This is *my* show. And I don't want anybody else in it."

CHAPTER XVI

THE year 1919 was, for Miss Verinder, quiet and uneventful. Magnificently equipped by that country which even peace had not robbed of its power to hustle, with such a splendid command as he had never till now enjoyed, Dyke reached Australian waters some time in the autumn. He called his ship *The Follower*, and in it he sailed away towards the darkness and the silence. About March, 1920, he must have taken up his winter quarters; and his southern advance would begin, "according to plan," with the opening of the Antarctic summer.

Early in September of 1920 the relief ship, named the *Heather Bell*, was to sail from Hobart; and thence onward Miss Verinder might begin to count the months. She could scarcely expect to receive any news till the end of January or the beginning of February, 1921; and until then there should be no real grounds for anxiety. Or, in other and more accurate words, the fate of the new expedition could not possibly be known until the new year.

Now, in this month of September of 1920, Miss Verinder received a cablegram from Hobart, saying that the *Heather Bell* and Twining had duly departed.

The message arrived in the morning, and after luncheon she amused herself by taking out and rearranging the contents of some of the little drawers in her bureau. She grew slower and more dreamy as the tidying process continued, because the sight and touch of these small treasured odds and ends carried her further and further backward into the past. Here, for instance, in a drawer by themselves, lay some pressed flowers. They had been picked in that courtyard garden behind the hotel at Buenos Ayres. Here was a photograph of the Mendoza valley. Here were a long white glove that she had worn at Mrs. Clutton's party on the night of their first meeting, the Hurlingham polo programme, one of her tiny lace handkerchiefs—things that Dyke had stolen from her, kissed a thousand times, and then after many years given back to her for safe keeping. She was lost in a gentle meditation when Louisa opened the door and announced an expected visitor.

"It's so kind of you to let me come," said Mildred Parker.

"I won't be a minute," said Miss Verinder putting the things away.

"I am not in the least hurry," said Mildred, with a nervous gasp.

Mildred was that pretty child to whom Miss Verinder had spoken kindly years ago, when the little thing was sitting on a pony outside her father's front door in Ennismore Gardens. Now she had become a glowing young woman. Daintily dressed in the prevailing gossamer style, with mauve-coloured stockings and grey *suède* shoes, with bare neck and looping curls, she had such brightness of attire and such a youthful bloom of complexion that, as she settled herself on Miss Verinder's sofa, she made the whole room and everything in it seem dull and faded.

"A place for everything and everything in its place," murmured Miss Verinder, flicking some dust from the treasures that had set her dreaming. "These are souvenirs—with only a sentimental value."

Then, after some conversation about the flat, she shut the last drawer and brought a chair to the sofa near Mildred.

"Now," she said, "I am all attention."

Mildred appeared to be overcome by shyness.

Emmie had divined that the girl had some small trouble of which she wanted to speak. But she was entirely unprepared for the actual fact. Knowing that the young Parkers were rather too fond of cards, even games of chance, she had guessed that Mildred had burned her fingers at poker and needed a small loan to tide over an awkward blank till her dress allowance became due. Seeing Mildred's confusion, she patted and caressed her, and further to encourage her firmly promised help.

But it was far more than a game of cards. It was love. Love, as Mildred confessed, had come upon her "like a thunder-clap."

Emmie drew in her breath, and sighed.

Mildred told the tale of how she had fallen desperately in love with a man; how her parents forbade her to love him, forbade her to meet him, forbade her to think of him; how Mr. Parker threatened her, bullied her, vowing he would take steps to separate her irrevocably from her beloved; and how, in consequence, that once comfortable house in Ennismore Gardens had become a place of torment and pain.

Listening, Emmie was stirred profoundly. As though the accident of those retrospective thoughts in which she had just been indulging had rendered her abnormally sensitive to emotion, she thrilled and quivered to the shock of Mildred's words. It seemed to her that she was hearing her own story from the lips of this innocent girl. It seemed to her that these obdurate parents who threatened and ordered and could not understand were Mr. and Mrs. Verinder, not Mr. and Mrs. Parker; that it was all in the past, not in the present; that the end of the story had been reached ages and ages ago, when the daughter walked out of the home that had become a prison-house and never came back again.

But Mildred was going on; assuring Emmie that she was very much in earnest. "It's no silliness—or infatuation, as mother says.... It's the real thing."

Then soon she said words so startling that they almost took Emmie's breath away.

"I would have you to know also that the man I've fallen in love with is very famous."

Emmie sat staring at her intently. The thing had become fantastic, like a dream.

"But it's nothing to do with his fame that has made me love him. Of course I don't mean to say that I wasn't influenced by all that. You know what I mean?"

Miss Verinder was breathing fast and moving her hands restlessly.

Then her whole heart melted in tenderness as the girl, analysing sensations, hopes, and fears, described the love itself. Yes, this was the real thing. This was the first wonder and glory of sudden overpowering love, of the love that takes possession and for ever changes its victim, and yet itself will never change. Miss Verinder recognized it and acknowledged it. All the bliss and torture that Mildred told of had been felt by herself a quarter of a century ago. And she was feeling it now while she listened; the years had gone; she and Mildred were both of them love-sick girls.

"You *are* so kind," said Mildred presently, conscious of the flood of sympathy that was pouring forth to sustain and float her onward in her romantic narration.

After a little while Miss Verinder asked who the famous man was.

"But *who* is he, Mildred? You haven't told me yet."

Mildred, smiling proudly, said he was Alwyn Beckett, the actor. At the moment he was not actually before the public, but he was understudying the two big parts in a play called *Five Old Men and a Dog*.

"Ah, yes."

An actor; a young actor! Miss Verinder at once became inwardly calm again. The young man was not of course truly famous; but some sort of unsubstantial fame he hoped to attain one day. Even the opposition of the parents was not solidly founded; they merely objected to the young man because they did not like his shadowy precarious profession, and because, further, they doubted if he would do any good in it. All her sympathy remained, but while Mildred went on talking about the attitude of Mr. and Mrs. Parker she ceased to listen with attention. This was a trifling commonplace little business when compared with the real romances, the big romances of life.

But then Mildred banged out something that gave her a violent shock; indeed it shook her to her very foundations. She gasped, and uttered a faint cry.

Mildred had been saying that she felt desperate, and inclined to run away.

"And marry him without your parents' consent?" Emmie had said dreamily.

"Or *not* marry him," said Mildred.

"Mildred!" said Emmie, uttering that little cry. "What *do* you mean?"

"Well, what I mean is that if they're so damned old-fashioned, I don't see why they shouldn't stew in their own gravy—at least for a bit. Don't you see? When they find I'm gone in that way, if they're really genuine in their feelings, it will be the regular mid-Victorian business. The lost child—our daughter gone to perdition. Get her married now to the scoundrel that has lured her away. Make her an honest woman at any price"; and Mildred laughed.

Although still preserving an aspect of calmness, Miss Verinder was greatly agitated by this monstrous suggestion. Again for a moment or two it seemed as if all this was a dream—or as if the innocent modern girl was mocking her with a travesty of her own ancient experience. How could she really contemplate taking so disastrous a step? With no insurmountable obstacle between her and her lover, with no irremovable cause to prevent their being eventually united, how could the child speak thus of throwing away her good name and bringing disgrace on all her family? It was fantastic.

"You and I must talk very seriously," said Miss Verinder, with firmness.

Louisa brought in tea, and throughout the meal Emmie was thinking. She watched little flashing palpitating Mildred with critical eyes but affectionate purpose. Mildred was only a child still, a child who must be prevented from doing idiotic things in a fit of childish impatience.

She thought of the thousand reasons why, even when driven inexorably, one should not do what she herself had done—the remorse for the pain one has caused to others, the crushing sense of being outlawed and proscribed, the slights, the humiliations, the meek submissions that one is called upon to suffer. Every year of her life, every day of it, had shown her another valid reason why any ordinary person should regret an act such as hers. She herself had never regretted. She had not been able to regret—because the thing had been done for Anthony Dyke. She had neither flinched nor faltered. But a pretty little flower like this would wither under the first frosty breath of disgrace. She would soon be sorry that passion had whirled her into a reckless deed. "She is not like me," thought Emmie, with a faint smile. "She is not by nature the sort of desperate character that sticks at nothing."

Besides, for Mildred to make a hash of her reputation would be a quite meaningless disaster. There was not the slightest necessity for heroic measures. If, as Emmie hoped and was inclined to believe, the young man proved worthy of such a nice girl, then those silly Parkers must be made to consent. And again Emmie felt a melting tenderness and sympathy for this pretty innocent little soul and her love-dream. It must, and it should end prettily; with music, marriage bells, and sunshine; with the bride all in white coming up the aisle upon her father's arm, to be given to her sweetheart amidst blessings and rejoicings.

So she offered Mildred—as has been already related—some very old-fashioned advice; and finally made her promise to abandon any idea of acting rashly and improperly. Mildred tore at her gloves, pouted, and shed tears beneath the chilling wisdom. But she in her turn was startled by one or two things that Miss Verinder said to her. Especially something quite inexplicable about no women ever ceasing to wait and to hope, moved her and made her wonder.

Miss Verinder was very severe about running away with people before you married them, no matter for what motive the unsanctified bolt might be undertaken.

"Believe me," she said, sitting beside Mildred on the sofa, and with an arm round her waist, "it is only the very strongest characters that can brave public opinion.... Yes, I am sure—to go right through with anything of that kind immense self-control, really almost an iron nerve is required. And," she added, "you musn't think I don't know what I'm talking about."

She said much more, but one reflection touched her young friend with greater strength than all the rest. "You have to think of your Alwyn and the effect it might produce on him." While she said it her voice grew soft and her eyes had an unexpected radiance. She was thinking of Anthony Dyke. "Perhaps," she went on, "it is only the very finest natures that can accept—ah—this particular kind of surrender or self-sacrifice from a woman, and still hold her quite as high in their minds as they did before—ah—the surrender occurred."

"There, Mildred dear," she concluded cheerfully, "I am going to help you for all I'm worth. And you are going to be wise. And don't—I beg you— forget this. I have my reasons for all I have said."

Mildred went away wondering what on earth could be Miss Verinder's reasons for one or two of the things said.

Emmie had promised to give help in this simple love affair, but truly it helped her. It charmed her and absorbed her, filling several of those months which had to be counted before definite news could come.

In accordance with her unfailing habit, she was writing every fortnight to Dyke, although all her letters must lie waiting at Hobart unseen by him for a long time; and she told him now about Mildred and Alwyn.

"...The young man was brought for me to see this afternoon, and I must say I was very much pleased with him. He is distinctly handsome with a good presence and a strong but yet musical voice, so that as far as one can judge he is well fitted for his profession. He is *very* ambitious, and I liked that too. But with the ambition he has that kind of helplessness that seems almost universal in this generation—as though they were not really grown-up, but like children trust everything to other people and make no effort themselves. He is only twenty-eight, and he left Cambridge, where he did a lot of amateur acting, in order to join one of the new battalions. He was twice wounded and mentioned in despatches. That is as it should be.

"I cannot tell you how much touched I was by Mildred's little proprietorial, almost *motherly* airs with him; so keenly anxious that he should make a favourable impression, and using all her innocent arts to show him off at his very best. O love, love! Is there anything else that is beautiful in the world beyond love, and the manifold effects that love produces? I assure you, dear Tony, that as I watched them, the past came right back again. It was not those two; it was you and I. It was the year 1895, and not the date that I have put at the top of this paper.

"To-morrow I am to see the brother. And after that I shall tackle the father."

Hubert Parker, Mildred's brother, had been at Cambridge with Alwyn Beckett; and he assured Miss Verinder that there was not a better fellow alive. He thoroughly approved of him as a husband for his sister. Alwyn, to his mind, was good enough for a royal princess. "I agree with Mildrings," he said, smiling. "I think the governor has been bitten by a mad dog."

Then Miss Verinder had Alwyn before her again. He sat in the middle of the sofa, facing her, while "Mildrings" stood behind him, put her hand on his shoulder, and told him not to interrupt but to listen, when he burst out with vows and protestations.

He was protesting because Miss Verinder said that there must be no more of these clandestine meetings. They were not fair to Mildred.

"Yes, but whose fault is that? If her people won't allow me to the house, if they treat me like a pick-pocket, if they—"

"Alwyn," said Mildred, with severity, "Miss Verinder is speaking."

Miss Verinder insisted on an assurance that the unlicensed interviews should cease forthwith, and it was given to her by both of them. She said it was necessary that she should feel on this firm ground before she approached Mr. Parker. She for her part promised to begin the attack at once.

"Mildred, could you get me asked to dinner informally?"

"*Rather*," said Mildred. "They'll jump for joy. They're getting rather stuffy because you always refuse."

"Then the sooner the better, dear"; and Miss Verinder smiled. "Don't be surprised if I seem a little artful—or even disingenuous. I think, just at first, I'll not say I know anything of your partiality for Mr. Beckett—or for Alwyn, if I may take the liberty of calling him by his Christian name."

"I should adore it," said Alwyn.

"It is all Christian names nowadays, isn't it?" and Emmie smiled again. "Then, as I say, I'll open a masked gambit for Mr. Parker to play to. You see, the great thing is to get him accustomed to the idea."

"What a dear funny old bird she is," said Alwyn, when he and Mildred were outside the door in Oratory Gardens.

"She's divinely kind," said Mildred with enthusiasm.

As she had predicted, there was no difficulty in regard to Miss Verinder's invitation.

"But are you sure she won't expect a regular party?" asked Mr. Parker.

"No," said Mildred, "she hates a crowd."

Only the family and two very old friends were present therefore, so that the conversation was general. Mr. Parker, who had recently flown to Paris and back in the day, just for fun, gave an account of his interesting experience, to which Miss Verinder listened with great attention.

Then, towards the end of dinner, she herself talking freely, told them about a very nice young man that she had met. She praised him for his modesty as well as his niceness. Quite the best type of the clever and yet not conceited youth of the present day! She understood that he had done very well in the war; and he was now on the stage—Mr. Alwyn Beckett. "By the way—I believe he said he knew you all, or some of you."

Only Hubert Parker spoke. "One of my best pals," said Hubert.

Mildred was staring at the tablecloth and crumbling the remains of a small roll; Mrs. Parker seemed to have been troubled with a twinge of toothache or rheumatism; Mr. Parker, suddenly red in the face, opened his mouth and, shutting it, breathed hard through his nose. It was one of those brief silences that appear to be long. Then Mr. Parker, recovering himself, asked Miss Verinder if she had read Mr. Locke's delightful new novel.

Following the modern fashion, the ladies and the men left the dinner-table together. Upstairs, in the double drawing-room, Hubert and Mildred soon set in action a monstrous gramophone of the latest model and most expensive style, both of them giggling hysterically while they assisted each other with the record and the mechanism.

"How can you be so ridiculous?" asked Mrs. Parker, speaking to them from the front room. "What *is* the joke?"

Mildred chokingly replied that there was no joke. It was only the gramophone that made them laugh. In fact, they had been overcome by the calm unscrupulousness of Miss Verinder's dinner gambit.

The two old friends liked the gramophone; and directly its crackling music began to fill both rooms, Mr. Parker seated himself beside Miss Verinder and explained to her that she had unwittingly touched on a very sore spot when she mentioned the name of "that young man." Mrs. Parker came and sat on the other side of her, and both together told her all about Mildred's absurd infatuation. Then they begged her aid in bringing Mildred to her senses.

"That is really why I have put you *au courong*," said Mr. Parker. "You have influence with her. A word in season from you may have great effect."

"Not if her affections are really engaged," said Miss Verinder, with one of her deprecating smiles.

"Oh, no, nonsense," said Mr. Parker, in a tone more irritable than any that he had ever employed when addressing this honoured guest. "Don't let's have any idiotic sentimentality, which would merely encourage her. We have never fostered anything of that sort, and Mildred, up to now, has seemed to have her head screwed on all right. I regard this as a passing craze—due, in great measure, to all this preposterous exaltation of the stage. Upon my word, the illustrated papers make me positively sick nowadays—nothing but photographs of actors and actresses. Miss So-and-So at play. Mr. What's-his-name on the golf links. Theatrical stars on the Riviera!"

A few days later Miss Verinder called upon the Parkers, and reported that, having sounded Mildred, she had no doubt that the young lady's feelings for the young gentleman were of a deep and serious character.

Mr. Parker immediately said that if he accepted even half the substance of this report, the time had come to put his foot down, and he would either send or take Mildred into exile on the continent.

"I'll keep her out of his way, until she has got over it."

An absorbingly interesting discussion ensued on the ethics of parental authority. Miss Verinder advised them not to attempt strong measures with Mildred; above all, not to put restrictions on her liberty here in London or to banish her from her native land.

"I really don't think," she said meekly, "that parents have the right to act in so violent a manner. And I am quite sure, Mr. Parker, that it never pays. As to banishment—well, you know, absence is apt to make the heart grow fonder; and if it comes to giving a young girl peremptory orders to stop being in love with somebody that she *is* in love with, I do really think it must always strengthen her resolve. She feels then that she is being unjustly dealt with. After all, it is *her* destiny that is at stake. She may love and respect her parents, she may regret—oh, yes, she may most bitterly regret giving them pain"—Miss Verinder's voice faltered, and she showed other signs of slight emotion—"but she *cannot* renounce the whole happiness of her life, because other people—even her father and mother—order her to do so. She herself *must* decide. Believe me, Mr. Parker, it isn't right to use more than argument and persuasion. Force is quite out of the question."

Mr. Parker walked about the room fuming; and it must be confessed that as Miss Verinder observed his frowning brows, his heightened colour, and the querulous lines at each side of his mouth, she felt for a moment an almost mischievous amusement in recognizing how little human nature had changed in the last quarter of a century. This room was very different from any room of that old house in Prince's Gate, and yet the atmosphere was the same. Emmie glanced round at the very modern decorations chosen by Mrs. Parker with so much pride and pleasure. This was the boudoir of Mrs. Parker, and she called it the Chinese parlour. The ceiling was red; the walls were black, with panels filled not by pale-limbed nymphs of Leighton or Burne-Jones, but by golden sprawling dragons, iridescent fishes, and impossible silver trees; the furniture, instead of being heavy and splendid, was light and fantastic. Mrs. Parker had no comfortable *pouf* to sit upon. But here was Mr. Parker, who believed himself to be full of liberal-mindedness and advanced up-to-date philosophy, who belonged to the Automobile Club and went by aeroplane to Paris, holding in all essentials the views that fathers held twenty-five years ago, or a hundred years before that. He believed not only that he had the right to dispose of his daughter's heart, but that if he showed firmness he would vindicate this right. He was more old-fashioned, further behind his times, than poor Mr. Verinder had been. He walked to and fro and gloured at Emmie.

"I hope," she said, "that you will not think me impertinent in venturing to give my advice."

"Oh, no. Oh, certainly not. I am very much obliged." Mr. Parker stopped walking, made some swallowing movements in his throat, and then spoke impressively but urbanely. "There are very few people for whose judgment I have so much respect as for yours, Miss Verinder. The position and the influence that you have rightly secured among all who have the honour of your acquaintance is, if I may say so, principally due to the very high standard of, ah, manners as well as morals that you rightly stand out for. I know that you do not tolerate subversive ideas. Otherwise, frankly, I could not have listened to you with the patience that I hope I have shown. But I cannot, I will not agree that it is my duty to allow a child of mine to make a fool of herself if I can prevent it. And what staggers me, what beats me altogether"—and he looked from Miss Verinder to his wife, with a suddenly helpless, baffled expression—"what utterly amazes me is the *change* in Mildred. I ask myself what has happened to her. Is she bewitched? It is not *like* her to oppose any headstrong wish of hers to the considered opinion of those older and presumably wiser. Up till now she has seemed to lean on one's advice, to crave for it. It is not as if she had ever been a disobedient girl. Why, good gracious, no. We used to say from the very beginning, even when she was quite a tiny little thing, 'There is never any trouble with Mildred.' One just told her what to do, and she seemed to take a positive pleasure in doing it. Is not that so?"

Miss Verinder said no more then; but before many days had passed she returned to the attack. Endeavouring to accustom Mr. Parker's mind to the idea, she extracted a statement of his objections to Alwyn as a possible son-in-law.

Mr. Parker said emphatically that Alwyn was not good enough for Mildred, and when gently invited to consider if in saying this he did not mean that Alwyn was not good enough for him, Mr. Parker, he owned that, beyond his distaste for the young man's profession—which he did not admit really to be a profession—Alwyn was a nobody in it. He had not "arrived."

"Oh, but he *will* arrive," said Miss Verinder. "You know, he had now been put on to play one of the principal parts in that delightful comedy *Five Old Men and a Dog*. I went to see it, and I was much struck by his performance. I really think, Mr. Parker, that you and Mrs. Parker ought to go yourselves."

"We shall do nothing of the sort," said Mr. Parker.

Then, very soon after this, Miss Verinder attacked in real earnest. She said that the result of arbitrarily closing the house doors against Mr. Beckett had been that these young people met each other in a furtive undignified fashion outside the doors; that they had promised Miss Verinder to discontinue the practice, and that they had discontinued it; but that she thought they would certainly withdraw the promise unless Mr. Parker adopted a more conciliatory attitude towards them.

"And then, Mr. Parker, who can say what may follow? At Mildred's age one is naturally impulsive, fearless, disinclined to attach importance to what is said or thought. She might so easily get herself talked about. And we don't want that, do we?"

Mr. Parker did not want it. The thought of gossip about his family life made him pale and grave.

The embargo on Alwyn Beckett was raised, and he was given entry to the house and access to Miss Parker in the capacity of her brother's friend and an ordinary visitor. But it was to be strictly understood by both of them that the possibility of an engagement was neither contemplated nor countenanced. This settlement was reached late one evening, and early next morning Mildred ran across the Brompton Road to thank and hug her dearest Emmeline.

And now Miss Verinder tackled Alwyn. One afternoon when Mildred had brought him to tea at the flat, she told him plainly that in her opinion he ought to bestir himself, and snatch success rather than wait for it.

"If I may say so, Alwyn, I think it is up to you to prove what you're made of."

Alwyn looked rather blank beneath this assault.

"Oh, but he *has* proved it already," said Mildred, at once defending the beloved object. "He tries so hard; he never spares himself. You forget how he played Mercutio at that charity matinée and what splendid notices he had."

"Yes," said Miss Verinder, "but he must go on doing it. He must strike while the iron's hot. He must impress himself upon the public."

Alwyn, interposing, dolefully said that this was just what he would do if he got a chance.

"What would give you chance?"

"A play and a backer."

"Well then, find them," said Miss Verinder.

"My dear good lady," said Alwyn, in a tone of distinct fretfulness. "That's easily said. But if you knew a little more about the theatrical—"

"Ally," said Mildred reprovingly.

"I mean to say, don't you know—"

"Ally," said Mildred again. "That's enough."

His classical features assumed a haughty expression, that olive complexion which Mildred thought the most beautiful thing in the universe perceptibly darkened; and he passed a hand backward from the brow, over his sleek, well-brushed hair, with a grand gesture.

"It's all mighty fine," he said to Mildred afterwards; "but I'm not accustomed to be talked to like that. And I don't like it."

Mildred was severe with him. "How can you be so abjectly ungrateful— after all she has done for us?"

But Miss Verinder intended to do much more for them yet.

Alwyn was a really good fellow, but, as is not infrequently the case with young actors who have not quite realised their full ambition, he was just a little touchy. Perhaps the slight prick given to him by Miss Verinder was really a valuable stimulus. At any rate, Mildred found that he had begun to bustle about with a new activity.

Next time he saw Miss Verinder he told her, rather grandly, that he had found a play. It was a very remarkable piece of work by that well-known author Mr. Sherwood—real literature, with psychology in it as well as characterisation, and, what was more to the point, a thumping fine part for Alwyn.

"Been the rounds for the last three years, but I don't mind that," said Alwyn, even more grandly. "That doesn't frighten me. It was too good for them to spot it. The same thing happened to *Ring a Ring o' Roses*"; and he named several other plays that, after being rejected by everybody, had made huge successes. "Of course, it's high-brow. But I want high-brow."

"Yes," said Mildred. "He *must* have high-brow stuff. I always tell him so."

Then, quite magnificently, he said he intended to approach Leahurst about it. He thought he might very likely be able to make an arrangement with Leahurst, who was always on the lookout for a really good thing. And he looked hard at Miss Verinder, to observe the effect produced upon her by this august name.

Unfortunately, she had never till now heard the name. Alwyn was compelled to tell her all about Mr. Leahurst; and, doing so, he abandoned his magnificent air and spoke with profound reverence of this Napoleon of the theatrical world. Mr. Leahurst owned or controlled half a dozen theatres, he sometimes had nine or ten shows going at the same time, his interests were so wide that you never got to the end of them. Wherever you saw a real success you might ask if he wasn't somehow in it. He had a marvellous *flair*. It was said, too, that why he scarcely ever went wrong, was because by his own business talent he could make a success of anything.

"Oh, then do approach him without delay," said Miss Verinder eagerly. "See Mr. Leahurst at once; and come straight here and tell me the result. I shall be longing to hear."

"Darling Emmeline," said Mildred, "you *are* so kind. It *is* such a support to both of us."

Not next day, but a few days later, she returned with an unusually excited Alwyn. The great Mr. Leahurst had considered his proposals in a most favourable spirit. He had, indeed, said that he might be inclined to do something with Sherwood's play if Alwyn had behind him somebody willing to come into it with a few thousand pounds.

"Tell him you have somebody," said Miss Verinder.

At first they did not understand what she meant, and then they said they could not possibly trade upon her kindness and generosity. Oh, no, it would be too mean and selfish to risk her money just for their advancement in life! But she was determined; and after yielding to her persuasion, Mildred fell into a sort of ecstasy of gratitude during which she uttered anything but compliments with regard to Mr. Parker.

"When I compare you with my own father, Oh, darling Emmeline, I do feel such contempt for him. It is *he* not *you*, who should be doing this for Ally. But would he have risked one penny-piece? No, not if we had crawled round Ennismore Gardens on our knees. If you only heard him grunting and grousing about the super-tax, when we all know he doesn't spend half his income. Oh, how I hate misers!"

"Mildred dear, don't. It is wrong to speak of your father like that. He only wishes you good."

For the young people there ensued a time of wild excitement; and Miss Verinder took her share in it, allowing herself to throb or shiver sympathetically with all their hopes and fears. Mr. Leahurst, like other potentates, proved difficult; one day, Alwyn said, he was shilly-shallying, another day blowing hot and cold, another day coldly doubtful. Then Alwyn gave a Sunday dinner-party at a restaurant, in order to clinch matters with Mr. Leahurst.

He implored Emmie to make herself very agreeable to Mr. Leahurst, and afterwards Mildred thanked her for her agreeableness.

Alwyn gave her many warnings and cautions. He said that Mr. Leahurst was not the kind of person that she had been accustomed to meet socially. How should he put it? "Not Eton and Christ Church and all that." He also said that she would certainly, sooner or later, hear tales about Mr. Leahurst. He added that Mr. Leahurst was fifty years of age or more. This, he concluded, was merely "preparing" her for Mr. Leahurst.

But no preparation could really prepare one for Mr. Leahurst. He was the most melancholy man that she had ever seen; in comparison, the sadness of her late partner, Mr. Gann, was gaiety. He did not speak to her or anybody else. He ate his food in profound silence and did not even appear to observe that there was a band playing. He smoked cigarettes, and had a dreadful trick with his lips, to get rid of bits of paper or tobacco—a perfectly dry manœuvre, but it sounded as if he was spitting. His cigarette case, Emmie noticed, seemed as big as a small dressing-bag; but he had no matches.

"Waiter," he said; and they all jumped because his speaking suddenly was such a surprise. "Waiter, 'blige me with match. Forgot my box. Thanks"; and he lit a cigarette. This was in the middle of the meal.

They talked of the play, and still he said nothing.

Then when the party broke up and he was going, Alwyn spoke to him about it.

"Oh, that's all right," said Mr. Leahurst. "Yes, I'll tell 'em to get on with it to-morrer."

"How can I thank you?" said Alwyn, humbly yet exultantly.

Mr. Leahurst made that ugly sound and lit another cigarette.

"You'd better come down to the theater to-morrer mornin'."

"Which theatre, Mr. Leahurst?"

"Duke o' Kent's. I've got it on my hands till Feb. eight"; and going, he turned. "If your thing *should* catch on, I'd have to shift yer."

The venture was fairly started now, and the excitement grew more febrile. There was difficulty in finding a good title for the play. The author's title had at once been condemned as "tripe." He had called his work *The Secret Disaster of Mr. Eadenwell*, meaning to convey thereby the main point of the fable—the disaster being that the imagined Eadenwell's private code of ethics would not work and was abandoned by him without anyone else knowing what had happened. Alwyn was in favour of calling it *The Danger Signal*; but somebody reported that Mr. Leahurst said the sort of titles he preferred were *Love Wins*, *For Two Bright Eyes*, and *The Tempting Sex*. Of course they might not use these, since they were titles of existing plays.

Miss Verinder and Mildred were present at the rehearsals. They could not keep away. This new strange aspect of a playhouse fascinated them—the darkness of the house itself, the seats all shrouded in white wrappers, with somewhere high up near the invisible roof a slanting beam of real daylight; and the stage brilliantly lit yet not like the stage, with odd bits of scenery, and the players unpainted, in commonplace every-day costume.

Miss Verinder sat in a stall next the central gangway, well back from the empty orchestra, and Mildred sat with her, except when for a few minutes Alwyn was unoccupied and could come down through the pass-door from the stage.

Mildred said, "We mustn't expect it to shape all at once."

That of course was what they were doing with the play, shaping it. Everyone was busy—the producer, Alwyn himself, Mr. Russell the stage-manager, a Mr. Holmdale with vaguely defined interests in Leahurst productions, and some one else who appeared spasmodically; so many that it seemed as if anybody who came in from the street took a hand at it. They chopped and changed little bits of dialogue, they transposed scenes, they worked hard.

People playing minor characters came down and clustered watching, and there were a few hangers-on in stalls at ends of rows; amongst them a rather miserable-looking man, very nervous and shy, who bowed and smiled at everybody. No one took any notice of him. A silly affected young woman playing the lady's-maid did not know her words, and with a shrill giggle said they were not worth learning. Miss Millbank, who played the principal female part, complained bitterly of the things she was made to say—"things that I simply don't *feel*."

"As if she could feel anything," said Alwyn scornfully to his backer. "She is made of wood."

At last Mr. Leahurst appeared. One morning he came mysteriously from the refreshment bar beyond the pit, walked down the central gangway to the orchestra, and returned again, with his hands clasped behind his back. Everyone fell silent, no one moved; it was as if waves of awe had begun to flow through stagnant air. One had a paralysing sensation of expectancy, one's heart gave heavy beats.

"Don't take any notice of me," he said, walking backwards and forwards.

The rehearsal proceeded.

Then almost at once he recognized Miss Verinder in her stall next the gangway. He stopped short in his walk and nodded to her.

"Well, how goes it?"

"I really think it is shaping all right," said Emmie.

"No, I don't mean the play. Yourself."

"Oh, very well, thank you."

"Move up one, will yer?"

And sitting down beside her, he remained silent, tapping himself on the chest and sides, and feeling in overcoat pockets. Then he called loudly.

Mr. Russell, the stage-manager, came down the stage at a run. The rehearsal stopped and there was dead silence. Mr. Russell leaned forward over the footlights, his face all lit up and a hand shading his eyes, as he peered into the dark auditorium and spoke anxiously.

"Was that you calling me, Mr. Leahurst?"

"Yes," said Mr. Leahurst. "Much ablige if you'll give me box o' matches. Somehow seem to have forgot mine." And he told the people on the stage to go on. "I beg your pardon. I didn't mean t'interrupt you. Very sorry, I'm sure"; and the rehearsal was resumed. "Ta, Mr. Russell."

He lit his cigarette, and turning a shoulder to the stage, talked to Emmie; while Mildred and Alwyn, spellbound, watched them from the corner by the pass-door.

"We shall lose our money over this," he said.

"Oh, I hope not, Mr. Leahurst."

"I wonder what made a lady like you take up such a game as this. Ever done it before?"

"No."

"No, so I thought. I was suprise when Beckett made me known to you. You follow what I mean? Nothing of the theatre about you. Just lending him a helping hand? Well, you're rich, I s'pose—so it won't hurt you either way."

"Oh, but my wish is that it'll be a great success."

"You won't get your wish," He nodded his head mournfully, and, removing his cigarette from his made that trumpeting sound with his lips.

"Don't you like the play, Mr. Leahurst?"

"I dunno anything about the play. It's Greek to me. But I know this: wrong season to produce anything important—stop-gap—no names in the cast"; and he made a movement with his thumb, as of Romans at a gladiatorial arena. "Right down—unless by a fluke Beckett draws the women."

Emmie pleaded against his dismal prognostications.

"Oh, please don't make me down-hearted."

"All right," said Mr. Leahurst, suddenly smiling at her. "I don't want to crab it. Cert'nly not—since you're so keen on it."

It was quite extraordinary, the effect of that first smile. Emmie, who had been afraid of him because everybody else was afraid of him, had now the weak instinctive gratification that even the best people feel when the ogre unbends to them. But it was more than that. She had a swift convincing impression of innate simplicity and good nature. Whatever the tales about him, there was something in this common illiterate man that you could not dismiss lightly. She asked herself what. Power, strength of purpose, or the concealed kindliness?

And without prelude he began to talk of himself—with a candour so astounding that Emmie was rendered breathless. He talked about himself as if there was no possible question that it was a subject of entrancing interest to all the world; also as if he had detected in Emmie complete sympathy, together with burning curiosity, and it would not be fair to keep back any detail from her. "Plays are all the same to me. The best of 'em—I mean what the critics call the best—give me an headache. I never went inside a theatre till I was thirty-seven—an' never wanted to. It was my late wife dragged me into the business. That's all it is to me—a business. She was an actress by profession—and a cat domestically. I gave way for peace and quiet. A lot o' money I spent on her, giving her shows in this and that, ramming her down the public's throat, and o'ny makin' 'em sick, all said and done. But I was loyal. I went on with it—till they came and told me I'd lost her. I don't want to say anything unkind about her. But that's why you see me here. I've learnt it now—and I wash one hand with the other. The people bred up in the business are like a pack o' children. Natchrally, any real business man does what he likes with 'em. Miss Verinder, tell me if you can: What is the charm of the theatre?" He did not wait for an answer. "Vanity, I suppose, at the bottom of it. Same with your friend Beckett! I dunno. I like Beckett because he's a manly young feller; not like these long-haired—" And to indicate the class of actors to whom he objected, he used a technical term that Emmie did not understand.

Then the producer spoke to him from the stage.

"Mr. Leahurst, a point has arisen."

"Go ahead, Mr. Hope," he said. "I leave it to you"; and turning his shoulder a little more, he went on talking to Miss Verinder.

"Take to-day—fine bright winter day. Fancy us coming stuffing in here, all in the dark. I don't play outdoor games myself. But surely to goodness one might take a 'bus and have a walk up Highgate way; or run down to Brighton in the *Southern Belle* and take a toddle on the pier. You like open air, don't you?"

"Yes, I do."

"Yes, I thought so. And cold water too, unless I'm mistaken. I mean, a tub every morning."

Emmie was embarrassed.

"So do I," said Mr. Leahurst, quite heartily. "Keeps one fresh—and young. I mean, young for one's age"; and he looked at her with another friendly smile. Then he became very confidential again. "But since I lost my wife I feel myself in a precarious situation. No proper home. Then, of course, these girls take advantage of me."

"What girls?" asked Miss Verinder innocently.

"Oh, I s'pose they've told you. I'm too easy. I dropped a lot o' money in putting up that revue—bother the name—for Mamie Cockayne. First one, then another"; and he made a gesture, waving the stump of his cigarette comprehensively.

While he brought out a fresh cigarette Mildred came sidling along their row of stalls, and whispered to Emmie.

"Tell him how bad we think Miss Millbank."

"Who's she?" asked Mr. Leahurst, when Mildred had sidled away again. "Understudy?"

"No, a friend of mine. Miss Parker."

"Nice ladylike person! S'pose she is a lady, if it comes to that—being a friend of yours."

Emmie presently conveyed to him the damaging opinion about Miss Millbank. "She doesn't seem to understand anything, and she is so hard—really as hard as nails."

"Is that so?" said Mr. Leahurst, glancing round at the stage.

"Of course, it's a Marian D'Arcy part; and Mr. Beckett says if you imagine Miss D'Arcy doing it, you see at once how dreadfully Miss Millbank falls short."

But just then a wrangle had broken out upon the stage and people were calling for Mr. Leahurst.

Miss Millbank declared that again she could not say such stuff.

"Well, cut it out," said somebody. "Or let her speak that line of Mrs. Harcourt's," said somebody else. "What's that bit of Beckett's?" said the producer. "'I wonder if women ever think that'—How does it go on? Give Miss Millbank the whole of that bit, Beckett. You can spare it. No, that won't do either. She can't say your line about poverty and her trouser pockets." And they all of them talked at the same time.

Then all at once they appealed to the unhappy-looking man in the corner of the stalls. "Is Mr. Sherwood there? I say. Can't you help us with a suggestion? Can't you write in some lines here? You must have some opinion. Sherwood!"

And Emmie with a shock of surprise understood that he was the author.

He said, "I think you're spoiling it."

They all turned against him in furious indignation. "Did you hear what he said? Mr. Leahurst, did you hear him? Here are we toiling for him—grinding our hearts out for him—and he says—Oh, great Scott, that puts the lid on everything."

Mr. Leahurst went down to the orchestra, and said, "There's no need for us to lose our tempers."

"Certainly not," said the producer, crimson with passionate wrath.

Miss Millbank, stepping forward, said she had never been asked to speak such tommy-rot. Stuff that she could not feel!

"My dear," said Mr. Leahurst, mildly and forlornly, "you are doing your best. It's not your fault if you don't quite hit it off."

This made Miss Millbank exceedingly angry. "What?" she said. "Don't you like my reading?"

"So far as I have been able to ascertain," said Mr. Leahurst, "it's a Marian D'Arcy part. Well, you aren't Marian, are you?"

The rehearsal went on again, and as Mr. Leahurst presently returned to his seat beside Emmie, she took the opportunity of telling him that, in the opinion of herself and Alwyn, the girl engaged for the lady's-maid was even worse than Miss Millbank.

Mr. Leahurst blinked his eyelids and very slowly lit a cigarette.

"Think so?" he said, after a pause.

"I do really."

"I dessay you're right."

This Miss Yates, the incompetent and affected lady's-maid, came into the stalls after a little while and talked to him in a friendly chaffing manner. But he did not stay; he got up and went off to some sacred managerial room. The young lady flopped down in a row of stalls at a little distance from Emmie, and occupied herself with a tiny gold-framed mirror and a lip-stick. She had brought with her also a large cardboard hat-box. Holding the box on high, she called to a pallid young man.

"Bertie! Be a dear, and put this in Mr. Leahurst's car will you? And ask some one to let me know as soon as he's ready."

Both Mildred and Alwyn had been as much amazed as rejoiced on observing Emmie's success with Mr. Leahurst. When the rehearsal was over, each of them in turn thanked her and congratulated her; and Emmie, pleased with herself without being vainglorious, told Alwyn how she had plainly said that Miss Millbank was no good.

"Splendid!" cried Alwyn.

"And I told him, too, that the other girl, Miss Yates, was no good either."

Alwyn nearly fainted.

"Oh, ye gods! Never mind. It can't be helped. Come along. Let's get some food."

Soon now people in this theatre and other theatres were asking a question. What was the matter with Mr. Leahurst? Unheard of things were happening. He regularly attended rehearsals, and telephoned for news when he was prevented from attending. He was showing the most active interest in what was, after all, merely a stop-gap or fill-in show.

He used to occupy the same stall, smoking, and talking to Miss Verinder. He told her that it rested him to sit like this and not be bothered for an hour or so. He said, too, in this connection, that she herself was "reposeful."

"Have you ever been told that? I s'pose you have, often."

At Emmie's suggestion he got the author to sit with them and explain the drift of the play.

"Very clever, I'm sure," said Mr. Leahurst, not in the least understanding.

Then one day, smiling, he asked her: "Have you set your heart on this being a success?"

"Yes, I *have*, Mr. Leahurst," said Emmie earnestly. "You don't know how much hangs on it."

"Well, we must see what can be done."

He tilted his hat to the back of his head, walked down to the orchestra, and clapped his hands loudly. Everything stopped, everybody was turned to stone.

"Mr. Hope," he said, addressing the producer, "I'm not satisfied."

"I am very sorry, Mr. Leahurst," said the producer, in a dreadfully crestfallen way. "I have done my best."

"The thing's not going to be ready by the tenth," said Mr. Leahurst. "We'll postpone production for a fortnight. Tell 'em there'll be no call to-morrer."

Then, in the most autocratic, Napoleonic style, he scrapped the company. Miss Millbank was whirled away in tears to join a tour at Scarborough. Marian D'Arcy, ruthlessly torn out of another play, replaced her. Two of the best-known and highest-priced character actors of Europe came in, and excellent trustworthy veterans were engaged to support them in minutely small rôles.

He had turned it into a star cast, and the word went round that no expense counted. Mr. Leahurst had set his heart on a success. He came every day "to put ginger" into the fresh producer; he consulted Alwyn about his press campaign; and already the advance paragraphing was tremendous. The new scenery, lighting, and dresses were described as likely to touch a high water mark of combined taste and costliness.

Everything was new, then—even the lady's-maid.

"I acted on your hint," he said to Emmie. "I gave her her marching papers—in all directions, I mean. Does that satisfy you?"

The excitement grew painful as the date of the postponed first night drew near. Now the bills were up, outside the theatre. The morning that they arrived, Mr. Leahurst invited Emmie into a little office near the stage door and showed her one of them pinned to the wall. She and Mildred studied it with rapture.

"Sole Lessee, Mr. Crauford. By arrangement with Mr. Somebody-else, Mr. Leahurst presents"—then came the gigantic lettering—"Marian D'Arcy and Alwyn Beckett in *The Danger Signal*."

"That's more like it, eh?" said Mr. Leahurst.

On the night itself Emmie and Mildred sat hidden in the recesses of a private box and trembled for forty-seven minutes—that is to say, till the end of the first act. After that they glowed and squeezed each other's hands ecstatically. The act-drop had been raised about thirteen times, of which the first four raisings were certainly in accord with the desire of the audience. After the second act there could not linger even a faint doubt. The thing was unquestionably a triumphant success.

During this interval Mr. Leahurst came into the box and trumpeted. Dressed in his ordinary costume of dark grey frock-coat and trousers, he kept well at the back of the box so as not to be seen by the public, and he carefully concealed a lighted cigarette with the palm of his hand in order that nobody should detect that he was breaking the Lord Chamberlain's regulations.

The ladies rose and went to welcome him with radiant faces.

"Oh, isn't it glorious?" cried Mildred, going close to him, and in her joy seeming as if she wished to throw her arms round his neck and embrace him. "But we owe it all to you, Mr. Leahurst—every little bit of it. Alwyn knows that well. And Miss Verinder knows."

"Don't mention it," said Mr. Leahurst, turning to go. "Bother. Burnt my hand!"

Next morning the entire press confirmed the triumph. "Acclaimed, without one dissentient note—" as the advertisements said.

Once again, then, a venture of the hardened gambler had turned up trumps. The money of Miss Verinder was not only safe, she had made the fortune of Mr. Alwyn Beckett. There were interviews with him; his photograph was everywhere—Mr. Beckett on the links, Mr. Beckett snapped in entering the stage door, Mr. Beckett hailing a taxi-cab. Full-page portraits of him enriched the illustrated weeklies. And he was nice in his new eminence, not swollen-headed, but modest and gay, just a manly young fellow, who, although so ambitious, valued success most of all because it brought him nearer to the lady of his love.

Mr. Leahurst, celebrating the affair in a manner quite alien to his custom, gave a magnificent supper-party at one of the most fashionable hotels, and Miss Verinder was placed at his side, in the place of honour. There were speeches, but he himself made none.

"Funny thing," he said to Emmie, during supper, "how things falls out. To-day I finally got rid of my late wife."

Emmie started, and looked at him in astonishment.

"What *do* you mean? Hasn't Mrs. Leahurst been dead a long time?"

"No, she's still alive. O'ny decree nisi. Made absolute to-day."

After supper he asked her if she was satisfied, and he added that he had given the supper on her account. "I have done everything that I have done for the purpose of pleasing you."

Emmie murmured a very faint acknowledgment; and, driving home, she felt grievously worried in the midst of her elation. Like others, she asked herself what was the matter with Mr. Leahurst.

But unlike the case of all the others, it was reserved to her to find out. He came to the flat next day and asked her to marry him.

She noticed how very smart he was directly he came in, also that he was not smoking; and she was at once fluttered by the complimentary things he said about the flat.

"Refinement—good taste"; and he glanced sadly here and there. "That's what you can't buy with money. This is a home, Miss Verinder."

Then he went straight ahead. "As things go, I'm a rich man. I don't ask you what you've got, and I don't want to know. You can keep yerself in clothes, p'raps? Leave it at that. I'm not after your money, Miss Verinder. It's you I want—and the refined comfortable home you can give me. Inferior by birth and education, granted. But if I can anyways rise to your level, I mean to try."

She stopped him as soon as she could, and said the dreadful conventional things that used to be said on such occasions during the middle period of Queen Victoria's reign—to the effect that she was honoured by his wish, although she could not respond to it, that she esteemed and respected him, and hoped he might later on be willing to accept her friendship in lieu of what he had asked for. But, curiously enough, the things were true. As Miss Millbank would have put it, she *felt* them. Through it all there was shining forth at her the unmistakable fact. This Mr. Leahurst was in truth a simple kindly creature—a good sort.

"Well, it's a hideous disappointment. I don't mind saying I thought the sympathy was mutual. There, it's my own fault. I told you, not accustomed to the ways of ladies—I mean, real ladies—and I mistook your polite manners."

"I am so sorry," said Emmie, in the same mid-Victorian style.

"Well, there's an end of it." He picked up his silk hat and malacca cane, which he had brought into the room just as he had always seen done by people on the stage. "I bear no malice," and he moved towards the door. Then he turned. "Would you mind telling me if there's anybody else."

"Mr. Leahurst," said Emmie, blushing hotly, "I don't think you ought to ask me that."

"Then one question. You're not hankering after that young Beckett?"

Emmie was indignant. "Mr. Leahurst! He is going to marry Miss Parker."

"That wouldn't need to make any difference. There's such funny arrangements nowadays."

"Mr. Leahurst!"

"All right." He spoke in a tone of invincible melancholy. "I'm very helpless. I s'pose I shall fall back into the clutches of those girls."

"Oh, no!" Emmie, scarcely knowing what she said, implored him not to do that. As in a dream, she heard herself assuring him that he was meant for a better fate; urging him to be true to himself, to keep his eyes on the heights, to climb upward from the slough.

He went out dolefully; giving Louisa a couple of one-pound notes, in order to prove that he bore no malice.

These excitements and interludes had helped her through some of the months that she had been counting. The pretty little love story was going to have a happy ending. Mildred, bouncing in and out of the flat, brimmed over with joy as she described the changed attitude of her parents. Indeed, if the dear child could have heard Mr. Parker talking at his club, she might have been able to report a more rapid progress in the desired direction. For certainly Mr. Parker showed at the club that he was at least accustoming himself to the idea of theatrical connections.

"That young man Alwyn Beckett," said Mr. Parker, "has been offered two hundred pounds a week to go to America. Till recently I had no notion that actors' salaries ever reached such a figure."

"Oh, that's nothing," said a well-informed member of the club; "nothing at all, compared with what they get for film-acting."

"Is that so? Well, Beckett is on the films too. It seems he has become a universal favourite. We know him personally. He and my son, Hubert, were up at Cambridge together, and they have never lost sight of each other."

Then one day towards the end of February, Mildred danced into the flat drawing-room and shouted that her father had nearly consented to recognize an engagement. A word to him from her angelic Emmeline might now make him surrender altogether.

"Oh, I'm sorry. I am disturbing you."

Miss Verinder was kneeling on the floor surrounded by maps and open books. One large map was spread out across the seat of a chair, and in her hand she held the magnifying glass with which she had studied its thin lines and minute signs. That dark hair of hers, still without a touch of grey, flopped loose and untidy; her face was haggard; her teeth showed strangely as she made a piteous effort that resulted in a wry, distorted sort of smile. Mildred drew back frightened, and then came forward with outstretched hands. This was a Miss Verinder that she had never seen before.

"I am glad, dear. He—he'll consent. But you mustn't count on me any more, Mildred. Yes, yes, yes, I have been upset. But you must leave me alone, please—you must leave me out of everything." And although the girl could see all the old affection in her eyes, her voice was almost harsh and forbidding. "I—I have no place among happy people."

CHAPTER XVII

NEWS had come; and it was bad news. Except that it conveyed desolation instead of comfort, she did not yet fully understand the long cablegram from Twining. Its one salient statement had been a blow sufficiently cruel to strike her down.

Twining had returned to Hobart in the relief ship. He had returned—without Dyke. He had brought back other people—but not Dyke.

The message had many map references, and she immediately recognised the first one—in Latitude seventy-seven degrees, forty minutes, south. That, of course, was Dyke's base camp on the Barrier, near the place from which Captain Scott started. So it had been arranged. He was to follow Captain Scott's line. He said it was a duty to the dead—to carry on the work.

Naturally it was to that point that Twining would go, to succour and relieve. The message said:—

"...Have taken away everybody from there. The large party that Dyke took with him all safe back. They left him Latitude eighty-five degrees south. Dyke going on with two."

Emmie's teeth, with retracted lips, began to chatter, and she repeated the words in a whisper. "Dyke going on—Dyke going on with two."

"I did not meet the *Follower*. As ordered by Dyke, *Follower* sailed October last for coast-line Latitude seventy-three degrees south, Longitude twenty degrees west of Greenwich. Gladstone instructed to make food depôts from Latitude seventy-four south, Longitude twenty-two west, to as far south as possible and to meet Dyke. Am refitting in haste to start for *Follower's* new station."

Twining had not seen Dyke's own ship, the *Follower*. The *Follower* was gone—somewhere else. Why? She could not understand. And what was the significance of that instruction to make more food depôts, when all depôts were already provided? On the supply of food from the base camp southwards depended all the security of Dyke's return journey from the Pole. Was there something wrong with the carefully planned arrangements? Surely this must mean that he intended to come from the Pole by a slightly different line? But then—oh, the danger, the horrible danger of altered plans.

Twining had broken up the original base camp; he had taken everybody away. It could have only one meaning: that Dyke was not coming back exactly the same way that he had gone. It could not mean—no, a thousand times no—that he had been so long that they did not expect him back at all? No, they expected him at this other place. They were to meet him there.

She fell into a fit of shivering as the thought came to her that all this had happened months ago. Twining was speaking of events that were over, done with, for ever. Already Dyke's journey was a thing of the past. At this hour Dyke and those two were safe, quite out of danger, or—

She threw herself face downwards on the bed, writhing and moaning.

Then after a while she set to work with the map again; trying to locate accurately that last map reference and find the exact point of the coast-line mentioned as the place of the new base camp to be established by the *Follower*. In spite of all her training, she was still apt to get confused in regard to Longitude. Latitude never troubled her.

Slowly the big map turned in her hands as she followed those thin north and south lines and the tiny numbers on the Antarctic circle; and as if with her weak trembling hands she had pushed the world itself round upon its axis, she stared in horror and amazement. That point to which Dyke had ordered the *Follower* was two thousand miles, a long sea voyage, away from the old place. It was right across the circle, on the opposite side of the map, facing Cape Horn instead of Australasia. The coast-line was in Coats Land. The new food depôts were to be made on the edge of that vast unknown which stretches from there to the Pole without a single mark on the map to indicate men's guesses at the secrets that it holds.

Then it was as if a bright light burst before her eyes, and she shook as if an explosion had set the room and the whole house rocking. She had understood at last the audacity and magnitude of Dyke's aim.

He had never intended to retrace his steps. He meant to go straight on past the Pole, through the unknown, unguessed-at regions on that other side, straight on, right across the circle.

Presently she was sitting on the edge of her bed, crying, and talking aloud. "O Tony, this is too bad of you. It isn't right. It isn't fair. You have broken the spirit of our agreement, if not the letter. You knew very well that I would not have allowed it, if I had been consulted. And you said I should be consulted—you said my word was law—at the time I gave you the money." She went on talking, half hysterically, just as a mother talks when news reaches her from a distance of a wild son's reckless and inexcusable behaviour; saying the things that even she, his mother, would have been forced to say to him, had he been here within sound of her voice. "No, Tony, I can't, I can't forgive you for this. You could not have done it if you had thought of me."

She went almost at once to Devonshire, in order to be with his father during this dreadful time.

Following on that cablegram from Lieutenant Twining to the unhappy patron and mock chieftain of the expedition, there came all sorts of messages from press correspondents in Tasmania. But evidently Twining had told them very little. They did not know what Emmie knew. Soon however the name of Dyke once more became prominent in English newspapers.

Silent and oblivious all this time, they now took him up again in the interesting uncertainty as to his fate. The famous explorer lost, became worth space again. Anthony Dyke missing, gone from human ken, long over-due, was naturally more valuable than Anthony Dyke alive and well, ready to answer our representative's questions at the end of a telephone wire. He took rank as a sensation that appealed to all readers, and was featured only less conspicuously than some Miss Jenkins, a pretty golden-haired flapper of seventeen, who started from home to go to a cinema palace three weeks ago and has not been seen or heard of since. A strange disappearance! His old photographs were brought out. His whole career was narrated—briefly, and without any intimate details that might discount his obituary notices. These were all ready, waiting.

As the weeks passed and the view of the newspapers grew more gloomy, their writers became more and more complimentary. They spoke of him as "the great Englishman." They said that even after a war which had shown us by hundreds of instances how the fire of patriotism can overcome the disability of age, one must yet feel dumb with admiration as one thought of such an enterprise as this being undertaken by a man of sixty-two. They wished they could entertain any real hope that he would ultimately work his way back to safety, but they must point to the adverse opinion of an expert (in another column) who reminded one that the factors of time and food allowed no possibility of delay. Neither seals nor birds would be met with. And to eat the sledge dogs, when it became necessary, meant destroying the means of rapid movement. They feared that, at this date, there could be little doubt that the tragedy of ten years ago had been re-enacted. Dyke and his two companions had perished on their way back to the base. And venerable admirals, writing in confirmation of this verdict, paid eloquent tributes and called it a national loss.

It was a part of Emmie's task at Endells to keep all these horrible newspapers out of reach of the poor old man. She said it merely lacerated one's feelings to read them, and, as they were without information that he and she possessed, their opinion was quite valueless.

Twining's letter came to her at Endells six weeks after his cabled message. He was scarcely more hopeful than the newspapers. And a little after this the newspapers themselves ceased to speak of Dyke. There was no more to be said.

Plainly old Mr. Dyke's bodily strength was ebbing fast. That seat on the cliff saw them no more. It was as much as he could do to walk to church, with the aid of Emmie's arm. In church he sat while others stood or kneeled; and always when the time came for the curate to read the prayer of promise that when two or three are gathered together in God's name their requests will be granted, Emmie saw his hands, and then his whole body, begin to tremble. He used to close his eyes, and Emmie, looking down at him, saw the deep lines on his shrunken cheeks, his veined eyelids, and his bloodless lips, all in a sort of fluttering movement that was produced by the rapidity of his breathing.

In the mild spring weather they drove in a little old-fashioned phaeton with a staid old pony—Emmie driving and the old man at her side—through the deep-sunk lanes, never on the high road, along the sheltered valleys and sometimes high enough on the hillside to find a point where, stopping for a few minutes to rest the pony, they could look through the bars of a field gate across sloping grass land to the wide calm sea. He loved these outings in the pony carriage, and they did him good. They talked all the while of Anthony; he as a rule telling her of incidents connected with his son's youth or early manhood, and she generally speaking of things that were to be done in the future. They comforted each other as best they could.

"As soon as he comes home, Mr. Dyke, he must help you to make the tenants do their duty in repairing these banks. They really are neglecting them."

"Yes, I'll get him to help me about that—and other matters. I am afraid I have been negligent myself this last year. But if Tony will settle down here, and—"

"Oh, he promised. He'll keep his promise. He promised us both that he would never go away again."

For although they did not attempt to conceal the torture of anxiety that both were suffering, neither had ever admitted even a transient fear that their belief in his return might not be justified. Nothing should shake her own faith, and she thought that the old man's faith was as firm. But then, during one of these drives, he unconsciously allowed her to divine that it was not so.

They had been almost laughing as they spoke of the remarkable fact that Mr. Sturgess, the doctor, had added a really new anecdote to his repertory.

"It would have amused Tony to know that," said Mr. Dyke.

"I will tell him in my next letter," said Emmie.

The old man turned his thin nose and dim eyes, and looked at her in startled wonder.

"Do you mean," he said, "that you are still writing to him?"

"Of course I am," she said, with a gasp. "I write every week now, instead of once a fortnight. Naturally there will be a great many letters—counting those that Mr. Twining had taken with him on the *Heather Bell*. And Tony won't get the rest till he arrives at Hobart. But he'll like having them, no matter how many they are"; and she tried to smile. "He can read them—or glance through them—on the voyage home." Then her voice broke. "Oh, dear Mr. Dyke, you have hurt me so dreadfully. Why did you seem surprised? Why did you look at me like that—as if you thought it was useless to go on writing to him?"

"My dearest Emmie, nothing of the sort." The old fellow made a gallant effort to speak firmly and cheerfully. "You are absolutely right. I don't know what I *was* thinking about. My mind had wandered—it does now, occasionally. Yes, tell him that Sturgess has been to London and learnt a fresh tale. Tell him all the news. Abertors! Don't forget to say that Abertors has been let furnished."

No one believed really, except her. Only she who did not dare to doubt, contrived to go on believing. The others merely pretended. In the village the kindly friendly little shop people assumed a pitying expression that betrayed them at once.

"Mr. Dyke du sim poorly. Very old he is, for sure," said Mrs. Prince, the post-mistress, to Miss Verinder, who was buying stamps. "A great age it is—and now what with his grief to—"

Miss Verinder, so firm as to seem stern and haughty, said that Mr. Dyke was feeling anxiety but no grief. Why should he grieve when there was nothing to grieve about?

"Oh, have yu a' had good tidings, miss?" asked the post-mistress eagerly.

"No, it is improbable that we shall have tidings of any kind for a long time. I have told you so, again and again. Don't you understand that the seasons are different down there?"

"Yes, miss, so you did mention to my husband."

"Down there the winter is beginning. The ship that has gone to look for Mr. Anthony will encounter frozen seas. Mr. Anthony's own ship—unless he has already got away—will be fast in the ice. If so, he cannot be expected at any navigable port until the autumn."

It was just the same with those old servants at the house. Talking to her of Master Anthony they spoke, as their master did, nearly always of his youth. Hannah, standing with Emmie in his dressing-room, pointed down into the walled garden and said how when he was quite a little chap, and she herself a young girl, he had a lovely black velvet suit with a lace collar; and wearing this much admired costume, he lay upon the grass down there on an April day. Then a sharp shower began; but Master Anthony, never seeming to notice the downpour, still lay there, till he was wet through and through. "Oh, there was a to-do, for fear he should take cold." Everybody in the house had loved the child.

All this was naturally put by Hannah into the past tense; but Emmie, wincing, noticed that Hannah still used the same tense as she went on to speak of later days, when she said how it was his kindness, his unfailing kindness, that had won the hearts not only of the tenants but of every man and woman for miles round.

"Yes," said Hannah finally, with a sigh, "he was a kind gentleman."

"He is a kind gentleman," said Miss Verinder. "And a great hero too. As you'll say, when he comes home and all the world is praising him."

"I'm sure we do hope so, miss."

But she knew that they merely acted hope; they had no hope, truly. She ceased to talk to them in the friendly open way that had become habitual. She let the house itself talk to her about him, and not its servants.

Everything spoke of him. There was not a room that had not legends to tell and memories to revive. Sometimes on these mornings of early spring she went by herself into his dressing-room, and remained there for a long while. It was a large comfortable room, beautifully neat and clean, smelling of lavender; with two spacious walnut wardrobes, a big writing-table, and chairs covered in newly-washed chintz—a room that seemed to have been occupied quite recently and to be waiting for some one to use it again to-morrow. She opened the latticed casements more widely to let in more air and sunlight, and stood looking down into the little garden, and thought of him, dreamed of him. In imagination she could hear him down below on the terrace, banging away at the cook's box as he and the electrician mended it—a splendid grey-haired giant, full of power and will. In imagination she could see him moving along the grass path between the crocuses and daffodils—a child dressed in black velvet and white lace; a child with a man's great soul already developing in him, careless of rain and storm, incapable of petty fears, daring and yet loving nature.

Sometimes she played with his things, rearranging the writing materials in the small cabinet on the table, or she opened the wardrobes, and fetching out the old-fashioned garments, shook them, brushed them, refolded them. This made him seem more certainly alive. These things were not a dead man's property.

"But he shan't wear them again," she said to herself. "We'll make a bonfire of them. It is absurd not to have got rid of them ages ago. I won't have him looking as he did that last Christmas, in this horrid little black coat. No, we'll have a bonfire."

At night when Mr. Dyke had gone to bed and all the house was shuttered and barred, she sat alone by the dying embers in the oak parlour, or stood looking into the round mirrors as if almost expecting that they would show a reflection of something more than emptiness behind her. She had then a feeling of vagueness and unreality, and it seemed to her that she too was acting. What was it all about—this tightening of the throat, this beating of the heart, this hot dull aching of the brain? Why had she begun to pace the room, like a tragedy queen, with clenched hands and wild eyes? Pretence? There was no real necessity for these exaggerated poses in order to shew an empty room and a vacant chair the ravages of mental agony.

"Courage, Emmie. Sit down. Don't walk about."

Who said that? She stood listening and trembling. No one, of course. But it was what he would have said, had he been here. The place was not really haunted. There are no ghosts—and if there were ghosts they must be ghosts of the dead not of the living. No one had spoken. She had merely supplied ordinary words to an ordinary thought.

She sat down on one side of the hearth and looked at the big deep chair on the other side of it. She had found him sitting there that Christmas eve long after she herself had gone upstairs, long after midnight. She had come down again. The fire had burnt itself out, the hearth was cold, and he was so completely lost in thought that he did not hear her slippered footfall. She had known then that she must let him go, that she could not keep him with her, that the sacrifice was inevitable.

"Tony," she had said, "this is disgraceful of you. What do you mean by staying down here, hours after you ought to have been in bed?"

"If it comes to that," he said, shaking off his reverie and speaking gaily, "why haven't you gone to bed yourself?"

And again it was as though she heard his voice, clear and distinct, speaking to her from the empty chair in this haunted room.

She was sleeping very badly at this time, often hearing the church clock strike the hours till dawn before she fell into light dozes. Now in the middle of the night there came a knocking at the door of her room. Startled, she called out loudly.

The door opened a little way, and the old man spoke to her.

"Emmie, forgive me. Can you get up? I have something to tell you."

She had turned on the light, and hastily putting a cloak round her she went to him in the corridor. He was wrapped in the loose folds of a dressing-gown, so white and feeble a thing as seen thus, so bony and thin, that his aspect gave her a new shock of pain. Because of the confusion of his spirit, forgetting the electric light, he carried a candle that was guttering and smoking in his shaky hand.

"What's the matter, Mr. Dyke? Are you ill?" And she took the candle from him and blew it out.

"No, dear—not ill. But I have been thrown into great agitation by a dream. Emmie dear, I am still under the influence of it. Help me. It was like a vision. But dare one attach importance to it? Emmie, it was so wonderful. I did not know I was asleep—but I suppose I must have been."

"Oh, Mr. Dyke, what was it?" She too was shaking now, so much that the candle fell from its socket and rolled against the wainscot. "Tell me what it was."

"Anthony," he said.

"Yes, Anthony. I knew it"; but she clung to him. "What did you see? What did you hear?"

"I saw him, but I could not hear anything."

"Dead?"

"No, alive. Oh, yes, I saw him move—he raised his arm, he seemed to hold his hand to his eyes, and then—But, Emmie, I heard nothing. That's what makes me so doubtful. Tell me what *you* think. No, don't tell me—I can't get rid of this agitation. I can't think clearly." Then it was as if the old man had suddenly convinced himself. "Why should I doubt? He is alive. My boy, my boy still lives. Some merciful power has sent me this message."

"Yes, yes—that is what we will think. But, dear Mr. Dyke, you mustn't stay here or you will catch cold." And with her arm round him she led him back into his room.

He looked about him vaguely.

"Get back to bed now."

"Yes, dear. But first I want to tell you all. I want to describe everything, for you to remember it. He seemed to be shading his eyes with his hand, looking forward. And when he dropped his hand I saw the face very bright, with a very strong light upon it—like the strongest sunshine. He wasn't alone, Emmie. There was some one else, on the ground by his feet. And then he seemed to be calling out—though I couldn't hear. Yet I seemed to understand that he was calling to me—asking me to wait for him—or to stay with him—not to desert him. Then, Emmie dear, though there was no sound to his voice, I spoke myself. I called to him to be quick, because I couldn't wait. Then, immediately it was gone—and I felt I must go to you."

"Yes, yes. I'm glad you came. But now—"

"Emmie, I don't like to ask you. Yes, I will. Pray with me a minute. When two or three are gathered together. Would you mind? You said once that you did believe in some universal power. Well, will you pray to that? I don't know if I believe in much else myself. Everything is slipping from me."

He sank upon his knees, and Emmie took the quilt from the bed and held it round him, kneeling by his side while he prayed. It was pitiful, heart-rending, the weak, weak voice quavering breathlessly in the silent night.

"O merciful God, make this thing true. O God of mercy grant our prayer. Have mercy on us, have mercy on us. Oh, spare my boy. Have mercy on my brave boy. Grant to us two who love him that he may come back to us safely."

She got him into bed again, covered him warmly, and he feebly pressed her hand.

"Thank you, dear Emmie. That was kind of you. Yes, when two or three are gathered together. Very kind. But you are always kind."

She stayed there for some time after he had fallen asleep, and then went back to her room. She was exhausted by the agitation that had been communicated to her; but before lying down she wrote a note in her memorandum book. "During the night of April 18-19, Mr. Dyke dreamed that he saw Tony," and so on. Then, worn out, she slept deeply, dreamlessly.

Louisa, rousing her in the morning, said that Mr. Dyke was ill and Dr. Sturgess had been sent for.

The poor old man was light-headed, babbling confusedly, unable to recognize Emmie or anybody else; and Dr. Sturgess told her immediately that the illness could have but one termination.

A little more than a fortnight later she was writing to Anthony to tell him of his loss.

"...We had Dr. Gordon Giles over from Plymouth, and two very good nurses from Exeter. We did everything that was possible. It began with a chill, then it was a dreadful rapid pneumonia that simply burned him up. He had no strength to withstand the disease, and both doctors agreed that in any case he could only have lived a very little longer.

"You know, dear Tony, that he felt himself that his course was nearly run. He said to me before you left that he would not be here to welcome you home. Of course you will grieve, but you must take consolation in thinking of his long, long life, and of all the pride and joy that came to him from being your father. He loved you so much. In the night when his illness began he had a very vivid dream about you; and I shall ask you later whether you were thinking of us at that particular time. On that same night I had myself a strange feeling that you seemed near to us. Can it be that, with your dear father standing on the borderland, and the veil, as they call it, become very thin, he was indeed able to reach you in the spirit? I wonder. You and I will talk of this.

"You know, dear Tony, that I loved him. Indeed, how could I do anything else, when he was so good to me from the very beginning?

"I have attended to all business matters with Mr. Sadler, and everything is all right. The house will be carried on as you would wish, and of course none of the servants will be dismissed. I know you would not like any petty economies to be made. You can trust old Hannah to keep order and see that your home is ready for you when you return to it.

"I am going back to London to-morrow."

She shut herself in the flat, and would see no one—not loyal Mrs. Bell clambering up those steep stairs breathlessly, not even affectionate, grateful Mildred lightly springing up them to be rebuffed at the guarded door again and again, not anyone at all. She had ceased to count the months now, dreading the tale of them, refusing to recognize their numbers. She only knew, by the warm air and the brilliant sunbeams that sent dancing fire between the leafy branches of the plane-tree, that it was high summer and that all the world of the noisy streets was gay.

Reverting to an old habit, she used to go out at night, and even then it was not dark enough to harmonise with her thoughts. Louisa always accompanied her. They crossed the Brompton Road, seeking the silence and darkness beside the closed churchyard, wandered through Ennismore Gardens into Prince's Gate; flitting like ghosts in the grey lamp-light and vanishing in the grey shadow—like two faded and fading ghosts that haunted the broad roads and empty spaces which they had both known in lifetime and youth. On into Queen's Gate, past its largest house, shrinking from those lighted windows and the sound of music; along the Cromwell Road, round and about the once animated neighbourhood; to and fro—thus they did their phantom walk, night after night.

She could not bear the sight of the daylight crowd. She felt hatred and contempt for these thousands of well-fed comfortable people who ate, slept, and amused themselves in mean security, while the great men, the heroes, the Dykes of the world, were giving their noble lives to distant peril and toil. Nothing short of an urgent call of duty would force her to face the garish sunlight and the heartless mob.

But such a summons came, and with Louisa she went for two days to that town in the midlands.

They returned by an evening train, sitting side by side at a table in the Pullman car; Emmie looking pale and well-bred, Louisa grey-haired, solid, severe, but so well-dressed and dignified as to seem a friend of the other lady and not her servant. No one would have noticed them or thought about them, if they had not aroused a little curious attention by asking for tea and eggs instead of the table-d'hôte dinner that the rest of the passengers were devouring. When they had finished their tea, Louisa put on spectacles and read the *Strand Magazine*; while Miss Verinder thought of what had happened at Upperslade Park, and of what this release might have meant to her once, a long time ago, many, many years ago. Coming now, it seemed like the last cruel mockery of fate.

That same night, although she was very tired, she wrote to Anthony to tell him of this second death.

"...Dr. Wenham says that in such cases the end very often comes like this, with haemorrhage (I do not think I have spelt it correctly) of the brain. Poor soul, she never recovered consciousness and she passed away quite peacefully without any suffering. And I want to say that I am quite sure she really loved you at first, dear Tony, and that, so far as anything like connected thought or sustained feeling was possible to a person in that darkened condition, she loved you to the last. She never forgot you; she always spoke of you.

"You will be surprised at my saying all this, but I will explain by telling you something that I have not told you till now. Only do not for a moment suppose that I kept it back because I was afraid you might not approve. I knew very well that you would think it right and wish me to do it; as it was what you used to do yourself until your work prevented you. I said nothing to you simply because I did not want to trouble you.

"For a number of years I have been in touch with her, and have regularly visited the asylum. Dr. Wenham seemed to think that my visits did her good, as proving to her that there was still somebody in the world who took an interest in her; although I cannot say that I ever could see that she felt this. At any rate, by going I was enabled to make sure that she was being well treated and having good food, and so on. This, I think, you will be glad to know. After the death of that hateful aunt of hers, it seemed that, except you and me, there was literally nobody who even knew of her existence.

"I will explain everything else about it when we meet."

She continued to write to him even more often; telling him about Louisa or the cat, telling him anything that could possibly interest him.

"They say the price of food has fallen again, but Louisa says the good shops are as dear as ever.... Mildred Parker is going to be married early in September. I wish I had you here to help me choose a present for her. I feel so dull and uninventive that I dare say I shall sneak out of the difficulty by sending a cheque. Mildred is a dear girl."

After the evening walk she used to sit at her desk, with only her reading lamp to make a bright circle of light and with all the rest of the room in darkness. If not writing a letter to him, she read his old letters to her. The thin paper rustled and shook in the lamp-light; and it seemed to her that the man whom all the world believed to be dead was standing close behind her; that at any moment he might step forward, put his hand upon her shoulder, and speak to her.

Did she still truly believe that he was alive? She went on writing to him. In some oppressively hot weather during the month of August she suffered from great lassitude; her head ached day after day, and noises in the head bothered her. Louisa wanted her to see a doctor, but she resolutely refused. Alone in the room, with the sides and corners of it all vague and shadowy, where the light of her single lamp did not reach them, she distressed herself by imaging that she could hear voices—not his voice ever, the voices of other people, strangers, talking about Anthony. It was not an illusion;

because she knew perfectly well that she was merely imagining it. This imagined talk was just a translation of her own thoughts. But she could not stop it; for a little while it was quite beyond her control.

These unknown imaginary people were saying that he was alive and they had seen him. They had met him in Bond Street. "Yes, I didn't recognize him at first. I thought, there's a thundering big man. Where have I seen those big shoulders before? Then I saw it was Dyke. You know, the man they said had perished five hundred miles on the other side of the Pole. Anthony Dyke. Dyke. Dyke. Dyke!"

And suddenly she began to laugh and beat upon the desk with her open hand. A thought had come to her that seemed to be at once tragic and ludicrous. "Am I going mad?" she asked herself; and for perhaps a minute she laughed unrestrainedly. "That would be too bad," she said, aloud. "No, I won't go out of my mind, Tony. It wouldn't be fair—for you to have had a mad mistress as well as a mad wife"; and she became quite quiet again. Then, looking round, she saw that Louisa had entered the room.

"I've nothing to do," said Louisa. "May I sit in here with you till you go to bed?"

"No," said Emmie. "Leave me alone, please."

"I fancied I heard something—as if you were making a noise."

"Don't believe what you hear," said Emmie, with a faint smile, "and only half that you see"; and the smile vanishing, her face became rigid.

On another night she suddenly sprang up from her desk, hurried across to the door, and turned on all the light switches. Every lamp glowed and grew bright. She had been on the point of starting a letter when an agony of horror and dread took possession of her. She stood now clinging to the back of a chair, her teeth chattering, her face ghastly. He was dead—while the horror lasted she seemed, in this brightly-lit room, to have visions of him. She saw him lying stiff on the snow, a huge black form stretched upon the dazzling whiteness. And she saw him seated, staring at her, with his hands clasped about his knees—like those frozen figures in the Andes—dead now for many months.

She made no noise. She fought the hallucination, she fought the abominable mind-destroying thoughts that had produced it; she fought, as if for her own life and his. And gradually the horror passed, the anguish lessened. Finally they were gone.

She sat down at the desk again, shaking and sobbing. Her tears fell upon the paper after she had written a few words, so that she had to tear it up and throw it away. Then, drying her eyes, she started once more.

"...You must never leave me after this. I have your solemn promise, have not I? I couldn't stand any more of it, the loneliness. I *must* feel that when I put out my hand it will touch you and not close upon the empty air. You must, you must give me a few happy years after all the waiting. You said once you could be happy with me in Devonshire—in the dear west country that people have called the land of sunsets. That'll seem the right place, Tony, for *our* sunset—I mean, the closing of our day.

"Oh, Tony"—and she had another fit of sobbing before she could go on writing—"God or Fate cannot mean to separate us. If you were dead I should die too. Not by my own hand. But I simply could not go on living without you.

"There." She was dabbing her eyes; and after forcing back the tears, she sniffed courageously. "You will read this and laugh your big laugh, and make a noise of crackers with your bony fingers, and think how cowardly and faint-hearted your little Emmie has become. I wasn't cowardly in the beginning, was I, darling? It is the waiting that has worn me out and broken my nerve. Good-night and God bless you and guard you."

She refused now even to glance at the newspapers; she would not look at anything that could remind her of the passing days—those days that she dared not count. September was close upon her, and still she went on writing to him.

Old Louisa came into the room late one night, to fetch the cat.

"Won't you go to bed, miss?"

"No," said Emmie, "I am busy. I have something to finish."

"Is it so very important?" asked Louisa. "Won't it keep?"

Emmie answered with great firmness. "No, it won't. The mail goes to-morrow. I am writing to Mr. Dyke."

Louisa looked at her.

"Why are you looking at me like that?" said Emmie, wildly and fiercely. "I tell you I'm writing to Mr. Dyke."

"Yes, miss," said Louisa; and she went out of the room very softly, leaving the cat. "I'll come back," she whispered, on the threshold.

Emmie wrote: "Darling, it is late, and Louisa is fussing. You know her ways. Well, I have told you all my gossip, and made it another long letter to add to the pile you will have to wade through. *Au revoir*, my beloved. Good-night. Good-night."

September had come; and Mildred Parker was talking to her on the telephone, reminding her that there would be no Miss Parker after Thursday next, but a Mrs. Beckett instead.

Mildred spoke of the wedding arrangements, the inexhaustible success of *The Danger Signal*, the amazing affability and good humour of Mr. Parker.

"He monopolises Alwyn. He trots about after him and crows over him as if Alwyn was a wonderful egg that he had laid, or a treasure that he had pecked out of the gravel. Sometimes I can't get near Ally because of him. Honestly, Emmeline, he and mummy both go on as if it was they who had found me a husband, and I ought to thank them on my knees for finding me such a nice one." And Emmie heard the girl's fresh young laughter.

Then Mildred spoke seriously and with intense affection. She said she knew quite well that Emmeline had some great sorrow, and it had almost broken her heart to be stopped always by that inexorable door, and never once to be allowed to give a hug of sympathy. She was thinking of Emmeline constantly. She hoped and prayed that Emmeline's private grief, whatever it might be, would presently pass away.

"Thank you, Mildred."

Then Mildred gave thanks for the cheque, saying she felt ashamed to take it because it was "such a whopper." And after that she said, although she must not urge Emmeline to come to the wedding itself, she wondered if Emmeline would feel up to coming to a little afternoon party at which friends would see the presents all laid out on tables.

"No, dear. I'm afraid you must excuse me."

"All right," said Mildred. "Then I won't be hateful and selfish about it. Only I hope you do know, darling Emmeline, what a tremendous difference it would make to us, and how dreadfully, *dreadfully* I miss you. I am so happy that I must not say it spoils my happiness. No, that would be wicked, and ungrateful too—when perhaps I really owe it all to you. But if anything *could* spoil it for me, it would be your absence.... One moment. Can you hold on, please? Alwyn wants to speak to you himself."

Then she heard the young man's voice, deep and strong, yet very musical; seeming to vibrate with tenderness although so firm.

"Miss Verinder, is that you? I wanted to say I feel just what Mildrings feels. It would make all the difference in the world to us. I must not press it, but I shall think it most awfully ripping of you if you do come."

She went. It was another fight with herself; but if her presence would really give any pleasure to this girl and boy, why should she spare her own pain?

Louisa dressed her with great care, in one of those greyish frocks covered in transparent black lace and gauze that, except for their length or shortness, belong to no particular age and fashion. Her shoes, stockings and hat were of the most modern style.

"Can I wear a veil with this hat?" asked Emmie.

"I should certainly wear a veil," said Louisa, looking at the dark circles round her eyes, and at that something more than pallor, the dull opaque waxenness of complexion that comes to people when for a long time they have been deprived of sunlight.

Like all such small parties, it was a very big one. The house in Ennismore Gardens was scarcely large enough for it. Mildred and her future husband devoted themselves to Miss Verinder, waiting upon her at tea, whispering the names of celebrated actors and actresses, then leading her through the throng, and taking her upstairs to see the lovely presents.

The presents and the long tables occupied both the back and the front drawing-room, and all about them there was pressure and excitement. The great majority of the guests were young people; their bright faces glowed with life and hope. The atmosphere seemed full of pretty, kindly thoughts. Even the stout and heavy elders felt a stirring of sentimental memories and an over-brimming sympathy. It was so pleasant to think of the happy young girl about to be united, amidst the joy and satisfaction of parents and relatives, to the honest young man that she loved.

Only here and there a matron of years pushed along the tables anxiously and murmured to herself or a friend. "I suppose it's here. But I haven't yet seen my silver and tortoise-shell pin tray."

Then all at once Emmie heard or thought she heard voices saying Anthony's name. It was like that semi-illusion of the flat—the imagined voices of strangers talking about him. "Dyke—yes, Dyke." These people just ahead of her were saying the words. She moved towards them, listening.

"Yes, found by the relief party.... Yes, Dyke. Anthony Dyke, the explorer.... Extraordinary. Given up by everybody. Risen from the dead, as it were. If he has a wife and children, what must be their feelings?"

She asked one of them what all this meant.

"That man Dyke has been found—alive, you know."

"But is it a fact?" she asked quietly. "Who says so?"

They said the news had been cabled; it was in the evening papers, at the clubs, everywhere.

She turned and took Mildred's arm.

"Mildred, dear, I want to go home. Help me to get away quietly. A taxi-cab."

"Yes, at once." Mildred, distressed and solicitous, took her down by a back staircase. "But dear Emmeline, what is it? You're ill. You're trembling—oh, you're crying."

"No, I'm not ill. Everything is quite all right. Only I'm a little hysterical—for the moment."

At the flat a cablegram was waiting for her.

"Done the trick. Coming home. Love. Tony."

CHAPTER XVIII

HE had got it now—the fame, the glory, the unsubstantial but glittering payment for a life spent in solid and incredibly arduous toil.

Never again would his name be left out of lists; never again would his publicity agent feel compelled to write reminders or corrections to the morning papers. As to the great achievement itself, very little need be said here. Indeed, as Emmie is already engaged in preparing for publication the two large volumes which will be entitled *The Sixth Cruise*, any attempt to give a detailed account of Dyke's final triumph would be at least premature, if not superfluous.

Suffice it then to say that with this last expedition there were no accidents. Not only the leader but his two companions won through to safety; and in regard to the minor journeys, the scientific researches, the geographical investigations, all went well. Everything scraped up from the bottom of the sea, the collection of minerals chipped off the land, the measurements, records, and diaries, were duly brought home to England. Honours from all countries, including his own, were showered upon the illustrious explorer. As has become customary on these occasions, it was immediately announced that the King had been graciously pleased to confer a knighthood upon Mr. Dyke.

To Miss Verinder that knighthood was a uniquely tremendous affair. She refused to remember that quite a large number of knights had been created during the last half century. Those did not count. She thought only of one or two who were like her man, real knights; and she added five or six more from Elizabethan times to make up the splendid company. Sir Francis Drake, Sir Walter Raleigh, Sir Richard Grenville, Sir John Hawkins, and Sir Anthony Dyke—the linked names rang grandly in her ears.

His title seemed to echo itself like music or the sound of bells, as she walked briskly away from the flat early one morning in October. She felt joyous and strong, not minding the fog, not fearing the motor traffic. It was not really a fog, rather a ground mist; an exhilarating morning of late autumn, with the sun and the mist contending for victory.

In fact, when she had left the Brompton Road, the sun showed itself behind her, high over the hidden houses, shining from a faint yet open blue sky. She stood for a moment at the bottom of Exhibition Road and admired. On this left-hand pavement a stream of students, girls and men, were hurrying onward to their classes and lectures. The right-hand pavement was quite empty; and, looking beyond it, one had a sense of vague grandeurs, a perception of domes high and still fog-shrouded. Ahead, the broad smooth road glistened like dark water beneath the shredding veils of whiteness; the long perspective line made by the unbroken cornice of the houses showed above the mist, and the side wall of a roof of one house, at the turning into Prince's Gardens, was all sunlit; nearer, the block of building that is known as the Royal College of Science was already emerging, freeing itself, getting definite and illumined, with its walls of delicate rose and upper story of yellow ochre, and a sketchy suggestion of columns; while the farthest end of the vista remained almost lost in the denser mist clouds that were rolling out from the grass of Hyde Park. The whole prospect seemed that of a larger, grander Venice, with the road converted into its splendid silent canal.

She walked on. Gradually and yet very swiftly, as she had seen happen once before, among the mountains of a distant land, the conquering sun tore the veils away and reached all things with its magic touch. Colour and brightness sprang towards the searching rays. Geraniums glowed in dilapidated flower beds of the sunk garden of the Natural History Museum; orange, crimson, and gold flashed from the dead leaves on its sodden paths. When she came to the first turn to the left, that road was quite lovely—an avenue of green trees, marble pavements, and tremulous light; the Imperial Institute seeming like a palace built of dreams; high towers without base or foundation, masonry swimming in air, domes and more domes; and over all, the dome of domes, the high vaulted sky.

She went through the avenue of wonder, into Queen's Gate. The sun had conquered. Light, not darkness ruled the world. And she thought that the world is beautiful, most beautiful, every part of it—even this Kensington, of straight lines, right angles, and stucco faces.

Miss Verinder walked on, with sunshine and joy in her heart, thinking that great things cannot perish in this beautiful world; thinking that fate gives freely and robs with regret; thinking that love is like the sunshine, the source and fountain of life; thinking that her hero had lived and not died, that her knight was coming back to her and soon would touch her hand.

Presently the newspapers were adding to profuse accounts of the home-coming what they called "an interesting announcement." They said that a delightful touch of romance had been given to the return of Sir Anthony by the fact (now for the first time disclosed) that he had come back "to claim a bride."

When claimed, Miss Verinder displayed coyness or diffidence; resuming that slightly mid-Victorian manner, while she asked him, in effect, if he really meant it, if he really wanted it, and so forth. It was only the second proposal of marriage that she had ever received; and perhaps the embarrassment caused by the first one automatically revived itself, making her a little uncomfortable now. As in the first case, the drawing-room of the flat served as scenic decoration or background to the romantic affair.

"What's that you're saying?" asked Dyke loudly, not catching the purport of her murmured doubts. He had come back in glorious health; but the deafness, of which he had once seemed to be cured, had again grown very apparent. He was distinctly hard of hearing.

"Emmie, my angel, I don't understand. What's that you're jabbering about serious wishes?"

Then Emmie became entirely her natural self; her gentle eyes filled with tears, and she asked him if it was worth while.

"Emmie, what on earth do you mean?"

"If we marry, won't it set people talking? Won't it seem undignified—even a little silly?"

"Oh, Emmie!" He looked at her reproachfully, and said what he used to say in the very beginning of things. "Oh, Emmie, don't spoil it for me."

And eagerly and ardently he told her that his real true joy in all the success and praise was derived from the knowledge that she could now openly share everything with him, that he would be able proudly to show her and boast of her to the world not only as his patron and financial supporter, but also as his *fiancée*.

"I've hundreds of people that I want to introduce to you—my *fiancée*." He said the word with a poor French accent but an immense relish. "So, no more nonsense, you angel. Tell me you didn't mean what you said."

Perhaps she had not really meant it. Or, at any rate, she had meant finally to do whatever he wished. Yielding then to his importunity—as the dear old conventional books used to narrate—she consented to name the day. It was not a far-off day.

He said he would not have a quiet wedding. No, certainly not. It must be a slap-up affair, with a huge reception at the Hyde Park Hotel. She shrank from this fuss, but he wanted it. That was enough for her.

Also he insisted that it should be a marriage by banns.

Immediately after the interesting announcement congratulations and presents began to pour in upon them. At tea-time on these jolly autumn afternoons spent by Sir Anthony and his *fiancée* in shops and streets and other public places, Louisa brought in with her tray prodigious piles of letters, which her future master tore open, read aloud, and tossed about the floor delightedly.

"One from old Barry! Bless his heart. Hear what he says, Emmie."

It was at the pleasant tea hour, while he opened more and more letters, that she asked about the date entered in her memorandum book before the death of his father. She wished to know if he had been thinking specially of home on that night of April 18-19.

"Well, you know, I was thinking about you all the time, off and on; but I can't say I remember thinking about you more on one day than another.... Postmark, Clapham, S. W.!" He was opening a letter. "No. You see, we had our work cut out for us. Our thoughts were pretty well occupied. By Jove. This is from dear old Cairns. I must write to Cairns—a special invitation for Cairns. What!"

He was like a child when it came to opening the presents. He could not wait a moment. He burst the stout string with his hands, he made the brown paper explode in tatters, he flung the tissue all over the room. His litter drove Louisa to distraction.

"What the devil are these? Menu-card holders! What the devil shall we do with them? All the same, deuced kind of her. Mrs. Slane-King! Yes."

He was also like a child—and a spoilt child too—with his press-cuttings. He had mock-modest smiles as he read the eulogies.

"'A glory to the Empire!' That's very handsome of them to say that. Emmie, that tickles my vanity." Then he roared with laughter. "How small we are, Emmie; how vain, how jealous. But you must check me. Hold me on a leash. Don't let me gas about things down in Devonshire when I begin to get old. Watch me then—and don't let me develop into a twaddling old bore."

He went on with the letters and parcels.

"Look here! Hamilton! 'I send this tribute from an old ship-mate. Hamilton!' Now that's very kind of Hamilton to remember me."

They all remembered him. No one forgot him—in his success.

On that first Sunday of their banns they sat in the church side by side; not minding now who saw them together, emancipated, acknowledging a companionship that had lasted during so many years. More than a quarter of a century's habit had not destroyed its freshness or robbed it of its charm; essentially their feelings at this hour were those of boy and girl lovers. Outwardly old, they were inwardly young.

Mildred Beckett, with her husband, was seated quite near in a side pew a little ahead, and looking round and watching them now and then she saw Emmie find his place for him in the prayer-book and hand him the book. Others too, many others, noticed them; not knowing who they were, failing to recognize Dyke—for, however famous a man is, however frequently photographed, and even filmed, there will still be people who do not know him by sight. But they were struck by the strong note of individuality—a couple that somehow *made* you think about them—this fine big old chap, with his shock of grey hair, intrepid blue eyes, and queer-coloured beard; and the tall, thin, faded maiden lady.

"I publish the banns of marriage between—" The clergyman had begun it, and Mildred looked round. The clergyman paused, as if startled.

Anthony Dyke was standing up. Emmie gently pulled his coat, and whispered "Sit down, dear."

"The banns," he said, in a gruff whisper, and because of his deafness louder than was necessary. "Get up, yourself."

"No, dear," she whispered, in a flutter. "It's not done."

But he was offering her his hand, as if to assist her, again inviting her to rise. It was the old country custom, still prevalent in the west of England when he was a boy, or at least practised in his father's church. Gentle and simple, the young squire and the colonel's daughter, the farm-hand and the dairy-maid, they all used to stand up to hear their banns read out—to let neighbours see who they were, to show that they themselves had nothing to be ashamed of, and that they were proud of each other. Dyke, in the Antarctic and other remote places, had not learnt that the practice was no longer usual and proper.

Then Miss Verinder, comprehending the cause of his solecism, rose at once; doing what she had always done for his sake, smashing through the barriers of convention, trampling etiquette under foot, caring not twopence halfpenny what anybody else thought about it. She stood by his side, proudly, yet demurely, as ready now to brave the world, to defy the universe, as she had been twenty-seven years ago.

Mildred, looking round, watched them; and because of her own happiness and something that seemed to her very wonderful in the expression of those two faces, she unexpectedly began to cry. As she said afterwards, the thing seemed to her, somehow, so sweet and touching.

The clergyman, after clearing his throat, had gone straight ahead with the little list:

"...Also between Anthony Penfold Dyke, widower, of the parish of Endells, in Devonshire, ... and Emmeline Constance Verinder, spinster, of this parish."

FOOTNOTE:

NOTE. Readers will of course understand that the author is not accusing this great traveller, nor hinting the faintest disparagement of his quietly matured plans. Miss Verinder's indignation is logically baseless. It is merely the characteristic of her extreme partisanship.